A TIME GONE BY

by William Heffernan

Also by William Heffernan

BEULAH HILL
CITYSIDE
THE DINOSAUR CLUB
CORSICAN HONOR
TARNISHED BLUE
RED ANGEL
SCARRED
BLOOD ROSE
RITUAL
THE CORSICAN
WINTER'S GOLD
ACTS OF CONTRITION
CAGING THE RAVEN
BRODERICK

A TIME GONE BY
by William Heffernan

AKASHIC BOOKS
New York

HICKSVILLE PUBLIC LIBRARY
169 JERUSALEM AVENUE
HICKSVILLE, NY 11801

This is a work of fiction. All names, characters, places, and incidents are the product of the author's imagination. Any resemblance to real events or persons, living or dead, is entirely coincidental.

©2003, 2005 by Daisychain Productions, Inc.
Published by Akashic Books
Originally published in hardcover by Simon & Schuster
All rights reserved
First paperback printing

ISBN: 1-888451-74-2
Library of Congress Control Number: 2004115504

Printed in Canada

Akashic Books
PO Box 1456
New York, NY 10009
Akashic7@aol.com
www.akashicbooks.com

H

For Leila, who joins Amber, Jennifer, Maia, Kayla, Tess, Ruby, Brishen, Taylor, Max and Parker in bringing joy to all.

ACKNOWLEDGMENTS

A special thanks to Gloria Loomis, who inspired the idea behind this book, and to Michael Korda and Chuck Adams, who saw its potential and offered support, encouragement, and guidance.

{ 1 }

New York City, 1945

I waited at the top of the stoop, like a wet cat hoping someone would come along and open the front door. Jimmy Finn stood beside me, a soggy cigar clamped in his teeth. Behind us the rain beat down on East Fifty-fourth Street, making the line of uniformed cops, who were keeping the press at bay, hunch into their rain gear. It was nearly midnight and the glow of the streetlights made the wet, black street glisten. Almost like a river, I thought—the big expensive cars glittering along the curbs looking a bit like powerful animals dozing on the banks.

I turned back to the door. "So this is how the swells live. Fancy town houses and shiny, new cars."

Jimmy gave me the eye from under the brim of his fedora. "Yeah, and they keep slobs like you and me standing out in a fookin' downpour."

"At least we'll get inside tonight. When I was in uniform I never got past the front door of a joint like this." I grinned as I watched the water cascade off Jimmy's hat.

Jimmy didn't think any of it was funny. "When we *do* get inside it's gonna be touchy. You better let me do the talkin'."

That was okay with me. I was a newly made homicide dick and although I'd covered half a dozen murders already, they'd been little more than ground balls. This was my first big case. Jimmy had been doing this for ten years, so I was content to keep my mouth shut and learn.

I looked back at the uniforms. They were set up in a human chain to keep about thirty reporters and photographers from storming the house. It was like I told Jimmy. At least *we'd* get inside. These poor slobs, cops and press alike, would just stand here and soak up the rain. A few months back, when I was still wearing the blue bag, I could have been standing there with them. I liked it a lot better this way.

The heavy oak door swung back and a uniformed lieutenant glared out at us.

"We're from homicide," Jimmy said. "I'm Jimmy Finn, and this is my partner, Jake Downing."

"You took your goddamn sweet time," the lieutenant snapped.

Jimmy and I stepped into a large foyer. Jimmy took off his hat and coat; shook them both to get rid of the excess water. I did the same.

"Watch the damned floors, for chrissake," the lieutenant snapped out again.

Jimmy stepped closer to him, using his great bulk like a threat. He's a bit over six foot and a good 230 pounds, and despite being ten years older than my twenty-five, every bit of it is rock solid.

Jimmy's lip curled into a sneer. "Look, we walk in the door and you jump on my ass, tellin' me we're late, when I only got the goddamn call fifteen minutes ago. Then you complain that we're wet, when we just came out of a fookin' monsoon. What's your problem?"

The lieutenant glared at him. "Whadaya mean you only got the call fifteen minutes ago? My men and I have been here two fuckin' hours."

Jimmy's eyebrows rose. "Have the forensic boys or the medical examiner gotten here yet?"

The lieutenant lowered his voice and inclined his head back toward a room off the foyer. It was closed off by a set of mahogany pocket doors. "The only people who've been here are the police commissioner, half the city council, and Manny Troy, himself. Commissioner Parker and Manny Troy are still in there."

I knew the name. Manny Troy was the indisputable boss of the city's Democrats. It was said the entire city council—and even our soon-to-retire Republican mayor, Fiorello La Guardia—did what Troy told them, or else.

Jimmy closed his eyes. "They been walkin' around the crime scene?"

The lieutenant kept his voice low. "You think I was gonna tell 'em to stay out?"

I saw the muscles dance along Jimmy's jaw. He has bright red hair, and now that color seemed to bleed into his face. "I thought the commissioner might."

The lieutenant snorted at the idea. "You're dreamin', mister." He jabbed a thumb into his chest. "And this here is one cop who ain't about to question what the commissioner decides to do, or doesn't decide to do. And you'd both be smart to do the same while you're here."

Jimmy eyed the man's name tag—Lt. Walter Morgan, it read—then drew a deep breath. "Where's the fookin' body?"

We climbed the stairs in tandem. Jimmy was in the lead with me behind, trying to hide the gimp in my bad leg, both of us taking care not to touch the banister or walls and add our prints to the dozens that were already there. It was a big house, a good third wider than most city brownstones, four stories tall with a center hall and an attic available for servants' quarters.

Lieutenant Morgan told us that the body was in a study, one flight up then down the hall to the rear of the house. The hall was partially covered with a long oriental runner. This time we stayed close to the walls, not wanting to step in any blood or fibers the killer might have left on the carpet. It was probably useless. Morgan had made it clear that half the city government had traipsed through the hall to ogle the body. But we did it anyway. It was part of the training, part of the way we were supposed to work.

The door to the study was ajar, and Jimmy used the tip of a pencil to push it open. It was a big room, plush and rich-looking. Across from where we stood, a set of French doors had been pulled back, revealing a balcony. There was a marble fireplace on the east wall. Opposite was a carved antique desk, and behind it, a high-backed leather chair now lying on its side. Next to the chair, extending out from the edge of the desk, I could see a man's arm, the sleeve of his white shirt soaked with blood.

Jimmy and I entered the room taking care not to tread on any obvious evidence. The heavy copper smell that always accompanies a large quantity of blood immediately assaulted our nostrils. As we stepped around the desk the body came into view. It lay on its back, legs crossed at the ankles as if casually resting, one arm extended above the head as if preparing to wave to some acquaintance. It was the arm I had seen from the door, the sleeve soaked with blood from the large pool that surrounded the head—or what was left of the head.

"Jesus," I said, as I turned my face away.

I had seen plenty of dead bodies, both as a cop and as a soldier. I had lasted one day in the war. A Jap Zero on a strafing run at Pearl Harbor had left me with my bum leg and a one-way ticket home. But before I packed it in, I had seen what was left of the guys who got it worse than me—the bits and pieces of them, anyway.

This was something else, though. Someone had taken something heavy to the man's head. And they had done it again and again and again, until the whole of his forehead was nothing more than a soupy mix of brain and bone and blood.

"Don't be a fookin' sissy," Jimmy teased. "You've seen far worse at automobile accidents."

I shook my head and turned back. What he said was true enough. I'd seen worse lots of times in lots of places. It was the way he was lying there, I guess. Here in this fancy room.

I looked back. "So that's the judge."

"That's himself." Jimmy ran a hand through his red hair.

"Judge Wallace Reed. Looked a bit better in the newspapers, didn't he?"

Jimmy was right again. Like most people, I had never seen Judge Reed in court. He seemed to handle only the biggest cases; not the kind young cops are often involved in. But I had seen his face in the newspapers countless times—distinguished and stern and fatherly. He had put some of the city's top mobsters away; had been the judge on some of Tom Dewey's biggest cases when he was the city's DA. Dewey had gone on to become the Republican governor. He had run for president last year, but FDR had chewed him up and spit him out. Now he was coming up for reelection, and Judge Wallace Reed had been touted as the man who could win back the governor's mansion for the Democrats.

"You think it coulda been some mobster the judge sent away?"

Jimmy wrinkled up his nose as if the idea didn't smell good to him, but before he could speak a voice came from behind us.

"That's exactly what we think."

We turned and found Manny Troy filling the doorway. Behind him, standing like his shadow, was Police Commissioner George Parker.

Jimmy took a halting step toward him. "If you could not come in, sir. We're tryin' to preserve the crime scene as best we can."

Troy ignored him and stepped into the room. The PC followed, giving Jimmy an icy look.

Troy was a big man with a broad chest and an even broader belly. He was dressed in a three-piece suit, and the buttons on his vest strained against his girth. He was somewhere in his fifties, but his hair was still dark and was slicked back with pomade. He had a large nose over a bushy mustache and a pair of blue eyes that were among the coldest I had ever seen. He looked past Jimmy and gave me a smile.

"You sound like a smart lad. What's your name, son?"

I told him, and introduced Jimmy as well.

"Downing's new to homicide." It was the commissioner this time, explaining away my youth. "He's just been moved up from the uniformed division. It's been hard to fill all the detective slots, what with so many boys off fighting the Jerries and the Japs."

Troy nodded. He was still smiling. "Looks like you made a good decision here, George."

Troy walked to the desk and leaned back against it, taking the weight off his legs. I could see the muscles do their dance along Jimmy's jaw, as he worried about any prints the man's ass might be wiping away. This time he kept his mouth shut.

"I wanted to let you boys know about some threats the judge had received," Troy said.

"How did you hear about those, sir?" Jimmy asked.

Troy gave him a smile that said there wasn't much he didn't hear. "The judge told me about them, during one of our many discussions. He said there were threats against his wife as well. He figured it was some guinea gangster he'd been hard on. He had some cases coming up, and he'd made it clear to their attorneys that he planned to lower the boom."

"Did he tell you who, specifically?" Jimmy asked.

Troy shook his head, his jowls quivering beneath his chin. "No, we didn't get into that. But I'm sure his clerk, down at the court, can fill you in."

"I was just wonderin' why he told you," Jimmy said. "I mean, sir, if he was that scared, I woulda thought he'd come to us."

Troy's eyes hardened. The man didn't like being questioned, I guess. He gave Jimmy a look that said he thought he was acting too smart by half.

"The judge wasn't afraid, Finn." He gave Jimmy a smile now. "There wasn't a guinea hood walking this earth that could put the fear in him." His eyes hardened again. I guess it was his way of letting Jimmy know that what he was about to say was none of his business. "Wallace told me about it because we were discussing his future. It's no secret that the party had big plans for the judge. And that makes this even more of a tragedy. That the people of this state will be denied the chance of having him as their governor."

I could see the boilerplate the press would be fed; the outraged headlines they would subsequently write. It was a nasty case to be dropped into, I decided. And it wouldn't take much for a newly minted homicide dick to find himself in some very hot water.

"What we're worried about now," Troy went on, "is that these dago gangsters will make good on their threats against Mrs. Reed as well. So we'll want her guarded until we catch the bastards who did this."

"We can arrange that, sir," Jimmy said. "We've got some good—"

Troy didn't let him finish. "No. You don't understand. We want you boys." He inclined his head toward Commissioner Parker, who was still standing there playing the dummy. "The commissioner tells me that you know how these hoods work, so we want you to handle it. It'll mean you'll have to work double shifts, but I'm sure you won't mind the extra money." He turned to me. "I hear your wife's pregnant with your first child, Downing. I imagine the extra dough will come in handy."

It surprised me—the man knowing so much about my life. I glanced at the commissioner. He gave me a curt nod.

"Does that mean we're off the investigation?" Jimmy asked.

He had directed the question to Commissioner Parker, but it was Troy who answered.

"Not at all, Finn. And the commissioner assures me you'll have all the help you need on that. In fact we're assigning Lieutenant Morgan—who I think you met downstairs—to help you. You'll be in charge of the investigation, but you'll work through the lieutenant. He'll coordinate things and report back to the commissioner. But understand me. I want Mrs. Reed protected, above . . . all . . . else." He had emphasized each word, and now held Finn's eyes. "Do we understand each other?"

Finn nodded. "We do, sir."

"Good. Then we'll want one of you to stay here tonight." Troy turned to me again. "You, Downing, I think. Mrs. Reed is understandably upset, and Finn, here—big as he is—might be a bit intimidating."

"Yes, sir," I said.

"Good, we'll get out of your way, then. Catch the bastards who did this. And do it as fast as you can."

When Manny Troy and Commissioner Parker left, Jimmy stood there stone-faced for several long minutes. It was a warning sign I'd already learned about in the few weeks we'd worked to-

gether. Jimmy had emigrated from the old country when he was
ten years old and his prolonged silences—together with a thick-
ening Irish brogue, when he did speak—were sure signs of his
anger.

"How's this for a lovely crock o' shit," he finally said. He ran
a hand through his wavy red hair.

"What do you think it means?" I asked.

He glared at me. "About this case? Who the fook knows? But
it sure in hell tells us who runs this police department, doesn't
it, now? And it also tells us the people running it have got their
own little informer in that lovely man, Lieutenant Morgan."

I didn't know what to say to that. "What do you want to do?"
I asked.

Jimmy glanced about, almost as if looking for someone he
could hit, his face now as red as his hair. "Let's check out the
room," he snapped. "See what we can find before Manny Troy
and his stooge decide we'll not be needin' any physical evidence
either."

"You don't buy his theory, then," I said.

"I'm not buyin' nothin'." He stared hard at me. "I'm not sellin'
nothin' neither. Not till I figure out what really happened here.
So make believe you're a fookin' detective, will ya, and help me
look around this fooked-up crime scene."

I left Jimmy to search the body and the area surrounding it.
I took the perimeter of the room, looking for anything the killer
or killers might have left behind. Near the open French doors I
found the clue that would come to haunt me.

"Over here," I called.

Jimmy and I stared at the bronze gavel that had been hidden
by one of the open doors. It was covered with drying blood. A
small plate that had been attached to its head, bearing the
judge's name, now hung off to one side, the force of the blows
apparently having dislodged it.

Jimmy nodded; then using a handkerchief carefully lifted it
from the floor. He weighed it in his hand, then put it back. "A
good weight for turnin' a man's head into mush," he said.

"There's something else." I used my elbow to carefully move
the door; then pointed to the gouges in the wood next to the
lock. "Doesn't look right, does it?" I said.

Jimmy stared at the marks and snorted. There were gouges on the exterior, but there were some on the interior part of the door as well—marks that shouldn't have been there, marks that were clearly made from the inside. "Looks just fine if you wanna break into a house from the inside," he said. He gave out a small laugh. "Or if ya wanted to make it look like somebody broke in, but didn't know how to pull it off."

"Have to be pretty stupid," I said.

"Or pretty scared," Jimmy countered.

I was grinning over my discovery, feeling quite full of myself. Jimmy looked up at me and shook his head. "You're a cocky young shit, ain't ya, boyo?" He returned my grin, and continued before I could answer. "But that's good. You can't be a good detective unless you've got a big pair hangin' between your legs, now can you?"

I gave him a nod and another smile; then I stepped through the doorway and out onto the small balcony to see if anything had been left there. The rain had finally stopped and the normally muggy August air felt cool and fresh and clean.

The balcony overlooked a long, narrow garden, thick with well-tended flower beds. There were stone benches set at each of the garden's corners, so a person could sit and enjoy the mingled fragrances that now drifted up to the balcony.

It was then that I first saw her. She was standing on a narrow, paved walkway beside one of the farthest benches, a cigarette held absentmindedly between her fingers. She didn't raise it to her lips. She just held it, seemed to have forgotten it was even there. She was dressed in a thin, gauzy dress that looked a very pale red under the glow of light that came from the house, and it gathered about her slender body, accenting every beautiful curve. Her head turned up toward the balcony, almost as if she had felt me watching, and the delicate lines of her beautiful face made my breath catch in my throat.

"There's someone in the garden," I said to Jimmy. "A woman."

Jimmy stepped beside me and followed my gaze. "That'll be Mrs. Reed." He kept his voice low, little more than a whisper, not wanting it to carry down to her. "I've seen her picture in the papers. Her and the judge were pretty big on the society pages."

"She's beautiful," I said.

"Yeah, she is that. Maybe you should clamp your jaw shut and go down and meet her, since you'll be stayin' here with her tonight. I'll stick with the body. I've got to get the ME and the forensic boys up here before Manny Troy tells me we don't need 'em."

There was a circular staircase leading from the balcony to the garden. The rain had destroyed any hope of fingerprints, so I took the staircase down and walked across the garden to where Mrs. Reed waited. I walked slowly, taking care to hide the limp that always showed when I moved at a faster pace. Coming from the house behind me, the sweet, mournful voice of Billie Holiday floated into the night. I couldn't make out the lyrics, but the magic in the voice was unmistakable, and when I reached Mrs. Reed I found her even more beautiful than I had thought, and I didn't know if it was the music, or the night, or the woman herself.

"You must be one of the detectives," she said. She had blond hair bobbed at her shoulders that accented the finely etched bones of her face. Her lips were full, her eyes a deep dark blue. She was much younger than her husband, no more than twenty-two or twenty-three. Judge Reed had been well into his fifties. There was no indication Mrs. Reed had shed any tears.

I introduced myself and explained that Detective Finn and I would be handling the investigation of her husband's death. I asked her when his body had been discovered and who had found it.

"I did." Her hands trembled as she spoke. "I guess it was nearly four hours ago, almost eight o'clock. We were supposed to go out to dinner. Wallace was working in his study while I got dressed. When I went to tell him I was ready . . . I . . . I . . ."

"It's all right. Take your time." I waited, but she didn't say anything more. "Did you hear anything? Any sound of someone breaking in, or the sound of a struggle?"

She shook her head, the ends of her hair moving about her long neck as though caressing it. "I was in the bath for a long time. The door was closed and the water was running almost constantly to keep the bath as warm as possible."

I fought off the image. I was standing close to her now, and could better see how the soft, gauzy material of her dress moved against her body with every gesture, every turn of her head. She folded her arms across her breasts and shivered.

"Are you cold?" I asked. "Maybe we should go inside."

She looked back at the house as if she dreaded that possibility. "I don't know how I'll ever be able to stay here." She looked at me with a deep sadness. "But I don't have anywhere else to go."

"Don't you have family nearby?"

"I don't have any family at all." Her voice was soft and frail, a whisper lost on the wind. She seemed to think about what she had said, then added: "Everyone in my life is gone now."

There wasn't much I could say to that, so as gently as I could I explained what Manny Troy had asked us to do.

"Does Mr. Troy think I'm in danger?" There was no hint of fear in her voice, and that surprised me. A great deal about her surprised me, in fact. For a woman who had just found her husband brutally murdered, she seemed remarkably in control of her emotions.

"I think it's more a question of not wanting to take any chances. And since Detective Finn and I will be investigating the case, he asked us to keep an eye on you as well. One of us will be here with you at all times, Mrs. Reed."

She considered what I had said and nodded once. "Then you better stop calling me Mrs. Reed. My name is Cynthia. My friends call me Cyn."

"If that's what you'd like. I guess you should call me Jake, then. And Detective Finn's name is Jimmy."

She stared at me with her deep blue eyes that had not yet cried. It was as though she was seeing me for the first time, perhaps realizing how taken I was with her beauty. A small smile flirted with her lips; then it disappeared. "I think I'm going to like you, Jake. You're tall, and I like men who are tall. I like your curly black hair and your green eyes. And you have a good, strong jaw. I think a good jaw is important. It lets you know you can count on someone. So I'm going to count on you, Jake. I'm going to count on you a great deal."

(2)

The sound of the priest's voice drove the memories away. Jake Downing looked back at his wife's casket, realizing how wrong it was to be thinking about Cynthia Reed; to be thinking about that time gone by that had forever ruined his marriage.

He stared at the casket suspended above the open grave where the Mary he had known would spend eternity. She's dead, he thought. And I'll never see her again; never talk to her again; never touch her again.

A gust of wind whipped across the cemetery, dislodging the single rose he had just placed on her casket. He watched it tumble then fall into the great hole beneath the coffin. He kept staring at where it had gone, barely hearing the priest's final prayer. He did recognize that it was being said in Latin. Mary had asked for that in those terrible final hours before her death—

that all the prayers be said in Latin. She had preferred it that way. She had been a good Catholic, devout in her way, but she had never approved of the change to English more than a decade ago. She thought it had robbed her church of its mysticism. He had never cared. He had never listened to the prayers anyway, had never believed what they said.

His daughter, Kate, took his arm. "Are you okay, Dad?"

He grunted in reply, not really sure how it would, or should, be taken. "As good as I can be."

The mourners began to file past. They were all there—the mayor, all the chiefs, all the senior commanders who wanted to kiss up. Many of the detectives he commanded were also there. He hoped at least they had come out of respect. As chief of detectives for the New York City Police Department, the book said, he was entitled to all respect due his rank at all times. It was a laughable notion, he realized, especially for those very few who knew his history.

The last person in the long line was one of those people. Jimmy Finn was sixty-five and retired from the department for the past decade. His hair was white now, the red having disappeared years before, and there were deep lines in his face, but he was still big and burly, still looked as though he could carry his weight in a dark alley.

Jake took his hand warmly. He, too, had changed over the years. There was gray at his temples now, and he was thicker in the body. But the biggest change was in his eyes. The cocky self-assurance those eyes had held when he and Jimmy were partners was gone now, replaced with a weariness that came close to despair.

"Thank you, Jimmy. Thank you for sharing this day with me." Jake tried to smile, but failed. "Will you have time to come back to the house? I really need to talk to you."

Jimmy placed a hand on his shoulder and gave a light squeeze. "Of course I will, Jake. I'll do whatever you want."

Jake Downing's house was in the Park Slope section of Brooklyn, only half a block down the sloping hill that fell away from Prospect Park and gave the area its name. Over the years the house had been through many transitions, almost as many as he had, himself. One hundred years ago, when it and those around it had been built, the stately four-story brownstones had been home to middle-class gentry, the doctors and lawyers and merchants of then fashionable Brooklyn. Later, as times grew hard, the homes had been chopped into tenements to house the flood of immigrants rushing to a better life. Later still, as those immigrants prospered, the houses became two- and three-family flats. It was then that Jake's father, a city fireman, had bought this house, turning it into a two-family residence—one to house his wife and two sons, and another to help pay off the bank. Upon his parents' death Jake had inherited the house—his brother having died in the Pacific during World War II—and he had lived there with his wife, Mary, and his daughter, Kate.

Now, in his prosperity, the house had been restored to its original glory. Now, with his wife dead, and his daughter married and gone, he had four floors of beautiful rooms in which to ramble about alone.

Jake saw to his guests as best he could. The politicians did not join the post-funeral gathering. Having done their duty to a senior chief who was nearing retirement, they had gone on to more important and potentially beneficial matters. Those who gathered were a clutch of family and friends, together with those police colleagues who felt compelled to attend, through either loyalty or expediency. It was mostly quiet conversation, recollections of Mary and the thirty-three years she had lived as a cop's wife. Some of it was clearly self-serving, subordinates wanting to curry favor by treating Mary's death as a near personal loss even though they barely knew her—most of them pleased that her passing provided a chance to do so. A local restaurant had supplied the food and drink, also pleased to be serving the chief of detectives, hoping for favors their efforts might one day bring. Jake suffered through it, remaining polite and political himself. Over the years, he too had played the same game more often than he cared to admit, so he played it again now from the other end with as much grace as he could manage. His daughter, Kate, was being the true hostess, making sure all had enough to eat and full glasses in their hands, and speaking about her mother with the only true feeling to be heard within those walls. So there was little for him to do except play his role as bereaved husband, the powerful chief brought low by his wife's passing. He quietly despised every moment of it.

After an hour, Jake took Jimmy Finn aside and led him to the small study he kept on the second floor. He poured them each a Bushmill's neat, and they took club chairs opposite each other—the chairs set before a cheerless, unlit fireplace that seemed suited to his mood. He rubbed his stiffening leg, Jimmy being one of the few people he would allow to see that perceived weakness.

"The leg botherin' you?" Jimmy asked.

"Just a touch." He paused a moment. "I'm reopening the case. I wanted you to know. I also wanted you to think about helping me."

Jimmy looked at him for a long time, but it wasn't due to any confusion. Jimmy knew which case. For each of them there was only that one.

"It's been thirty years, Jake," he finally said. "Is it because of Mary? Has the guilt of it come rushing back at you now that she's dead?"

"It's because of me," Jake said. "It's something I have to do."

Jimmy shook his head. It wasn't a negative act, more an uncertain one. "Why? What can it do for you now? Except maybe take away everything you have."

"What I have doesn't seem very important right now. It hasn't seemed important for a long time."

"Then do somethin' that'll *feel* important. Hell, Jimmy Hoffa's been missin' for two months now. Find where the mob buried the sonofabitch and be a hero. Or find Patty Hearst and show everybody what dummies they got workin' in the FBI. But don't do this. Don't pull skeletons out of your own closet."

"Will you help me?"

Jimmy studied his shoes and drew a long breath. "I've got no reason not to help you," he said without raising his eyes. "The statute's past, and I've been away from the job long enough I don't give a damn about my reputation." He looked up now. "But you're still young, Jake, and you'll have your choice of cushy jobs when you decide to throw in your papers. You've come a long way, boyo, and you've deserved everything that's come to you. You were a good cop and a damned fine detective."

"Except that once," Jake offered.

Jimmy gave him a pained smile. He had been Jake's conscience all those years ago. But his young partner had refused to listen. "Yeah, except that one time." He raised his glass in what could have been a salute. "Instead of beatin' on yourself, have you ever wondered how many could say as much?"

Jake sipped his drink. It was true enough, he told himself. In his thirty-three years on the force he'd played it straight—at least straighter than most. Oh, he'd bent the rules when they needed bending to make the system work. But never for himself . . . except that once. He drew a long breath and thought over Jimmy's words, thought about how they were both kidding themselves. Yes, he'd been an honest cop. There was no tin box buried in his backyard. But he also knew there were things far worse than taking money.

"So, will you help me?"

Jimmy stared at him, then finished off his drink in one swallow. "Of course I will. I don't know what good it will do, the case bein' as old as it is. What about the evidence we gathered? Surely it's gone missin' after all these years."

"I still have it."

Jimmy stared at him, incredulous. "Where? Not under your bed, I hope. It won't be worth a fiddler's fart if it's been out of official custody."

Jake shook his head. "It's been in the secure warehouse, under lock and key. I've checked on it, gone through it from time to time, but it's never left the building."

"You've gone through it? Why, for God's sake?"

Again, Jake shook his head. "I guess I was looking for some mistake we might have made—something that would justify what we did."

"And?"

Jake finished his drink now, got the bottle and poured them each another. "We didn't make any mistakes, Jimmy." He returned to his chair. "We knew who killed the judge. We just didn't take the final steps to prove it." He watched his old friend take a long pull on his drink. "We let the wrong person go to the electric chair. That's the worst of it."

Jimmy's temper flared. "He was a murderous bastard. And

he deserved gettin' the juice. He deserved it five times over by my count."

"You're right." He kept looking at Jimmy's face, watching the emotions twist and change. "He just didn't deserve it for *that* murder. That's the bottom line."

Jimmy stared off at nothing, his large hand tightening on his glass until Jake thought it might break. "So, it wasn't just Mary that made you want to do this."

"She's part of it. I won't deny that." Jake leaned forward, his elbows on his knees. "Did you know that we never slept together afterward? That after Kate was born we always had separate bedrooms?"

Jimmy looked back at him now, his eyes filled with a deep regret. "I knew it started out that way, when she first found out. You told me about it then. But I never suspected it went on all these years."

Jake gave him a weak smile. "She could never forgive me, Jimmy. She still loved me, I think, but . . ." He let the sentence die.

"But she didn't know? Not about everything, I mean?"

"No, she only knew the part that mattered to her. I never told her the rest." He gave Jimmy an even weaker smile. "I couldn't do that."

Jimmy stared at his shoes for a long time. "It's a helluva thing to be askin' at the poor woman's funeral, but why didn't you ever separate?"

Jake sat back, cupping his drink in both hands, allowing their heat to warm the Irish whiskey. "Mary was a devout woman, and she wanted Kate raised with two parents. I don't think the idea of divorcing me and marrying someone else ever occurred to her." He stared into the glass, as if the amber liquid might hold a better answer. "And me? I didn't want to lose my only child as well."

Nearly a minute passed without either of them speaking. "There's been another woman," Jake finally said. "There've been a few, actually, over the years. But these last six there's been someone special." He thought over what he had said. "The others never really mattered. They just filled the emptiness. This last one matters a great deal."

Jimmy shook his head vehemently. "You can't blame yourself for that, Jake. You never signed on to be a priest. You did the right thing for your daughter. And you did what Mary wanted. I'm glad you did what was right for yourself, too."

Jake leaned his head back and stared up at the intricate pattern in the tin ceiling. A small, weary smile came to his lips. "Right and wrong, Jimmy. People think it's simple, but it's always such a complicated question, isn't it?"

The door to the room opened, keeping Jimmy from offering any reply. Kate stood there, a worried look on her face.

"Am I interrupting something important?" she asked.

"No, not at all. Jimmy and I are just kicking around some old memories."

Relief seemed to wash over his daughter's face. "Thank God. Could Sean stay here with you? He's driving me crazy out there."

Jake saw that his daughter had one hand behind her back, and he realized for the first time that she was using it to restrain someone or something. Now she released that pressure and a small bundle of energy raced past her into the room.

"Grandpa. Grandpa, Grandpa." The words came in a high, shrill voice, as a small boy of five ran across the room and jumped into Jake's lap, almost dislodging his drink.

"Have you met my grandson?" Jake was nearly breathless as he tried to contain the wriggling child.

"Looks like we may have to cuff him," Jimmy said, grinning at the small blond head that was emitting a stream of giggles as Jake began to tickle his stomach.

The boy held out his tiny wrists. "Put your handcuffs on me, Grandpa," he demanded. "Do it now. Please."

Jake pulled the boy's head against his chest. "I don't have them with me."

The boy looked across at Jimmy. "Do you have some?"

"No. I'm not a cop anymore. I used to be, and I used to specialize in locking up little villains like you. But that was long ago."

The boy turned back to Jake. "Why don't you have yours?"

"I didn't think I'd need them today."

The boy seemed to think that over. "Is it because Grandma's dead?"

"Yes, Sean. That's why."

The boy thought that over as well, seemed about to say something—perhaps about his grandmother, Jake thought—then decided not to. Jake wondered if his daughter had told the boy not to say anything that would make his grandfather sad. It would be like her to do that—like her mother before her, they were that much alike.

Jake looked across at his old partner. "I think I'm going to take Sean out in the garden for a bit. Would you be willing to meet me at the warehouse tomorrow morning? We could grab some breakfast afterward."

Jimmy nodded, then stood and stretched his back. He looked around the room as if analyzing it. "Have you ever noticed how much your house—now that you've fixed it up so grand and all—resembles the house Judge Reed . . ." He stopped himself, glancing at the boy.

"Yes, I have," Jake said, relieving him of the need to finish the thought. "It's not as big, not as grand at all, but I've noticed the similarity."

Jimmy looked at him for a long moment, then nodded. "What time tomorrow?"

"I was thinking nine o'clock," Jake said.

"I'll be there."

Jake's driver, Detective Pete Tedesco, waited in the hall by the front door, as the final guests began to leave. He was a tall, fit, muscular thirty-year-old with curly black hair and a cocky manner that Jake always associated with good detectives. He was not a handsome man, his large nose and bushy eyebrows eliminating him from any beauty contests. But he was thoroughly competent. It was Tedesco's job to play bodyguard, as well as to shepherd the chief of detectives from place to place. He had held the job for the past three years, half as long as Jake had held the rank.

When he bade his last guest goodbye, Jake turned and placed a hand on Tedesco's shoulder. "I won't need you anymore today. But I'll need you to pick me up tomorrow morning."

"You're working, Chief?" Tedesco was clearly surprised.

"After a fashion." Jake paused a moment. "What I'll be doing is police business, but it's something I'll want to do quietly. In fact I'll be doing a lot of it over the next few weeks. Do you have a problem with that?"

Tedesco shook his head. "Not at all, Chief. Nothin' goes beyond the car, or the office. You know that. Personal or business."

Jake patted Tedesco's arm and made a mental note not to involve him in the case. It could only harm the young detective's career. "I'll be ready at eight. But wait here a minute. I want you to give my daughter and grandson a ride home."

Jake found his daughter in the kitchen, supervising the cleanup the restaurant had included in its catering service. His grandson, he knew, was asleep on a parlor sofa, worn out by the excitement (or boredom) of the day.

"Leave this to the pros," he said, taking his daughter's arm and guiding her out of the kitchen. "They're not going to break the chief of detectives' dishes. Or steal them."

He led her into the room where his grandson lay sleeping. Kate was thirty, slightly plump, but in a pleasing way, he thought, and looked very much like her mother. She had dark hair and warm blue eyes, a few freckles about her nose and cheeks and a comely, maternal way about her. She was separated from Sean's father, a stockbroker and proven jerk, and the irony of that situation, juxtaposed with his own, was not lost on him.

"I've asked Pete to drive you home," he said, keeping his voice low so as not to awaken his grandson. "And I want you to do me a favor over the next few days. I want you to consider the possibility of you and Sean moving in here . . . permanently. The place is so big. Too big for just me."

His daughter stared at him for several moments. "I thought you'd want your . . . your friend to move in," she finally said.

Jake looked down at the floor, then back at her, and she could see the hurt in his eyes.

"I'd never do that. This was your mother's house. I'd never bring someone else to live in it."

A touch of color came to Kate's cheeks. "I'm sorry. I just thought . . ." She looked down at her sleeping son. "Will you see her later today?"

"Yes, I will."

Kate nodded, resigned. "Let her know that I appreciate that

she didn't come to the funeral. I know it must have been hard for her. I'm sure she wanted to be here to give you comfort."

Kate had never met the woman. She had seen them together once and had asked who she was. Jake had told her. Kate had known since childhood about her parents' estrangement and he hadn't wanted to lie to her.

"Molly's a good person, and she understood how you'd feel about it." He let the subject drop. "Please consider what I asked you—about you and Sean living here."

"I will."

Jake reached down and picked up his grandson. The boy didn't stir, or even blink. He kissed his forehead and carried him out into the hall.

Molly Reagan's apartment building was at the bottom of Fifth Avenue overlooking Washington Square Park. Jake had taken a taxi from Park Slope, preferring the expense to the aggravation of finding suitable parking for his personal car. The area around Molly's building, dominated as it was by New York University, seldom offered any space, and he disliked leaving the car on the other side of Sixth Avenue in the rabbit warren of narrow Greenwich Village streets.

The doorman sent Jake on up, having been previously instructed to do so by Molly. They had always kept his arrivals and departures as formal as possible, for the sake of his position as well as her own.

When the door to her apartment opened, Molly stepped into the hall and put her arms around him. It was an unusual public display of affection. Her voice whispered against his cheek. "You look tired, Jake. Come inside and let me fix you a drink."

He followed her into a large, comfortable living room with wide windows that overlooked the park ten stories below. The stereo was playing softly, and he recognized the voice of Janis Ian, one of Molly's favorites. He walked to one of the windows and looked down. They often stood before that window together, watching the eclectic mix of people, some sprawled on the benches and grass, others meandering along the walkways that crisscrossed the small park. The young, some students, some merely wanting to be perceived as such, always dominated the fountain at the park's center. There were mothers with children occupying the grassy areas, and the elderly taking up most of the benches. At the park's westerly boundary chess players congregated, often drawing crowds for a particularly good match. Collectively it was like a soap opera, so many of the characters unchanged from week to week. He and Molly had their favorites; had even given some of them names.

"Are the rooster and his girlfriend still fighting?" He raised his chin, indicating the area around the fountain. The rooster was a young man with red hair, cut in the style of a cock's comb. He and his girlfriend, a skinny child/woman in tattered clothing, sat at the fountain each day and argued.

"He seems to have a new girlfriend," Molly said. "Now they fight."

Molly came up to him and stroked his cheek. She was forty-two, an assistant medical examiner he had met six years ago as a newly made chief directing his first high-profile homicide, and today he found her even more beautiful than he had all those years ago. It wasn't an arresting beauty. Not the kind that made people stop what they were doing when she entered a room. It was subtler than that. Molly was average height, with a trim, attractive figure. Her hair was dark, cut just above the shoulders, her eyes a soft light brown. Her face was full and pleasing, unremarkable until she smiled. When she did, everything about her—everything around her—seemed to glow.

"Was it difficult?" she asked. "The funeral, and afterward?"

Jake smiled at her. "Not particularly. It went smoothly enough. I think Mary would have been pleased, if anyone could be pleased about their own funeral."

"Are your daughter and grandson all right?"

"Kate's fine. I think the fact that it was cancer made it easier. She had time to prepare herself for the idea, and then felt relief that her mother's suffering was over." He hesitated a moment. "Kate wanted me to thank you for not coming. I think she was worried you would—that it might be awkward." When Molly didn't respond he went on. "Sean was a devil. He drove his mother nuts, wore himself and everyone else out, and then fell asleep on a sofa."

Molly smiled at the image. She had met the boy numerous

times when Jake had taken him on afternoon outings. She had never had children of her own, and Sean provided vicarious pleasure, a substitute for the maternity she had sacrificed for her career.

"You should have handcuffed the little rascal," she said.

"That's what Jimmy Finn said. Sean was all for it."

"Jimmy Finn was there?"

Molly had never met Jimmy, but she knew who he was. She also knew the story that lay behind their friendship. She knew Jimmy's part in it; Jake's part—knew how it still haunted him. He had told her all of it five years ago, when he was certain that he loved her, certain that he wanted her in his life until the end. Outside of those who were there thirty years ago, she was the only living person who knew it all.

"Jimmy and I are going to reopen the case." He spoke the words in a matter-of-fact tone.

"Why, for God's sake?" Molly seemed truly incredulous.

"That's the same thing Jimmy asked." He smiled at her. "I guess it's like the man who climbed the mountain, then told everyone he did it because it was there."

Molly took his hand and led him to the sofa. When they were seated she took both his hands in hers. "It's a bad reason, Jake. I hope you have a better one. You'll be throwing away a great deal."

"Call it conscience, then."

"That's a better reason. But there are other ways to salve your conscience."

"I don't think anything but the truth will work." He paused, wondering if he should go on with the rest of it. He decided he had to. "I'll need your help to do it right."

Molly let out a long breath. "What exactly will you need?"

Jake stood and began to pace, allowing the first bit of nerves to show. "I've still got the evidence. It's as pristine as possible after thirty years. I've made certain it remained that way."

"So this is something you've always known you'd do?"

He thought about that. "No." He paused again, not sure how she would take it. But there was no choice now, only complete honesty. He gave her a regret-filled smile to soften the words. "I knew I couldn't while Mary was alive. I couldn't risk hurting her again."

"And now you can do it . . . even if it hurts you." She shook her head.

He ignored her last words. "Now I can do it."

Molly studied her hands, pressed them together, and then raised the tips of her fingers to her lips. When she lowered them again, she looked up at him, her eyes sad. "What will you need me to do?"

Jake had forced himself to stop pacing, and stood over her now. "There are still samples of dried blood. Most of it belongs to the victim. Some, I think, may have been the killer's. There's also some tissue that was under the victim's fingernails. It's still sealed in a test tube. Also some fibers and hair follicles. I'll want it all tested. There are things we can find out now that we couldn't back then."

"You're talking about some pretty sophisticated tests. It will be expensive, so you'll have to authorize it . . . officially. With this fiscal crisis we're in, with all the talk that the city may even default on its bonds, any extra expenditure is going to draw a lot of attention."

"I know. So we'll start slow; get to the heavy ticket items if the early stuff proves out. For now, just review the autopsy and the other forensic evidence we found at the scene. The reports back then . . . well . . . let's just say they weren't as complete as they should have been. I'd like to see what you can find."

Molly looked down at her hands again, refusing to meet his eyes. "You're asking me to do things that could destroy your life if I'm successful."

Jake took the seat next to her again. "No, that's not what I'm asking. I'm asking you to help me take my life back."

(3)

"Good morning, Chief. You here to look at your pet case again?"
The words came out of Charlie Donahue's mouth respectfully,
but with a hint of mirth to them.

Donahue was a sergeant closing in on his thirty years—an
old hairbag in department lexicon, a term used to describe an
aging and often useless cop who was just biding his time until
he could get out. In Donahue's case it wasn't deserved. He had
been badly wounded in the line of duty more than a dozen
years ago and had opted to remain in a desk job rather than
take a disability retirement.

Jake Downing nodded. "One more time." He glanced at his
watch. "I've got my old partner, Jimmy Finn, coming by in half
an hour. Bring him back to me when he gets here, will you?"

"Sure, Chief." Donahue paused a moment, his round red
face pregnant with the question Jake knew he had wanted to

ask for several years. Now Jake had a reason to give him an answer. Not the right one, of course, but one he might pass on to anyone who started nosing around later.

"You'd like to know what I'm doing with this old case, wouldn't you, Charlie?" He grinned at Donahue, who was his own age but whose full head of silver hair made him look ten years older.

"Ain't my business, Chief." He returned the grin. "But if you're offerin'."

Jake laughed, keeping the moment light. "I'm planning on writing a book after I toss in my papers, Charlie. Some of the tougher cases I've had. That's why I've got Jimmy Finn stopping by. I'm hoping he'll help jog my memory."

"Should be a great book, Chief. I'll make sure to buy one myself."

"I'll count on it." Jake started down the long, bare corridor he had traveled so often over the years. "I'll even sign it for you."

Jake arranged the evidence on a long table that took up most of the small, bare-walled room he had commandeered. Every piece of physical evidence, every report filed, every notebook listing his and Jimmy's observations was there—the edges of the notebooks and reports now yellow and brittle with age. He stared down into the center of the table where one of the most crucial pieces of evidence sat, then he reached out and picked up the plastic-encased gavel—its heavy bronze weight filling his hand, the crusted, dried blood still visible on its head. There are things you'll tell us now, he thought. Things I've waited a very long time to hear.

MANHATTAN, 1945

I watched her throughout the wake and thought I'd never seen a woman more beautiful in mourning. Jimmy and I had positioned ourselves so we could keep her in view at all times, but I have to admit, had that not been our assignment, I would have tried to do so anyway.

It wasn't that we bought the argument, the one that said Cynthia Reed was in danger. Jimmy surely didn't, and I had very strong doubts that her husband's killer was out to get her, too. But that was the official line, and the men who expected us to act as though we believed it were all sitting nearby— Commissioner Parker, the mayor, the members of the city council, and most important, Manny Troy himself, the provider of the theory.

We were in the Walter B. Campbell Funeral Home on Madison Avenue, the official place of death and mourning for the city's upper crust. The body was laid out in an open casket in the funeral home's largest room. All the stops had been pulled out, including Manny Troy's summons to every Democrat, big or small, to make an appearance for the great man.

That was how Judge Wallace Reed, or rather his corpse, was being portrayed. The great man taken down by the criminal element he had fought against all his life. Maybe it was true, but somehow I didn't quite buy that either. Jimmy didn't buy it at all. He had actually held his nose when Manny Troy had laid it out for us that morning. Of course, he waited until Troy had left the room before he did it.

I had laughed at the gesture and Jimmy wagged a finger at me. "Have no doubt about it, boyo," he had said. "At that level they're all a bunch of thieves. Trouble is they're also the ones who make the laws, so ya can't even lock 'em up when they pick yer fookin' pocket."

Manny Troy turned to look at me, just as I was recalling Jimmy's words. He held my eyes, almost as a warning that he could read my mind. Then he nodded and turned his attention back to the casket. It was a small, subtle gesture, but it sent a chill down my spine.

It took two hours for the party faithful to pay their final respects. Throughout it all Cynthia Reed sat on a small settee to the right of the casket with Troy at her side. She was dressed entirely in black, a delicate hat on her head, its veil concealing her face. There was a lace handkerchief clutched in one gloved hand, and occasionally she brought it up beneath the veil, as if dabbing tears from her eyes. I couldn't help wondering if the tears were real, or if they existed at all. There were no sobs. None of the movements you'd expect, the slight tremors that always accompany a woman's tears.

Occasionally Troy would pat her hand, or lean in for a whispered word, as if helping her bear up to it all. Again, I wondered about the need. Cynthia Reed sat erect and beautiful, accepting the condolences of strangers with a quiet elegance that seemed almost . . . bored.

We left the funeral home at nine, the widow joining Troy in the rear of his Packard; Jimmy up front playing bodyguard as I followed in our unmarked sedan. It was my night to stay at the house again, and when we arrived I placed a quick call to Mary to make sure she was all right. She was eight months along now, and this final stage of her pregnancy had us both a bit on edge.

"Everything okay?" Jimmy asked when I had finished my call.

"Yeah," I said, nodding with more conviction than I felt. "Her sister stays with her whenever I'm on duty. Just so she isn't alone."

"I can cover for you if you want to get out to Brooklyn for a bit," he said.

I shook my head. I was too new to homicide to be taking any liberties. "I'll do my bit," I said.

Jimmy gave me a little cuff on the shoulder, then inclined his head toward a small sitting room. "Let's go in there," he said. "There's some things I want to fill you in on."

We went inside and closed the door behind us. It was an elegant little room with damask-covered settees, brocaded drapes and a fine oriental rug sitting on highly polished oak. It was like every other room in the house, I thought. It made a loud, clear statement. The people who live here never want for anything.

Jimmy sat on one of the settees and took out his notebook to make sure he didn't leave anything out. "The canvas of the neighborhood and all the judge's friends and associates is finished up, and it gives us one big goose egg. The judge's aide did confirm what Manny Troy said about the judge gettin' some threats, but he acted like that was pretty much par for the course, and he sure as hell didn't make a deal out of it like Troy did. Speakin' of Troy, I got him printed, along with everyone else who was in the house, so at least we can rule out prints that shoulda been there. But as far as prints at the murder scene go, we're comin' up goose eggs again." Jimmy flipped to another page. "The autopsy report came in, and based on the angle of the blows it seems the judge was flat on his back when the mortal ones were struck. Maybe even unconscious, or close to it, since there weren't any defensive cuts or bruises on his hands or arms."

"So you're saying somebody knocked him down, then finished him off with the bronze gavel?"

"Or he slipped and fell. We only know two things for sure. One is that he was down, maybe even out, when somebody turned his head into soup. The other is that it didn't take somebody with a lot of strength to do it. Poor bastard was pretty much helpless; didn't have a fookin' Chinaman's chance."

I digested what Jimmy had said. "You're thinking the wife?"

Jimmy inclined his head to one side. "It's like the great Irish poet once said: 'A pity beyond all telling, is hid in the heart of love.' And that, my lad, means that I'm sure as hell not countin' her out. I haven't exactly seen a river of tears flowin' out of the woman. And did ya notice that nobody showed to hold her up durin' the wake—except Manny Troy, that is."

"She told me she didn't have any family."

Jimmy raised his eyebrows. "Did she now?" He ran his tongue along the inside of his cheek. "Well that's interestin'." He took me by the arm and lowered his voice. "I did a little checkin' on the lady. Her maiden name is Marks, and she comes from a small town upstate, not far from Utica. The judge met her three years ago, about six months after his first wife died. The new Mrs. Reed was only twenty then, and accordin' to some friends of the judge she was workin' at the Stork Club at the time." Jimmy gave me a knowing smile. "Seems the records of that job have disappeared, but with the plans Manny Troy had for the judge that doesn't surprise me none. Anyways, it was a whirlwind romance, I'll tell ya that, with them gettin' hitched at City Hall three months later." Jimmy glanced over his shoulder at the closed door. "Interestin' thing is that the marriage register lists an Oliver Marks as a witness. It also identifies him as the brother of the bride."

I nodded slowly. "He could be dead. What with the war and all."

"Yeah, he could be. She could also be lyin' through her teeth; not wantin' us to know about this brother of hers."

"You think, if it was her did the judge in, that maybe the brother helped her?"

"Or vice versa." Jimmy waved his hand, taking in the room. "The judge was no pauper, boyo. So I'm thinkin' we can't afford to overlook the possibility that the lady and her brother decided to collect themselves a nice inheritance. I'm also thinkin' you're in a pretty good spot to ask her—easy like—about this brother she says she don't have."

I nodded. "I'll try. I'll try tonight."

Jimmy cuffed my shoulder again. "Just cozy up to her. Don't make too big a deal out of it. See what she says. I'm gonna make a call tomorrow to a cop I know up in Utica. See what he can find out about this pair."

After Jimmy left I found Cynthia Reed alone in the parlor. The strains of "Sentimental Journey" coming from the radio led me to her. She was sitting on a sofa, smoking a cigarette, her eyes fixed on a window and the dark night beyond. There was a large jasmine plant on the table beside her and its delicate scent mingled with the smoke coming from her cigarette. She hadn't heard me come into the room, and I watched her for a while. She looked small and lonely and lost.

"Are you okay?" I asked.

She didn't respond at first, or look at me. Then she turned her head slowly. "Hello, Jake." She took a long drag on her cigarette, still not answering my question. "Do you like this song? 'Sentimental Journey'?"

"Yes, Mrs. Reed. I do."

She held my eyes for a long moment. "I asked you to call me Cyn. Did you forget?"

I shrugged helplessly. "It seemed out of place, what with the judge . . ."

She smiled. "That's very . . . thoughtful, Jake. But it will make me feel better, make things seem . . . more normal. Will you do that for me? I need things to seem normal right now."

She was the kind of woman who made men melt, I thought. And there was very little that the average Joe wouldn't do for a woman like that. I nodded slowly, thinking that over. "Yes, I will . . . Cyn."

She seemed to inflate a bit; pleased I had done what she wanted. "You know you don't have to tiptoe around me, Jake. I'm not the grand lady Manny Troy would like everyone to think I am." She looked out the window again, as if seeing something no one else could. "My people were poor—dirt poor. I came to the city when I was eighteen to try and make something of myself, but I didn't do much of a job of it. I was only a hatcheck girl when I met my husband." She gave out a short, harsh laugh. "When we suddenly married, Manny Troy was beside himself. He had already picked Wallace to be the next governor, and I didn't quite fit the image of a governor's wife." She continued to stare out the window into the darkness beyond the glass. "But they fixed it. They created a job at party headquarters—one that I was supposed to have worked at for over a year. And they told me what to say and what to do." She turned back and gave me a wry smile. "And I became a grand lady, just because they said it was so." The sarcasm in her voice was palpable. She waved her finger as if it were a wand. "It was like magic, Jake. Hatcheck girl to grand lady. And you saw me tonight at the wake. Wasn't I grand?"

I wanted to tell her she had looked beautiful there, but held myself back. "It must have been very hard for you," I said instead. "All those people, and you knowing so few of them."

She tossed her head, making her hair sweep back from her cheeks. "Oh, that was easy. That was one of my first lessons when I married Wallace. They told me you only have to remember the names of the people who matter. The others just get a smile. But *everybody* gets the smile, Jake. Everybody."

"How do you tell the difference? I mean the ones who matter and the ones who don't?"

She turned back to the window again and her thoughts seemed to drift a bit. "That's easy too, Jake. They tell you who the important ones are, the people who really matter. That's what's truly amazing. How few people there are who matter in this world."

"Is that what Mr. Troy was doing tonight—when he leaned in to whisper something in your ear?"

A bitter laugh escaped her lips, and she turned to me and smiled. "Yes. When someone important came up to offer his condolences, Manny leaned in and whispered his name. You're a good detective, Jake Downing."

I gave a small bow of thanks. Cyn's sudden candor had turned everything around on me, but it had also opened a door. I decided it was a good time to push for the information Jimmy had told me to get.

"Still, it must have been hard with no family to help you through it. Not even your brother." Her eyes snapped to mine, full of concern or suspicion, I couldn't tell which. I hurried on. "But I forgot, you said you had no family left."

She looked down into her lap, a small smile playing at the corners of her mouth. "I was right. You are a good detective." She looked up at me now. "I have a brother. His name is Oliver. But he no longer chooses to recognize our relationship. So I do him the favor of not acknowledging him."

"And he chose not to come to your husband's wake?"

"He wasn't there, tonight, was he? And I doubt he could have missed the news."

"Does he live here in the city?" I tried to make the question seem innocent, but of course it wasn't.

Her eyes didn't meet mine. "I suppose he does, but I don't know where. We haven't been in touch for quite a while. The last I heard he was working in a bar on Third Avenue. A somewhat disreputable place under the El. It's called Brady's, I think." Now she raised her eyes and met mine fully, almost defiantly, I thought. "I'm sure you'll be able to find him."

I held up my hand, annoyed with the clumsy way I had handled it. "I didn't mean it the way it sounded . . . I . . ."

"Of course you did. But that's your job, isn't it? Finding out everything you can about everyone who was connected to my husband." She turned back to the radio. Frank Sinatra was singing "Saturday Night Is the Loneliest Night of the Week." She listened to the lyrics for a moment, then reached out and turned it off. "I think it's time for me to go to bed."

I was standing close to the sofa, and when she stood we were only a foot apart and I could smell the faint, delicate aroma of her perfume. It was jasmine, like the plant on the table beside her. I took a step back, but she reached out and laid a hand on my chest. "Would you do me a favor, Jake?"

"If I can."

"Oh, you can. It's very simple really." She moved a bit closer to me. "Would you put your arms around me, and just hold me? I'd just like to feel that there's still someone alive who wants to hold me. It doesn't even matter if they mean it . . . just so long as they do it."

I felt dumbstruck, but I took a half step forward and slipped my arms around Cynthia Reed's waist. It was stupid and I knew it. If someone walked in on us, I could never explain what was happening and why. But right then it didn't seem to matter. Right then her body seemed to melt into mine as her hands went to the back of my shoulders. So I just stood there feeling every part of her, all of it yielding, all of it soft and sensuous, every passing second making me want to do much more than give her momentary comfort.

Then she stepped back and sighed. There was the faintest smile at the corners of her mouth again. "Thank you, Jake," she whispered.

"You're welcome, Cyn."

I watched her walk toward the hall stairs; watched as she moved slowly up until she disappeared from sight, and even when she was gone I could still smell her perfume, still feel her soft, beautiful body pressed against mine.

{ 4 }

Jimmy stared at the evidence spread out like a feast across the long, narrow table. Almost imperceptibly he shook his head. Then he picked up a bundle of reports, tied together with twine, the edges now discolored by thirty intervening years. "It's all here, then, is it? Everything we put down on paper?"

"All of it." Jake reached out and gently tapped a small cardboard box that had been taped shut. "Plus our notebooks, which included some things we didn't put in the reports."

Jimmy glanced at him, then back at the table. "I seem to remember tearing some pages out of my notebooks." He looked at Jake again. "You didn't?"

Jake shook his head. "It's all there."

Jimmy began walking along the table, allowing his hand to brush against the evidence. Jake studied him closely. He was still a commanding figure, and the wavy white hair that had replaced the red added a touch of distinction he had lacked as a younger man.

"It should be interestin'. Readin' through these old reports again; holdin' the evidence in our hands after all these years." Jimmy stopped and looked up. He held Jake's eyes. "Like havin' ta look at the stains on yer own decrepit soul." He shook his head. The gesture seemed filled with regret. "I wonder if at my age, it'll be a good thing to read about my past failures. Or even at your age."

"I've already done it. Over the years I've done it more times than I can count."

Jimmy shook his head again. "Sweet Jaysus. You've been hauntin' yer own self. Do you know that?"

Jake winced inwardly at the rebuke. "I was never able to let it go, Jimmy. I was able to hide it, sure. But I could never completely get rid of it. It kept popping back up and sneering at me." He paused a long moment before asking what he had to ask. "Are you telling me it wasn't the same for you?"

Jimmy tightened his jaw. "I'm not tellin' you nothin'. I'll help you, because you asked. But I'll not be encouragin' this madness by openin' myself up to these dark thoughts." Jimmy reached out and picked up a book of matches that bore the name of a Third Avenue saloon. He tapped the matchbook against his palm, then held it out so Jake could read the name.

"This is where it all started to go wrong, you know. When we went to Brady's Bar and talked to her brother."

Jimmy pulled the car to the curb in front of Brady's Bar. He picked up his hat from the seat, checked it to make sure there were no dents in the crown. He never wore his hat when he drove, never risked battering it when he got in and out of the car. He was fastidious that way, almost comically so.

A train roared along the El as we climbed out of the car, and the flashes of electricity above our heads flickered against Jimmy's red hair. He put on his hat and looked at me across the roof. "Let's feel this fella out." He inclined his head toward the saloon's front door. "I know this rat trap. If he works here, like his sister said, we won't be dealin' with high-class goods. But let's play it easy for now. Just see what he has ta say. I don't wanna take any chances he'll go squealin' to his sister. Then have her decidin', all of a sudden like, that she's gotta protect her lovely brother. She may claim they're on the outs, but those things have a way of changin' once a cop gets involved." He raised his eyebrows knowingly. "You got my meaning there, sport?"

The instructions, as I had come to learn, were typical of the way Jimmy thought. A good detective didn't make problems for himself. He played it loose and easy, eyes always open. "I gotcha," was all I said. But I meant it. I was still watching and learning.

The interior of Brady's was typical of low-class Third Avenue saloons, a mix of dim lighting and dirt, blended with an overriding smell of stale booze that so permeated every crack and crevice, no amount of cleaning would ever remove it. The bar itself was a long mahogany affair, the surface deeply scarred by years of broken bottles and glasses. Behind it mirrored shelves displayed the bartender's wares, mostly the varieties of cheap rotgut preferred by the regular clientele. It was nearly eleven P.M. and a dozen still lingered on their stools, none apparently having a better place to be—or at least a better place that would have them.

We ambled up to the bar and Jimmy ordered us drinks, telling the bartender we'd take them at a table near the door. The bartender was a flat-faced mug, an ex-prizefighter, I guessed, with a nose spread across his face from too many sharp jabs. He eyed us, as did several of the regulars, all of them certain they knew who and what we were.

"Do ya know about this place at all?" Jimmy asked when we reached our table. He had kept his voice low and I followed the example.

"Can't say I do. I never worked this precinct when I wore the bag."

Jimmy nodded. "Well you're not wearin' the bag now. You're a fookin' detective, so you better mark this place down in yer book. The guy behind this joint is Owney Ryan."

"The Irish thug?"

"None other than." He tapped a thick finger on the table.

"And everybody who works here, works for Ryan. You get my meaning?"

"Cynthia Reed's brother works here."

"That's right. And that's why I didn't ask the bartender if he was here. He made us for cops, no doubt about that. So I thought we better just sit tight and wait for somebody to start sayin', *Hello, Oliver*, or, *Goodnight, Mr. Marks*, before we made our move. No bartender workin' for Ryan is gonna point a finger for a cop. Not unless he fancies losin' his meal ticket, and maybe more."

"So you figure Marks for a hood."

Jimmy tapped the side of his nose with one finger. "If he works here, he works for Ryan. And if he works for Ryan, he ain't no regular at Sunday Mass."

I knew Ryan, or at least I knew of him. He was an Irish gangster, a big, bluff thug who liked to portray himself as some kind of living criminal legend, one who supposedly ran the East Side of Midtown Manhattan. His power base was said to be the meat cutters union and the slaughterhouse it controlled on First Avenue. Part of Ryan's *legend* involved the number of gangland rivals who had hung on slaughterhouse hooks while awaiting more permanent disposal in the nearby East River.

"What about that upstate cop you were going to talk to? Did he know anything about the brother, or about Mrs. Reed?"

Jimmy leaned in close, still keeping his voice low even though Woody Herman's "Apple Honey" was now blaring from the jukebox. "I've been savin' that, 'cause I wanted you to get yer own read on the brother before I filled you in. But, yeah, I did." He gave me a knowing grin. "It's like I told ya, they hail from this small town outside Utica, so my friend didn't know nothin' from any personal dealin's. But he checked with a copper he knew who worked in that one-horse burg, and that boyo knew 'em good. Especially the brother." Jimmy offered up an all-knowing nod. "Said the rest of the family was okay. Didn't have the proverbial pot, but they was good people. Poor but honest folk, like they say in the pulps. He said the sister—that'd be Mrs. Reed—was always a haughty little thing. Walked with her head high, even though her shoes were fulla holes. Pulled it off 'cause she was such a looker, even as a kid."

"But nothing criminal."

"Not her. Not her folks neither."

"But our boy Oliver?"

"Ah, that's another story. This small-town copper tells my friend that Oliver was a punk, start to finish. If he wanted somethin', an' it wasn't tied down, he'd fookin' steal it. Had a juvenile rap sheet a yard long, and did one six-month bit in reform school. This flatfoot says he was always braggin' to his fellow villains, how when he turned eighteen he was gonna move to one of the big cities an' join up with a gang. That was the little bastard's ambition. He wanted to be a professional hoodlum." Jimmy grinned at me. "Got his wish, looks like. According to the copper, Mrs. Reed pulled out of that little town when she was eighteen. Came here to the big city. Then Oliver follows her two years later, when *he* turns eighteen. That'd be three years ago, and already he's tied in with Mr. Owney Ryan."

"This cop have anything else on him? Like maybe he went home to visit his folks and was bragging to his buddies about what he was doing down here?"

"No such luck. Besides, punks like him don't go visitin' their ma and pa. Not unless they're lookin' for a place to hide out. This copper did give my friend a description, though. Said Oliver was a tall, skinny kid, with real light blond hair—almost white, he said—and blue eyes that were so pale it looked like the color had faded out of 'em. He shouldn't be hard to spot."

We spotted Oliver an hour later. He arrived with a group of thugs headed by none other than Owney Ryan, himself.

Ryan was shorter than I expected. No more than five-eight. But he had a bull neck and thick shoulders, and he moved like someone who was sure about handling himself in tight spots. The thugs surrounding him were bigger and even rougher-looking. All except Oliver. He was the tall, skinny drink of water the upstate copper had described, right down to the pale blond hair and even paler blue eyes. The only thing the copper hadn't mentioned was the gold tooth that flashed in the front of his mouth, but that was probably something new—something he had added since joining up with Ryan.

The group hadn't noticed us when they entered, our table being tucked back at an odd angle from the door. But less than a minute passed before the bartender gave them the eye and made sure they knew we were there. A quick buzz went around their table, and each of them took a turn looking us over. It brought a big smile to Jimmy's mug.

"Well, looks like Oliver has arrived with his boss. Now they're all sittin' there wonderin' what the two dicks in the corner are up to." He gave me a long wink. "I think we should go an' tell 'em."

We walked toward their table under a shower of cold stares. I moved slowly, hiding my limp, not wanting these thugs to perceive any weakness. When we reached the table Ryan's square-jawed face broke into a grin that didn't carry to his eyes.

"Well, well, if it isn't Jimmy Finn. I didn't recognize you from across the room. I think my eyes are gettin' weaker." The false smile widened. "Christ, I'll be fifty next week, don't you know."

"You shoulda smelled 'em, even if ya din't see 'em."

It was one of the goons. Everyone at the table except Ryan laughed, and I noticed that Oliver laughed longest and loudest of them all. Ryan raised both hands, calling for silence. The gesture had a touch of benevolence to it. Jimmy gave the goon who had made the crack a long look, then turned back to Ryan and smiled.

"I gotta tell ya, Owney, that yer boy here is gonna look silly walkin' around with my blackjack hangin' out of his ear."

The thug who had shot off his mouth started to rise from his chair, but Ryan extended his hand again and motioned him back down.

"Now we don't want any trouble with these two fine detectives." Ryan had big horse teeth, I noticed, and he was using all of them now. I was sure Jimmy would like nothing better than to plant his fist right in the middle of them. Ryan leaned back and extended his arms in another gesture of benevolence. "Now what can I do for you, Finn?"

Jimmy returned the smile. "Not a thing, Owney. Not a blessed thing." He turned his stare on Oliver. It was as if a spotlight had just illuminated him on a darkened stage. All eyes turned to his tall, lanky body, and he squirmed slightly under the sudden attention. "It's Mr. Marks here I'm needin' to talk to. Would ya care to be steppin' outside with us, Mr. Marks?"

3 1911 00476 7159

HICKSVILLE PUBLIC LIBRARY
169 JERUSALEM AVENUE
HICKSVILLE, NY 11801

Oliver's mouth moved soundlessly for a second or two, then he stiffened his narrow shoulders with false bravado. "I ain't got nothin' to talk about." He had a high, reedy voice; more of a boy's than a man's, I noticed.

Jimmy shook his head and his eyes hardened. His earlier admonition that we treat Marks with kid gloves disappeared just as quickly. "That may be, *sonny.*" He emphasized the final word. "But I'm needin' to talk to *you.* So you can either step outside, or take a ride downtown. It's up to you." He jerked his head toward the door. "Right now would be a good time ta decide how ya'd like ta have it."

Oliver seemed lost; clearly uncertain about how he should handle Jimmy's demand. You could tell it was important to him to make the right choice in front of Ryan, and I could hear his feet shuffle nervously under the table as he threw his boss a questioning look. But Ryan just shrugged his shoulders, indicating there was nothing he could do.

Slowly, he rose from the table. "I ain't got a lotta time," he snapped. "I'm supposed to be workin'."

"We understand," I said as I stepped in front of Jimmy. I gave Oliver a friendly pat on the back that also propelled him toward the front door. "We won't take up a minute more than we have to."

Given that verbal concession in front of Ryan, Oliver stepped toward the front door with a slight swagger in his step. I wondered how Jimmy managed to keep from booting him in the ass before he reached it. I knew I was tempted to myself.

Outside on the sidewalk we squared on the younger man and watched his eyes dart nervously back toward the door, hoping without hope that someone would come out and back him up.

Jimmy started it off. "I guess you heard inside that my name is Jimmy Finn. *Detective* Jimmy Finn from homicide." Jimmy inclined his head to me. "This here is my partner, Detective Jake Downing."

Again, Marks shuffled his feet. "What's homicide got to do with me?"

Jimmy took an exaggerated step back; then turned in a half circle, a baffled look on his face. "Now could it be he doesn't know?" He asked the question as if addressing some invisible gathering, perhaps even the night itself. "Could it be his dear sister's husband went and got himself murdered and Oliver here doesn't know a thing about it?" He turned back to Marks. "Have you not seen the papers for the last day or two?"

Marks stared at him sullenly. "I seen 'em."

"Well, thank God for that. Then you know somebody went and murdered Judge Reed, your sister's own husband. When you didn't seem to know why two homicide dicks were standing on the sidewalk talkin' to you, I started to wonder. Especially since ya didn't show at the wake, and your poor, dear sister grievin' so."

Marks let out a snorting bark of a laugh. "Yeah, she's all broke up all right. She's probably countin' the judge's money, an' gettin' it all wet with her tears."

Jimmy turned to me and raised his eyebrows. It was all for show, all part of the game he was playing. "My, my, now," he said, turning back to Marks. "No wonder you didn't come to the wake, you feel that way about the poor, dear girl."

Oliver sneered at each of us in turn. "All I know is that she ain't gonna give me none of the judge's money. That's for sure."

"And should she be givin' you some?"

"Hey, why not? I'm her brother, ain't I?"

"Oh, I see. I thought maybe you felt she owed you for somethin'. Like maybe for some little favor you did her."

Marks's eyes became suddenly wary, like a rat watching a distant cat, I thought. "What's that supposed to mean?"

Jimmy spread his hands wide; let them fall to his side. "I dunno. Why don't *you* tell *me*? We're just two cops pokin' around. That's what we do. So why don't ya start by tellin' me when was the last time you saw yer sister and her poor dead husband?"

Marks shuffled his feet again, and I could tell he was trying out different answers, figuring which would be best. "I dunno," he finally said. "I don't keep track of stuff like that. Maybe a cuppala weeks ago, maybe more."

"It wouldn't have been a few days ago?" I offered. "Say like the day the judge was killed?"

Marks rounded on me. "Hey, whaddaya tryin' ta pull? Me and the judge, we got along just fine. Everything was jake between us."

"Oh, it was, was it?" Jimmy stepped in close, crowding him. "Why don't ya tell us about that?"

Marks stared at him, then shook his head in disgust. "All this, just 'cause I didn't go to a stinkin' wake?" He turned away, shook his head again, and finally looked back at us with a sneer. "So wakes make me nervous, what can I say? They have ever since I was a little kid." The sneer seemed to turn in on himself. "Besides, my sister wouldn't want me there. I ain't the kinda person she likes to associate with now."

I turned to the sound of movement. The sidewalk was shrouded in heavy shadows, the steel girders that supported the Third Avenue El blocking out much of the already inadequate street lighting. To my left a drunk staggered down the sidewalk, reeling in and out of the shadows, taking two steps to the side for every step forward. He had the look of a neighborhood regular patrolling his turf, and he was headed straight for us, his eyes filled with the hope of a handout. I pulled my tin when he was two steps away and held it out in front of his nose. "Beat it," I snapped. "And make it fast."

The drunk started to mumble under his breath, but I distinctly heard the word "fuck," and assumed it was meant for me. I ignored it. Oliver, meanwhile, had reached into his pocket and removed a roll of bills. He pealed off a five spot and handed it to the drunk. The word "fuck" was mumbled again as the drunk snatched the offered bill, turned and lurched away. I wondered if it was the only word left in his gin-soaked brain.

"That's pretty generous," Jimmy said. He raised his chin toward the pocket into which Oliver's bankroll had disappeared. "But it looks like you can afford it." He raised his chin again, this time indicating Brady's Bar. "Workin' in a saloon must be payin' better these days."

Oliver looked back toward the bar. "I don't work here no more."

"Ah, and where do ya work now?"

"I work for the meat cutters union."

A broad smile filled Jimmy's face. "Ah, Owney Ryan's little union, is it? Well I'll be. Seems like you're comin' up in the world. Now what is it you'd be doin' for that esteemed labor organization?"

Marks seemed uncertain again, but perhaps he was just trying to figure out what he actually did do for the union. "I just do
stuff," he said at length. "Whatever they need."

"Ah, kind of an all around factotum sort of fella. Is that what
you are, then?"

Marks momentarily struggled with the word, or perhaps the
suspicion that Jimmy had just insulted him. "Yeah, I guess." His
eyes were wary again.

"So let's get back to the judge," I interjected. "You said you
two were tight."

"Hey, why's that a big surprise? I was his brother-in-law,
right? He asked me to do him a cuppala favors an' I did 'em. He
liked that."

"*You* did the judge some favors?" Incredulity filled Jimmy's
voice.

"Yeah, what of it?"

"What kind of favors?" I asked.

I caught movement out of the corner of my eye and turned
and saw the same drunk weaving toward us again. This time his
eyes were fixed solely on Marks.

Marks saw him as well, and his displeasure with us seemed
to pass on to the staggering rummy. "Hey, I already took care of
you," he shouted. "Now get outta here."

The drunk stopped and looked back over his shoulder, as if
checking to see if his benefactor might be speaking to someone
else. Then he mumbled something and turned away. I was certain I knew what he had said.

Oliver watched him stagger away. "The nerve of some guys.
Just 'cuz they see you got a few bucks they think you owe them
one handout after another."

Jimmy grinned at him. "Sort of like you and your sister, eh,
kid?"

Marks turned back slowly and glared at Jimmy.

"So tell us what kind of favors you did for the judge," I said.

Oliver was momentarily sulky. "Hey, just stuff, ya know."

"No, we don't know," Jimmy said. "That's the trouble. So let's
just make believe we're a couple of guys don't know shit from
shinola." He stepped in closer, crowding Marks even more.
"What stuff?" His voice carried a touch of snarl to it now.

Marks seemed to sense what Jimmy was doing and he stepped back, buying himself some room. He gave a broad, expansive, self-important shrug. "The guy was a politician, right? He wanted to run for governor, right?" Another shrug. "So he heard I was workin' for the union, and he wanted to meet some union people. You know, to sort of try an' get their support."

"How'd he find out you were workin' for the union?" Jimmy gave me an amused glance. "I don't remember no announcement in the newspapers. You remember an announcement in the newspapers, Jake?"

Oliver caught the sarcasm and glared at him again. "Hey, musta been my sister who tol' him. All I know is he knew and he asked me to see what I could do."

Back in the car Jimmy placed his hat on the seat between us. "Interestin' story Mr. Marks tells." He grinned at me. "If ya believe any of that shit, that is."

We were still parked under the El. Jimmy had wanted to wait and watch. See if Marks left in a hurry after going back inside and reporting our conversation to Ryan. Nothing happened. He started to say something just as a train passed overhead, the sound so overpowering it deadened everything else, even momentarily shook our car as it moved through.

"Seems like we've got ourselves a few contradictions," I offered when the train had passed. "Mrs. Reed tells us her brother works in a Third Avenue dive. The brother says she knew about the union job and probably told the judge about it."

Jimmy smirked. "Yeah, lovely. And I can just see the judge reachin' out to some twenty-one-year-old junior gangster to get himself set up with some union people. As if Manny Troy couldn't do that by crookin' his little finger. More'n likely Owney Ryan found out the little squirt's sister was married to the judge and sent him sniffing around to see what good it might do him. More'n likely he found out before he ever gave the little punk a union job in the first place."

"You think the judge would have been dumb enough to let himself get mixed up with a thug like Ryan?"

Jimmy grinned at me. "Laddy, the more I see of politicians, the more I'm amazed at what they'll do when the hunger seizes 'em."

I laughed at the term. "The hunger?"

"Power, laddy. Prestige. Gettin' a shot at bein' the 'Big Dog.'" He put the final words in quotes with his fingers. "Or whatever job they think will take 'em there. What I'm talkin' about is—"

"Greed," I said, finishing the thought.

Jimmy grinned at me again. "Now you're gettin' the picture. But remember one thing. Greed covers a lotta ground. And it's not always a straight shot to where the money's kept. Some fellas, they go after power, 'cause they know it'll take 'em to the back door of that lovely bank vault."

"But it's always money in the end," I offered.

"That's what they tell me." He tapped the side of his nose. "All that time you spent at City College, before you joined the cops. You ever hear of that Eye-talian philosopher, Machiavelli?"

The question caught me off guard, coming as it did from the big, bluff, street-smart Irishman seated next to me. "Yeah, I heard of him. But just barely."

"Well, ya oughta have paid more attention. Then ya'd know how the merchant seeks wealth to gain power, and how the politician seeks power to gain wealth." He tapped his nose again. "Course ya mighta learned it by just watchin', too."

"Who should I have been watching?"

"The big dogs, that's who. Then ya woulda discovered the one truth of politics—how money always finds its way to the big dogs."

"And that's why you think the judge might have gotten mixed up with a thug like Owney Ryan. Because he wanted to be a big dog."

Jimmy gave me an exaggerated shrug. "No question he wanted it. We already know that. An' bein' the governor of New York . . ." He shook his head. "Well, there's only one dog bigger'n that, isn't there?"

Jimmy dropped me at the Reed house and I found it took some effort to climb the ten steps of the front stoop. It was my night to play watchdog, and as the uniform stationed at the front door let me in, all I could think about was finding myself a soft chair. There would be a second uniform in the rear garden and my official job was to stop anyone who got past either of them . . . if I could stay awake. My real job was to keep Manny Troy happy and play along with the idea that somebody wanted to harm the judge's widow. That, and to get whatever information I could from Cynthia Reed.

It was two in the morning and the house was dark. I settled into a chair in the parlor where they kept the big Zenith console radio and turned the dial until I found Sarah Vaughn singing "Lover." I was just starting to doze a little when Cynthia Reed stepped into the room. She was dressed in a thin silk robe, with an equally thin nightgown beneath, and the backlighting from the hall revealed every soft curve of her body.

I stood quickly. "I'm sorry. Did the radio wake you?"

She shook her head. Her eyes darted around the room as if checking to see if anyone else was there. Her hands were clenched in front of her, and she twisted the fingers of one and then the other. "My brother telephoned a little while ago. He woke me." She paused, staring at me with an open, nervous skepticism I hadn't gotten from her before. She seemed to be trying to decide what she wanted to say. "Why did you question him about my husband?" she finally asked.

I made a helpless gesture with my hands. "We're questioning everybody who knew the judge. It's just the way it is with a murder investigation."

There was a look of distrust in her eyes. "Do you think he was involved in my husband's death?" She stepped toward me as she spoke, her eyes still fixed on my face, as if this might reveal any lie in my words.

"We don't just talk to people because we think they're involved. We want to find out what other people knew about the victim. Find out everything we can. Sometimes it's those small things that lead to big ones."

She continued to stare at me, analyzing my face. "Don't believe anything Oliver tells you," she finally said.

"I'm sorry, I don't understand."

"Just don't believe him. No matter what he tells you, it will be a lie. Oliver lies very well, and he lies about everything."

I took a step toward her, but she spun away and moved back into the hall.

"About everything," she said again. Then she was gone.

(5)

Mary came into the kitchen, each step looking like a struggle. One hand was under her belly and she hiked it up with each stride forward, almost as if she were hauling her stomach across the room. When she reached a chair she turned her back to it, then placing a hand on the kitchen table and still holding her belly, she eased herself down in that way pregnant women have—like an ungainly bird settling on a nest. She finished it off with a long, weary breath.

"Did you have a bad night?" I asked.

She hesitated a moment, then looked up at me as though I was daft.

"Can you remember the last time I had a good one?"

The wrong question, I thought. "Do you want me to rub your back . . . if it hurts, I mean?"

"It always hurts."

I started around the chair but she waved her hand, telling me I shouldn't bother. "It won't help," she said. She looked at me again, seemed to take in the fact that I was dressed in my good, blue suit. "Are you going back to work already?"

"I have to. It's the judge's funeral today. You know the old saw. Detectives have to go to the funeral to see if the killer shows up."

She ignored my attempt at humor. "When did you get home?"

"About an hour ago. I just came to shower and shave and to change into some clean clothes."

"It's not fair, you being away all the time."

She was looking down into her lap, or what used to be her lap. I went to her, stroked her cheek and pushed an idle strand of brown hair back behind her ear. Her shoulders began to shake and I could tell she had begun to cry. She cried a lot these days. I knelt down in front of her, lifted her chin with one finger, and began blotting the tears with my pocket-handkerchief. She looked haggard; these last months of her pregnancy had taken a toll. She was still beautiful. Her face, like the rest of her body, had become plumper, but her eyes were the same warm, vibrant blue and the faint smattering of freckles about her nose and cheeks still offered that hint of mischief I had always found so appealing. Mary had been my high-school sweetheart when I was young and strong. She had come to me as I lay in an army hospital after Pearl Harbor, and she had continued to love me despite my ugly, mangled leg, and I knew I loved her then and now, and that I always would.

"I can't take the day off," I said.

She shook her head. "It's all right. We need the overtime money for the baby."

She started to cry again, and I reached around her as best I could and pulled her against me.

"You'll wrinkle your suit."

"It's all right. I don't care. Do you want me to call your sister?"

She shook her head again. "She's coming over later. I have a doctor's appointment this afternoon."

I felt like a heel. I'd forgotten all about the doctor. "I'll try to get off. I'm pretty sure Jimmy will cover for me."

"No, don't." Her head was still against my shoulder and I could still feel the tremors from her tears. "You'll lose overtime if you do, and we'll need every extra penny when the baby comes." She sat back and took my face between her hands. The tears were running down her cheeks again. "I don't mean to be such a baby." She sniffed deeply. "It's wonderful you got the promotion when you did, and that you're working all these extra hours now. I don't know what we'd do without the money it brings in. It's just that I miss you and want you here, and I'm a little bit scared, too, and I don't want to be." She smiled at what she was saying. "I know it's all silly, especially the part about being scared, but I can't help it." She wiped away her tears with the back of one hand and forced a laugh. "I want you here and I want you to earn all that overtime. Do you think you can split yourself in half and give me everything I want?"

I leaned in and kissed her nose. "I'll see what I can do," I said, realizing I hadn't the faintest idea what that meant.

Cynthia Reed stared at me across her husband's grave. She seemed very alone and very vulnerable as she stood beside the flag-draped casket dressed in a simple black suit and veiled hat. When I arrived at her house a few hours earlier she was aloof, almost as though I was a stranger, and she remained so during the two short rides we took together, first to the funeral home, then behind the hearse as it traveled to Saint Patrick's Cathedral. I had hoped she might continue the conversation she had initiated early that morning, but there was only silence between us.

Any chance that might change disappeared when we reached the church. Manny Troy joined her there, and the madness that was to take over the day began as reporters and photographers descended on her the way they always seemed to squeeze in on people who sat at the heart of a big story. It always made me wonder if that's what the term "press" really meant, rather than some vague reference to the machines that printed out the daily rags.

To her credit Cynthia Reed hadn't wilted under the onslaught. She had done the only thing she could. She had hidden behind her veil and endured the popping flashbulbs and shouted questions. Now, standing at the graveside, she was still hidden behind the veil. But somehow the light seemed to catch her just right, and despite that dark, gauzy shield I could tell she was watching me.

It was a bright, sunny day, better suited to a ball game than a funeral, and Jimmy and I were standing well to the rear of the crowd on a slight incline that allowed us to see everyone gathered at the grave. Lieutenant Walter Morgan, the commissioner's flunky whom we'd been told to work through, was standing behind Cynthia and Manny Troy, freeing us from our phony guard duty, and giving us a chance to look over everyone who had come. Yet my eyes were fixed on only one person, Cynthia Reed.

As I returned her stare I felt a nudge in my side when Jimmy leaned in and whispered in my ear even though we were far enough away from the crowd not to be overheard. "What's with you and Mrs. Reed? You two have been starin' at each other ever since we got here."

I hadn't told him about our early morning conversation when I returned to her house after our visit to Brady's Bar. So I drew him back further from the crowd and did.

"Now that's an interestin' tidbit," he said when I had finished. "Little brother went straight to the phone soon as we left, did he?"

"Seems like. And there's no question that it shook her up. Not so much that we talked to him, I think. But more about what he might have said. She definitely wanted us to know what a liar he was."

"Like we couldn't have figured that one out." Jimmy let out a little snort, then became more thoughtful. "I wonder what worried her . . . what it was she thought he might tell us."

"Maybe he hinted at it."

"And what was that?"

"That she was only in the marriage for the money."

Jimmy let out another snort. "Hell, she's gotta know that people have been thinking that ever since her and the judge tied the knot."

"Yeah, you're probably right. But she's still come a long way from where she started, and it could be she's afraid her hoodlum brother might start spreading stories about her that could drag her back down."

Jimmy chewed on that. "There could be another reason she don't want anybody talkin' to her brother. Maybe the same reason she didn't want anybody to know about him in the first place." He tapped his nose with one finger.

That little habit was beginning to annoy me. I also saw where he was going and shook my head, letting him know the idea didn't work for me.

Jimmy wouldn't let it go. He raised his chin toward the judge's casket. "If she did it, if it was her who killed him, I don't see her doin' it alone. The judge was a big man. Putting him on the floor wouldn't be easy."

Now it was my turn to persist. "I think you're putting too much into what she said. I was there and it wasn't like that."

"Then how was it?"

I tried to think that through. "I think her brother scares her. I think she knows what he is, and that any connection to him could hurt her. And if we're listening to him, then *we* scare her, too."

"Christ, we're not gonna arrest her on rumors, or on something her hoodlum brother says about her."

"I don't think she's worried about being arrested."

"Then what the hell is she worried about?"

"I think she's worried about what will happen if certain things come out; things about her and her brother. That maybe people won't consider her a lady anymore." I could see the doubt clouding Jimmy's eyes so I pressed on. "Remember, she grew up poor, and she came here to escape it. Well now she jokes about it, about working in a nightclub when she met the judge, and how she suddenly became a grand lady after she did. But I think it's important to her that people think about her that way, even if she won't admit it. And I think she's afraid her brother can take all that away from her."

Jimmy inclined his head as if considering the idea. "I think there's more to it than that, boyo," he said at length. "I think the lady's up to her ears in it. I'm not sure exactly how, but she's in it somewhere. I can feel it in my gut." He looked toward where she was standing, then back at me. "Don't go soft on her, Jake. Don't let those well-shaped legs turn your head."

I bristled under the admonition. "I don't intend to." There was a bit of a snap in my voice.

Jimmy grinned at my annoyance, then he let it go and pushed ahead. "I got somethin' for you to do after the funeral." He took out his notebook; found the page he was looking for, tore it off and handed it to me. It was a woman's name and an address in the Yorkville section of Manhattan, better known to the people of that neighborhood as Germantown.

"I want you to check this lady out without her knowin' it."

"What's her connection to the case?" I asked.

"That's what you're gonna find out." Jimmy stepped in close again, dropping his voice back to a whisper. "The lady's phone number was in the judge's address book. No name, just the number with a hand-drawn star next to it. I found it our first day on the case but it took since then to get a name and address outta the phone company." He gave a little tilt to his head. "Look, maybe it's nothin'. Maybe she's the cleanin' lady. Or maybe the judge had somethin' goin' on the side. Or maybe she's been holdin' him up for a kid he squired a dozen years ago. But the fact that he kept her number, but not her name, in his book makes me suspicious. And that means we gotta check it out."

"And that's why you don't want her to know we're checking. You want to find out what the story is before we brace her."

"That's right, boyo. It's hard to learn anything from people who know you're after 'em. You gotta get the lowdown before they start lookin' over their shoulder. And this one's gonna be harder than most." He tapped the name on the sheet of paper in my hand. "Lilly Straus of 1669 Second Avenue. That would put it right near the corner of East Eighty-sixth Street, and you're not gonna get a lotta help findin' out about a kraut woman in the heart of Yorkville. Not with all the nervous Germans up there." He gave me an all-knowing look. "And nervous with good reason. They didn't call East Eighty-sixth Street *Hitler's Broadway* for nothin', boyo."

I stood on the corner of East Eighty-sixth and Second Avenue with a German newspaper tucked under my arm. It was as close to a disguise as I was going to get and I had little hope it would do much for me. I was across the street from a German beer garden with tables set out on the sidewalk, and I was already catching furtive glances from some of the patrons. Before Germany's surrender much of the area had been openly pro-Nazi, a hotbed of Often Bundists, anti-Semites and outright spies; so thick that the FBI kept the entire area under constant surveillance. Now, despite the fact that Hitler and his boys had bit the dust more than three months ago, half the people on the street acted as if the war were still going strong. Or as if they all had something to hide. What the hell, I thought. Maybe they did.

Lilly Straus's building was three doors down from the beer garden. The address was solidly upscale, fourteen stories with a doorman out front, and rents guaranteed to be so far up there, I knew I wouldn't find any cops living in the building—at least not any honest ones.

Right now I was concentrating on the doorman. He was in his mid-fifties with a broad Irish mug, and I had him pegged as a retired cop or fireman. I was just biding my time, waiting for traffic in and out of the building to hit a lull so I could go over and brace him. It turned out to be the right move. Twenty minutes after I started my surveillance a car pulled up and Owney Ryan climbed out and headed straight inside. I decided to wait longer, rather than risk having him come out while I was talking to the doorman. He had seen enough of me last night to make me on the spot. Again, it was the right decision. Ten minutes after Ryan walked through the front door, a second car disgorged none other than Manny Troy. I stood there stunned, feeling like I had just stumbled into a gold mine that I didn't want to find.

Troy and Ryan left the building thirty and thirty-five minutes later, coming out the front door five minutes apart, not enough time to fool anybody watching, but just enough to keep any dawdling passerby from making a connection. Now I moved in on the doorman. There was one question I needed to ask, and I was sure I already knew the answer.

The doorman was seated behind a small desk just inside the front door. Even seated you could tell he was a big guy, and he had a wavy shock of white hair that accented a permanently flushed complexion and a road map of burst capillaries running through his cheeks and nose.

"Do somethin' for ya, mister?" he asked as I stepped up to the desk.

I flashed my tin and identified myself, and it brought a sardonic smile to his lips.

"I'm Johnny Collins, and I gotta tell ya that you bein' a copper ain't a big surprise." He raised his chin toward my badge. "Half the neighborhood had you pegged for either a city cop or a fed when you was standin' across the street. Don't tell me ya didn't notice?"

"Yeah, I noticed. What's with the neighborhood? They don't know the war with Germany's over?"

Collins chuckled over that idea. "Most of 'em are still waitin' for the other shoe to drop on the stuff they done over the last couple a years. Hitler had a lotta buddies in Germantown. Shit, he still does. Day after the little creep bumped himself off half the people around here was sportin' black armbands." The chuckle turned into a laugh. "Hell, some of 'em are even rootin' for the Japs now. I heard a couple of 'em in a bar last night. They were talkin' about those two big bombs we dropped on 'em a couple a weeks back, an' how those Nips still wouldn't give up. Said it like they hoped those bastards would keep on fightin' no matter what we did."

I shook my head at what he told me, more to curry favor than anything else. I could give a damn what a bunch of old Nazis thought. "So what's *your* story?" I asked. "You retired from the job, or what?"

"Fire Department," he said. "Thirty years and enough smoke in my lungs I can blow rings without a cigarette. What're ya nosin' around for?"

I glanced back over my shoulder, then gave a quick look toward the elevators to make sure the coast was clear. "Two guys left a little while ago . . ."

He started to laugh before I could finish. "Owney Ryan and Manny Troy. I noticed. In fact I notice them goin' in and outta here lotsa times."

"Who do they go to see?" I asked.

He raised his eyebrows. "Question like that could get a guy fired. And in case you ain't figured it out yet, jobs are gonna get tight with all them guys comin' home from the war."

I pulled out my wallet and handed over a five. He looked at it like it wasn't enough, then stuffed it into a pocket. "They both come to see the same woman. Cute little kraut broad named Lilly Straus, apartment 4B."

"What can you tell me about her?"

Collins gave a broad shrug, then looked at me as though he expected another five spot. "Hey, be friendly and helpful," I warned.

He shrugged away his disappointment. "What can I say? I don't figure her for a hooker, 'cause there ain't enough guys comin' by. Just Ryan and Troy and another bigshot. Except he ain't comin' by no more."

I held my breath. "Why not?"

" 'Cause he's dead. It was that judge got himself knocked off a couple days back."

"Wallace Reed." I said it flat out as a statement, not a question.

"Yeah, that's the one. For a while there I thought maybe she liked to have three guys at once. Then I figured they was just usin' her joint as a place to meet up." He grinned at me, then added, "Quiet like, if you know what I mean."

I thought it over and decided on one final question. "How would I meet up with this lady, if I wanted to?"

His smile broadened. "Hey, you want a lot for one picture of Lincoln."

I took out my wallet and withdrew another five. Mary would have a stroke if the department didn't reimburse me.

Collins's pocket swallowed the second Lincoln. "Meetin' her is easy. Every night after dinner she heads over to a bar on Second Avenue, has herself a couple of shots, then comes on home."

"Alone?"

"Usually alone. Couple of times she brought company. What the hell, it's a lonely world, right?"

Collins was grinning again, but I didn't join in. "What's the name of the joint she goes to?"

He told me and I placed my fists on his small desk and leaned down, bringing my face close to his. "I got one more thing I need you to do. And I need you to do it just because you're a good citizen."

He snorted, then offered up a regretful shrug that I took for agreement.

"I'm gonna go back across the street, and when Lilly Straus comes out I want you to give me the high sign. Got it?"

Collins nodded. Then the sardonic grin returned. "Least I can do for the city what gives me a pension."

Lilly Straus turned out to be a short blonde with heavy breasts and hourglass hips, all of it molded into a solid little package and a saucy, look-at-me sort of strut. I followed her down Second Avenue and watched her well-rounded butt gyrate with each step. She might as well have had flashing neon lights accenting each stride. But, like Collins said, it's a lonely world. Especially with all the men off to war.

The joint Lilly favored for her nightly drop-in was a small German bar that advertised a bratwurst and sauerkraut special in its front window. The interior was brightly lit and decorated like it belonged in some alpine resort, each wall holding an assortment of well-worn skis and travel posters depicting snow-capped peaks. Behind the bar four rows of elaborate beer steins gave it a finishing touch. Across from the bar there were a few tables scattered along one wall, occupied mostly by men who had hung their coats on the backs of the chairs. All the pictures of snow and the accompanying cold weather accoutrements didn't stop the place from being a sweltering hellhole in the August heat.

I spotted Lilly as soon as I entered. She was seated at the bar, as I had hoped she would be, and I moved to a stool two down from her and ordered a draft of Becks. There was a mirror behind the bar, and as the bartender served up a frosted mug I caught her looking me over. It was clearly an appraising look, as if she was deciding what I might have to offer.

I smiled, but she looked back at her drink without responding. So much for my good looks and instant charm, I thought.

Then she did something that almost knocked me off my seat. She picked up her drink and moved two stools down so she was seated next to me. She looked at her glass, then at me; then she smiled. "My drink iz almost empty," she said. She had a heavy German accent, her voice so low and throaty that it reminded me of the actress Marlene Dietrich. But then any good-looking German woman would remind me of Marlene Dietrich.

"It won't be empty for long," I said, as I nodded to the bartender.

He filled the glass quickly, removed enough money to pay for it from my small stack of change on the bar, and walked to the cash register to ring it up.

Lilly Straus turned to me and smiled. "You are a man of action," she said. "I like zat." She had crooked teeth that detracted from her looks and she seemed to know it because the smile disappeared quickly.

"Glad to please you. The name's Jake Downing. What's yours?"

"Lilly Straus." She rolled the "r" on her last name, and continued to watch me, almost as if she wanted to see my reaction to her accent. She started to smile again, but stopped herself. "Zo you zay you like to please me. Zen you do one zing more, yes?"

I was still wearing my hat, having only tilted it back on my head when I sat down. Now she reached up and took it off. "I zon't like it when a man vears his hat inzide. Bezides, you haf zuch nice curly hair." She reached up again and played one finger through my hair, then softly along one cheek.

I looked more closely at her blue eyes and realized that this trip to her neighborhood tavern was not for her first drink of the day. Lilly Straus was a little drunk, and the knowing smile I caught on the bartender's lips told me it wasn't the first time he'd seen her play this "friendly game."

Lilly finished toying with my hair and cocked her head to one side. "Zo tell me zumzing. You are not from here. I haf not zeen you before. Vere are you from?"

"Brooklyn. Out near Prospect Park. You know the area?"

Lilly nodded, then seemed to forget what she was doing. Her head kept moving up and down for a full ten seconds before she spoke again. It was as though her brain had to float through a sea of booze before it could reconnect. "I haf been to zee muzeum zere," she finally said. "You know it?"

"The Brooklyn Museum, sure. Right on Flatbush Avenue, just up from Grand Army Plaza. I grew up in the neighborhood so I've been there lots of times. Me and the other kids on my block, we used to visit the mummies whenever it rained on a

Saturday afternoon. Unless we could get our fathers to give us a nickel for the movies, that is."

Lilly laughed at the image I had offered her. When she did the lines around her eyes and mouth showed through the heavy layer of makeup she had applied, and I suddenly realized she was older than I thought, probably well into her forties.

"Vat do you do now?" she asked. "Now zat you are not a cute little boy anymore. For your bizness, I mean."

I had thought about this while I was waiting for her to leave her apartment and had come up with a ready lie. "I work for the city. In the office that issues construction permits." I actually had a friend who did work there who could cover for me if it ever went that far. "What about you?"

Lilly gave a small twist of her head, indicating her job wasn't much. "I vork for a real estate company. Vee buy property und hope vee can zell it zumday."

"You do the buying yourself?"

"No, no." Lilly shook her head emphatically. "My boss, Mr. Murtaugh, he does all buying, und all zelling. At least he buys und zells vhatever *his* boss says to buy und zell. I'm just zee secretary."

"And who's his boss?" I asked the question as innocently as I could.

"His boss iz Mr. Troy, but he iz almost never zere." She grinned drunkenly. "Actually, I am really Mr. Troy's secretary vhen he iz zere, und Mr. Murtaugh's ze rest of ze time." She shrugged and looked slightly sad. "But still just a secretary. Zey don't let me buy und zell nossing."

"That's okay, maybe you'll be calling me for a permit some-day." I could feel my stomach close to somersaults. But I had to be careful, and I still had to establish her connection to the judge. Lilly had finished her drink and I quickly ordered her an-other. I didn't want to push her too far, not yet, not until I'd had a chance to check with Jimmy and see how he wanted to play it. Right now I just wanted to soften her up, and I'd settle for the address where she worked and her home phone number. I wanted to leave an opening to see her again.

The bartender served her new drink, and she turned to face me. There was a coy look in her eye now.

"Zank you," she said.

I gave her my best smile, then spoke loudly enough to make sure the bartender could hear me. I didn't want to leave Lilly sitting there feeling like she'd been given the breeze in her neighborhood saloon. "This is kind of a busy night for me," I said. "In fact I'm supposed to go to a coworker's house for dinner, and I just stopped in for this one beer to kill some time." I broadened the smile. "But I sure am glad we met, and I'd really like to see you again some time."

There was momentary disappointment in Lilly's eyes, but she quickly forced herself to brighten up a bit. I could tell she was a woman who was used to promises that were never kept.

"I vould like zat," she said.

I picked up a cocktail napkin and placed it in front of her, then dug a pen out of my pocket. "Write down the name of your company and your home phone number, so I can get in touch," I said.

She brightened a bit further and did as I asked.

It was eight o'clock when I got back to the Reed house and found Lieutenant Morgan pacing the floor of the sitting room. He did not look happy.

"Where's Jimmy?" I asked.

Morgan hit me with a dark scowl. He had a narrow, pointy, ratlike face and thinning greased-back hair. He was under thirty, young for a lieutenant. He either had a very good rabbi in the department, or, like me, he'd benefited from the war. Right now none of that mattered to him. He glared across the small room, trying his best to intimidate me.

"Jimmy got called out," he snapped. "And he stuck me here, doin' *his* job." He picked up his hat from a chair. "Now you can take over till he gets back."

"When will that be?" I asked. "I got a pregnant wife at home, and I'm supposed to be off tonight."

Morgan held up a hand and started for the hall. "I don't wanna hear your problems. Either you or Finn are supposed to spend the night here. Those are the orders. And Finn ain't here, so I guess it's you." He kept walking, still holding up his hand. "And before you ask again, I don't have any idea when he'll be back.

He didn't say. He got a phone call and he just took off, leavin' *me* holdin' the bag. Now it's your bag. Goodnight."

I watched him disappear into the hall, heard the front door open, and listened to a brief exchange with the uniform outside. Then the door closed with a snap. "Shit," I said. I thought about Mary, realizing I needed to call her. I had tried earlier in the day when I knew I wouldn't be making it to the doctor's office, but she'd already left for her appointment.

There was a phone by the stairs in the hall and I went to it and dialed my home. Mary answered on the fourth ring and sounded as if she'd been asleep. I told her what had happened, that I didn't know when I'd be home.

"What did the doctor say today?" I listened as she gave me a rundown, and found out that the doctor had done what all doctors do. He'd told her the obvious—that she was still pregnant and that things were going as they should be going. Then she added the kicker.

"The doctor says no more . . ." She paused. "Well, you know. No more of *that*."

I drew a long breath. There hadn't been much of *that* anyway for the past few weeks. "Well, we knew it was coming," I said.

She paused again. "Are you disappointed?"

"Sure I am."

Another pause. "Do you think you'll have to stay there all night?"

I answered as truthfully as I could. "I really don't know. If Jimmy finds out I'm here, I'm sure he'll come back as soon as he finishes up whatever he's doing. But if he thinks he's sticking the lieutenant with the job, who knows?"

The answer didn't seem to please her, and I quickly gave her the phone number of the Reed house, telling her she could call me there if she needed to. I knew she wouldn't, but she'd been so down on herself lately I just wanted to assure her I was really working, not staying away from home because my wife was pregnant and not available to me in bed.

When I finished with Mary I called the desk sergeant at the precinct and left a message for Jimmy. Then I went back into the sitting room and settled down for what I hoped would be something less than the entire night.

The flash of a cigarette lighter made me jump in my chair.

"Hello, Jake." Cynthia Reed exhaled a long stream of smoke. She was seated across the room in a darkened corner that left her nearly invisible.

"Jesus, you scared the hell out of me." I shook my head and gave out with a nervous laugh. "I guess I'm not much of a body-guard if I can't see the person I'm supposed to be guarding when they're right there in the same room with me."

"I came in while you were on the phone." Her voice was soft and silky. "I was in the kitchen getting myself a glass of milk and I came in through the other door. That's why you didn't see me." She paused a beat as if deciding something. "Was that your wife you were talking to?"

"Yeah. I was due home tonight, and I had to tell her I wasn't going to make it until Jimmy got back."

"Is he coming back?"

"I'm not sure."

She paused again. "You don't have to stay. There are police officers in front and back. I'm sure I'll be safe."

I shook my head. "We can't take any chances on that."

She sat forward and I could see her now. She was still wear-ing the simple black dress she had worn to her husband's fu-neral, minus the veiled hat and gloves. Her shoes and stockings were also gone, and her bare legs seemed surprisingly erotic, and I realized how beautiful she looked sitting there in that dimly lit room.

"You don't really think I'm in danger, do you?" Her words had a light, airy sound to them, really more of a statement than a question, but I couldn't be sure if she wanted me to dismiss the danger or not.

I decided to play it out. "Why do you say that?"

She took another long drag on her cigarette and let the smoke out in a slow, steady stream. "I think you're guarding me because Manny Troy says you have to. But I don't think you be-lieve that the person who murdered my husband wants to harm me as well." She tapped the ash of her cigarette into an ashtray then brought her eyes back to mine. "You may even suspect that I was involved in my husband's death, and that would mean I wasn't in any danger at all."

I was momentarily stunned, and had to fight it off. "Why would we suspect you?"

The cigarette trembled in her hand and she quickly put it out. "I suppose you could say there are a lot of reasons. The difference in our ages. The fact that he had a great deal of money. Or maybe just because I didn't love him." The final words seemed to catch in her throat.

"Why didn't you love him?" The question came out before I could stop myself.

She looked away, and then back. "Because he was cruel." She tried to laugh but it came out harsh and brittle. "Everyone thought he was the great man, the oh-so-benevolent judge." Her mouth twisted as she said the words. "But he was the cruelest man I ever knew." Her face seemed to collapse. She stared at me, eyes filling with tears, jaw trembling. "He was completely consumed with himself. He was evil, Jake. Everything about him was selfish and evil."

Cynthia stood and started to move toward the hall. I was up before I knew exactly what I was doing. All I knew was that I didn't want her to leave. Not yet. I reached out and took her arm.

She turned to me, tears running down her cheeks. I could feel her arm trembling beneath my hand. "I loved him at first. I truly did. I didn't marry him for his money, or his position, or any of the reasons people said."

There was nothing I could say; nothing I wanted to say. I took my handkerchief out and began dabbing the tears away. She stared at me as I wiped the tears from her face. We were no more than a foot apart and her eyes seemed so large and so close they were all I could see. I remember letting the handkerchief fall to the ground and feeling her body lean in against me. Without thinking I reached out and took her other arm and pulled her even closer against me.

Our first kiss was hungry and full of everything we suddenly wanted from each other. There was no reason, no rationality to any of it. It was like falling into a black hole that I knew I would never climb out of. And right then I didn't want to.

{ 6 }

Jimmy Finn climbed the stairs to his apartment, noting, as he often did, that every crack and crevice in the wood, every blemish on the wall, seemed like an old friend. In one sense it was comforting; in another he found it a bit depressing. He had lived in the building for almost thirty years, and the building itself often seemed like a second skin. Sometimes that very sensation made him feel older than he wished. Or perhaps it was just that he had always lived here alone.

When he reached the third-floor landing he automatically turned to his right and stopped before the faded red door that marked his home. He inserted his key into the deadbolt lock and felt the familiar roll of tumblers as the bar slid back. Most New Yorkers had at least two locks on their doors, but Jimmy's years as a cop had taught him that no number of locks would stop a thief intent on getting inside. Instead he always left a fifty-dollar bill on the small table that stood just inside the door. It was a simple solution. He knew that most break-and-entries were the work of junkies who would be content to grab the first thing they saw, providing it was enough to temporarily satisfy their habit. They would be back, of course, usually within a few days. They weren't fools, after all. But when they returned they would find a retired cop waiting for them. Since his retirement Jimmy had collared four junkies that way. The first one he had taken to his neighborhood precinct for booking. That had produced a countercharge from the junkie, accusing him of unlawful imprisonment, and he had wasted two days in court before that charge against him was dismissed. He had treated the next three junkies differently. He had taken a blackjack to their kneecaps and elbows and had thrown them down the stairs. Word gradually got around. He hadn't had a "visitor" in over a year.

As he swung the door back Jimmy noted the fifty-dollar bill untouched on the table. He nodded, then drew a deep breath, taking in the scents of his life—the faint odor of stale tobacco, the hint of bourbon that came from the unfinished drink he had left out when he went to bed the previous night. It was all the same for him now, day after day, a routine that took him through a life with little to do. Maybe it would have been different if the life he had planned with Betty had ever materialized. He had met her shortly after the Reed murder had been "solved," and he had rented this apartment a few months later when they had become engaged. It was to have been their first home together. What was it now, twenty-nine years since those grand plans blew up in his face? He let that memory sit a moment then sent it away. It was all for the better, he told himself. Cop marriages never lasted anyway.

A melancholy smile accompanied that thought as he entered his living room. It was an overcrowded affair with far too many chairs and tables wedged in together. He wasn't sure how it had gotten that way. Over the years it just seemed to happen, and he had decided long ago that it would take too much time and trouble to change it.

There was a cardboard box on the sofa table and he sat down in front of it. He had taken it out of storage to prepare for his meeting with Jake. The box held all his notes on the case

Jake planned to reopen, all the observations and bits of evidence he had never put in official reports. He had told Jake that they no longer existed, that he had torn those pages out of his notebooks. It was a lie, of course. He had simply recopied his notebooks before he turned them in, leaving out things he wanted no one else to know. He had kept the originals, and he was certain his old partner knew he had. They had always been good at seeing through each other's lies.

He reached out and touched the box. So here it is, he thought. Now, between us, we have all the evidence we ever had. The idea produced a bitter smile. Not that it'll do us a damn bit of good, he thought. Manny Troy stopped us thirty years ago, and even though he's been long in his grave, his hand'll reach out and stop us again. He let out a small grunt, then reached into the box and pulled out a worn notebook. Slowly, he began flipping through the pages.

I took in his smug look and all I wanted was to reach across that small table and wipe the self-satisfied smirk off his face. But that was only a vision, a fookin' pipe dream. We were in Delahanty's, me and Mr. Manny Troy, himself. He had called me at the Reed house an hour earlier and told me he wanted to see me. Then, without waiting for any reply, he told me where I should come to and at what time, and I had done what any smart New York cop would have done. I hopped to it.

Now Troy sat there smiling at me, his oversized belly pressed against the table. He was an ugly man, with a big nose and a bushy mustache and dark hair that was slicked back with pomade, and you could tell how much he liked giving out orders and seeing people dance to whatever tune he played. I had another vision, this one of him as a fat little kid—the kid that everybody in the neighborhood beat on, the smart kid who took violin lessons and who always went around dressed in a clean white shirt and neatly ironed knickers, the kid who nobody liked. Now that kid was all grown up and he was getting back at everybody who had ever hung a "kick me" sign on his back. I smiled at the image, but it was probably just wishful thinking. Troy was probably nothing like that as a kid. Most likely he was the one who organized all the others to do whatever he wanted.

You didn't get to be boss of New York without lots of practice for a lot of years.

I looked around the bar, waiting for him to tell me what was on his mind. Delahanty's was a fancy joint with a thick carpet on the floor and lots of polished brass. It was only two blocks from City Hall, a place the politicians headed for when they wanted to wheel and deal over a stiff drink. I didn't like the looks of it a bit.

Troy tapped his fingers on the table, drawing my attention back. "I got a tip today that I wanted to pass on to you." He folded his hands on the table and gave me another smile, but it carried no warmth. It was cold, like the cold blue of his eyes, a deep, deep cold like the kind you'd find in a lake way up north, the kind of lake that never got warm at all, even in the middle of summer.

Troy kept staring at me, so I dutifully took out my notebook and pencil and placed them on the table in front of me.

"Louie Grosso." Troy watched me as I wrote it down.

I knew the name. Grosso was a guinea leg-breaker who last I heard worked for Frank Costello; a low-level thug who Costello used to keep people in line. We suspected him of bumping off half a dozen other hoods, but I couldn't imagine Costello sending him after somebody like Judge Reed. He was good enough blasting away in some Brooklyn spaghetti house, but he lacked the finesse for going after somebody like the judge. But then, the judge hadn't been done in with a lot of finesse.

"Where'd you get this from?" I asked.

Troy gave me a shrug. "Let's just say a little bird passed it on. A bird who doesn't want it to get around that he's singing."

"Did your bird have any idea about a motive?" I watched Troy's eyes harden, as if questioning his information was some kind of affront. I thought I'd better smooth his feathers. "I'm talking about what his beef was with the judge, or if maybe he was sent by somebody else who wanted the judge dead."

The explanation seemed to satisfy him and he folded his hands across his belly like a man getting ready for some lengthy discourse. "You're wondering if Frank Costello sent him."

I nodded my assent.

"No, not a chance. I've met Costello"—he gave out a bark of

a laugh—"hell, everybody in city government has met Frank Costello. The man hits all the nightspots. Makes sure he meets everybody." He waved a hand as if dismissing the information as irrelevant. "No, and according to my friend, Grosso may even be working for somebody else now. But it wasn't Costello, in any event. My friend was sure the judge had something on Grosso, himself, and that he was ready to take it to the DA."

"Did your friend have any idea what the judge might've had on Grosso?" I felt like the man was spoon-feeding me the information and then watching as I digested each bit. It was almost as if he was checking to see what part I'd swallow and what part I wouldn't.

"He found out that this Grosso character had attacked a woman. Sexually attacked her." He waved his hand in the air as though dismissing the word because he found it offensive. "This Grosso dated this woman a couple of times, and then, when she wouldn't put out for him, he beat her up and forced her. Afterward he threatened to kill her if she went to the cops."

"So she went to the judge instead?" I let a touch of incredulity seep into my voice just to see what it produced.

"That's right. She knew the judge somehow. Or somebody she knew did. I'm not sure about the connection." He waved his hand again, dismissing any need to discuss it further. "The judge told her to take a vacation; go visit some friends out of town so this Grosso guy couldn't find her. Then he went to see this hood."

"Why? I mean why would he go and see this Grosso character himself? Why not send a cop?"

Troy glared at me, unhappy with the interruption. He leaned forward and rested his forearms on the table. His eyes had grown even colder, which seemed impossible to me, and everything about his demeanor had become aggressive and threatening.

"It was the kind of man he was." Troy's voice was almost a growl now. "It was his nature to be fair. Even to a known hood like Grosso. It was just the way he was. He had to know the truth of it himself before he turned it over to the DA."

Despite his displeasure, I couldn't let go of it. "But why do it alone? That's the part that doesn't make sense to me. He could have had a dozen dicks shaking Grosso's tree five minutes after he picked up a phone."

Troy's eyes hardened. "I told you. He wasn't that kind of man." He paused, making sure I saw the displeasure in his eyes. "But I am," he finally added. Another pause. "So I want you to get a dozen dicks if you need them, and shake that bastard's tree until he falls out. Am I making myself clear enough?"

"Clear as a bell." I ground my teeth, keeping my head tucked down into my notebook so it wasn't noticed. When I looked up I was in control of my features again. "What's the woman's name? The one who was Grosso's victim?

A small smile played at the corners of Troy's mouth, and again I wanted to reach across the table and slap the satisfaction off his face.

"Her name is Lilly Straus." He gave me a cold smile. "She lives on Second Avenue, a few doors from Eighty-sixth Street."

{ 7 }

Walter Morgan was dressed in full uniform when he stuck his head into Jake Downing's office. "Can I have a minute, Jake?" he asked.

It was eight in the morning. Jake had come in early to go over some reports. There had been three murders the previous night. Two were ground balls, but one was certain trouble—a young woman beaten to death in her East Side apartment—the type of case the media would be all over. Normally, with that kind of morning facing him, Jake would have put off any visitors, but the timing of this visit suggested some urgency. Besides, he had been expecting Morgan to come sniffing around. It was only a question of when.

Jake extended a hand toward one of the visitors' chairs set before his desk. "Sure, Walt. Grab a seat."

He watched Morgan close the door behind him, then carefully adjust the creases in his sharply pressed uniform trousers before he slid into the offered chair. Jake remained silent, studying him. Except for the lines and crevices imposed by time, the man still had the same narrow, ratlike face he'd had thirty years ago. The only other difference was his once-thinning hair. Now, except for the well-barbered tufts above his ears, it had thinned down to pure skin. He smiled at the notion. Yes, those were the only differences, as long as you ignored the fact that Walter Morgan was now chief of patrol and an even bigger sonofabitch than he had been all those years ago.

Jake held the smile as if it had been intended for Morgan. "Something I can do for you, Walt?" he asked.

Morgan slowly shook his head, then took a moment to look over Jake's office, almost as if assuring himself that it remained as Spartan as it had always been; that nothing of status had been added since his last visit. Satisfied, he leaned back in his chair and offered a consoling smile. "How are you feeling, Jake?" The question had a pro forma quality to it, and he hurried ahead without awaiting a reply. "Frankly, I was surprised when I heard you weren't taking some time off. Everyone would have understood if you took a week, even more. Mary was a great loss."

"Yes, she was." Jake wondered if his own level of sincerity sounded as bogus as Morgan's. "But work is better. It keeps my mind occupied."

Morgan nodded sagely. "Thought you might take time to work on your book." He dropped the idea casually, without any sign of concern—like a good actor using a throwaway line. And Morgan was that, if nothing else. One damned fine actor.

Jake eased back in his chair. The warning signals were all up now, and Jake wanted to appear casual, unconcerned. "How'd you hear about that?" He asked the question with a broad smile. "The book, I mean. I haven't told but a handful of people."

Morgan tapped his nose with a long bony finger. "Not much escapes." He let out a soft chuckle. "It's how I've held on to the job for the past ten years. By making sure I know things. Whether the information is important or not." He waved a hand, as if dismissing what they were discussing, then paused again, still smiling. "While we're on the subject, though, I hope you aren't planning on going into a certain old case that we both remember." His eyes narrowed almost imperceptibly. "You aren't, are you?"

Jake tilted his chair forward. "The Reed case. It's curious you should bring that up. I was going to call you and ask what you remembered about it."

Morgan was momentarily silent. "So you are," he finally offered. He, too, leaned forward, his demeanor turning quite somber. "You think that's wise?" He shook his head as if answering the question himself. "I'm thinking the public doesn't need to be reading about old cases like that one."

Jake formed a steeple with his fingers and began tapping them together. "I'm not looking at it for any book, Walt. I only said that to keep unwanted noses out of my business." He watched relief momentarily flood Morgan's face, then change quickly back to concern.

"Not for a book. For what, then?"

"I'm reopening the case. It's why I've asked Jimmy Finn to come back and help me." He paused. "Unofficially, of course."

Morgan stared at him in disbelief. "Are you mad? Why in hell would you want to do that?"

"Bring Jimmy into it? You think that's a mistake?" Jake forced a look of dumb surprise onto his face. He smiled inwardly. Walter Morgan's not the only actor in this room, he told himself.

"I think reopening the damned *case* is a mistake." Morgan was on the edge of his seat now, leaning even further forward for emphasis. "What good could it possibly do?"

"I think we arrested the wrong man." Jake paused. "He got the chair, if you recall. The State of New York fried his sorry ass based on our investigation."

Morgan stared at him, his face filled with incredulity. "And who the hell cares? The man was scum. He killed a half dozen people, for chrissake." He raised a hand, prepared to stop an objection that was not forthcoming. "Oh, I know, I know, we could never prove any of the others. But, dammit, we knew it was true."

"But he didn't kill the judge. And, sadly, we knew that, too."

Morgan sat back and pressed the palms of his hands together.

"Jake, Jake, Jake. This is crazy. You and Jimmy Finn were the arresting officers. Why in hell would either of you want to tarnish your reputations for scum like Louie Grosso? And why in hell tarnish the department's good name?"

Downing rested his arms on the desk and stared at his fellow chief. "Walt, tell me something. Did you ever wonder if maybe we both got to where we are because of that case? Oh, I don't mean as a direct result. I mean about it being the big boost that sent us on our way."

Morgan's eyes hardened. "No, I haven't. Not once. Not ever."

Jake nodded, sat back and steepled his fingers again. "I've thought about it a lot. I've also thought about the fact that the real killer—or killers—are still out there. Or, maybe they're lying buried somewhere with golden reputations they don't deserve."

Morgan shook his head. "Again, at the risk of repeating myself, who gives a fiddler's fart?" He began waving one hand in a small circle. "So what's the point of it, Jake? To pay back a long-dead killer at the expense of . . . of those of us who got themselves sucked into that damned mess?"

"Is that what you think happened to us, Walt? We got sucked into it?"

"You're damned right, I do." He had raised his voice, seemed to realize that he had, and forced another false smile. "Look . . . Jake . . ."

"What if the killer's not dead?"

Morgan's smile vanished with the interruption. "And what if he's not? Christ, man, it's been thirty goddamn years. Even if you find this supposed killer, you've got a snowball's chance in hell of convicting him. And in the meantime a lot of reputations go straight into the crapper. Yours and mine among them, not to mention the department's."

Jake lowered his eyes, stared at his desktop for a moment, then slowly brought them back to Morgan. When he spoke his voice was light, almost amused. "Maybe our reputations will improve. Maybe it will show that we're willing to face up to our mistakes." He gave Morgan a small shrug. "And even correct them."

Morgan let out a mean-spirited laugh. "Oh, certainly, Jake. That's just what will happen. No doubt about it. I can see the newspapers right now. Christ, I can almost read the headlines. And those sweet little blow-dried boys and girls on TV, too. All of them, every single one, they'll just praise us to the heavens. Never mind that we sent Louie Grosso to the electric chair. They'll just pat us on the back for correcting our mistake." He raised a hand. "Oh, and of course they'll gladly overlook the fact that it took us thirty goddamn years to do it." He shook his head, then glared across the desk, jabbing a finger toward Jake's nose. "Now you listen up a minute, Jake Downing. You do this thing, and before those bastards are through with us, the public will think we dragged that piece of scum out of some fucking seminary and strapped him in the chair with our own hands. They'll dig up every relative that rat bastard ever had, and they'll be telling the world how he used to be a choirboy, and how he loved his pet pooch, and was just the sweetest son to his dear old mom. Hell, before they're finished the fucking pope will be ready to canonize that piece of shit. And there won't be one word about what he tried to do to you." He paused for effect. "You remember that part, don't you, Jake? You remember what he did to you?"

Jake ground his teeth. "I remember. It's not something you forget."

Morgan stared at him, letting the long-ago image sink in. "And you'd still do this thing?" he finally asked.

"Yes, I would."

Morgan closed his eyes and shook his head like a man suffering some great weariness. Then his eyes snapped open in a challenging stare. "And I suppose you'll get Molly Reagan to help you on the forensic side." He caught the surprise in Jake's eyes, then slowly shook his head again, this time as a tribute to Downing's foolishness. "Yes, I know about her, too, Jake. As does half the department. It's another of your not-so-well-kept secrets."

Morgan had let the sarcasm drip from his voice, and Jake could only lower his eyes, smile, and shake his own head. "I never was much for secrets, Walt."

"No you weren't, Jake." Morgan paused again. "But I'll promise you this, my friend. You'll keep this one, or I'll fight you to hell and back to see that you do."

Jake nodded. "I wouldn't expect you to do anything else, Walt."

"How much harm can he cause you?"

"It's not just me. He can hurt you, too. He was letting me know that."

They were seated in Molly's office, a small, cluttered mess in the medical examiner's building on First Avenue. The sandwiches Jake had brought for their impromptu luncheon were spread out on Molly's desk.

"You think he was threatening me as well?" Her voice was filled with doubt.

"Not directly. Any threat against you might backfire, and he knows that. Morgan's not that reckless. But that's the message he wanted to get across." Jake studied his shoes for a moment, not wanting to look at her. "He wanted me to know that you'd suffer whatever befalls me if I go through with this."

Molly gave him a long, steady look. "I don't see it, Jake. I'd just be doing my job. You'd make an official request, and I'd conduct the forensic and pathological side of the investigation. It's what I do when an old case is up for review."

Jake stood and walked in a tight circle. Molly's office, small and cramped to start with, was overflowing with a collection of reports and medical books that covered every available smooth surface. The overflow covered parts of the floor. Jake liked to pace when he thought, and her office left little room to maneuver. "How can you ever find anything in here?" he asked.

"Don't change the subject. Tell me how I'm vulnerable to Walter Morgan."

Jake turned to face her. "Our relationship, for starters. Morgan's argument against what I'm doing would be that it's bad for the department. He'd go up the line with that story. First to the other chiefs, then all the way to the commissioner if necessary. He'd get them to pressure me to drop the case—'for the good of the department.'" He made little finger quotes around his final words. "If that didn't work they'd start pressuring me to resign, or face dismissal by the commissioner. Chiefs serve at his pleasure, as you know, so it would be a legitimate threat."

"Yes, but one that you could fight. It's really the mayor who picks the chiefs—or fires them."

"Yeah, but the mayor's a wuss. If the PC goes to him and says he's got a chief who's involved in an investigation that will bring shame on the department and the city, the mayor is going to listen. Hell, he'll do more than listen. He'll wet his pants. It's a cardinal rule of politics. Shame must *always* be avoided. So in a case like that, I doubt the mayor will ignore his own commissioner. It'll be safer and easier to just kiss my Irish ass goodbye." Jake started pacing again to keep the thought flowing. "So if it gets to the mayor it's over. The real battle will be with the commissioner. It'll be a question of how far he wants to go with it; how much trouble he thinks I might hand him if he tries to dump me. If he thinks I'll go to the media and make it a public fight, he might just back off." He shrugged. "But that might also fall under the category of wishful thinking on my part."

"I don't think so. Not from the little I've seen of the man," Molly said. "How long he'd back off, that's another question. And I still don't see where I fit in. I'm not starting any investigation. And it's not up to me to call it off."

Jake gave her a regretful look. "You're helping, and you also happen to be the lady I'm romantically involved with. And that's probably something Morgan could prove if he had to. That would make you part of the problem, at least as far as the opposition was concerned. So if we move ahead on this, and they find they can't pressure me, I'm sure Morgan and his friends will apply pressure at this end, where you are. When that happens you can expect your boss to drop by and suggest that you have better things to occupy your time than a thirty-year-old case."

Molly looked down at her desk, then back at Jake's eyes. They seemed very sad at the moment. "And if I choose to ignore that suggestion?"

Jake went back to his chair and sat. "You know the game as well as I do. If you ignore the request, nobody's going to stick their neck out and force the issue. But there will be some immediate reevaluations of your other work. And, not surprisingly, it will be found wanting. Enough to get you suspended, pending a more thorough review."

Molly leaned back in her chair, her teeth clenched, the forced rictus of a smile spread across her face. "So when are you sending me the material on the case?" she asked.

"That's one amazing broad," Jimmy said.

Jake nodded. He knew Jimmy meant it in the best possible way. "More than you know." He hesitated, uncertain how much he wanted to tell Jimmy, how much he wanted to reveal about his and Molly's relationship. He thought about that, then shook his head and smiled. What did it matter now. Everyone in the department seemed to know anyway.

They were seated in a small coffee shop not far from Jimmy's apartment. Jake glanced around to see who might be listening, then lowered his voice for good measure. It was more out of habit than anything and it, too, caused him to smile. "I told her I didn't want her doing it for me; that I'd ask another pathologist."

"And . . . ?" Jimmy had also lowered his voice.

"She told me to get my ego under control, that she wasn't doing it for me; she was doing it because it was her job to look at evidence when the resolution of a case fell into question. She said she wouldn't turn her back on any case like that, no matter how old it was or who asked for the review, and especially not one where an innocent man was sent to the electric chair." He laughed softly. "She also told me she'd go to the media and scream bloody hell if she was ever asked to back off a case—*any case;* said she'd let her boss know that in no uncertain terms if he ever came around suggesting anything like it."

Jimmy snapped his fingers. "And she'd have another job just like that if they fired her. It wouldn't be New York. But it would be somewhere decent. Experienced MEs—especially ones with the kind of experience you get here—aren't exactly a dime a dozen."

"Yeah, but that's not something she should have to do. That's the rub in it all. If Morgan hadn't known about us . . ." he let the sentence die. "Hell, I can stop Morgan if I have to. But I want the consequences to fall on me alone if everything turns shitty. Not Molly. And especially not because we care about each other."

"She would still be pressured to back off, even if you two weren't involved." Jimmy waggled his hand. "She wouldn't be told to refuse the work, mind you, just to drag her feet a bit, or lose the request at the bottom of a pile."

Jake thought about Molly's office. That second approach wouldn't be too hard, he thought. "You're right. Even if we didn't know each other she could have been handed the case and found herself in a pile of shit. But right now she has it because of me, so I still want to take it slow. I want to move ahead without Morgan knowing that I am. We may still have to fight the battle, but let's not do it until we're ready."

Jimmy nodded. "If we can name the real killer—and prove it—it'll be pretty hard for anybody to tell us to ignore it." He paused, studying Jake's eyes, looking for some degree of doubt. There was none to be found. "So, how are we going to do this?"

"We'll get the material to Molly without Morgan knowing. I've already found out when his spy at the warehouse has his next day off. We'll do it then, and do our best to make the record of the transfer as obscure as possible."

Jimmy thought that over; was certain it could be done. He took a deep breath and studied Jake's eyes again. "You sure you want to do this?"

"Yeah, I'm sure."

Jimmy studied his eyes again. "Do you know why, Jake?"

"I think I do, Jimmy. I think I do."

Jimmy wondered if that were true.

{ 8 }

I could see the angry look in Jimmy's eyes, and my first thought was that somehow he knew what had happened. Maybe one of the uniforms guarding the doors had seen me with Mrs. Reed, had seen that all-too-intimate moment in the parlor and had turned me in to Jimmy, or worse, to Morgan. Or maybe Jimmy had gotten my message and had come back to the house when I was upstairs in the lady's bed. None of the possibilities seemed very appealing, but there was nothing I could do now, so I sucked it up, expecting the worst. "You don't look happy," I said. He glared at me; grunted something unintelligible, waved a hand in disgust. I started to offer an excuse, not at all sure what I was going to say. "Look . . . I . . ."

"It's not your fault," Jimmy snapped. He placed his hands on his hips, drew in a breath, and studied his shoes for a long minute. "I suppose we should even be grateful. Hell, the case is practically solved."

"What . . . ?"

"You don't know what in Christ's name I'm talkin' about, do you?" He laughed at himself. "Of course you don't. The great detective, Mr. Manny Troy, probably hasn't talked to you yet." Jimmy slipped his arm around my shoulder and began walking me around the small parlor. It hit me then. Jimmy didn't know. No uniform had seen Cyn and me together. Jimmy had never even gotten my message the night before. He had never come back to the house; didn't have a clue that I had spent the night here, filling in for him. As far as he was concerned Morgan had been stuck with the duty and I had just shown up for work ahead of him. Actually, I had just come back from Brooklyn and a quick change of clothes, and I was glad he didn't know any of it. It was like somebody had lifted a ton of bricks from my shoulders.

"What's this about Manny Troy?" I asked, happy to talk about anything other than what had happened last night.

"He's solved the case for us, that's what. All we have to do is get in our car, find the slob he fingered, and slap on the cuffs."

I laughed at the idea. "So who's the killer?"

Jimmy kept walking me in a small circle. "A punk named Louie Grosso. He's a leg-breaker, works for Frank Costello, last I heard. Seems like the judge was investigating him because some broad the judge knew said he did her wrong." He gave me a big smile. "Wanna guess who the broad is?"

"It's too early to play twenty questions. Why don't you just tell me?"

He laughed. It was as though he was starting to enjoy the absurdity he was explaining. He stopped walking and looked me in the eye. "A little lady by the name of Lilly Straus."

It felt like the bricks that had just come off my shoulders had fallen on my head. "Oh, shit," I said.

"Yeah, exactly."

I waved off Jimmy's words. "No, you don't understand. I was trying to get ahold of you last night . . . to fill you in on that surveillance I ran."

"Lilly Straus."

"Yeah, that's right. But while I'm watching her place she has some visitors, who according to the doorman are regulars."

Jimmy raised his eyebrows. "And who would *they* be?" Suspicion was full in his voice.

"Manny Troy. And five minutes before he got there, Owney Ryan walked through her door."

Jimmy's mouth was uncharacteristically open. "You're sure," he finally said.

I nodded. "The doorman says the pair of them meet there like clockwork. And not just the two of them. He said until a few days ago there were usually three; said if they'd been anybody else he'd have thought maybe the lady liked her lovin' in bunches."

"And the third guy?" Jimmy gave me a hard stare.

I let him wait while I just stood there grinning.

"The judge, himself," he said, not waiting for me to answer. He shook his head. "Sonofabitch."

"I also got to meet the lady. Cozied up to her in a gin mill she haunts. Guess who she works for?"

Jimmy closed his eyes. "Like you said, forget the twenty questions. Just tell me."

"Lady works in a real estate office. Said her boss' name is Murtaugh, but the real boss is a *Mr. Troy.*"

"I'll check this Murtaugh out; find out who he is." He started to laugh. "Jaysus H. Christ. A crook, a politician, a judge and a real estate office. Put 'em in a pot and stir." He slipped his arm back around my shoulders. "And that, my boyo, is a surefire recipe for criminal behavior." He laughed again. "And there you have it: lesson number one in Jimmy Finn's detective school. Five dollars please. Pay the cashier on your way out."

"Yeah, and now we just have to find out what it means."

"Well, for starters we know the three of them was usin' this Lilly Straus as a beard. We also know it probably means that Louie Grosso assaultin' Lilly Straus is one big, fookin' red herring, somethin' to point us away from a real motive, or at least away from whatever the judge was doin' before he got himself knocked off."

"And the two things—the murder, and whatever the judge was up to—aren't necessarily connected," I offered.

"You're right on that. But I'd sure as hell buy it if I found it. Graft gone bad would stir my embers a lot more than some guinea gangster bumpin' off a judge over some rough sex with a Germantown floozy. Think about it. Even a thickheaded leg-breaker like Grosso would know that any charges filed against him was nothin' more than a 'he said, she said' deal. And even if he didn't, he'd sure as hell know that if he wanted it to go away, leanin' on the broad was a lot easier play than leanin' on a judge."

"So we need to find out about the real estate angle," I said.

Jimmy nodded. "Whether it's connected or not, I wanna know about it. And I figure I know two ladies who just might know the answer to that story."

I cocked my head to one side. "Lilly Straus and . . . ?"

Jimmy jabbed his thumb toward the ceiling, indicating Cynthia Reed. "And we can't play hardball with either one of them. Not unless we want 'em running to Manny Troy." He paused a beat, thinking it through. "What'd you think of this Straus broad?" he asked at length.

"A floozy, like you said."

"Somebody I'd have a chance of cozyin' up to?"

I laughed. "No offense, Jimmy, but a gorilla with bad breath could cozy up to that lady. She's that hungry."

Jimmy ignored the jibe; took some time to think about what I'd said. "I was kinda hopin' we could divide them up," he finally began. "But since this Straus woman has already seen you maybe you should keep that goin'. That way one of us could tail her without tippin' our hand. But you also get along with Mrs. Reed a lot better than I do, so I think you should stay close to her, too."

I felt a rush of guilt; a certainty that I should tell Jimmy just how close I had already gotten to Cynthia Reed. But the words I needed to speak seemed to catch in my throat.

"I hate to ask it, what with your wife so close to havin' the baby. It's gonna take more overtime than you should be puttin' in. But it looks like the best way to handle it—you dealin' with both women and leavin' me to do the grunt work."

Again I felt the need to say something more, and again I found I could not. "Where are you going to start?" I asked instead.

"I'm gonna find out everything I can about Louie Grosso. I'll start with his boss, Frank Costello, and work back from there. I wanna know if there's some reason Manny Troy has tapped him as the fall guy."

"Damn," I said. "I'd like to be with you when you brace Costello. He's a goddamned legend in this town."

Jimmy grinned at me, amused no doubt with my naïveté. "Come if you want. He eats his lunch every day at '21.' Meet me there at one o'clock and we'll take him on together. Morgan will be here by then, and we can let him play bodyguard for the afternoon."

Cynthia Reed came downstairs about an hour after Jimmy had gone. She was dressed in white silk slacks and matching blouse with a pale blue scarf knotted at her throat, and she looked like she had just stepped off a movie set. The slacks and blouse were loose-fitting and flowed about her as she moved, all of it alluring and provocative in a way I had never before known.

She seemed to sense the effect it had on me, and she stood there in the doorway of the small parlor letting me get my fill. I had spent the night in her bed, lying there with that same soft, silky flesh moving against me. Now the clothing draped along her body seemed to bring it all back, and I could feel myself growing rock hard just looking at her.

She came across the room and melted into my arms, her lips caressing my ear. "I've been lying in bed, hoping you'd come back up. But you didn't and I got so excited waiting for you, thinking about you, I had to pleasure myself."

I pulled my head back from her cheek and pressed my lips against hers. Her tongue filled my mouth and I felt myself hard against her and I pressed forward and listened to her moan with pleasure. I had listened to that pleasure throughout the night. Even my hideous leg hadn't intruded; she seemed not to have even noticed it, and I knew with absolute certainty that I had never known anyone like her, never known the pure agony of want I felt every time I saw her. Everything she did and said seemed to excite me. She was so unlike my wife—sweet, innocent, quiet Mary, always so chaste, so . . . good. Cynthia was different. She was . . .

I pulled back at the sound of the front door opening and stepped away from her just in time. Walter Morgan filled the doorway, just staring at us, and I could feel the blood rush to my cheeks.

"Hello, Lieutenant, can I help you?" Cynthia turned to face him, her voice cool and calm and fully in control.

Morgan nodded, stared at me for a long moment, and then smiled. "I need to talk to Detective Downing."

"You can have him in a minute. I'm almost finished with him." Cynthia's voice didn't waver under Morgan's suspicious gaze. "I was just telling the detective that I want to go to the Stork Club tonight, and I'll expect someone to accompany me." She turned back to me, her voice crisp and commanding. "I'll expect you here by nine."

I croaked out a reply. "I'll be here, Mrs. Reed."

She looked me up and down. I was dressed in a freshly pressed white shirt, my best suit and tie. "What you're wearing is fine. You won't have to take time to change." She said it curtly, almost rudely. Then she turned and left the room without another word.

Morgan watched her walk down the hall, and I could feel his eyes following the sway of her hips, and I hated him for it. Then he turned and stepped into the parlor, the hint of a smile on his lips. "What was that all about?"

"Just what she said. She was giving me my marching orders." I shook my head. "The woman thinks we've got nothin' better to do than squire her around; like investigating her husband's murder is something we should fit in when we're not tagging along after her." I turned the subject in on him. "Which reminds me. I've gotta meet Jimmy at one. We gotta check out a guy we got a tip on. So I'll need a backup here."

Morgan watched me, as if searching my eyes for some lie. "Yeah, okay. And when you see Finn tell him I got a tip for him."

"Why don't you just tell me?"

Morgan seemed reluctant, but shrugged it away. "This snitch I know claims he saw a guy leavin' this house the night of the murder. Says he recognized him."

"How'd the snitch happen to be here?"

Morgan gave me a sour look, as if he thought it was a stupid question. "Says he was just walkin' by. Says he wouldn't have noticed except he knew the guy."

"He give you a name?"

Morgan nodded. "Says it was a hood named Louie Grosso."

I tried not to show that I recognized the name. "Who's the snitch? And where can we find him?"

"His name is Willie Riley. He hangs out in a Hell's Kitchen gin mill called the Aces and Eights. It's at the corner of West Thirty-third and Ninth. You go there this afternoon, you'll find him." He reached in his pocket and took out a slip of paper. "You miss him, this is his home address."

I nodded and tucked the paper into my pocket.

Morgan gave me a well-practiced sneer. "Just don't forget where you got it when you and Finn are takin' all the bows."

"Now ain't that convenient. Another stool pigeon just floatin' out of the woodwork like that." Jimmy gave out with a harsh, barking laugh, and then clamped the cigar he was smoking back between his teeth. "Damn if it doesn't look like everybody and his brother is developin' evidence that points to Louie Grosso." He smiled around the stogie, holding that bitter-looking visage as he continued. "Even a certain police lieutenant, who just happens to be in our beloved police commissioner's pocket, who himself happens to be in Manny Troy's pocket, who also just happened to drop the same fookin' name just twenty-four hours ago."

"It's a miracle," I said.

"It's a miracle Morgan didn't mention Lilly Straus as well. Somebody must've forgot to tell him that part of it."

We were standing outside "21" on West Fifty-second Street, all ready to waltz into that posh eatery and spoil Frank Costello's lunch. It was certainly an appropriate place for an old bootlegger like Costello to chow down every day. Now replete with ornate iron gates and hitching-post statuary, "21" was known during Prohibition as Jack and Charlie's, one of the city's more notorious speakeasies, a then-faceless building in whose hidden cellars the hoi polloi and gentry gathered together to soak up forbidden booze. Today it was different. Now only the swells could afford to show up, with lunch costing as much as a day's pay for the average bozo like me.

Jimmy inclined his head toward the front door, which glistened under a heavy coat of black paint. "Let's you and me go inside and see what Francesco Castiglia has to say. Maybe he can tell us why Louie Grosso bumped off the judge. Maybe he even knows what the man did to the lovely Lilly Straus. Hell, everybody else in this fookin' city seems to know all this stuff. Everybody except you and me, that is."

"Who's Francesco Castiglia?" I asked.

Jimmy grinned at me. "That was Costello's name before he changed it." His grin widened. "The nerve of that fookin' guinea, eh? Takin' a lovely Irish name like Costello for his own."

We pushed through the front door like we owned the joint, and after Jimmy flashed his tin a tuxedoed maître d' led us to a table at the rear of the restaurant. The interior wasn't half as glamorous as I'd expected, but the clientele obviously was, and as we approached his table it was clear that Frank Costello fit in perfectly. But why shouldn't he? During Prohibition there were unproved rumors that he owned the joint. Of course, he was also supposed to have owned El Morocco and the Stork Club and even Toots Shor's.

Sitting there now, he looked like all those rumors might have been true. Right down to his manicured fingernails, Costello seemed more the slick businessman or Broadway sugar daddy than the supposed "prime minister" of organized crime. He was a blocky sort of guy with a thick waist and thinning hair brushed straight back. The suit he wore clearly cost more than I made in three months, and if you could ignore the four thugs who filled the table to his right you might mistake him for one more business exec stuffing himself with an overpriced lunch.

One of the thugs rose protectively as we approached Costello's table, but was ordered back to his seat with a wave of his boss' hand.

"Hello, Finn," Costello said in his trademark gravel voice. "I didn't know cops could afford to eat here. The pad must be better than it was in the old days."

Jimmy pulled out a chair and sat. "You'd know better'n me, Frank."

Costello eyed me as I sat next to Jimmy. "Hey, I ain't bribed any of you guys since Prohibition," he said, still watching me. "It ain't worth it anymore. Besides, I retired from all that stuff.

I'm strictly legit now." He raised his chin in my direction. "Who's your partner?"

"Jake Downing. Another honest dick."

Costello snorted. He inclined his head toward the thugs at the next table. "The only difference between my guys and you guys is that you guys carry badges."

Jimmy hardened his stare. "We get paid less, too."

Costello let out a laugh and slapped a hand on the table. "That's good, Finn, I like that." Now Costello's eyes hardened. "So what can I do for you? No offense, but havin' you at my table don't do nothin' for my digestion."

Finn leaned forward. "Tell us about Louie Grosso."

I watched Costello's eyes turn suspicious, his lips curl in a small, unfriendly smile. "I ain't seen Louie in months, maybe a year. What'd he do? Forget to pay his parking tickets?"

"I thought he worked for you," Finn said.

Costello shook his head. "He never worked for me. He *tried* to work for me, and maybe I gave him one or two things to do so I could check him out, see if he was worth botherin' with."

"But he wasn't?"

Costello shrugged. "I never found out. Louie was an impatient guy. He was also a little crazy, a little uncontrollable, if you know what I mean. Last I heard he went to work for Owney Ryan." He snorted again. "That mick'll hire any rat bastid comes his way, so long as he's got a big mouth and some iron in his pocket."

Jimmy gave a noncommittal nod, then leaned forward again. "You hear anything about Grosso havin' a beef with Judge Reed?" He let the question drop as casually as he could, but it still produced a raised eyebrow from Costello.

"That's what you're thinkin'?" Costello let out a low chuckle that sounded like rocks rubbing together, then lowered his voice so nearby tables wouldn't overhear what he was saying. "You gotta be kiddin' me. Hey, let's be serious. I mean the guy's no Einstein, I'll grant you that, but he ain't stupid enough to bump off no judge."

"You hear anything about who might have?" I asked.

Costello gave me a long, steady look. "I don't hear talk like that." He seemed to think over what he had said. "All I ever heard about the judge was that he had trouble at home."

"What kind of trouble?" Jimmy asked.

Costello gave him an almost indiscernible shrug. "Wife trouble. Like how *his* used to have a boyfriend before they got married—a certain singer, works with the band at the Stork Club." He tapped a finger against his oversized Roman nose and added: "Like maybe how he's *still* her boyfriend."

"You know the lady?" What he had said hit a nerve, and I struggled to keep an edge out of my voice.

Costello seemed amused by my question, or my attitude, or both. He hit me with that small, unfriendly smile he had used with Jimmy. The way a cat might smile at a mouse, if cats smiled. "I seen her around. She used to be a hatcheck girl at the Stork." He nodded approvingly. "Good-lookin' kid. But real young and still had some hay behind her ears, you know what I mean. Then all of a sudden she's married to the judge and she's back at the Stork sittin' in the Cub Room with all the swells." He gave us both the smile this time. "But that's life, right? That's America."

Jimmy and I found Willie Riley at the Aces and Eights just like Morgan said we would. It was a seedy Hell's Kitchen bar, one of those beaten-down places where the stench of stale beer went all the way out into the street. Inside it was even worse, mixed with the rancid odor of defeat, the kind of smell that warned you to walk easy, or risk getting a shiv stuck in your back.

Willie Riley was seated in a booth with a racing form spread out in front of him. He was the only guy in the joint whose clothes didn't have holes in them, so I guessed that he had been doing pretty well picking the nags. There was a toothpick dangling from the side of his mouth, which was small and tight and fit neatly into his narrow, pinched face. He looked up as we approached and motioned toward the opposite side of the booth.

"I figured you guys would be around." He kept his voice low, little more than a whisper. "The cop I talked to said he'd pass it on to the dicks handling the case." He glanced furtively around the room. "Let's just not make it real obvious. You know what I mean? This ain't a very public-spirited place. Maybe you could make like you're bracin' me or somethin'. That way I don't end up in some alley with my throat cut."

Jimmy ignored the cautioning words. "Just tell us what you saw," he said as we slid into the booth.

Riley grinned at us with rotting teeth. He wanted to be our friend. "Just like I tol' the lieutenant. I saw Louie Grosso the night the judge got put on ice. He was comin' out of the judge's house, maybe eight-thirty, nine o'clock."

Jimmy nodded and gave Riley the same kind of smile Costello had given us at "21." He took time to light a fresh cigar, made sure it was going good, then blew a lazy smoke ring up over Riley's head. "What were you doin' on East Fifty-fourth?" he finally asked.

Riley gave us a broad shrug. "Just walkin'."

"Out for a stroll, eh?"

"Yeah, out for a stroll. My evenin' constitutional." Riley let out a harsh cackle.

Jimmy tapped a cigar ash into the overflowing ashtray. He glanced at me. "Now if Mr. Riley here told me he was out casin' somebody's house I'd believe him. Wouldn't you, Jake?"

"Without a doubt." I turned to Riley. "So you were just walking, taking the air?"

"That's right, just walkin'. Hey, it ain't against the law, is it?"

I ignored him. "And you saw Louie Grosso coming out of the judge's house sometime around eight-thirty, nine at night?"

"Yeah, that's right." Riley's voice was filled with resentment at not being immediately believed. I tried not to smile. It was hard.

"What was he wearing?"

"Whaddaya mean?"

"Hey, it's a simple question. What was he wearing? Was he all dressed up in a tuxedo? Was he wearing a Hawaiian shirt and sunglasses? Was he carrying an umbrella? What was he wearing?"

"He was wearin' a fuckin' suit." He looked to Jimmy for help. "What was he wearin'? What kinda question is that?"

Jimmy glared at him. "Was he wearin' a hat?"

"Jesus Christ, not you, too."

"Answer the fookin' question."

"Yeah, all right, he was wearin' a fuckin' hat. Okay?"

"My partner here asked you if he was carryin' an umbrella?"

Riley looked at him as though he was daft. "No. No fuckin' umbrella."

"Was he wearin' a raincoat?"

"No."

"Were you wearin' one?"

"No."

"Why not?"

"What the fuck do you mean, why not?"

"Because there was a fookin' monsoon that night, you dim-witted bastard. That's why. But neither you or this Louie Grosso was wearin' a raincoat or carryin' an umbrella. You were just out takin' your evenin' constitutional in the middle of a fookin' downpour that would drown a fookin' horse. No rain-coat. No umbrella. Just strollin' along like some goddamn dim-wit, and you just happened to see Louie Grosso traipsin' out of the judge's house in the middle of that same rainstorm without so much as a newspaper held over his fookin' head." Jimmy stared at him for a full ten seconds, then reached out without warning and grabbed him by the throat. "Now tell me the truth, you lyin' little cocksucker, or I'll rip your fookin' throat out."

Riley made gasping, gagging noises. I glanced around to see if anyone was coming to help him. Nobody was. The handful at the bar had their backs carefully turned away from us. They were listening to the Tigers-Yankees game on the radio. As I watched, the bartender reached out to turn up the volume and drown out Riley's gags.

When I turned back, Jimmy's knuckles had turned white from squeezing and Riley's eyes were bulging out of his head. "Jesus, ease up before you kill him," I said.

"I wanna kill the lyin' bastard," Jimmy said.

"Well, then take him out back. There are too many witnesses in here."

Riley's eyes darted to me, then rolled up in his head. Jimmy turned him loose and pushed him back against the bench seat.

"Oh, Jesus. Oh, Jesus." Riley spoke through a deep, rattling wheeze.

"Shut up," Jimmy snapped. "Don't say a fookin' word until you're ready to tell me the truth."

Riley looked at me with beseeching eyes. "What does he want me to say?" The wheeze had turned into a croak.

I leaned across the table and smiled. "The truth, you fucking weasel."

"Jesus, I wish you guys would make up yer minds." He ended the sentence with a gasping cough.

"What does that mean?" I asked.

Riley shook his head. "First Morgan tells me I gotta tell the truth. Then he tells me what it is I gotta say. So I say what he tells me and you guys come here and half kill me for sayin' it." He coughed again. By morning his throat would be so swollen he wouldn't be able to talk at all, I guessed.

"So what is it you did see?"

Riley stared at me, his eyes red with burst capillaries. "I saw anything you say I saw. Or I didn't see nothin'. Whatever you want."

"Were you on Fifty-fourth Street that night?" I asked.

Riley shook his head. "I dunno. You tell me."

"You little shit," Jimmy growled.

Riley shrunk back, trying to make himself melt into the bench.

"Hey, I'm just tryin' to get by here. That's all."

"What does Morgan have on you?" I asked.

Riley looked at me, as though ready to offer a quick denial. Then he looked at Jimmy and thought better of it. "He caught me with some slips."

"Numbers?"

Riley nodded. "I run a little policy. Nothin' big. It ain't even my own. I just run some numbers for somebody else. It puts a few bucks in my pocket."

"And Morgan caught you."

Riley nodded.

"So where were you the night the judge got iced?" It was Jimmy, his voice suddenly calm now.

"You tell me, and that's where I was."

Jimmy leveled a finger at him, holding it only inches from his nose. "You get lost for a while so Morgan can't find you. At least three or four days, more if you can manage it. And when he does find you, you tell him you hadda go out of town. Tell him your auntie died. Tell him any fookin' thing you want, except that you talked to us. Understood?"

Riley held up his hands in surrender. "Whatever you want."

Jimmy glared at him. "What I want is for you to fall in a fookin' sewer and drown. But I'll settle for you doin' a rabbit."

"I'm gone." Riley started to rise as he spoke. "If that's what you want, I am Bugs fucking Bunny."

Jimmy and I grabbed a table in Jack Dempsey's Broadway Restaurant. The Manassa Mauler, himself, was seated on a high stool by the front entrance, greeting people as they came and went, and when they were beside each other I was surprised to see that Jimmy had the old champ by a hard twenty pounds. The champ was fifty now and hadn't stepped in the ring in thirteen years, but despite his greater size I doubted Jimmy could stand up to that crushing right hand, even now. If Dempsey were in his prime, I'd even have doubts about the current champ, Joe Louis.

Jimmy hadn't said much on the ride over, except that he was hungry. He was still steaming over our session with Willie Riley and everything that had led up to it.

"They're playin' with us," he said now, as the waitress put corned beef sandwiches and glasses of beer in front of us.

"So we ignore them," I said.

"We can't ignore them. Not if we want to stay on the case."

"So what do we do?"

Jimmy looked around the room as if surveying the other patrons for one who might have an answer. Dempsey's, as always, had a mixed crowd. Half were regulars who had adopted the ambiance and the food. The other half were tourists who wanted to tell their neighbors they had shaken the old champ's hand and had eaten their lunch surrounded by the many framed photos of his glory days in the ring. Jimmy turned back to me and ground his teeth. "I'll tell you what we do. First we make 'em think we're a pair of dummies who are doin' what they want." He shook his head in disgust. "It's clear enough they already think that anyway. But while they're thinkin' it, you and me gotta get busy and find out *why* they're playin' with us." Jimmy jabbed a sausagelike finger into the tabletop. "We do that and I think we'll find out why the judge met his maker, and who it was who sent him there."

I took a sip of my beer and sat back. "Okay, I'll buy all of it. So let's see what we've got. First, the day of the murder, two hours went by before we got the call. Unusual, to say the least. And when we finally got to the house, we find that Morgan, the commissioner, Manny Troy, and God knows who else had already gone stomping through the crime scene."

"And God knows how much time went by before they even called Morgan and his boys in."

"But we have a hint about that," I said. "Mrs. Reed said her husband was working in his study while she fixed herself up to go out to dinner. It was almost midnight when I interviewed her for the first time. She told me she went into his study and found his body. She also said it was four hours earlier when that happened, which would make it a little before eight o'clock. That means at least an hour went by before *any* cops were called. Then, from what Morgan said when we got there, another two hours went by before we were called. And during that time Manny Troy and a bunch of politicians were in the house."

"Which probably means Mrs. Reed found the body and called Troy before she called the cops," Jimmy said.

"Or he happened to stop by." I raised a finger. "But what's interesting is that Willie Riley was told to tell us that he saw Louie Grosso leaving the judge's house as late as eight-thirty, maybe even nine o'clock."

A grin broke out on Jimmy's face. "Which means that somebody didn't know what Mrs. Reed told you, and wants us to think Morgan and his uniforms got there within a half hour of the murder, not an hour or more later." He let out a soft chuckle. "I think we're gonna make a detective out of you yet. Yes I do."

I was pleased with the compliment, but tried hard not to show it. "So now we have to find out what went on before the murder was called in."

Jimmy raised a finger. "We gotta be careful on that one, boyo. And we sure as hell better have our ducks lined up before we call down Manny Troy or any of his cronies. Remember, we don't even know how long the commissioner was there, or what *he* was doin'. But one thing's for sure. We try to brace Manny

Troy about this before we've got all the answers, and the commissioner will fall on us like a building."

"Looks to me like the time of death will answer some of our questions."

"Yeah, but that's a tricky business. We haven't got the autopsy results yet, but I don't expect any great help there. Rigor mortis had already started by the time we got to the judge's study. I checked that myself. But rigor doesn't mean a helluva lot. It varies too much. It usually starts two to four hours after death, depending on a lot of factors. You usually see it first in the jaw and neck. Then it goes head to foot, and is complete in eight to twelve hours, and starts to disappear in eighteen to thirty-six hours. But there are too goddamn many variables." Jimmy began to tick them off. "Fat people don't always develop it. Skinny people develop it fast. Heat speeds it up, and cold makes it last longer. If the victim was in a fight before he died, or if the body experienced some kind of shock, it usually happens faster. But the basic rule is that no two bodies develop it at the same time, so it's fookin' useless in pinpointing the exact time of death." He paused to take a long pull on his beer. "An old ME I knew when I was a young dick taught me a trick that works better. You feel the underarms, and if they're still warm, death probably came less than three hours earlier."

"Did you feel the judge's underarms?"

Jimmy nodded. "There were as cold as a fookin' mackerel."

"Then I think I better ask Mrs. Reed a few questions when I take her to the Stork Club tonight."

Jimmy gave me an exaggerated wink. "There's some answers I'd like to hear, too. Like what time their dinner reservation was for that night? And how did Manny Troy happen to get there before the cops?"

I held back, avoiding the other question I didn't want to ask. Jimmy stared at me, then finally smiled and nodded, sensing the unspoken concern that sat there between us. Then he raised it himself. "What if Troy was already there when she found the body?"

(9)

"So you never gathered any hair, tissue or clothing samples from Manny Troy, or Oliver Marks, or Owney Ryan?"

Jake Downing shook his head. "Afraid not. We did get everyone's fingerprints. Even Manny Troy's. We used the argument that we needed to eliminate prints that *should* be in the house. It was true, of course, but it was only part of the reason. We were hoping to find someone's prints on the murder weapon. But there weren't any. At least nothing clear enough to get a positive match."

"But nothing else. No hair or tissue or clothing samples."

Jake shook his head.

Molly gave him a smile that summed up what she thought of that answer. She glanced at the notes she had brought with her. "What are the chances of getting them now? I know Troy is dead. He was retired and somewhat obscure, but there was still a rather lengthy obituary in the *Times* about five or six years ago. I remember reading it."

"Nine years, almost ten," Jake said. "Oliver Marks is dead, too. He was shot outside a Brooklyn spaghetti house two years after Grosso was electrocuted. It was a separate incident, unrelated to the judge. I went to the funeral, hoping to see his sister, but she never showed."

Molly looked at him steadily for a moment and then went on. "Well, I suppose we could try and have their bodies exhumed if we have to. What about Grosso? Did you at least get samples from him?"

"We weren't quite that incompetent. On Grosso we gathered everything. We even took swatches from every piece of clothing he owned."

"And?"

"Nothing matched with any of the evidence found at the scene."

"But he was still convicted."

Jake nodded. "The press had the electric chair dusted off before he even walked into court."

"Who orchestrated it?"

"Everyone."

"You and Jimmy?"

Jake studied his shoes. "We never said anything. But then, we didn't have to. Our part in it—the way it all went down at the arraignment—garnered some big headlines. What Grosso did then . . . especially what he did to me and to Cynthia Reed . . . well, it pretty much turned the trial into a fait accompli. All we had to do was keep our mouths shut and look the other way." He stared at her with eyes as sad as any she had ever seen, then drew a deep breath and shook his head. "Forget Jimmy. The point is, *I* never said what I should have. And that's one of the things that still haunts me."

It was early evening. They were in the living room of Molly's Greenwich Village apartment, seated on opposite facing sofas. Molly had received the case materials from the NYPD warehouse that afternoon, and had promptly conducted her initial review. She was acutely aware that despite Jake's efforts it was only a question of time before Walter Morgan found out that an official transfer of evidence had been made. When he did, the battle lines would be drawn. It also meant that Jake needed some hard evidence to keep Morgan at bay, and she intended to provide whatever help she could, as quickly as she could. But first she needed some things only Jake could provide, so she had asked him to meet her right after work.

"Jake, the evidence you sent me is remarkably well-preserved, and the photographs of the murder scene are especially good, but I'm going to need help on this. Basically, I want a good criminologist to work with me. Preferably someone Morgan can't bully." Molly dropped her notes on the cocktail table that sat between them. "This will do two things for me, Jake. First, it will give me some help in areas where I'm not terribly strong. I'm talking specifically about some techniques that weren't available in '45, when you were working this case, like recovering hidden fingerprints with chemical and laser technology, along with some of the newer methods of analyzing blood splatter evidence."

"What else do you think a criminologist will do for you?"

She gave him a wry smile. "It's like you said the other day. Once Morgan realizes I'm actually working on the case, he's going to try to get the investigation stopped. To do that he's going to gather as much support as he can at One Police Plaza—all the way to the commissioner's office if he can manage it. Then he'll use that support to put as much pressure as he can on my boss." She gave him an exaggerated shrug so filled with innocence he almost laughed. "So . . ." she continued, "when all that pressure comes down . . . I may have to make it appear that I'm *not* working on the case. If I have help, I can do that."

Jake tilted his head appreciatively. "You're a sly lady."

"Always."

"Who do you suggest we use?"

Molly's eyes glittered with excitement. "I want an expert from outside the department. Specifically, I want somebody I know I can work with; somebody who will accept my direction, and somebody who won't spend half his time listening for Morgan's footsteps." She tilted her head to one side. "The person I want will be expensive. I don't know how you're going to pay for it without attracting attention, especially with all the financial pressure the city's under, but I hope you can."

Jake nodded. "We've got some funds in our intelligence unit that I can tap. It's money even Morgan won't be able to trace."

Molly raised her hand. "Don't tell me about it. I don't even want to know."

"Who do you want to hire?"

Molly answered without hesitation. "Barry Hamilton. He's the best forensic consultant I know. He's retired FBI, strictly a behind-the-scenes lab guy, very low profile. And he's from D.C., so Morgan probably won't even know the name."

"You know him personally?"

Molly nodded. "We've worked a couple of cases together."

"Do you think he'll take this one on?"

Molly smiled across the small divide that separated them. "I know he will. I spoke to him this afternoon."

Jake returned the smile, genuinely pleased by the way Molly had thrown herself into the case. He sat back, momentarily relaxing in this room that had become a haven for him. The first haven he had known since . . . He thought about that, realizing it was the only safe and secure place he had known since 1945. Since he threw away his life with poor dead Mary. He looked back at Molly now, grateful she was there, hoping he would always deserve her loyalty.

"I guess Jimmy was right."

"How so?"

"He told me you were an amazing broad." He raised a protective hand. "That's his word, not mine. And he meant it in the nicest of ways."

Molly arched an eyebrow, letting him know she questioned both the distribution of blame and the use of the term in a kind-hearted way. Then she gave in and laughed. "Jimmy and I have a thing going."

"Even though it's clear he's an unredeemable chauvinist?"

"I make exceptions for *him*." She laughed again. She wanted things on a lighter note now, to get Jake away from the blame that seemed to engulf him whenever they discussed the case. "Jimmy just has that effect on me." She let out an exaggerated sigh. "I can't help myself."

"I was afraid of that." Jake got up, moved around the small table that separated them and slid in beside her.

Molly arched her eyebrow again. "Uh, uh." She placed a re-straining hand on his chest. "Keep your distance, Chief."

"Why?"

"New rules. Since we're working together now, we can't have any physical contact."

"Why?"

"It might be misconstrued as sexual harassment."

"Who's gonna do the misconstruing?" He leaned in closer.

"That's a point I hadn't considered." Her hand dropped from his chest. "Well, we certainly can't do anything in public."

Jake placed one hand along her cheek and lightly kissed her lips. "Don't want to frighten the horses." He kissed her again, even more softly.

"Certainly not. Or give anyone the wrong impression." She slipped both arms around his neck.

"I hate giving people the wrong impression." He started to unbutton her blouse.

"It's so easy to do. Give the wrong impression, I mean." Molly's breath was coming quickly now.

"Um. Impressions are always worrisome." Jake lowered his lips to her breast.

"I think we should go into the bedroom," she whispered. "It's less public."

"I was hoping you'd think that."

Dinner came two hours later and just the thought of the cir-cumstances surrounding it made Jake smile.

"Why are you grinning like some old Cheshire Cat?" Molly asked as she set plates of grilled chops, steamed broccoli and salad on the table.

He waved his hand, taking in everything around him. "It just pleases me."

"What pleases you? The food?" She rolled her eyes.

"No, the sex. It pleases me that two middle-aged people can get so horny for each other that they have to knock off a piece before dinner."

Molly raised her eyebrows. "Knock off a piece? Is that what we did?"

"Yeah, that's what we did." He grinned again.

"Well, for your information, I didn't consider it knocking off a piece . . ." She stopped herself, fighting back a smile, then continued. "And I also don't consider myself middle-aged. I'm forty, in case you managed to forget. *You're fifty-five.*"

His grin widened. "Okay, I'm middle-aged and you're still a chippie."

"I was *never* a chippie."

He gave her a long wink. "You were a little while ago."

She jabbed her fork at him, again fighting off a smile. "Stop it and eat your dinner. You're starting to sound like a teenager."

He let out a low growl and got another eye roll in return.

They took their after-dinner coffee into the living room and resumed their earlier positions facing each other across a low cocktail table.

Molly casually brushed a strand of loose hair off her forehead. "I want to ask you something about the case," she began.

"Shoot."

She sipped her coffee, taking her time. She wanted it to seem that what she was about to ask didn't really matter. "Well, I've skimmed some of the reports—although I do intend to read them more thoroughly over the weekend. But for now there's one impression I've come away with. Jimmy seems to have had some pretty strong suspicions about Cynthia Reed."

Jake nodded. "I think that's a fair assumption. But it's also fair to say that he still had a lot of questions about some other people as well."

They were quiet for a moment. "Who did you suspect?" Molly waited, watching various emotions play across Jake's eyes as he considered how to answer.

"I'd rather not say. I don't want to prejudice your thinking. And I say that because I might very well be wrong."

"But you don't think so."

He slowly shook his head. "No, I don't think so."

Molly sipped her coffee, then placed the cup on the table between them and sat back. "Tell me about Cynthia Reed. I don't mean who she was, I mean *what* she was."

Again, varying emotions ran through Jake's eyes, including something Molly hadn't seen there before, a slow simmering anger.

Jake leaned back and steepled his fingers. "She was very different from anyone I had ever known. She was very beautiful, strikingly so, and very sad at the same time. It was a combination that was new to me back then, something I hadn't seen, or if I had, that I hadn't recognized." He paused, thinking over his own words. "I think she knew that, too. She knew I was really taken with her beauty, with her style, with everything about her." Again, he paused. "Maybe taken *in* is a better way to put it. But I was young. A lot younger than I thought I was back then." He smiled at her, at himself as well. "And the sadness I saw in her, that really got to me. It didn't seem to fit . . . with a woman like her. I mean, somebody so beautiful. Living in that big house. A person who obviously had whatever money she needed." He smiled again at his own words. "And she wanted *me*. Or at least I thought she did—a guy with a mangled leg, who didn't attract a lot of beautiful young women; a guy who probably wouldn't even have gotten a job with the cops if the war hadn't produced such a manpower shortage." He stopped as if recognizing the bitterness in his words, and then continued, his tone more controlled. "And at the same time I knew what she had come from. It wasn't very different than me, really—growing up without much more than the proverbial pot." Jake took time to sip his coffee. "You see, it's like I told you. I was very young. I was too young even to realize that you could have a lot of stuff—success, money, whatever—and still be unhappy."

"But the sadness you saw in her . . . it got to you?"

"Oh, yeah. It got to me big time. Not right away. But it got to me. And you see, she knew it would. She knew just how to play the part—that little girl lost bit."

"So you think it was mostly an act." Molly fought to keep any judgment from her voice. She watched Jake fight his emotions as he considered her statement.

"No, it wasn't an act. Not all of it, anyway. There were things . . ." He stopped himself and shook his head. "I'd rather let you read about them in the reports. Take them the way they happened. The way we found them."

Molly nodded as she continued to study his eyes. It's all right, Jake, she thought. You told me what I wanted to know. Cynthia Reed hurt you. She hurt you badly. And you haven't for-

gotten. You haven't forgotten any of it. And I think you might
even still hate her for what she did.

I had heard about the solid gold chain, but I had never seen it.
We had entered under the green canopy, perhaps the most famous in New York, the one that bears only the name *Stork Club*
and the numeral 3 that marks its place on East Fifty-third
Street. We had glided past the blue-uniformed doorman who
had pulled back the heavy bronze door; the doorman nodding
respectfully to Cyn, acknowledging her as someone who belonged; not looking at me at all.

Cyn's house was only one block north and two blocks east,
but she had insisted we arrive by taxi. *No one walked to the
Stork Club,* she had explained, and as our cab pulled into a line
half a block long I saw why. On both sides of the canopy wooden
barriers held back crowds of celebrity hunters, every set of eyes
eager and hungry as the line of taxis and limousines deposited
their quarry before them. While we waited our turn I noticed
that some of those eyes turned envious when a car door opened
and revealed someone they did not recognize. These were the
city's gentry, not celebrities in their own right, but men and
women whose money made them a part of this café society the
newspapers wrote about, whose money made them "good
enough" to travel in the same circle as the celebrities these
gawkers adored. But to those who waited, these others didn't
really count. Only the celebrities mattered. When these moneyed
folks arrived, the hands offering autograph books were with-
drawn, held in check for the next movie star who would walk
on past them as if they didn't exist at all, who had already done
so time after time, night after night, but who this hungry crowd
still found worthy of worship.

Inside, as we stood before the gold chain, I noticed that the
hatcheck room lay beyond that point of acceptance. And I
wondered about those who were turned away, who were forced
to walk back out through those bronze doors and again face
the crowd that had witnessed their grand entrance. I was feeling quite grand myself, realizing I would not be among those
who were turned away—not as long as I was with someone
who belonged.

I leaned in close to Cyn and whispered, "This must have been what it was like in the Roman Colosseum, everybody sweating it out, waiting for the emperor to give them a thumbs-up or thumbs-down."

Her back stiffened as I made my little joke, and I realized how much all of this mattered to her. I glanced toward the hatcheck room where she had once worked and tried to understand the transformation that had taken place, the one she had spoken to me about only a few nights ago, that sudden change from hatcheck girl to "grand lady." She had tried to make it seem that she was mocking the idea. I had had my doubts about that then. Now I was sure.

"When we get inside," I said, trying to ease the tension, "how much should I tip the hatcheck girl?"

She turned to me, her voice only a whisper. "Don't tip her anything."

The reply stopped me cold. "Why?" I asked.

"They don't get the money," she whispered. "The money goes into a slot in the counter, and straight into a lockbox."

"Who gets it?"

Cyn gave me a small shrug. "The club sells the hatcheck rights to somebody, I don't know who that somebody is."

"Didn't you work for whoever it was?" I asked, still whispering.

She shook her head. "The girls work for the club. The club pays them twenty-eight-fifty a week and has the right to hire and fire them. But the hatcheck room itself is a concession. It's one of the ways the club pays protection to the mob, I think. The same way they have to rent all their linens from a certain company. At least that's what I was told."

I had known about the linen scam. Together with jukeboxes and pinball machines, and the new cigarette and candy machines that had just begun to spring up around the city, it was one of the mob's biggest but least publicized rackets. The hatcheck operation was new to me, but I could understand why a place like the Stork insisted on hiring its own girls. Had that item been left to the mob, the hatcheck room would have been filled with young ladies offering a helluva lot more than coat hangers.

When our turn came at the chain, the maître d' offered Cyn his condolences over her husband's death and told her he'd have

a table for her "and the gentleman" as soon as I'd checked our
coats. When that was done he led us across the foyer, Cyn first,
then me trailing behind and starting to feel very much the lackey.
But lackey or not, I was getting some envious looks. Cyn was
dressed in a loose-fitting black dress that satisfied her status as
a new widow, but just barely. The dress, like all her clothes,
seemed to move with her, accenting every part of what I had
come to know the previous night, and together with the way she
wore it, garnered appreciative stares from every man we passed.

Our little stroll took us by a boisterous bar, then past a
smaller room off to our left, and I saw Cyn hesitate and glance
inside before continuing. Then her back seemed to stiffen as it
had while we were standing behind the gold chain. We were approaching a larger L-shaped room, this one marked by mirrored walls, gold silk draperies and table chairs upholstered in
yellow and gray satin. There was a bandstand to one side where
musicians were just beginning to set up, and a massive crystal
chandelier at the room's center that reflected every flash of
light, be it from cigarette lighter or diamond necklace—and
there were plenty of the latter in evidence. Taken all together
the room was more elegant than anything I had ever seen and I
wondered why Cyn seemed suddenly upset by it.

Before I could ask, a large, bluff, red-faced fellow in a double-
breasted suit hurried toward us. He had a square jaw that jut-
ted out over a severely knotted necktie, and his eyes seemed
angry and filled with rebuke. When he reached us his eyes softened momentarily, and he took Cyn's hand and told her how
sorry he was that he had missed her husband's funeral, explaining that some problems within his own family had unexpectedly
come up. Cyn thanked him, not bothering to tell me who the
man was, perhaps assuming that I'd know, simply telling him
that I was a detective looking into her husband's death. That's
what she called it, looking into his death, not investigating his
murder. She quickly added that I was also guarding her, as a
way of explaining why I was standing there beside her.

The man gave me a grunted greeting and looked me up and
down as if assessing what good I'd be if protection proved necessary. He didn't seem very impressed. Then he turned to the
maître d', his eyes glaring again with undisguised anger.

His voice, too, was snappish and filled with rebuke. "Mrs. Reed sits in the Cub Room. She always sits there. So does any guest she brings with her. Is that understood?"

The maître d' flushed and lowered his eyes. "Of course, Mr. Billingsley. It was my error." He turned his attention back to us, or rather to Cyn. "Please follow me, Mrs. Reed. I'm sorry for the mistake."

I recognized the name, even if I had not the man himself. Sherman Billingsley was the owner of the Stork, although many insisted he actually worked for his long-time Prohibition buddy Frank Costello. True or not, the suspicions weren't surprising. Billingsley was somewhat of a legend in New York's café society. He supposedly began his career in his native Oklahoma selling liquor on Indian reservations when he was still a kid in short pants, then moved on to New York during Prohibition for a brief stint in bootlegging and a longer one as proprietor of a speakeasy. Now fully legit—at least on the surface—he ran the Stork Club like some petty dictator, deciding who was socially acceptable and who was not. And for some reason people accepted his rulings. To be barred from the Stork was a major blow to any celebrity. And to make matters worse, the city's top knife-'em-in-the-back gossip columnists, including Billingsley's good buddies, Walter Winchell and Dorothy Kilgallen, eagerly reported those banishments.

It was all a mystery to me, and just a little amusing. What I didn't understand right now was the significance of the Cub Room, and I wondered about it as we were led there and seated at a smallish table. The room was certainly elegant, though considerably undersized compared to the one we had just left—and not nearly as grand. Here celebrity photographs had replaced the mirrored walls and golden draperies of the larger room.

"So what's with this Cub Room?" I asked, after we had ordered drinks.

Cyn gave me a quizzical look. "You really don't know?"

I offered her a regretful shrug. "Hey, I've only been a detective for a few months. The closest a patrolman gets to places like this is handing out tickets for double parking. And I never worked this precinct, so I didn't even do that."

Cyn nodded her head as if dismissing her earlier question. "I suppose I just expect everyone to know about this place. I mean the gossip columns and society pages are always so full of it."

I grinned at her. "If they wrote about it in the *Daily News* sports columns or in the *Police Gazette* I'd know about it," I teased. "At the precinct the lieutenants and captains usually snag the society pages before the rest of us have a chance to look at them."

She laughed at that, then turned serious again, and waved her hand, taking in the room. "Some people call it the 'snub room.'" She tried to laugh the words away, but couldn't, and hurried on. "If you're seated in here it means you're considered a valued and important customer. It's where all the movie stars and politicians are seated, along with people who are famous in other ways—writers, Broadway producers, newspaper columnists. The duke and duchess of Windsor sit in here when they're in town. So does J. Edgar Hoover—right next to Frank Costello sometimes—Charlie Chaplin, Frank Sinatra, everybody who's anybody. They had a big party for Clark Gable when he came home from the war with his Distinguished Flying Cross. If you're here, you're important. If you're seated anywhere else it tells you you're just a customer, a nobody. You see what I mean?"

"And you sit here," I said.

Cyn lowered her eyes. "My husband was a well-known judge, and he was about to run for governor. I just went along for the ride."

"But you're still here."

Cyn looked up at me, her eyes sad, almost waiflike now. "That's Mr. Billingsley's doing." She paused as if deciding how much she wanted to say. Then she seemed to surrender to it and continued. "When the judge and I were married there was talk—some of it pretty nasty at times—talk that said I was a gold digger and social climber. Well, Mr. Billingsley had always liked me, and since he came from a poor background himself, I guess that talk kind of rubbed him the wrong way." She shrugged. "Anyway, he became somewhat protective toward me."

I studied her beautiful face. It seemed to hold an odd mix tonight—sadness and defiance all blended together in one neat package. But the beauty was there, too. It always was, and it made it easy to lose focus, to forget you were a cop. I decided it was time to do my job and push her a bit.

"I heard you used to date one of the singers here." I had been hoping to slip the question into our conversation tonight, and thought this was as good a chance as any.

Cyn stared at me for several moments, holding my eyes, the defiance winning out now. "You're always working, aren't you?" she asked at length. "I thought after last night . . ." She let the sentence die, then straightened in her chair. "His name is Bobby Ramirez. He's a crooner with the Latin band that plays here. Sometimes he gets out on the dance floor and does a little rumba for the ladies. He's got good hips and the ladies like him." She glared at me, her eyes challenging, almost insolent. "I liked him, too. At one time I liked him a lot." She continued to stare me down. "I like men, Jake. I always have. Maybe that makes me a bad sort to some people. But I don't think I am. I was kind of hoping you understood how it was with me. After last night I thought you would."

We ate dinner mostly in silence. Even though I tried as hard as I could to make light conversation, the question I had asked about Bobby Ramirez seemed to hang between us, dampening any hope for a pleasant evening. Halfway through dinner the society band that had been setting up in the main dining room when we arrived was replaced by the Latin band, and I could hear the energetic voice of a male singer over the din of conversation that filled the Cub Room. Cyn gave me a look when Bobby Ramirez started to sing, but said nothing, and I didn't dare satisfy my curiosity by getting up to take a look at him. Sooner or later one of us would, of course. Either Jimmy or I. We'd brace him, get his story, whether Cyn liked it or not. It was what the job required.

It was eleven o'clock when we got back to the Reed house, very early for a night on the town. Early even if you just did the Stork and bypassed other obligatory stops at the Copacabana or La Vie Parisienne, as we had. But then Cyn *was* a widow, and I was a cop and a bodyguard, not a date. At least I didn't think I was, despite what we had gotten into last night.

We went past the uniform stationed at the front door and into the long hall that divided the house in half.

"I'd like a drink before I go up." She turned into the small parlor, allowing her wrap to fall from her shoulders. "Will you join me?"

I picked up her wrap and glanced around, making sure we were alone. "I shouldn't but I will." I followed her into the small parlor where the drinks were kept and let her do the honors— single-malt scotch over ice for her, bourbon for me.

She gave me a long, steady look, then asked, "Are you staying here tonight?"

"Yes. Tonight's my watch. Tomorrow it will be Jimmy's."

She kept staring at me, then placed her drink on a side table, took mine from my hand and placed it next to hers. Then she slipped her arms around my neck. "I'm sorry I got angry tonight," she said. "My husband was very jealous about Bobby, about the fact that we were once . . . close. When you asked about him, it just hit me the wrong way." She raised herself up on her toes and gently kissed my lips. "Is that all right?" she whispered.

"That's fine," I said.

"Good." She was smiling now. "I want you to kiss me. Do you think you can do that?"

I nodded; any answer I might make suddenly caught in my throat.

After I kissed her, she leaned her head back, eyes still closed, mouth still slightly parted. "That's so good." Her voice was little more than a whisper now. She opened her eyes and stared at me. It was a hungry look that sent a chill down my spine. "It's good. But it's not enough, not nearly enough. I want you to take me upstairs and I want you to touch me, Jake. I want that a lot. I want it an awful lot. Can you do that for me, too, Jake? Can you make me feel good; make me feel happy again?"

I could feel my heart beating in my chest. "Yeah, I can do that." My breath felt short, ragged. "I can do anything you want."

I awoke at six the next morning. Cyn lay beside me, a sheet draped loosely around her body. There was a spray of blond hair hiding most of her face and I propped myself up on an el- bow and with one finger brushed the hair back. Then I just looked at her, that beautiful, finely etched face, the high cheekbones and the soft, smooth shape of a nearby shoulder, the bit of breast visible beneath her arm. I used the same solitary finger to trace along her spine, slowly sliding back the sheet as I moved down the length of her body. I stopped when the sheet fell away just above the sharp curve of her buttocks. There, a jagged scar marred the silky surface of her skin. It was fairly recent, still had that raw look of a fresh wound. I had not noticed it the previous night when we were together, but it had been dark then, and I had left Cyn's bed before dawn. Now it was visible in the morning light, and it momentarily startled me, jarred my senses, seemed somehow wrong and inexplicably out of place.

Cyn stirred and slowly opened her eyes. Lightly, I touched the scar. "How did you get this?" I asked.

She reached down and pulled the sheet over the scar, her sudden movement making her hair fall back over her eyes so I couldn't see them. "It's something I don't want to talk about," she said.

I knew what she meant. My own mangled leg, the gift of half a pound of Japanese shrapnel, lay hidden beneath the sheet, just where I wanted it even though Cyn had already told me that it didn't bother her at all.

"It's only a scar," I lied. "And it's in a spot most people never see."

"That's the best place to leave a scar, isn't it?" she said. "In a place no one is able to see."

The words hit me hard. I'd been a street cop long enough to get my share of domestic calls, seen more than enough wives who'd been worked over by their husbands; girlfriends used as punching bags by the heroes they dated. A lot of those guys—worried about what their friends and neighbors might think—had learned to dish out punishment in places where it wouldn't show.

"Are you telling me your husband did this?"

Cyn turned away and pulled the sheet up around herself, creating a safe little cocoon. "I'm not telling you anything." She spoke in a whisper I could barely hear.

I leaned down and kissed her shoulder softly. "Maybe it's something I should know about." I tried to keep my voice gentle, nonthreatening.

"It's nothing you need to know. It's not part of your case, so you don't have to worry yourself about it."

I kept my lips against her shoulder. "If you were hurt, it worries me." I was suddenly surprised how true that was; how much I meant it.

Cyn turned over slowly and looked into my eyes. She seemed to be searching them, as if trying to find some lie there. Then she reached up and drew me down to her. She kissed me, then pressed her cheek against mine. "I haven't done anything wrong." She was whispering again. "No matter what you and Jimmy Finn think, I haven't done anything bad."

"Tell me about the scar."

"Don't ask me about that. Not now. Just protect me, Jake. Can you do that? Can you just protect me for now and forget about everything else?"

I kissed her cheek and then her neck, and felt myself wanting her more than I could remember ever wanting anyone. "Yes," I whispered. "I can do that for you."

I still had my jacket over my arm as I came down the stairs. It was seven o'clock and the front hall was deserted. I had just reached the bottom of the stairs and was slipping my suit coat on when Jimmy stepped out of the parlor.

"You and me have to talk, boyo."

I looked at him and felt guilt spread across my face. His hard eyes bored into me, and I was certain of only one thing. Talking to Jimmy Finn was not something I wanted to do just then. "Talk about what?" Even my voice sounded guilty.

Jimmy took my arm and guided me toward the front door. "Let's take a walk. The lady will be fine for a few minutes, and what I have to say needs a bit of privacy."

Jimmy walked me halfway up the block. Just far enough to keep us out of earshot of the uniform guarding the front door. Then he turned on me, eyes as hard as I'd ever seen them. "Now tell me what the fook is goin' on."

A half dozen lies had been running through my head as we moved away from the house, but the look in Jimmy's eyes told me they were useless. I abandoned them all.

I studied my shoes. "The lady and I have gotten a little closer than we should have."

Jimmy stared at me. "That's a lovely way to put it." He looked away, shaking his head. "Did it ever occur to you that we might have to arrest her one day for knockin' off her husband? And that you—one of the fookin' detectives assigned to the case—just might be fookin' up the whole case by crawlin' around under the sheets with her?"

I kept my eyes averted. "She didn't kill him." I could hear the weakness in my voice, the uncertainty, and immediately hated the sound of it.

"Oh, you're sure of that, are you, Sherlock?"

The sarcastic contempt in Jimmy's voice forced my eyes up. I glared at him. "Ninety-nine percent sure. Yes."

Jimmy nodded. "Well, that's wonderful. And what about this crooner the lady was supposed to be screwin'? The one we heard about from Frank Costello only yesterday. You think maybe that gave her a motive to want her husband dead and gone?"

I could feel my face begin to color, more from anger than embarrassment. I couldn't deny what Jimmy was saying. I could still hear the defiant words Cyn had spoken just last night playing out in my mind. "His name is Bobby Ramirez. I asked her about him and she told me they had been close. *Very close.* But that was before she married the judge." My mind filled with Cyn's further words that her husband had been jealous of that old relationship, but I kept them to myself. I also kept silent about the scar I had seen on her back, and how I thought it had gotten there. I had no intention of providing Jimmy with any additional motives. "I plan on talking to Ramirez today." I threw the last out defiantly.

Jimmy smiled at me, his face a mix of wonderment and disbelief. "You are a fookin' marvel, you are. Let me tell you somethin' right here, right now. If it weren't for the fact that it'd give Mr. Manny Troy even more leverage than he's got now, I'd bust your ass with the bosses down at headquarters and have you taken off the case like that." He snapped his fingers for emphasis. "And I wouldn't give a fiddler's fart that I'd be kissin' your ass right back into uniform, because I'd figure you'd brought it on yerself by bein' such a stupid sonofabitch."

I stood there growing redder by the minute, thinking how I'd like to grab Jimmy by the throat and throttle him, no matter the consequences. But I knew he was right, so my hands stayed at my side, and I listened and just took it.

"Now, since I'm the one who's in charge of this investigation, I'm gonna tell you what's really gonna happen. First"—he jabbed his thumb into his chest—"*I'm* gonna talk to Bobby Ramirez. In fact I already started to do some checkin' on that fine gentleman." Now he sent his thumb jabbing over his shoulder back toward the direction we had come. "A fine gentleman, I might add, who's been known to pay the occasional visit to the judge's home. And accordin' to the people who told me this, those visits happened durin' the day, when his honor's fat ass was sittin' in court."

My jaw tightened and I stared out into the street. "What do you want me to do?"

"Three things. First, I want you to take the afternoon off. I want you to use that time to go home and see your wife. That's that pregnant woman who lives in your house, in case you've forgot. Then I want you back here by five and I want you to explain to Mrs. Reed that from now on your dick is gonna stay in your pants where it belongs, no matter how much she'd like it someplace else." He stared hard at me. "You got that?"

I could feel the blood rush to my face and my jaw clench. "I got it."

"That's very good. And when you finish with all that, I want you out and about tonight with Lilly Straus. I want you to get the lady as drunk as you can get her, and then I want you to find out everythin' you can about what she's been up to with Owney Ryan, Manny Troy and our dearly departed judge. You got that, too?"

"I got it."

Jimmy gave me a large smile that held all the sincerity of a Times Square grifter. "That's very, very good." The smile disappeared and the eyes hardened again. "Then I think you should get the fook outta here and make sure I don't see your sorry ass again until five o'clock."

The house in Brooklyn and all its furnishings had passed on to me when my father died last year. My father's will actually had

divided the house in two with my brother, Tim, getting an equal
share. But Tim never made it home from the Pacific. He was
killed somewhere on Corregidor, and even though our dad out-
lived him by two years, he never changed his will. According to
that document, the two lower floors were to be mine; the upper
two were for Tim. That's how our father had planned it. Except
now the upper floors housed a family the old man had never
met—the tenants whose monthly rent supplemented my salary
as a rookie detective.

I entered the house through the garden-level door, which
was just beneath the front stoop. As with most brownstones, the
entry was to one side of the building, with the rooms on each
floor running straight back railroad-style off a main hall. The
garden level of our flat held a dining room and kitchen and a
large pantry. The second floor was made up of two oversized
parlors with fifteen-foot ceilings and massive pocket doors to
set them apart, and a smaller room normally used as a study.
One of the larger rooms now served as our bedroom, the second
as our formal sitting room, with the third, smaller room already
outfitted with a crib and layette for our coming child. It was a
sizable amount of space for a newly married young couple, especially in New York, and the income from the upstairs flat was
an added blessing. All of it a gift of my father, who spent his
adult life running into burning buildings as a member of the
city's fire department, and who suffered the agony of burying
both his wife and his eldest son.

I called out to Mary as I entered, but got no reply. When I
reached the kitchen I saw her through the rear window, out in
her garden, kneeling before one of the flowerbeds she tended
with such care. The kitchen radio was on the windowsill, facing
out, and she was listening to *Arthur Godfrey Time.* I watched her
for several minutes. She looked large and heavy now, no longer
the slim, lithe, raven-haired woman I had married two years before. Now every movement seemed slow and tired, her rounded
stomach brushing against her thighs each time she shifted position, every breath heavy and labored. I felt a sudden rush of
guilt just having those thoughts and I moved quickly to the
kitchen door and out into the garden.

"You shouldn't be doing all that. You'll wear yourself out."

She looked up at me, a strand of dark hair plastered against her sweaty forehead. "So you're finally home."

I looked down at my shoes. "I'm sorry. It can't be helped." I forced a smile and raised my chin toward the garden. "Let me change my clothes and I'll do that for you."

"It's all right. I'm finished." She drew a deep breath, then placed a hand on her knee and pushed herself up. It was an awkward, lumbering movement and I hurried quickly to her side and reached for her elbow in case she fell.

She brushed my hand away, annoyed by my belated concern. Then she seemed to regret it. "I'm all right. I just feel so heavy when I have to get up, or sit down. It's like there's a sofa strapped to my stomach."

I took her arm again and met no resistance this time as I guided her to the kitchen door. "Let's go in and sit, and I'll make you some tea."

Mary didn't say anything; she just followed my suggestion and lowered herself into a kitchen chair as I got busy at the stove setting the kettle to boil.

"How's your big case going?" she asked, when I joined her at the table.

"Slow. All the time we spend guarding Mrs. Reed cuts into the time we have to investigate the crime."

"So why don't they assign someone else to guard the woman, or someone else to do the investigating?"

"That's a good question. I wish I knew the answer."

Mary pondered it herself. "It almost sounds like they don't want the investigation to go anywhere."

The kettle started whistling and I got up to get our tea. "That thought has crossed our minds." I spoke the words over my shoulder as I poured water on the tea bags. Lipton, the same tea Arthur Godfrey was advertising at that very moment.

When I returned with the tea I tried to change the subject. Cynthia Reed's protection wasn't something I wanted to talk about—especially right now. That was something I had learned from the crooks I'd dealt with during my time in uniform. Always avoid subjects that can get you nailed, and when you can't, just play dumb. Some people claim that cops and criminals are a lot alike. They just work different sides of the street. The truth is they learn a lot from each other. Hiding guilt is one of those things. An experienced crook never lets his nerves show. Neither does a smart cop.

I placed Mary's tea down before her. "So tell me what the doctor said."

"I told you on the phone."

"I know, but tell me again."

She looked at me oddly, then a small smile formed. "Are you excited it's getting so close?"

"Of course I am. A little scared, too. When did he say it'll be?"

Her smile widened. "Anywhere from a few weeks to a month. He's just not sure when . . . it happened, is all."

"Why isn't he sure? I thought they had ways to tell those things."

"I asked him that." Mary lowered her eyes. "He said if we only did it once a month they could tell for sure. But I'd already told him how you wanted it almost every day—how you'd come home for lunch if you could." She let out an embarrassed laugh. It was something good Catholic girls didn't talk about—even when they were married and it was okay to give your husband a little dance under the sheets.

"So because I lusted after you we're stuck guessing when the baby will get here? Somehow that doesn't seem fair. Being denied information because you worked too hard at something."

Mary blushed and kept her eyes on her tea. "It wasn't that much work, was it?"

"Of course not."

When she looked up at me her eyes took on a fearful cast. "Do you still lust after me, Jake? Even though I've gotten big and fat?"

The guilt rose again. I felt like such a sonofabitch. "Of course I do."

"But you never come home like you used to—all . . . hot to trot and all." She blushed again at the use of the phrase.

I reached out and placed my hand over hers. "It's just the new job. All the work, and me just learning. And it's your condition, too. I'm afraid of hurting you, or hurting the baby. The doctor said we should stay away from it, didn't he?"

Mary nodded. "Yes." She paused. "But I still miss you, Jake. I really do. I know that makes me sound like a terrible tramp but I can't help it."

"It doesn't make you sound terrible. I wouldn't want it any other way."

Mary lowered her eyes again. Then she drew a deep breath. "But you're out and about every day, seeing beautiful women and all. And then you come home to this." She waved a hand, taking in her enlarged body.

I laughed and squeezed her hand. "Hey, what do you think Jimmy and I do all day long? Sneak off to burlesque houses when we're supposed to be working?"

She smiled at the idea. "I wouldn't put it past you, either one of you." Her eyes became serious. "I've seen Mrs. Reed's picture in the papers. She's sure beautiful. What do you have to do when you're guarding her?"

I put on my best poker face, like any good crook would do when braced with a question he didn't want to answer. "Mostly, when she's in the house, I just sit in the parlor and listen to the radio. We've got uniforms at the front and back doors, so my only job is to be there if somebody gets by them. That, and to follow her if she goes anyplace."

"Has she gone anywhere?"

I kept my face as blank as possible, pushed the guilt down, hard. "Well, she went to the funeral home all those times, of course. And the funeral." I thought about the possibility that our picture might appear in one of the newspapers. The flash-bulbs were certainly popping at everybody who entered the Stork Club. I drew a breath. "And last night she went to the Stork Club."

Mary's eyes widened. "The Stork Club? With her husband just fresh in his grave and all? Sweet Jesus."

I felt immediately defensive. "I think she just needed to get out."

"Well, couldn't she go to a movie, then? God, there's *Going My Way* with Bing Crosby and Barry Fitzgerald showing now."

I smiled at the idea of Cyn going to a movie with Bing Crosby and Barry Fitzgerald playing a pair of Catholic priests. Maybe *Spellbound* with Ingrid Bergman, given what the gossip columns were saying about her penchant for bed-hopping. But I sure couldn't tell Mary that. "Yeah, I guess she could. I think it's just that she doesn't have any family here in the city, and the few people she knows are at the Stork Club. She used to work there before she married the judge." I didn't know why I was defending Cyn this way, why I'd risk tipping my hand and all. But after my conversation with Jimmy I couldn't seem to help myself. Right now I was thinking about one person Cyn had worked with at the Stork, a café singer named Bobby Ramirez. I couldn't help wondering how Jimmy was getting on with him.

"Worked at the Stork Club?" Mary seemed shocked by the idea, and her sense of great surprise irritated me far more than it should have. "What did she do there?"

"Hatcheck girl." I snapped out the answer, then took a quick sip of my tea to hide my annoyance.

"Dear God, the papers never said anything about that. All they talked about was how the judge could've been the next governor, and her the first lady of New York." She shook her head, her eyes full of wonder. "A hatcheck girl as first lady." She looked at me eagerly now. "What's she like?"

I sipped my tea again, knowing I had to avoid the subject. "She's just like anybody else, I guess. I mean she doesn't exactly confide in me, or tell me her thoughts. I'm just a cop who's there to protect her."

"Is she really in danger?"

"I don't know. The commissioner seems to think so. And so does Manny Troy. That's all that matters for Jimmy and me."

"But you don't think so?"

I considered what she had asked and realized that the answer was no. I didn't think Cynthia Reed was in danger. At least not from any killer. "No, I guess I don't. I don't think whoever killed the judge has any interest in her. If she had seen what had happened maybe it would be different."

"But she didn't."

"No."

"Are you sure?"

I thought about that and realized the answer was no again. "As sure as I can be, I guess."

"Maybe the commissioner and Manny Troy aren't as sure as you are."

The comment stopped me cold, but before I could think about it she was off on another tangent. "What's the house like? The judge's house, I mean. Is it very grand?"

"No grander than this one," I said. "It's really laid out a lot like this house. Except it's a bit bigger and has a center hall. They had it all to themselves, of course. It wasn't chopped up for two families." I reached out and took her hand. "You know, being there and all, it's made me think how one day—when I'm making more money and we can afford it—how we could turn this house back into a one-family place. It would be pretty grand if we did."

Mary smiled at the idea. "Oh, God, it certainly would." Her face colored again. "We'd have to have a big family to fill it up, though, wouldn't we?"

"Yes, we would." I squeezed her hand. "A real big family."

{ 10 }

"What was it like for Jake back then? What was his relationship like with Cynthia Reed—and with his wife?"

Jimmy Finn studied Molly's face, looking for some hidden reason behind the question. "Is this to help you with the case, or are you just curious?"

"A bit of both. But it *will* help me understand the evidence better if I understand the circumstances surrounding the investigation."

Jimmy chewed on that. "Jake was twenty-five." He said it as if that answered the question in itself.

"And . . . ?"

"And . . . that means he was doin' most of his thinkin' with a certain part of his anatomy in his hand." He saw Molly's eyebrows arch and quickly continued. "That doesn't mean he didn't do good work. That he wasn't good at his job. It just means this woman, this Cynthia Reed, had a way of gettin' to him, and let's just say he was ripe for the gettin'."

"Was he in love with her?"

Jimmy nodded slowly, then finished with a shrug. "Toward the end I think he thought he was."

"But you don't think so." Molly offered it as a statement, not a question.

Jimmy drew a long breath. "I don't know. I do know he loved his wife. When it was all finished and done, Mary was the one he wanted." He shook his head. "When he lost her, when he realized his own foolishness was the cause of it all, it nearly drove him nuts."

They were in Molly's small, cramped office. Jimmy had come at her request to fill in the blanks about the reports he had never filed. Molly, in a fresh lab coat, was seated behind her desk, Jimmy in the lone visitor's chair facing her.

"What did you think about her? About Cynthia Reed?"

Jimmy inclined his head to one side. "She was a looker, that's for sure. The kind of woman every man dreams about having, but few ever do. Very aloof, very sexy; glamorous, I guess you'd say."

"You think that's what got to Jake? The glamour?"

Jimmy nodded. "That was part of it, sure. You got to remember, he was just a kid, and even though he grew up in the city, even though he'd been off in the army, he was still wet behind the ears when it came to that kind of woman." He smiled and leaned forward, warming to the subject. "Jake was a poor kid from Brooklyn. Oh, he didn't know he was poor. I mean his father was a fireman and there was always food on the table growing up, but when it came to real money he was poor, all right. Then, with this Reed woman, he sees up close how the other half really lives. I mean here he is goin' to the Stork Club and sittin' with all the swells and the movie stars and all. And he's with this beautiful woman—this really beautiful woman— who lives in this big house on Fifty-fourth Street. I mean here's a twenty-five-year-old kid with a gimpy leg he's always tryin' to hide, and all he's got at home is a pregnant wife and a lot of bills. Sure the glamour got to him. All of it did. It had to."

"And Cynthia Reed used it." Again, Molly words were a statement, not a question.

"She played him like a fookin' fish." Jimmy caught himself. "Sorry. It slipped out."

"I've heard the word before." She smiled at him. "Not said quite so quaintly, though. I've even used it on occasion."

Jimmy nodded, grateful for the reprieve. He leaned forward again. "There's one more thing I gotta say on this. Just to give Jake a fair deal and all."

"What's that, Jimmy?"

Jimmy studied the floor for a moment. When he looked up again there was a small smile on his lips. "Let's just say there aren't many men who wouldn't of let Cynthia Reed put her shoes under their bed."

Molly sat back and steepled her fingers in front of her face. She felt a surprising tinge of jealousy for something that had happened so long ago. "What did *you* think about Cynthia Reed?"

"I think she knew who killed her husband."

"Do you think she was involved?"

Jimmy gave her a broad shrug, then a wink and a smile. "Do I know for sure? No. Do I think she was involved? Up to her pretty neck."

Now Molly leaned forward, intent on Jimmy's answers. "Why? Because of that singer . . ." She looked down at the notes on her desk. "This Bobby Ramirez?"

"That could of been a part of it. But I was never sure."

"Tell me about it."

Bobby Ramirez looked about to wet his pants when I flashed the tin at his front door, but he covered it quickly. He lived in a semi-rat-trap, just off Tin Pan Alley on Forty-eighth Street west of Broadway. It was a fourth-floor walk-up with peeling paint and the smell of cabbage embedded in the walls. I decided right off that either Bobby was making piss-poor wages crooning at the Stork, or he had some expensive habits that were soaking up his cash.

He let me in his one-bedroom flat and showed me into a sparsely furnished living room. There was only one window and it opened onto a ventilation shaft. I walked to the window and looked out at another staring back at me.

"Nice view. I bet it really jacks up the rent."

Bobby ignored the jibe. He was a tall, slender guy with slicked-back black hair and a well-barbered Errol Flynn mustache. He was wearing a white silk shirt that looked soft even from a distance and a pair of pleated black trousers set off by a gold key chain. All together, standing in that battered room, he had the look of a down-at-the-heels gigolo. But he was definitely a handsome guy, no question about it, and in better surroundings I had little doubt he'd give the ladies a case of the flutters. It was something I'd never been able to do myself, so right away I decided I didn't like him, and my gut reaction was to loosen a few of his shiny white teeth.

Bobby had shrugged away my comment about his view, making a very conscious attempt at bravado. He seated himself in a battered overstuffed easy chair. The only other place to sit was an equally battered sofa, so I plopped down on it and gave him a cat-and-canary smile.

"So tell me about Cynthia Reed."

"What do you want to know?" He enunciated each word like it was a little jewel in itself, and there was an underlying hint of a Spanish accent that, to my ear, sounded put on. His bravado was still holding, but just barely, and I knew it wouldn't last much longer. His eyes had darted about a bit when I threw the question at him, and I knew he was getting ready to lie right through those pearly whites.

"Make it easy on yourself." The cat smiled at the canary again. "Tell me all you know."

"She's a good kid." The eyes were still darting about. "I liked her a lot. A real looker, too, if you know what I mean. We went out a couple of times." He raised a cautioning hand. "But that was before she met the judge and got married."

"You ever see her after she married the judge?"

"Hey, look—"

"Never mind the *hey, looks*. Just answer the fookin' question."

Bobby shifted uneasily in his seat and I could see a thin line of perspiration forming along his well-barbered mustache. "Yeah, we stayed friends. Like I said, she's a good kid. Even after she married the judge, she didn't have her nose up in the air like most of the women who come into the Stork. Some of

them, they get on a rich guy's arm, they forget where they came
from, you know what I mean?"

"Ever visit her after she was married?"

Bobby's whole body jerked with the question. "Hey, what is
this? I don't have to answer that kind of stuff."

His umbrage made me smile. I reached into my side pocket
and took out my blackjack, let it slap my palm a few times. "Oh,
you're gonna answer, boyo. One way or another you're gonna
answer every fookin' question I ask. How your kneecaps and
your elbows are gonna feel after you answer them, well now,
that's what we don't know, isn't it?"

Bobby stared at me and I could tell he believed every word
of it. All the bravado suddenly went south and he folded like a
cheap suit. His jaw gave a little quiver. "Okay, so I visited her a
couple of times. But it wasn't what you think."

"What is it I think?" I was grinning again. It seemed to make
him nervous.

"You know. That I was having my way with her." Bobby was
twisting in his seat again.

I threw back my head and laughed. "Havin' yer way with
her?" I leaned forward, all the laughter gone now. I stared him
down. "You mean fookin' her? Is that what you're afraid I'm
thinkin'?"

He began to stutter. "W . . . W . . . Well . . . yeah."

"Were ya?"

He twisted in his seat again. "No, not after she got married.
Never."

"So what'd ya do when ya went to her house—went there
when you knew the judge wasn't home? Did ya play Parcheesi
maybe?"

"I . . . I . . ."

I didn't let him finish. "What did the judge think of you
comin' there when he was sittin' on his bench sending dirtbags
off to prison?"

"I . . . I don't know. He never said anything to me." The perspiration on Bobby's upper lip and forehead was heavy now and
he was still squirming in his seat.

"You don't know much, do you?" I jabbed a finger toward his
face. "Okay, try this one. Did the judge like you?"

Bobby was perplexed by the question. He shook his head as if hoping an answer would rattle out. "I don't know if he liked me." He seemed to realize that saying *I don't know* again was the wrong approach. "I mean, we never said much to each other. Sometimes, when I stopped by their table at the Stork he'd say hello. That's all."

"When was the last time you were at his house?"

"I don't know." He shook his head, grimaced. "I mean I don't remember the last time I was there."

"Was it the night he got himself murdered?"

Bobby jumped up from his chair. "Hey, no. No. I wasn't anywhere near there that day."

"Sit down." I snapped out the order and watched Bobby do as he was told. "So you weren't there that day? Not at any time?"

"No."

"Where were you that night about eight o'clock?"

"I don't know." He shook his head, as if trying to chase those forbidden words away. "I was here, I guess."

"Not at work?"

"No. I never get there until ten."

"Were you there that night at ten?"

"Yeah."

I lowered my voice to almost a whisper. "Some people there said you looked a little upset that night. You wanna tell me about that?"

Bobby squirmed again. "Aw shit. I don't believe this. Okay, look, I was at the track that afternoon. I lost my shirt on a nag that was supposed to be a sure thing." He let out a snort and shook his head. "The piece of shit belonged in a glue factory. Came up lame at the quarter pole. I was upset about it because I lost everything I had, even my rent money."

I glanced around the apartment and understood why a cabaret singer with a good gig would live in a shithole like this. "What was the name of the nag? And don't doubt for a minute that I'm gonna check out if he ran that day and how he finished."

"Sunbeam. The horse's name was Sunbeam. It was the fifth race. You believe me, don't ya?"

I grinned at him, gave him a little bark of a laugh. "I'll tell you what I believe, boyo. I believe a deadbeat dirtbag like you just might think that Cynthia Reed was gonna come into some big bucks if her husband up and got himself dead. I think that same piece of worthless shit might even be so desperate that he might help the old boy along. Or maybe even do his old girl-friend a favor if she asked him real nice like."

"Hey . . ."

"Just shut your trap." I stood up, twirled the blackjack on my finger and slid it back into my pocket. "So I'll tell you what you're gonna do. You're gonna come to the precinct with me, and you're gonna give me a set of your prints. Then I'm gonna check those prints against the ones we found in the judge's house, and if any of them match I'm gonna come back and you and me are gonna do a little dance. You got that?"

Bobby Ramirez nodded, his eyes frozen on mine.

"And I'll tell you one other thing, boyo. You even *think* about leavin' this city before I tell you it's okay, you and me are gonna spend some time together that'll make you wish your mama never spread her legs for your dear old dad. You got that, mister?"

Bobby Ramirez nodded his head again and didn't say a word.

{ 11 }

Jake cooled his heels outside the commissioner's office for twenty minutes, the requisite time to tell all concerned that Paul Sutcliff, the boss of New York City's cops, was not pleased with his chief of detectives.

When he was finally ushered into the office Jake received an equally cool welcome as Sutcliff gestured to a chair opposite his desk. It was another clear sign of the commissioner's displeasure. The PC's office was on the top floor of One Police Plaza. It was an extremely formal room, covered in a thick red carpet with a wall of red-draped windows that overlooked the East River. Sutcliff's desk was set squarely in the center, a massive piece of Victorian walnut that had once belonged to Theodore Roosevelt when he was the city's police commissioner. To the left of the desk was a long conference table, a working area only used when the PC presided over staff meetings. To the right was a comfort zone consisting of a leather sofa and matching club chairs. When private meetings were friendly Sutcliff used the sofa and chairs. When they were not he enthroned himself behind his desk and used his considerable authority like a club.

"How have you been, Jake? I haven't had a chance to talk to you since Mary's funeral." The question was clearly a formality and held no warmth at all. Sutcliff was in his early sixties, but his age was deceptive. He was tall and lean and still more physically fit than most men twenty years his junior. He was not a handsome man, nor did his thinning gray hair make him look particularly distinguished, and the lack of either attribute often made others underestimate a sharp and penetrating mind. He had a long, homely face that could seem as comfortable as an old pair of shoes when he was pleased, or somber and rigidly judgmental when not. Right now it was very judgelike.

Sutcliff watched Jake closely. Almost as though he expected him to lie about how he had been since Mary's death. But that was to be expected. The PC had been a cop himself for thirty years, rising to the rank of chief of department. Then he had retired, only to be brought back as commissioner. Now he worked directly—some said solely—for the mayor, and was even more of a politician than he had been as a chief. Jake momentarily wondered which hat made him the more suspicious man—cop's or politician's.

Jake drew a shallow breath, prepared to play whatever game Sutcliff had in mind. "Thank you for your concern, Commissioner, but I've been fine." He spoke slowly, softly. "It's an adjustment, of course. But Mary was very ill for a long time, so it was almost a relief to have her suffering end." He fought off a grimace, recognizing how hackneyed and practiced the reply sounded.

Sutcliff didn't seem to notice. He nodded, a bit sagely, Jake thought. "I was surprised you didn't take some time off," he finally offered. "You know the loss of a loved one can be a hidden weight. It can even affect the decisions one makes."

Here it comes, Jake thought—through the back door.

"Well I haven't seen that yet, Commissioner. But I'll keep an eye out for it." Normally the various chiefs would speak to Sutcliff on a first-name basis, except in public. But the formality of today's meeting precluded that.

Sutcliff drummed the fingers of one hand on his desk, then stopped abruptly and leaned back in his plush executive chair. "Others have noticed some things, Jake." He let the statement hang out there for Jake to field.

Jake decided he'd be equally obtuse. "Really."

Sutcliff waited for more, his eyes narrowing when nothing was offered. "It's a concern," he finally said.

"I see that. I'm just not exactly certain about the cause."

Sutcliff leaned forward and began drumming his fingers again, a bit more rapidly this time. It was another practiced signal of irritation, and it made Jake wonder why all these signs of displeasure were in place. It wasn't a question of what he had done to earn the man's dissatisfaction. That was clear enough. What wasn't clear was how he had made Sutcliff believe that he was vulnerable to such blatant attempts at intimidation.

Finally, Sutcliff folded his hands and leaned forward. "I've heard some things. Disturbing things about you opening up an old case. A case, I might add, that can only bring embarrassment to you, and possibly shame to the department." He stared across the desk, as if defying Jake to deny it.

"Who'd you hear this from?"

Sutcliff wasn't biting. "That's unimportant. What I want to know is if you've set yourself on something that will tarnish this department's good name, something that will bring shame and embarrassment to all of us."

Jake crossed his legs and studied his shoe tip for a moment as if considering that possibility. "I don't think shame or embarrassment really fit here." He appeared to think about that again, but the gesture was all for effect. "I think the department could only earn praise if it acknowledged a bad piece of investigative work and tried to correct it."

Sutcliff exploded. "For God's sake, a man was executed! He was strapped in the goddamn electric chair and fried until his eyes boiled in his head. And that same damned chair is still sitting up at Greenhaven Prison. It's probably the most famous electric chair in the country; the same one they fried the Rosenbergs in." He leveled a finger across his desk. "You do this, Jake, and pictures of that wooden monstrosity will be on the front page of every damned newspaper in this country and on every

TV screen as well. Good Christ, man, it's only been three years since the Supreme Court knocked down just about every capital punishment law in this country. It's still a hot-button issue, dammit, and the press will be all over it like flies on a load of fresh crap."

The outburst was very unlike Sutcliff, the profanity even more so, and it took Jake momentarily aback. It reminded him of the anger his plan had produced with Morgan. Now it had been passed on to the PC and Jake was surprised by just how good a job Morgan had done stirring the man up.

Sutcliff also seemed to realize his outrage was a bit untoward. He drew a breath and eased back his chair. When he spoke his voice was calmer, more modulated. "Let's put it this way, Jake. I do not intend to see this department's good name tarnished. Not while I'm commissioner. Nor will I allow the acronym NYPD to become synonymous with the execution of an innocent man. Do I make myself clear?"

Jake put his palms together and rubbed softly. "I think someone has sold you a bill of goods, Commissioner."

Sutcliff's eyebrows rose. "How so?"

Jake readied the lie he had decided on weeks ago. "First, I'm in no way convinced that Louie Grosso was innocent. I believe it's possible, but far from a certainty."

"Then why the hell are you even bothering with this?"

Jake raised his hands. "Let me finish, and I think you'll see my point."

Sutcliff made a circular motion with one hand, like some king or pontiff granting a subject permission to speak. Jake almost smiled at the gesture.

"First, Grosso deserved the chair five times over, so I'm not terribly concerned the press will rush to his defense. What I am concerned about—and don't forget that Jimmy Finn and I were the primary detectives on this case—is that we missed something that allowed someone else who was involved in this killing to go free."

Sutcliff cocked his head to one side. "What are you saying? That someone might have hired Grosso?"

Jake hadn't anticipated that conclusion, but grabbed at it. "It's possible, Commissioner. It's one of the things I'm looking at."

"So it would be someone in addition to Grosso, not instead of." Sutcliff spoke the words as a comforting fact, not a question.

Jake fought off another smile. "If I had to say right now, that's the way I'd be leaning."

Sutcliff steepled his fingers before his nose and shook them back and forth. "Well, that's quite different, isn't it?" Suspicion crept back into his eyes. "But why bother, after all these years?"

Jake looked down at his shoes again. It was time for a personal touch that he knew Sutcliff would buy. The commissioner prided himself on three things: being an honest cop, a staunch Catholic, and the ultimate family man.

"There's another element involved here." Jake put the sound of the confessional in his voice.

Sutcliff brought himself forward, hands folded before him on his desk, then listened intently as Jake told him about his affair with Cynthia Reed, and the havoc it wreaked on both the investigation and his marriage.

"Mary was never able to forget," he confessed. "I'm certain she tried, but . . ." He ended the thought with a shake of his head. "She died without ever forgiving the dishonor I brought into her life."

Sutcliff nodded thoughtfully. "So it destroyed your marriage." Again, it was a statement, not a question. He gazed into space, as if further wisdom were to be found there, then finally added: "And it could just as easily have destroyed your career."

Jake imitated Sutcliff's thoughtful nod. "Jimmy Finn saved me from that. Jimmy, and the way it all ended."

Sutcliff nodded again, and Jake wondered if they had begun playing the role of two wise men pondering errors of the past. Either that, or two old coots about to fall asleep, he told himself.

"Yes, I remember that," Sutcliff said. "You and Finn were quite the heroic pair. The newspapers and the radio were full of it. It was a big boost for your career." He seemed to think that over, then added: "If the rest had come out . . . well . . ." Sutcliff eased his chair back, steepled his hands again and stared at Jake over his fingertips. "Is it guilt, then—what you did to your wife—is that what's behind this now?"

Jake called up his acting skills. Cops were either actors or bullies. The truly good ones were a bit of both. He studied his shoes, then offered up what he hoped would be taken as a smile of surrender. "You're very perceptive, Paul." Jake instinctively knew they were back to first names now. "But then you always were." He paused for effect. "But it's also a question of doing the job right." He set his jaw. "This is the one case that I didn't handle properly when I could have . . . should have." He waved his hand as if sensing Sutcliff's objection to that statement. "This is the one case where someone who was guilty may have gotten away because of my own failures." He shook his head. "I excuse it because I was young. But that doesn't mean the record shouldn't be set right."

Sutcliff raised a cautioning finger. "But no harm to the department. That's something I insist on, even if it means the guilty party escapes justice." He held up both hands now in a request for understanding. "After all, Jake, it has been thirty years." He paused and thought that over. "Of course, it would be quite a coup if justice was served after all that time." Another pause, and again the finger went up. "Providing, of course, that it didn't also bring out any impropriety that was best left buried. It wouldn't, would it?"

"Not that I know of, Paul." Jake kept his gaze steady; marveled at how smoothly the lie rolled from his mouth.

The commissioner sat back. "Very well. I won't order you to drop this matter. I can see it means a great deal to you, and that it could be a benefit to the department if you're successful. But there's a strict caveat involved here, and I think you understand what it is." He waited while Jake nodded agreement. "I'll also expect regular reports on this—progress reports, so to speak, every week. Understood?" Again, Jake nodded. "And one other point. If, at any time, I feel this investigation is endangering the good name of the department, I intend to pull the plug. And I'll expect you to respect and abide by that decision."

Jake nodded solemnly. "I do and I will, Paul."

The commissioner slowly nodded his head. But despite that gesture of acceptance, there was a clear note of suspicion in his eyes.

(12)

"Do you think he believed you?" Molly leaned forward, eager for his answer.

A small smile appeared. "That depends on what you mean."

"What I mean is, does he believe you'll step away from the case if he orders it?"

Jake flashed all his pearly whites. "Not for a minute."

"Then why did he agree to let you go ahead?"

"It allowed him to avoid the alternative."

"I don't understand."

"Sutcliff knows this is something I've set my mind on. I'm sure Morgan told him how I've safeguarded the evidence all this time, and that's a bit of a tip-off. So he has to suspect that I'd go ahead anyway, even if he orders me to stop. He also knows that to stop me he'd have to fire me for refusing a direct order." Jake grinned again. "That's a tough one when you're talking about the chief of detectives. The press would be all over it, demanding to know what order the commissioner gave that I refused to obey."

"And the commissioner knows that sooner or later *somebody* would tell them." Now Molly was grinning. "Hmm, that's a press conference I'd really like to see. The police commissioner explaining that the chief of detectives was fired because he refused to back away from an old case that may have sent the wrong man to the electric chair."

They were in Molly's office, awaiting the arrival of Barry Hamilton, the retired FBI forensic scientist Molly had brought into the case. Jimmy Finn was due to join them for what would be Hamilton's first look at the thirty-year-old evidence.

Finn and Hamilton arrived together fifteen minutes later, and as they walked through the door of Molly's office Jake was struck by the uncanny resemblance they bore to each other. Juxtaposed they could have passed for a pair of sixty-something brothers. Like Finn, Barry Hamilton was a big, bluff, red-faced man with a shock of white hair that, given his complexion, must once have been red. They were the same size, both a bit over six feet and an easy 230 pounds. The only thing that truly set them apart was their dress. The former FBI criminologist was fitted out in a sharply pressed pinstriped suit, a crisp white shirt and a blue and red regimental necktie. Jimmy wore a well-used polo shirt under a badly wrinkled sports jacket that clearly showed the bulge of the pistol he still carried on his hip.

Molly made the necessary introductions, after which Hamilton put on a pair of bookish spectacles and began sifting through the evidence. After nearly fifteen minutes he pulled the spectacles down on his nose and looked in turn at Finn and Jake.

"This is what you've got? This is all of it?"

"That's it," Jake said.

Jimmy eased forward in his chair as if preparing to speak. A bulky manila envelope rested on his lap and his fingers played nervously along its edges. Then he sat back. Not yet, he told himself. And maybe never. He felt the envelope beneath his fingers and wondered why he had even brought it with him. He pushed the thought away. First things first, he told himself. Right now he needed to see what this Hamilton guy was about.

Hamilton picked up the bag that held the gavel. "You put this in a plastic bag recently? I mean, I know your department didn't use plastic bags back in '45. Hell, nobody did." He picked up a second plastic bag that held only a badly aged brown paper bag and inclined his head questioningly at Jake.

"That's the original bag the gavel was in. All the evidence was transferred to plastic about ten years ago, but we kept the original containers as well, just in case any trace evidence was transferred inside them. Blood samples and other body fluids taken from the physical evidence was kept separately and stored in sterile containers. Everything's been marked."

Hamilton replaced both items and rubbed his hands together. "That's good, very good. Did you also log that change?"

Jake nodded. "You'll find the evidence log among the materials you have there. The change is noted inside. The log is our primary means to establish the chain of evidence, but it's also backed up by individual reports. We call them D-D-5s. You'll find those there as well, along with the notebooks of everyone who worked the case."

Hamilton nodded approval as he removed a magnifying glass from his briefcase and studied the gavel through the plastic bag. Then he began reading through the reports detailing the fingerprint analysis.

"You have something?" It was Jimmy this time.

"Could be." Again, Hamilton looked at each of them in turn. "There are two partial bloody prints on the handle of the gavel that are listed as latent prints, meaning that the print man who dusted the crime scene decided they were from skin secretions left there when fingers came in contact with the surface of the gavel. He also decided that those prints were *underneath* the blood." He gave a small shrug. "He didn't do anything with them, first because he didn't have today's technology, and second because the old technology would have required removing the blood, which would have destroyed the prints. So he listed them as unusable partials and never went any further." Hamilton raised a lecturing finger. "But I think he was wrong. The crime scene photos show us there was blood on the floor that could have been transferred to the gavel if it was subsequently dropped. The gavel was found a considerable distance from the body but it already had a substantial amount of blood over most of its surface. This would support the theory that it was dropped into the blood and later moved away." Hamilton stopped for a moment and grinned. "I think the print man who worked this case in '45 made a very understandable mistake. I think what we have here is a patent print caused by a bloody finger touching the surface of the gavel, which was subsequently covered by more blood when the gavel was dropped. This means the patent print would have gotten there *after* the victim was initially attacked, with additional blood covering the print *after* that attack. And that makes it even more valuable to us, because it also eliminates the possibility that the print was already on the gavel before the murderer first picked it up."

"I don't think I understand," Molly said.

Hamilton grinned at her, obviously pleased with himself. "It's pure speculation, of course. And it will only be borne out if I'm right about it being a patent fingerprint. But I'm guessing that someone already had the judge's blood on their hand when they handled the gavel. This left the patent print on the surface. Then they dropped the gavel into the pool of blood on the floor and that blood covered the patent print."

"Can you enhance what's there?" It was Jake again.

Hamilton nodded. "I'm certain I can."

"Enough for a positive ID?"

"Well, as you all know, there's positive and then there's positive. Enough for a court? I don't know. Enough for us to be certain who held the gavel in their bloody hand? Yes, I believe I can do that. Especially since your reports indicate that the Reed's cleaning woman worked in that room two days before the murder."

Jimmy inclined his head to salute Hamilton's thoroughness. "That's right. I wrote that up myself. And if you're right about these fingerprints I can't wait to see what else you come up with."

"Neither can I," Jake said. He turned to Jimmy; looked pointedly at the manila envelope in his lap.

Jimmy ignored him, laying his large hands atop the envelope, almost hiding it from view. Not yet, he told himself. First, we'll see what Hamilton comes up with.

(13)

"Jimmy caught me coming downstairs this morning. He knows we were . . . together last night."

I watched Cyn gather in that bit of information, and I could see her mind working it around, looking at it from different angles, deciding what each possible scenario might mean for her. We were in the rear garden of the Reed house. The air had begun to cool and she had retreated there to escape the summer heat trapped inside the house. I had found her seated in the shade of a small tree when I returned at five o'clock, reluctantly ready to carry out Jimmy's instructions.

Cyn seemed to read that capitulation in my eyes, for her jaw suddenly tightened, forcing her lips into a straight line. "If he tries to keep us apart I can make trouble for him. If he tries to hurt us I can see that he gets hurt, too."

I glanced over my shoulder at the uniform guarding the rear

door. I had kept my voice low when I spoke, but Cyn hadn't bothered to follow that example.

"Let's go inside. I don't want everything we say repeated back at the precinct."

I followed her into the house, watching her hips sway beneath the thin blue dress that accented every curve of her body, catching the straight seam of her nylons as she climbed the stairs that led to the parlor floor. It brought back the previous night, and as I followed her I knew one thing with complete certainty. No matter what Jimmy had said, no matter the consequences to the job, I knew I wanted her to keep climbing those stairs straight to her bedroom.

She went into the small parlor, right to the cabinet where the liquor was kept, and I watched her pour a drink with trembling hands. When she turned she raised her chin back toward the cabinet. "Help yourself to anything you want." There was a tremor in her voice as well.

"No thanks. I have to work tonight." I thought about Lilly Straus. I had called her that afternoon and made a date for seven o'clock, just as Jimmy had ordered. I hoped that part of the night would be easier than this, but I doubted it would turn out that way.

"I meant what I said outside." Cyn's voice was hard and angry, interrupting the thought. "I'll make trouble for him. I'll go to Manny Troy if I have to."

I studied my shoes for a long minute. "And what will you tell him?" I slowly raised my eyes to her.

She began pacing, drink in hand. She made quick little steps with quick turns, moving back and forth in front of me. "I'll tell Manny that Finn's being rude to me. I'll tell him he's harassing me. I'm not sure what I'll tell him, but I'll tell him something. And he'll believe me. I know he will."

"And what if Jimmy tells Troy about us?"

The question stopped her cold, and she turned toward me and stared, her face suddenly confused, filled with incredulity. "He wouldn't dare."

"And why not?"

"Because I'd deny it. And you'd deny it, too."

I shook my head sadly. "I couldn't do that," I said. "I couldn't

put Jimmy in a box like that. He hasn't done anything to deserve it."

She stared at me, incredulous again. Then she did something
that surprised me. She actually stamped her foot in frustration.
"Yes, he has." Her voice was almost a wail. "He's doing it now.
And he'll keep doing it because he hates me and he wants to
hurt me. He thinks I was cheating on my husband, and because
of that he thinks I deserve anything that happens to me. I think
he'd even like to convince everyone that I was involved in
Wallace's murder. And don't tell me it isn't true. I can see it in
his eyes every time he looks at me."

I reached out and took her shoulders between my hands.
She was close to hysteria and I needed to calm her before this
whole thing blew up in my face. "Look, it's not what you think.
Jimmy isn't out to get you. It's just that we're getting a lot of
pressure to have the case turn out a certain way. And that's not
the way any cop likes to work. You're just seeing his resentment
about being pushed. It's nothing more than that."

Cyn seemed uncertain at first, then what I said seemed to
click and her entire face suddenly filled with a hungry interest.
The near hysteria was gone now and her eyes took on a look of
cunning I had never seen there before.

"What are you being pressured to do?"

I shook my head. "That's not something I can talk about.
Let's just say somebody's name keeps coming up, and we keep
getting pushed in his direction."

"Who? Whose name?"

"I can't tell you that. Not yet, anyway. Maybe when it's all
finished."

Cyn seemed frustrated by my answer, and for a moment I
thought she might stamp her foot again.

"But I might be able to help."

Again, I shook my head. "Look, I'm only telling you this
much because I want you to know what's bugging Jimmy. It's
not you. It's the outside pressure we're getting."

She stared down at her drink, then placed the glass on a side
table. "I hope the person you're talking about turns out to be the
one who killed Wallace." She looked up at me and her eyes were
hungry again. "Then it would be over. Then our lives could be

the way they should." She stopped speaking and stepped in closer. We were only inches apart. "Will you stay here tonight?"

"It's Jimmy's night to stay. If I try to change the schedule . . . especially after what he saw this morning . . . it just might cause trouble."

"But you'll be here tomorrow night?"

I drew a long breath. "I don't know. I don't know what's going to happen." I took hold of her arms again. "But I want to be here. You have to know that."

She gave me a small smile. "You'll be here. No matter what Jimmy Finn says, you'll be here."

There was a different doorman working the lobby of Lilly Straus's building when I arrived at seven o'clock. He was a short, stocky guy with a bored face and a bored manner, and I was certain he'd forget all about me as soon as the elevator doors closed. That was all to the good as far as I was concerned. The ex-fireman I encountered on my last visit had been helpful, but only after I made sure his palm was well greased, and a guy like that couldn't be trusted to keep his mouth shut. Not if he thought blabbing would make him a few extra bucks. And right now I didn't want anybody telling Lilly Straus that her date was a cop.

Lilly was all smiles when she opened the door to her apartment. She wore a brightly patterned summer dress and fresh coat of makeup that hid the lines and wrinkles I had seen the last time we met. The youthful dress and concealing pancake made her look ten years younger.

"You are right on time. I like zat in a man. Come inzide und have a before-dinner drink."

I caught a faint smell of booze on her breath and realized she had already had one or two herself, and as I followed her into a large living room I noticed a slight sway in her walk. Just as well, I thought. It would make what I had to do that much easier.

Lilly poured us drinks and took hers to one of two matching settees that had been set up on either side of a fake marble fireplace. The living room was cluttered with more furniture than was needed, all of it formal, delicate stuff, the kind of furniture

you never felt comfortable sitting on. There was also bric-a-brac
covering every surface. It was on the mantel, on ornate shelves
that hung on the walls, on every table—tiny porcelain figures of
animals and elves and cupids and all sorts of things—and I
imagined bumping into a table and setting off a chain reaction
that would send everything crashing down like a wall of domi-
noes. It was an old lady's apartment, the kind of place somebody's grandmother might live in, a place where you'd be afraid
to touch anything, one that would drive you nuts if you had to
live there. It also made me wonder if Lilly had an ancient
mother stashed in one of the bedrooms. It was a question I
needed to know the answer to before it jumped out and bit me.

"So," I began, putting on my best smile, "do you live here
alone?"

She seemed to take the question as a hint of some romantic
intent on my part and it brought a coy smile to her lips. "Now I
do. My mosser used to live vit me. But she died last year."

"Oh, I'm sorry." I lost the bright smile.

"No, no. It is all right. She vas very sick. It vas better."

I brought the smile back. "It's just that I know so little about
you. Tonight you have to tell me all about yourself. The last
time all we talked about was me."

Lilly returned my smile with her crooked teeth, genuinely
pleased with my interest. Then she leaned forward to put her
drink on the low table that separated our matching sofas. The
summer dress she wore had a scooped neckline and the movement gave me a good look at the heavy breasts beneath—just as
she intended.

"But I told you, I vork for a real estate company. Vee buy
properties vee hope to zell. Vee buy zem cheap und zell zem
high." She gave a small laugh. "Zat is our hope anyvay."

I laughed at her little joke. She had told me the first time we
met that she was only a secretary at the real estate office—
Manny Troy's secretary—and right now I wanted to make her
feel important. I also wanted her to think I was real impressed
with just how important she was. It was one of the first things I
had learned as a cop. When people thought they were impress-
ing you, they couldn't stop flapping their gums.

"So what kind of big deals have you got going now?" I asked.

I gave her a conspiratorial wink. "You know, I can speed up construction permits if I know ahead of time what's coming down the pike. Sort of grease the wheels, if you know what I mean."

Lilly gave me a coy look. "Oh, I know vat you mean. Mr. Murtaugh says he spends more money on zis grease zen on anysing else."

We both laughed at that. All of a sudden we were just two happy people—a crooked city employee and a crooked real estate lady. What could be more natural?

"So what have you got in the works?"

Lilly gave me another coy look. "Oh, it is zumzing quite big. Zumzing zat vill surprise everybody. But I must not zay any more. I could end up vit no job if Mr. Murtaugh hears I zay even zis much."

"Well, we sure don't want that. So why don't we do something else instead." Now it was my turn to play coy. I threw in a suggestive pause and finally added: "Why don't you take me to the best restaurant in Yorkville."

Lilly laughed. "I sink I am going to like you. Yes I do."

The restaurant she took me to was small and elegant and very German. Lilly smiled and laughed and tossed her shoulder-length blond hair, and in general played the role of the beautiful young woman out on the town. It was a role that, though once undoubtedly true, was now little more than a fast-fading memory.

Lilly also drank. First cocktails, then wine, until I began to wonder if I had enough cash to cover the bill. I also wondered if the department would balk at picking up the tab. If they did my very cash-conscious wife would have my ears. But the drinking served a purpose. By the time we hit dessert—strudel and a large brandy for the lady; coffee for me—Lilly was like an overprimed pump, ready to spill.

"So tell me about this big project you've got going." I had leaned forward, making the moment more intimate. Now I reached out and gently took her hand. "You've got me all curious. You can't just drop little hints like you did at your apartment, and then leave me guessing."

"Zo you are curious, are you?" Her words were slightly slurred and ended with a big grin that seemed slightly misplaced, slightly out of focus like her eyes. "I vill tell you a little bit. But I can't tell you everysing."

I gave her a little shrug and followed it up with a smile and a squeeze of her hand, hoping that all of it suggested promises I had no intention of keeping. "Tell me what you can."

Lilly sat back, but held on to my hand. She was clearly enjoying the power of her position, being able to spoon-feed me whatever information she chose. The waiter came by to see if we required anything else and she waved him away, too intent on the game she was playing to even think about another drink.

She waited until he had left, then leaned forward again. "Do you know zee slaughterhouse on First Avenue?"

"Yeah, sure. Everybody knows that place."

"Und vhat vould you zay if it zuddenly disappeared? Vhat vould you zay if somezing replaced it zat vas zo big zee whole vorld vas talking about it?"

"You mean like the Empire State Building?"

She shook her head. "Not big like zat. Big like being important to people."

I shrugged, but my stomach was suddenly doing backsprings. "I dunno. That's too big for me to even think about."

She smiled, pleased with my answer. "Und zat is how big it will be."

Lilly was almost gone when we got back to her apartment, and it didn't take much to send her the rest of the way—just another drink and a little hugging on one of her uncomfortable settees and she was out cold for the night.

The idea had come to me in the restaurant. Now with Lilly unconscious I didn't waste any time. I opened her handbag and found her keys. There were two sets. I tried them out and found that one set fit the two locks on her apartment door. The second set I assumed—and hoped—were for her office. I found a phone on a table next to her bed, the phone directories in a lower drawer, and I checked the yellow pages for all-night locksmiths and found one only four blocks away. I telephoned, told him who I was, and arranged to meet him in ten minutes. Then I checked Lilly again and headed out the door.

I got back to the apartment forty-five minutes later, my fingers firmly crossed that Lilly was still dead to the world. Just in case, I had stopped to pick up a deck of condoms. If she asked where I had gone—and more important, how I had gotten back into her apartment—I intended to tell her that I had taken her keys to go out and pick up some romantic essentials. Then I'd have to find some way *not* to go to bed with her—and do it without getting thrown out on my ear. Pulling that off would require one helluva tap dance.

It all proved unnecessary. I found Lilly where I had left her, curled in a fetal position on the small settee, emitting a faint little feminine snore like a well-satisfied drunk. I smiled, relieved. Sometimes things just worked out the way you wanted, I thought, as I draped a throw blanket across her body. When she awoke in the morning, Lilly might be a bit disappointed, maybe even a bit embarrassed, but she would think of Jake Downing as a proper gentleman, not the sneak thief he was fast becoming—and would continue to be—providing Jimmy Finn approved of my plan.

Jimmy not only approved, I thought he was going to kiss me when he pulled up in front of the Second Avenue building that housed ABC Realty Ventures, Incorporated. I had telephoned him at the Reed house, explained what I had done and asked him to meet me outside Manny Troy's realty company office.

"I knew you had the makin's," he said, as he cuffed me on the shoulder.

The praise felt good after our confrontation that morning. "Of what?" I asked, keeping it light. "A detective or a second-story man?"

He gave me a wink. "Sometimes the only difference is motive. And we're doin' it for one that's as pure as the pope's underwear." He let out a bark of a laugh. "Next Saturday you remember to tell your confessor you got that straight from Jimmy Finn."

One of Lilly's keys opened the ground-floor door of the building, and once inside a directory on the wall told us that ABC Realty Ventures was located on the second floor. We took the stairs, rather than the small elevator in the lobby, just so we'd be familiar with that route of escape if it proved necessary. But I doubted it would. Security didn't seem to be a big item for either the landlord or Manny Troy. Maybe Troy figured nobody would dare rob him. Maybe, like the landlord, he was just too cheap to spend the money. Either way, it worked for us. We checked for alarms, found none, and entered the second-floor office using another of Lilly's keys. It was one of four, the other two being the smaller type that might fit a desk or a filing cabinet.

The office was far from grand, just two rooms, an inner and outer office, both sparsely furnished with used desks and chairs and a pair of well-worn sofas for visitors. The only new item was in the inner office, a locked file cabinet with heavy, thief-resistant drawers that nothing short of a sledgehammer would open. Fortunately for Mr. Manny Troy, one of Lilly's keys made brute force unnecessary.

While Jimmy concentrated on the files, I searched both desks, neither of which had locks. Neither did they hold anything worth finding. When I joined Jimmy he looked completely frustrated.

"Not a fookin' thing." He stood there shaking his head. "I don't get it. A file cabinet worthy of Fort Knox and not a damned thing in it worth protectin'." He threw his hands up in disgust. "Come on, let's get outta here."

We were almost at the front door, when I took his arm, stopping him. "Hang on a second," I said. "Lilly had four keys on this office set. One for the front door downstairs, one for the office door and one for the file cabinet. What's the fourth one for?"

Jimmy raised his chin toward Lilly's desk. I shook my head. "Neither desk had locks. But something else in here does."

Jimmy raised his eyebrows and without further comment we started to search. It took us fifteen minutes before we found the flap in the carpet. It was a nice snug fit, almost invisible, located in the kneehole of the inner office desk, the one we had figured out was used by Murtaugh and Troy, depending on who was running the show that day. When we pulled the flap back we found a two-foot-square strongbox built into the floor.

It was a treasure chest, starting with a stack of money—all

hundreds and fifties—wrapped in rubber bands and sitting on top of the files we'd been looking for. Jimmy peered at the money, then at me, and grinned. "Be an easy way to pay the expenses of a new baby, eh? Kid would start out with just about everything it needed."

I shook my head in wonder. "Hell, it could even have a new car." I let out a long breath. "Please get it out of my sight before I'm tempted."

He laughed and put the stack of money on the desk, then began to pull out the files.

"Clever bastard, that Troy," Jimmy said as we began sorting through the files. "Buys a big, strong file cabinet to attract attention, then fills it with shit." He laughed. "All the while everything that matters is stuffed under the rug. Oh, yes indeed, that's one clever fella we're dealin' with here. If we ever search his house, remind me to check under his fookin' mattress before we look anywheres else."

The first papers we found were the articles of incorporation for ABC Realty Ventures and for the First Avenue slaughterhouse that employed the members of Owney Ryan's union. Also included were all the required filings with the secretary of state's office of all officers and stockholders for those concerns. Jimmy started chuckling as he began reading through them.

"Well, well, isn't that interesting." He handed me the first stack of papers. "Seems like the First Avenue slaughterhouse that Owney Ryan's union has a labor contract with is about to be sold to ABC Realty. And just look who ABC is plannin' on sellin' that slaughterhouse to, and what that somebody is plannin' to put in its place."

I stared at the papers in disbelief. "But I thought that was supposed to be built in San Francisco. At least that's what I've been reading in the papers."

"Don't look like it, does it?" Jimmy handed me another stack of papers, the incorporation documents for ABC Realty. "It also seems like Mrs. Reed's brother, Oliver, isn't the snot-nosed little villain we figured him to be. Seems like he's a boy genius. Only twenty-one years old and fresh outta the boondocks and already he's a vice president and major stockholder in a big city real estate company."

I read the documents, then nodded as I thought it through. "But who's he a front for—Owney Ryan or the judge?"

"My guess is the judge. You see that second name—Vincent Murtaugh—the one Lilly mentioned to you. He's listed as president of ABC. Well, unless there's two of them, he's one of Manny Troy's top henchmen; runs most of the Brooklyn machine for him."

"Okay," I said. "Let's say you're right. That gives us beards for the judge and for Troy. Where does Ryan fit in? He sure as hell has to get his cut in all this."

"Oh, he gets it, boyo." He handed me a second file. It held a partnership agreement for the First Avenue slaughterhouse that showed Owney Ryan as a fifty percent shareholder.

"Now that's interesting. Ryan all of a sudden is a fifty-fifty partner in the slaughterhouse where all his meat cutters work. Must make it easy to negotiate new labor contracts." I looked up from the papers. "So ABC buys the slaughterhouse and sells it to . . ." I shook my head and started to laugh. "I still can't believe that part. It's so goddamn big."

"Believe it," Jimmy said. "And to pull that part of it off they have to buy a slaughterhouse where Owney Ryan just happened to suddenly become half owner." He barked out a laugh. "It's lovely, isn't it? That way, Owney gets his end up front and even if it comes out later that Manny Troy and the judge were partners in a real estate deal, there's nothing to tie them in to a hood like Ryan. All anybody sees is that the judge and Troy were smart investors. As far as Ryan goes, he just happened to be part owner of some land they bought."

"Yeah, that's pretty cute. And I'm sure the owners of the slaughterhouse had a lot to say about making Troy a partner, or for that matter about selling the land their business sat on."

Jimmy feigned a look of shock and surprise. "Of course they had a choice. This is fookin' America. They could sell the land, or they could turn Owney and his friends down. Then they could hang from their own meat hooks until Owney decided when he wanted to dump 'em into the East River. And I'll bet my badge it was put to them just that way."

"Be lovely if we could prove it."

"Now you're dreamin', boyo." He looked at the clutter of papers scattered around us. "We better put this place in order, so Mr. Troy doesn't know he had visitors."

When the papers were all back in the strongbox, Jimmy picked up the stack of money. "Ah, what a shame." He drew a deep breath and laid it atop the papers just as we'd found it.

Jimmy locked the strongbox, refitted the carpet and then stopped and gave me a long, steady look. "We need to find out what Mrs. Reed knows about this real estate deal."

I returned his steady gaze, fighting to keep a smirk off my face. "Why are you telling me? You gave me my orders about her this morning."

Jimmy's eyes hardened. "Don't be a smartass. If I could keep you out of it, I would. But the lady sure as hell ain't gonna tell me about her husband's crooked real estate deals, is she? But she just might tell you somethin'." He paused for effect. "But do you think you could leave her skivvies on when you're askin' her?"

"I'll try."

"See that you do."

(14)

Jake's driver, Detective Pete Tedesco, turned off Forty-second Street onto First Avenue and headed uptown. Jake looked to his right at the imposing glass tower of the United Nations and tried to remember what it had been like thirty years ago when that very site and the land around it had housed Owney Ryan's slaughterhouse. He shook his head. He still marveled at it, still marveled that no one knew the story. And no one ever will, he thought. Not unless you do your job right this time.

Pete turned left onto Forty-fifth Street, then left again on Second Avenue, before he pulled to a stop in front of The Palm. Jake was meeting his daughter, Kate, for lunch. The Palm was one of her favorites—good food and a celebrity clientele—a place where she could mingle with people she only saw in magazines or on television, a momentary escape from her life as a single mother from Brooklyn. It was also a place she could afford only when her father was buying.

Kate was already seated when Jake entered and the maître d' hurried him through the already crowded restaurant to the choice rear table he had reserved for the city's chief of detectives. He bent, kissed his daughter's cheek, thanked the maître d', and then seated himself with a great exhalation of breath as if that might explain his tardiness.

"Sorry I'm late, honey. We had a triple in Queens early this morning. Mother, father and a daughter in her twenties. All with a shotgun. Very messy. The press was drooling."

Kate didn't bat an eye. She was used to these off-the-cuff comments that would horrify most sane people. She had grown up with it. For her it was talk about the weather. She reveled in the grisly details, loved to quiz him just like another cop might. "Was it drug-related?" she asked now.

"Not this time. But it's what the press was hoping for. Turned out to be a ground ball. Daughter's lunatic boyfriend. A couple uniforms nabbed him at a laundromat trying to wash the blood out of his clothes."

They ordered lunch, a petite steak for Jake and a lobster salad for his daughter, and changed the conversation to more mundane subjects, mostly the latest antics of his grandson, Sean, and his continued hope that his daughter would move into his house in Brooklyn.

"It would save you quite a bit of money. You could sell the co-op you got in the divorce and do whatever you wanted with the money, maybe even put it aside for Sean's education. Plus you'd save all those mortgage payments and the maintenance fees, and I'd guarantee you all the privacy you'd want. Hell, I'm hardly ever there, you know that, what with all the maniacs loose in this city."

Kate looked down at her plate. The same worried look creased her brow that his late wife, Mary, had so often displayed. Kate was so much like her, in so many ways, that being with her often tugged at the guilt that still filled his heart.

"What about *your* privacy?" Kate asked.

Jake stared at his now-empty plate. "I told you before, no one would ever be coming to the house. I wouldn't bring someone else to your mother's house, no matter how much I cared for them." He looked across the table and saw the doubt in Kate's eyes. It saddened him, but there was nothing he could do about it.

Kate used her fork to toy with the last of her salad. He could tell she was trying to get up the courage to say something. He decided to wait her out, not to push.

"Dad, will you tell me something?" Kate said at length.

"If I can."

"You can. In fact *only* you can." She paused again.

The waiter came and they both declined dessert, ordering only coffee.

When the waiter left Kate leaned forward and lowered her voice. "I want to know about the woman you were involved with when Mom was pregnant with me. I want to know why that happened."

Jake was stunned. Very few things caught him off guard, but this one had come out of left field and floored him. "Her name was Cynthia Reed—"

"I know that," Kate said, cutting him off. "I know about the case you were working on and what happened, and all of that."

Again, he was stunned. "How do you know those things?"

"Mom told me. I asked her about it when I was a teenager. I asked her why you never slept in the same room together. I asked her how she could love you and not want to be with you that way. Because she did love you, Dad. I know she did. She told me so."

"What else did she tell you?"

"Just about the affair; who the woman was; what the case was you were working on when you met; how you had to spend nights at her house guarding her." She paused again, and Jake could tell she was getting to the part that was hardest for her. Kate drew a long breath. "But she never told me why, Dad. She never told me if you were in love with her or not. Maybe she didn't know. Were you, Dad? Were you in love with Cynthia Reed?"

"Did you ask her what she thought?"

"Yes, I did. It was years later. But she wouldn't tell me. She would never talk about it again. Just that once, that was all."

The coffee arrived and Jake was grateful for the momentary reprieve. But when the waiter left again Kate's eyes were still riveted on him.

"Was I in love with her?" He asked the question of no one in particular. "That's a tough question thirty years later, especially after everything that happened." He began to reach for his coffee, then stopped. "I suppose at the time I thought I was." He gave a slight shake of his head and offered up a wan smile. "Cynthia Reed was a very beautiful and glamorous woman—at least she was to a twenty-five-year-old kid from Brooklyn." He raised a hand, putting off an anticipated objection. "Oh, I'm not trying to make excuses. I was an adult. I was a cop. I had even been wounded in a war. I wasn't exactly an innocent. And, yet, in some ways I was. At least as far as she was concerned." He shook his head again. "Your mother and I had known each other since high school. But we weren't always together. I'd been with other women before your mother and I married, so I wasn't innocent in that respect. But I'd never been with anyone like Cynthia Reed. Everything about her—the money, the glamour, that café society life she led—all those things were stuff I'd only seen in movies. Oh, I'd seen it from the outside as a cop, but never up close. Never the way she showed it all to me. And, God help me, I wanted it. It happened almost before I knew it. And then it was too late. I wanted it all so much I could taste it."

There was a look of confusion on his daughter's face. "Then why didn't you go off with her? Why did you come back to Mom? Was it because you loved her more? Was it because I was born? Why?"

Jake looked down at his plate and gritted his teeth. If ever he had wanted to lie to his child, this was the time.

He raised his eyes slowly and felt his hands begin to tremble. "I wish I could say it was for all those reasons. I wish I could say that I came to my senses about the whole thing. But that wouldn't be the truth, Kate. And I don't want to lie; not about something that's so important to you."

"Then why? Why did you come back to us? I need to know."

Jake clenched his fists to stop the tremors in his hands. "I came back because in the end Cynthia Reed sold me out."

(15)

Cyn gave me a big smile when I told her I was going to pull guard duty that night. I was pretty pleased myself, and not just because of that. It was August 14 and Japan had just announced its surrender. The war that had ended for me on December 7, four years earlier, had just come to an end for everybody else.

"I'm glad you're wearing a good suit," Cyn said. "There's a big party at the Stork Club to celebrate the end of the war. It's invitation only, and we're invited."

"We, as in you and *me*." I tapped a finger to my chest and let my incredulity fill my face.

"Well, *I'm* invited. And you're my escort. It's the same thing." She widened her smile.

"Not quite," I said. "But I'll take what I can get."

We were in the parlor where I usually set up shop on guard duty nights, and she glanced toward the door to make sure no one else was around, then stepped in close until our bodies were touching. "There's a lot you can get." She lowered her voice. "I've been thinking about you all day, thinking about all the things I want to do to you. All the things I want you to do to me." She smiled again, impishly this time. "But not now. Right now I just want to store that hungry feeling inside; save it until I can't stand it anymore; until it starts to drive me crazy."

"And what will you do then?"

Cyn didn't answer. She only smiled.

The number of gawkers and autograph hounds gathered outside the Stork Club had tripled since our last visit. Cyn guessed that word had gotten out about the "invitation only" party, a sure sign that every celebrity who happened to be in New York would make an appearance. Inside, the atmosphere rivaled New Year's Eve. Party hats were being passed out as guests made their way through the gold chain, at which point everyone was told to sit wherever they chose. Since every guest was already on the club's "A" list, the Cub Room—or *snub room*, as it was called—was suddenly insignificant. At Cyn's insistence, we opted for the main room so we could listen to the rotating bands and dance.

Sherman Billingsley had stationed himself between the two rooms and was nodding and smiling at everyone as they passed by. You could almost see the mental calculations taking place behind his eyes, checking off those who had heeded his call as the self-declared leader of New York's café society. I was sure later that night he'd be putting mental stars alongside the names of those who had come to celebrate Japan's demise and black marks beside those who had not. Just from the set of his jaw I could tell there might be a realignment of the *snub room's* membership in coming days.

Cyn and I were the last couple of one entering group, and Billingsley took extra time with us as he awaited the next wave.

"Great day, isn't it?" Billingsley's voice boomed out with heartiness and cheer. He turned his attention to me. "I bet you wish you'd been a part of it, don't you?" He gave my shoulder a comforting squeeze. "I sure wish I'd been young enough to fight those Nips."

The implication was clear that I *was* young enough. I was ready to set him straight, but Cyn chimed in before I could. "Jake's more of a lover than a fighter. You can tell that by his curly hair." There was laughter in her voice, and what she said, or her way of saying it, made Billingsley laugh as well.

I felt myself bristling. "I had my chance, but it didn't last very long." I looked Billingsley square in the eye. "I was wounded on the first day. At Pearl Harbor."

Billingsley's eyes widened. "No kidding." He clapped me on the shoulder this time. "I've only met one other guy who was actually there." He shook his head with genuine sadness. "Cut down before you even had a chance to fight those devils. That's a stinker. Well I'll tell you this, my friend, your money's no good here, tonight. And I'll tell you something else. You come here any time you want, and anybody gives you a problem about getting in you just send them to me."

When we were seated at our table Cyn leaned in close. "So I have a date with a war hero." She gave me a coy, impish look. "You never told me. And now I'm very impressed. Do you have any medals?"

She was teasing, but she was doing it in a fun way now. And there was even a hint of pride in her voice. All together it was a lot better than before.

"As a matter of fact, I do. I've got a Purple Heart. They give you that one when you forget to duck."

She turned momentarily serious. "Do you mind talking about it?"

"Not really. There isn't much to talk about. I had just gotten out of bed when the Jap planes came in on their first bombing and strafing runs. All we had time to do was grab our weapons and run for cover. We all thought they were softening us up for an invasion; that troops would be coming ashore as soon as they knocked out our defensive positions."

"Were you on one of the ships?"

I shook my head. "I was army. We were attached to one of the airfields just outside Pearl." I shook my head remembering it. "The Japs hit the airfields hard; knocked out over two hundred planes. Most of them never got off the ground, never got a chance to fight back, and the ones that did, well . . ." I gave her a shrug, indicating the helplessness we had all felt back then, and realized I was feeling it again now. "Anyway, they knocked out most of our antiaircraft guns, too. The rest of us were left firing rifles at the planes as they came in. And that didn't work too well."

"And then you were wounded." The tone of her voice told me she wanted to hear more.

"Yeah. I was trying to help one of the guys from my barracks who'd been hit. But when I got to him he was already dead, so I started to run for cover and this Jap Zero came in on another run and I took a load of shrapnel." I tried to shrug away the wound. "You've seen my leg. There's not much meat left on it." I smiled, a bit weakly, and hurried on. "Next thing I knew I woke up in the base hospital. And I'll tell you something. That was the scariest time of all. First just lying there, hearing the bombs hit, knowing I couldn't even run for cover. Then later, when the bombing stopped, waiting for the Jap troops to come ashore and bayonet us in our beds. They passed out rifles to those of us strong enough to hold them. I remember being propped up against a wall, hanging onto my rifle for dear life, so full of morphine I hardly knew where I was, and shaking like a leaf while I waited for the first Jap to come through the door."

"It sounds frightening."

"Yeah, it was." I smiled across the table. "Before the first bombs hit we all thought we'd pulled such great duty, getting sent to the Pacific, to a tropical island, no less. Palm trees, beautiful native girls, year-round sunshine, a real paradise." I shook my head, recalling how we had thought of it then, the irony of it. "But even though it turned out bad, I still got off pretty easy. There were three thousand killed or wounded that day, with most of the wounded a lot worse than me. And the next four years weren't much better. I was one of the lucky ones. My brother was on Corregidor. He never made it back. Me, I ended up in an army hospital in San Francisco with a million-dollar wound."

It was the same as it always was whenever I spoke about it. I could still see the torn bodies, still hear the screams, but it was distant and fuzzy, as though it had happened to someone else. Even in the hospital, back in '41, it had all seemed like a bad dream, none of it real, none of it truly a part of my life. Back then, it was as though I was someone else, someone outside my own skin. I was back in the States in an army hospital in San Francisco, but the reason I was there didn't seem to make any sense. The doctors said I was hiding from everything that had happened, hiding from the fear. Then one day I woke up and Mary was sitting beside my bed. She'd come all the way from New York to be with me, and that's when I knew it had actually happened. But I also knew it was over; that I was alive and safe and there was nothing else to be afraid of, not even my ugly misshapen leg. Not as long as Mary was there.

She stayed for a month while they operated twice on my leg—living in a rundown rooming house and barely eating so she could make her money last. I didn't know about it then, of course, didn't know she was doing all that just to be with me, just to sit there holding my hand every day, trying to make me forget that I'd have a bum leg the rest of my life. Joking about it to make me feel better. *When they sent you to Hawaii, I thought you'd meet some girl in a grass skirt, and she'd steal you away and I'd never see you again. Then you went and got yourself shot instead.* Her eyes glistened as she spoke the words and I can still remember how she laughed. *I guess I'm lucky it wasn't another girl,* she had said.

"You sound like you almost feel guilty about it. About surviving it all." Cyn's words pushed the memory away, bringing me back.

I nodded, a bit absently. "Sure," I said. "A little bit, anyway. But not enough to take the place of anybody who didn't make it."

"That's the right way to think about it. Life can be pretty lousy, especially for people like us, who aren't born into a nice cushy family. And when you're not, and when you happen to catch a break, even if it doesn't seem like one at the time, you've just got to grab onto it and be thankful it came your way."

I looked at her, thinking about what she'd said, thinking that there were a lot of things I felt guilty about. Someday I'd have to tell her about them. I decided for now I'd let it pass.

The society band finished its set and the Latin band took over. Bobby Ramirez took center stage, placed one palm on his stomach and began swaying his hips to a little rumba beat. It was the first time I'd seen him, and I could tell right off that he was a favorite of the ladies—at least the ones in the café society crowd.

I felt a small twinge of jealousy, and when he started to sing it increased a bit. He was good, and he knew how to play up to an audience, especially the female part of it. It was interesting to see how the men didn't pay much attention. They just kept on drinking and socializing. But the women, that was a different story. Most of them had their eyes on those swaying hips, or the flashing white teeth that sat behind that little Errol Flynn mustache. I glanced at Cyn and saw that she was watching me instead.

"That's Bobby Ramirez," she said.

"Tell me about him," I said.

"I'm sure Jimmy Finn can tell you everything you need to know. Right now, I'd rather have another drink."

Cyn got her drink, and when the set ended she also got Bobby Ramirez. As soon as he left the bandstand he began making the rounds, stopping at a few tables, just smiling and saying hello. But his route led straight to Cyn, and it was clear—to me at least—that it was our table he was headed for from the start.

"Mrs. Reed, hello." He spoke the words as he reached us, his face slightly somber. He glanced at me, not quite certain who I was, a date or just some friend who was accompanying a new widow. Cyn seemed to sense his discomfort, and a small smile played on her lips.

"Hello, Bobby," she said.

Bobby turned to me. "Excuse me, I know it's a bit unusual, but I wonder if I could speak to Mrs. Reed privately for just a moment." He turned back to Cyn, seeming uncertain about what to do next. "Maybe we could step out into the lobby."

Cyn smiled. "I don't think so, Bobby." She glanced at me, then back, and her smile took on a touch of meanness. "Jake, this is Bobby Ramirez. Bobby, this is Jake Downing. Detective Jake Downing." She paused to let the words sink in. "Jake's investigating my husband's death, Bobby, and he's also making sure nobody harms me. I don't think he's supposed to leave me alone with anyone." She turned back to me again. "That's right, isn't it, Jake? You're not supposed to leave me alone, are you?" I shook my head and she turned her attention back to the crooner. He had grown a bit pale. "But you can say anything you want in front of Detective Downing, Bobby. I don't really have any secrets from the police, and I'm sure you don't either."

Bobby began to stutter just a bit, and all the smoothness he had exuded on the bandstand seemed to evaporate. A thin line of sweat appeared just above his thin mustache and he shifted his weight from one foot to the other, each one just the kind of *telltale* that every detective looked for. This guy, Ramirez, had suddenly turned into a living, breathing *tell*.

"I just wanted to let you know how sorry I was . . . about your husband." He hesitated, seeming to realize how lame the statement was. He drew a deep breath. "I also wanted to let you know a detective had come around to talk to me about it." He glanced at me and smiled weakly. "But I guess you already knew that."

"No, I didn't." Cyn's expression didn't change. It remained cool and calm, and still a bit mean. "But I expected they would. I imagine they'll talk to everyone who knew my husband or me." She turned to me again. "Isn't that right, Jake?"

"That's right."

When Bobby had beaten a hasty retreat I leaned in close to Cyn. "You were pretty rough on him."

"I told you we used to be friends. The important words in that sentence are *used to be*. We're not friends anymore."

"What put an end to the friendship?"

She looked at me coolly. "He tried to borrow money from me. I didn't like that."

Cyn made love to me that night with a frenzied abandon that left us both exhausted and bathed in sweat. As we lay recovering in her bed I again traced my fingers along her back, again stopping at the small, jagged scar just above her buttocks. When I first discovered the scar she had refused to speak about it. Now I wanted the truth about it, certain I would need it if I was going to keep my promise to protect her.

"Tell me about the scar." I kept my voice low and soft.

"I told you it's nothing. It has nothing to do with your investigation."

"I can't protect you unless you tell me everything."

Cyn stared at me for a long time, the expression in her eyes changing from uncertainty to gratitude to fearfulness and then back through that entire range of emotions. "Do you really want to do that, Jake? Do you?"

I pulled her close to me and stroked her hair. "I thought you knew that."

She let out a long breath that sounded far too weary for her age. "Sometimes I know it, or I think I do, but then, when you're not here, I have trouble convincing myself it's true. It's just that I'm so alone, Jake, so alone most of the time."

"I'm here. You're not alone."

"Yes, I am. I always have been."

"Tell me what he did to you. Trust me that much."

She hesitated, then let out another weary breath. "If I tell you he hurt me it gives me a reason to have killed him, doesn't it? What is it you detectives call it?"

"Motive." I spoke the word and let my mind fill in the rest. And you were in the house with him. And you were alone except for the killer—if there was someone else—and that gives you the second criterion: opportunity.

"Yes, a motive." She began to laugh as tears appeared on her cheeks. "I definitely had a motive." Cyn was lying on her stomach staring at her pillow, almost as if it provided a vision of her past. "I told you once that Wallace was cruel." Her eyes filled with bitterness. "Sometimes that seems like a gentle way of describing him." She turned to face me, the tears drying on her cheeks now. "He enjoyed his cruelty; took pleasure in it. You know how some little boys torture their pets—how they're always taunting them and teasing them—and then, if the animal does something they really don't like, how they hurt them?"

"Yeah, I knew a kid like that growing up."

She let out a short, bitter laugh. "I think everyone knows someone like that growing up." The laughter disappeared and her face became cold, filled with hate. "Wallace was like that as an adult."

"You mean he liked to hurt you." I said it as a statement, not a question she had to answer.

"I mean he liked to hurt everyone—anyone at all, anyone he could. He liked to use his power. He'd come home and tell me about lawyers that he'd humiliated in court, about defendants he'd berated and sentenced to maximum terms." She closed her eyes and drew another long breath. "Sometimes humiliating me would be enough. Sometimes it wouldn't. Sometimes he'd just get angry. Sometimes he'd be angry at me, sometimes he'd be angry at something that had happened . . . and I'd just be in the wrong place, I'd be close enough to strike out at . . . I'd be *convenient.*"

I reached out and stroked her arm. "I'm sorry."

"Yes, I am, too." She closed her eyes and turned over on her back, and drew the bed sheet up to her chin, as if hiding her wounded body from me, from everyone. I knew exactly how she felt.

"Did you know about a real estate deal he was involved in?" I asked the question offhandedly, not making a great deal of it.

She shook her head.

"It was a deal he was in with Manny Troy and a man named Owney Ryan."

"He never spoke about it." She lay there quietly for almost a minute, then turned and raised herself up on one elbow. There was a quizzical look in her eyes. "That name. Owney Ryan. It's familiar. Is he the gangster I've read about?"

"Yeah."

She gave her head a small shake. "Wallace would never do that. He would never put himself in a position where he could be tied in with some gangster. He was very careful about his reputation." She hesitated and finally laughed. "But then it never stopped him from beating me, did it? He just made sure he hurt me in places that wouldn't show."

"You could have told someone."

She laughed at the suggestion. "Who would have believed me? If I had come to your precinct and filed a complaint, would your captain have sent someone out to arrest him? Or would he have just telephoned my husband, or maybe Manny Troy?" Again, she shook her head. "No, he knew he had nothing to fear from his wife—a former hatcheck girl. The people who mattered would just say I had proven them right, that I had finally showed my true colors as a gold digger, and now I was setting Wallace up for a big divorce settlement."

Cyn stopped talking and turned on the bedside radio. She tuned in a music station where Josh White was singing "One

Meatball," a Depression-era song about a man who goes to a restaurant and discovers that the only thing on the menu he can afford is one meatball. I couldn't tell if Cyn was listening. I guessed she was thinking over what I had said about the real estate deal. I remained silent, giving her space to think it through, hoping she'd have more to say when she had.

"Besides," she added at length, "Wallace didn't need money. He was financially secure. He came from that kind of family— not filthy rich, but one that left him well off."

"This deal would have made him filthy rich." I laid it out now, making it as tantalizing as I could.

Her eyes widened slightly as she thought that tidbit over. When she had she shook her head again. "No, he still wouldn't have allowed his name to be tied to a gangster."

"It wouldn't have been. They wouldn't have taken money from the same pot. Ryan would have gotten his cut first, and then Troy and your husband would have waltzed in and made their money. Ryan would have been out of it before either one of them made a dime."

Cyn was quiet for a long time. "If it involved a lot of money, and if it wouldn't hurt his reputation, then Wallace would have done it. He loved money, and even though he had enough to be secure, he always talked about getting more."

She was silent again, and so was I. I still wanted her to think it through further, see where it led her.

"Is the deal off now?" she asked at length. "Did Wallace's dying put an end to it?"

"I don't see why it should have. The papers I saw the other night indicated that your husband had already put some money into it. I'm surprised Manny Troy hasn't mentioned it."

"So am I," Cyn said.

"One other thing." I was going to push it now, push for the whole ball of wax. "Have you ever heard of a woman named Lilly Straus?"

A curious look came to Cyn's eyes. "A blond woman, who tries very hard to hide her age?"

"Sounds about right. What do you know about her?"

"I met her once. She was with my brother, Oliver, when he came to the house one night. He said she was his girlfriend."

{ 16 }

Molly struggled through the last of the paperwork on a small, cleared-off section of her cluttered desk. A strand of dark brown hair fell across one eye and she brushed it back with a touch of irritation. It had been a long day—four postmortems, the last a five-year-old victim of child abuse—and still more than an hour of paperwork ahead. And it was already five o'clock.

A light rapping of knuckles against the doorframe made her look up. Dr. Vincent Martone, the city's chief medical examiner, filled the doorway looking every bit the *dapper doc* the newspapers had dubbed him. Obviously leaving for the day, he was dressed in a gray pinstripe set off by a silky flash of pale blue Countess Mara necktie and glistening black Bally loafers. Unlike his predecessor, who had been legendary not only for his forensic skills but for his total lack of sartorial style, Martone was a delicate-looking man, an acknowledged fashion plate and a self-styled bon vivant, known more for his political skills than his scientific talents. And he never works ten minutes past quitting time, Molly thought. And that just plain pisses you off.

"How did that juvenile post turn out?" Martone asked the question without preamble, clearly in a hurry to get on with his social life.

The five-year-old had been the daughter of James Radcliff, a well-known Queens Republican who had been a repeated and unsuccessful candidate for city council. Although it had not yet become the feeding frenzy that lay ahead, several members of the press were already camped outside awaiting the results of the autopsy.

"It's homicide." Molly said it bluntly and watched Martone grimace. "Death was due to internal bleeding caused by severe trauma to the liver, kidneys and spleen. The spleen ruptured, but if it hadn't the other injuries would have killed her."

"Any chance it was due to an accident?" Martone readjusted the cuffs of his shirt as he asked the question. He was short and effete and he was always fussing with something, a man never satisfied that things were as they should be. "Perhaps a fall off a bicycle? That seems to be what Mr. Radcliff has told the press."

Molly shook her head, sending the errant strand of hair across her eye again. She brushed it back. "No chance at all. The injuries were caused by blunt trauma, each one separate and distinct and consistent with the size of an adult fist. That's what my report will say." She patted the papers that lay before her for emphasis.

"You're certain? We wouldn't want a mistake, given who's involved."

"I'm positive. The forensic evidence is indisputable."

Martone made a point of looking at his watch. "Well, pass on what you have to homicide. But let's not release anything from here tonight. I'll deal with the press tomorrow, if I have to. Hopefully the boys in blue will have made an arrest by then and any controversy will be in their laps, not ours."

Molly fought back a smile. Dr. Vincent Martone did not like controversy. It was the one thing that could threaten his lofty position, and even if it failed to do that, it would definitely cause him to spend extra hours in these less-than-elegant First Avenue offices, rather than more suitable social surroundings.

"I think any controversy will be laid on the doorstep of a certain Queens politician. And, if Mr. James Radcliff committed this horror, I hope they nail his ass to the wall."

"No question they'll do exactly that." Martone gave Molly a lingering false smile, then continued, "One other thing, while I have you. I was at a meeting at One Police Plaza today and I was asked about another case you're supposedly working on. I was told it involved a thirty-year-old homicide that the chief of detectives has dredged up. It was also rather clear that not everyone is pleased that he has."

Molly studiously avoided Martone's eyes, turning her attention back to her report as if what he was saying had little meaning for her.

"Yes, I have it, Vincent. But right now it's not much of a priority. In fact, I haven't really had a chance to read all the reports or look over the evidence."

"Well, don't do any somersaults getting to it." Martone gave her a false little chuckle. "The powers that be don't share the chief's enthusiasm. In fact, I got the distinct impression they'd be grateful for a little foot-dragging on our part."

Molly looked up and saw that Martone's beady eyes were boring in on her. The message he had gotten had obviously been a strong one. Perhaps he'd even been told about her relationship with Jake. She gave him a look of bright innocence. "Well, that's a refreshing thing to hear. With an average of four fresh homicides a day, a little foot-dragging for one that's thirty years old seems more than appropriate."

A broad smile erupted across Martone's face, revealing a too-perfect line of bright white teeth. It made Molly wonder if he'd recently had them capped. "Well, that's good; that's settled then." He glanced at his watch. "Oops, I'm late. Have to run. Try not to work into the wee hours, now."

Molly returned his smile, wondering if it appeared as false, hoping that it did. "I'll do my best."

"My boss came to me today and asked about the investigation."

Jake was standing at the window in Molly's apartment, looking down into Washington Square Park. The rooster was at his usual place by the fountain, gesturing wildly as he argued with his new girlfriend. Another romance headed for the dumper. He turned to face Molly. "And what did your boss, the dapper doc, have to say?"

Molly smiled at the reference. "Just that I shouldn't bust my buns getting to it; that the powers that be at One Police Plaza are *not* looking for a speedy resolution."

"Sounds like Morgan's been busy. He's a man who doesn't like to lose." Jake turned back to the window. The rooster's girlfriend was stalking off. Molly came up beside him and slipped her arm around his waist. "So what did you tell the dapper doc?"

"I gave him a song and dance about how busy things were, and how nice it felt to be told to drag my little tootsies for a change."

Jake drew a long breath. "I think it's time for me to put a little pressure on Morgan, otherwise he'll never get off our backs."

"Have you got something on him that will let you do that?"

Jake smiled down at the rooster, who was shouting after his girlfriend. "Oh, yeah. I was just hoping I wouldn't have to use it."

Jake's beeper cut him short. It would be the Queens homicide unit, the one handling the Radcliff case. He had been expecting the call. He went to Molly's telephone and spoke to the lieutenant heading the unit. When he replaced the receiver he stood quietly shaking his head. Then he picked up the phone again, telephoned his driver and told him to come and get him. When he finished he turned to Molly. "I have to head out to Queens."

"Radcliff?"

"Yeah. Seems like he and his wife are pointing the finger at their housekeeper. She's an illegal alien from Bolivia, barely speaks English. My boys aren't buying it, and fortunately for the lady the doctor in the emergency room says that Radcliff claimed he was there when his daughter fell off her bike. Now he's insisting he wasn't, that the housekeeper was watching her at the time, and *told* him it was a bicycle accident. He says maybe she was lying. That maybe she hit the child and was afraid to admit it."

"That will be a tough defense to sell—pinning it on the housekeeper—unless she happens to have unusually large hands for a woman."

Jake turned to her, raising his eyebrows. "The trauma was caused by someone with large hands?"

"Definitely."

"The injuries couldn't have been caused by a weapon—a club, maybe, or by someone kicking the child?"

Molly shook her head. "A club or the toe of a shoe leave distinct injuries. They're long and narrow. This was caused by something large and square. No question in my mind it was a fist administering numerous blows, each one consistent with the other. You see the same type injury when a professional boxer is killed in the ring."

"That's good enough for me."

"Are you going to charge him?"

"That's up to the DA. But he's a Democrat and Radcliff is a Republican, so I don't think we'll have the usual political crap getting in the way when we're ready to move. Right now my boys are sweating him, just to see what other inconsistencies they can come up with. He hasn't been bright enough to ask for an attorney yet."

"Ego."

"Yeah, there's more than one jerk doing time because of that." Jake took Molly's hand and led her to the sofa. "Come sit with me. And tell me what your buddy, Barry Hamilton, has come up with."

Molly sat next to him and rested her head against his shoulder. "Hamilton hasn't come up with a thing that I know of. But you know how these FBI geniuses are. Even retired ones. They're very, very thorough, and they play it very close to the vest until they're sure they have something. At least that's the excuse they give for taking twice as long as anyone else. But he is working on it. I understand he's gotten some lab space at NYU. I could probably walk over and check on him. The building he's in is just across the park."

Jake shook his head. "You've had enough of the case for one day, what with your boss bugging you and all, and I've had enough of it, too." He paused a moment, deciding how much he wanted to say. Then he pushed ahead. "I had lunch with my daughter today, and right out of the blue she started asking about it."

Molly sat up and gave him a slightly mystified look. "What could she want to know? She wasn't even out of the womb when most of it happened."

"Well, it wasn't really about the case. Not the particulars of it, anyway. She wanted to know about Cynthia Reed. Seems her mother told her what happened between us."

Molly noted his choice of words. It was always the same whenever he spoke about Cynthia Reed, which was rare in itself. Yet, when he did, he always used similar words, something along the lines of *what happened between us*, never anything more descriptive; anything more accurate. She wished just once that he'd speak about their love affair. That just once he'd refer to the woman without a sense of coolness, with just a hint of the affection he must once have felt.

"Your daughter's upset, I take it."

"Yeah, she is." He lowered his eyes. "She tried to mask it as simple curiosity, but yes, I think she's upset."

"It makes sense." Molly took his hand. "Her mother was pregnant with *her* when it happened. It's natural for her to feel hurt, maybe even to wonder if you really wanted her back then."

Jake blinked. Her words had hit like a slap. He sat quietly for almost a minute. "God help me, but I can remember thinking back then how much simpler everything would be if Mary wasn't pregnant." He turned to her, a look of urgency in his eyes. "But it was just a thought. I didn't really mean it. Kate's meant so much to me over the years."

Molly reached out and stroked his cheek. Yes, and Cynthia Reed, and all the glamour that surrounded her, meant so much to you, too. Molly gave him what she hoped was a comforting smile. "I'm sure Kate knows how much she's meant to you."

Jake stared out into the room. "That was something I never doubted." He turned back to Molly. "Now, all of a sudden, I wonder if she does."

The homicide detectives who had been assigned to the Radcliff case were working out of the Forest Hills precinct. Initially, when the child's injuries were thought to be accidental, uniforms from that precinct had handled the case. Then an emergency room physician raised a red flag, a concern later supported by the medical examiner, and suddenly everything changed. Now Queens homicide had been brought in to bring the case to its conclusion.

Jake stood behind a two-way mirror in a small windowless room that allowed him to watch two of his homicide dicks interrogate James Radcliff, the father of Vanessa Radcliff, whom someone had beaten to death ten days shy of her sixth birthday. Radcliff was in his mid-thirties, with a once-athletic body that was quickly going to seed. He had a puffy face and broken capillaries that were just beginning to show in his cheeks. Jake had never heard that the man had a drinking problem, but the signs were definitely there.

Radcliff did not seem particularly nervous, and Jake wondered if a man could hurt his child so terribly and still be able to hide his emotions. He thought back to the unpleasant memory of that afternoon's lunch and his own attempts to cover up his feelings. Yeah, you could harm a child in a great many ways, he told himself. Granted, some were worse. Some crippled or even killed. But there were other ways to do serious harm, and often they were just excused away.

Jake refocused on the interrogation, noting that Radcliff's hands were quite large, watching as he ran one through well-barbered black hair. A detective had just asked him why he had told the emergency room doctor that he had been present when his daughter had supposedly fallen from her bicycle, rather than explain that his housekeeper had told him she had. It was the first sign of nervousness Jake had noted, the first *tell*—detective shorthand for a telltale sign—that the man was lying. The detectives had seen it, too, and they began bearing down.

Radcliff shifted in his chair. He was wearing a blue blazer and tan slacks. His shirt was a blue button-down, sans necktie, and it had begun to wilt after several hours of questioning. It was the only visible sign of stress. And that was a great deal of composure for a man whose child had just been murdered. More if he was, in fact, the killer. But Jake had confronted murder suspects like that before. A few had been sociopaths who had never revealed any sign of regret. The others had eventually cracked, and when they had it had been quick and overwhelming. He wondered how it would be for Radcliff.

Jake listened as Radcliff told the detectives that he had been trying to protect his housekeeper; that he had been aware of her illegal immigration status, and had wanted to keep her out of the investigation, if possible. Then, when he had learned that his daughter's injuries were not the result of a fall, he realized he had made a terrible mistake.

Jake's facial expression mimicked those of his two homicide detectives—blank and disbelieving. He watched Radcliff study the two detectives, first one, and then the other. After a long silence he pushed back in his chair.

"I think I better have my lawyer." Radcliff spoke the words calmly and without apparent concern.

Before Radcliff could say any more Jake left the observation room and entered the detectives' bullpen. Moments later the two homicide detectives emerged from the interrogation room.

They were older men, both in their late forties or early fifties, both approaching thirty years on the job. Mike Mulligan was tall and heavy-set with a thick shock of gray hair and the rosy cheeks of a man whose high blood pressure would pursue him to the grave. His partner, Len Kowalsky, was the exact opposite, short, slender and balding, with a complexion like library paste. Both detectives spotted Jake immediately and came directly to him.

"You here about our case, Chief?" There was concern in Mulligan's voice.

Jake understood. Chiefs seldom showed up at crime scenes unless they anticipated problems, and the good ones like Jake stayed away even then. They simply did not interfere with their subordinates unless someone screwed up badly. In this instance he had decided to break that personal rule. He had come for only one reason, to make sure there was no political interference. At least that's what he had told himself—that his reopening of Judge Reed's murder had sensitized him to the possibility.

Jake borrowed an unused office and took both detectives inside. He sat both men in chairs and used the edge of the desk as his own seat. He smiled, trying to put them at ease. "I listened to part of your interrogation and thought you both did a good job. Is Radcliff calling his lawyer?"

"Yeah, we turned him over to a uniform while he made the call." It was Kowalsky this time. "I expect the lawyer's gonna tell him to keep his trap shut."

"I expect so." Jake rubbed his hands against his thigh. His bum leg had started to ache. He leaned forward. "Any problems with anybody at the DA's office?"

Mulligan shrugged. "So far so good. You think we might down the road, Chief?"

"I have no reason to believe you will. But if you do, you let me know right away."

Small smiles creased both detectives' lips. "You bet, Chief," Kowalsky said.

"One other thing. Have you interviewed this housekeeper?"

Kowalsky fielded the question. "Yeah, we saw her this afternoon. She was all broken up about the kid. Doesn't realize yet that the parents are fingering her."

"She a big woman? More specifically, does she have unusually large hands?"

Mulligan and Kowalsky looked at him curiously. "No, sir." It was Mulligan this time. "She's a little pudgy, but she's a tiny little thing, no more than five feet tall."

"And small hands?"

"Yeah, small hands," Kowalsky said. He was still giving Jake a curious look. "Why do you ask, sir?"

"Just before I came out here I spoke to the ME who handled the post. Molly Reagan. She said death was not only the result of a beating, but that the perp had unusually large hands. You both noticed Radcliff's hands, I take it."

Both detectives smiled more broadly now. "Yes, sir, we noticed," Mulligan said.

Jake nodded, then pushed himself off the desk and led the men out into the squad room. He stopped and looked around. "It feels good to get back out where the real work is done." He turned and looked at both detectives in turn. "Now I'll get out of your hair. Just don't let this prick get away with it. Nail his ass to the wall."

I met Jimmy at the squad room at eight A.M. Detectives were still wandering in from home; a few appeared to have worked through the night. Already the smell of cigarette smoke and stale coffee permeated the room, mixing there with the fear-induced smell of sweat that always seemed to be present. This time it came from two young toughs seated at Johnny Morrow's desk. Both wore handcuffs and both looked as though they were about to wet their pants. Johnny, an old pro in homicide, had a satisfied look spread across his wide, flat face. He was a big, beefy guy with fists the size of hams, and I'm sure just looking at him added to the kids' fears.

"What's with the two punks that Johnny's got?"

Jimmy and I sat at desks that abutted back to back so we faced each other over a single, cluttered surface. He raised his chin toward the two kids, both of whom looked no more than seventeen or eighteen. "Those two little charmers rolled some old doll over on West Fifty-first yesterday. Got themselves seventy cents. Unfortunately the old dame also hit her head on the curb and croaked. More unfortunately for those two was the fact that there was two witnesses—two fookin' nuns from St. Paul's who were on their way home from an afternoon stroll." Jimmy glanced at the two kids again and shook his head. "The warden's already dustin' off the hot seat up at Sing Sing, and those little shits know it. So does Johnny. It's why he's got that big grin spread across his puss."

I glanced at the two kids and felt an inexplicable sense of regret. Two more wasted lives. You'd think the war had already produced enough of those. I caught myself, but not before Jimmy sensed what I was thinking.

"Don't go gettin' all dewy-eyed over that pair of punks," he said. "A couple of years from now and they'd be inta bigger heists and sure as hell they'd end up pullin' guns on the cops who had to chase 'em down. Better we get rid of 'em now and keep our own outta the funeral parlors."

I nodded. "Yeah, you're right. It's the only way to look at it."

"You bet your ass it is. Couple a weeks from now you're gonna have a kid to start worryin' about. So you ever find yourself feelin' sorry for punks like those two, you just keep rememberin' that your kid's gonna need you comin' home each night."

Though he didn't know it, Jimmy's words nagged at my gut, brought out feelings of guilt that were already hanging on me like a wet shirt. He added to it with his next question.

"So how'd things go with Mrs. Reed last night?" He lowered his voice. "You behaved yourself, right?"

One of the two young men at Johnny Morrow's desk let out an obscenity-laced complaint that made Jimmy and I turn our heads. The distraction also allowed me to slip Jimmy's question.

The young man kept shouting something about the unfairness of his situation, or his life in general, or who the hell knew what. Johnny let him finish his diatribe, then slowly eased out of his chair. His motions were almost placid, so much so that the speed of his fist lashing out caught everyone—especially the young loudmouth—by surprise. Light laughter filled the squad room as the baby-faced killer flew from his chair and hit the floor with a thud.

Johnny looked down at him and shook his head. He didn't offer to help the kid up, didn't say a word to him or in any way indicate that anything else, good or bad, would follow. He simply eased himself back into his chair and returned to his paperwork as if nothing had happened. The kid lay there for a moment, then wiped blood from his lip with the back of one handcuffed hand, struggled up and climbed back into his chair.

We were still chuckling when Walter Morgan approached Jimmy's desk, his lieutenant's uniform crisply pressed, his brass and his black brogans glistening under the overhead lights. Jimmy gave me a warning look as Morgan stopped in front of our desks. He fixed his gaze on Jimmy.

"I've had Manny Troy all over my ass about this Grosso business," he snapped. "He said he hasn't been able to get ahold of you, and he wants to know what the fuck is happening with the lead he gave you."

Jimmy pushed back in his chair. "Does he now?"

Morgan glared at him, his narrow ferret face and ratty eyes looking particularly feral. Jimmy seemed not to notice, or wanted Morgan to think he didn't.

"I've got an interview with Lilly Straus today." Jimmy made a point of looking at his watch. "In about thirty minutes, in fact."

"What the hell are you wasting time with her for? I told you that Willie Riley saw Grosso coming out of the judge's house just before his body was found."

Jimmy gave his head a sad shake. "Yeah, well that information didn't turn out as good as we hoped."

"What the hell do you mean?"

"Well, your boy, Willie, kind of backed away from what he saw. Said he was only tellin' us what he thought we wanted to hear." He hurried on before Morgan could object. "The DA's not gonna like that. Also, the time he says he saw Grosso was a bit off."

"Whadaya mean, off?" There was a clear note of challenge in Morgan's voice now.

"Well, Grosso supposedly left the judge's house at eight-thirty, at least he did if Willie Riley decides to stick with his original story. But Mrs. Reed told us that she found her husband's body a little before eight. She also told us that she called Manny Troy and he came to the house straight away. So if Grosso was seen leavin' at eight-thirty, then he was there at the house with Mr. Troy and the lady, and I don't think we wanna be sayin' that."

Morgan stood grinding his teeth. You could almost see his mind going through the possibilities. You could also see he was coming up empty. "So what are you gonna do?"

"Well, I haven't given up on Grosso, that's for sure. But I've got to start at the beginning with his motive for killin' the judge. And to do that I've gotta talk to Lilly Straus."

I could see Morgan seething inside, but there was little he could do or say. Jimmy had boxed him in pretty well. He had followed up on Grosso just as Troy had wanted. In fact, he'd even pursued that lead using an informant that Morgan had conveniently provided. But Morgan's informant had turned out to be a bust and, if anything, had delayed any hope of tying Grosso to the judge's murder. It was a clever little shell game Jimmy was playing. And it had done one important thing. It had bought us time. And the only person Manny Troy could blame was Willie Riley, and through him, Morgan, himself.

Morgan didn't seem to know what to say. He shifted his weight from foot to foot and ground his teeth. "Just understand that Mr. Troy wants some action on this," he finally managed.

"Oh, I understand that." Jimmy's voice was full of false sincerity. "Please tell him so when you talk to him. And tell him I'm sorry I didn't get back to him. I just never got his message."

We watched Morgan leave, struggling for whatever dignity

he could manage. I didn't envy him having to explain it all to
Troy, but that was his problem. I turned back to Jimmy. "Funny
how you never got Troy's message."

"Indeed it is. I never got any of the blasted things."

"How many were there that you didn't get?"

"Six. I'll have to speak to the desk sergeant. Things are gettin'
pretty sloppy around here." He gave me a wink. "Now tell me
what you found out from Mrs. Reed."

"First of all, she doesn't know anything about the real estate
deal."

"You're sure? You don't think she's just playin' dumb?"

"I'm sure." I leaned in toward the desk and lowered my
voice. "But I got the distinct impression that she intends to find
out about it."

Jimmy grinned. "That's interestin'. It also means she'll be
askin' Manny Troy." His grin widened. "Seems like he'll be
havin' more than one unpleasant conversation today. I'd sure
like to listen in on both of them."

"She told me something else you're going to like."

"What's that?"

"She knows Lilly Straus."

"You asked her that?"

"I did."

"And?"

"She met her once."

"Did she now?"

"Wanna know where?"

"Don't play with me."

I waited, fighting to keep a smile from my lips. I intended to
make Jimmy ask.

"Where, dammit?" he finally said.

"At her house." I watched his eyebrows rise. "She came with
Oliver." His eyebrows went up a bit further. "Oliver told her Lilly
was his girlfriend."

Jimmy started to chuckle. "Holy shit." He shook his head.
"This *is* a timely bit of news."

"You mean for the interview with her?"

"I do. All I was gonna do was take her statement about Louie
Grosso 'raping her.'" He made little quotation marks around the

final two words to let me know he still thought Manny Troy's tip was a load of crap. "Now I got a real question I can ask her."

"I'd like to be in the observation room while you talk to her."

"I wouldn't have you anyplace else."

Lilly arrived on time. She was wearing a light summer dress, well-suited to a day when the temperatures were expected to climb into the mid-nineties. But everything else about the dress was wrong. It was seersucker with a scooped neck and puffy sleeves and a small bow at the back. It was a dress intended for a young girl—a very young girl. It might have seemed coy, maybe even provocative on a young woman, but not on a woman who had already pushed forty over a cliff. Now, on Lilly Straus, it just looked sad.

Lilly sat in the small, windowless interrogation room. Jimmy had provided a fan, but it did little more than move the damp, stagnant air about. Lilly had her own as well; a small folding fan made of rice paper, the kind you find in every shop in Chinatown. She used it to flutter the air about her heavily made-up face.

Morning was not Lilly's time, I decided, as I watched her from the secluded viewing room. Bright lights, like the ones overhead, were also not especially flattering. She looked decidedly older than she had on the two previous occasions when we were together. Here, under the lights, the heavy makeup failed to do its job. It only accented the fact that it was there, that it was hiding something, and that it was doing so with only limited success.

Jimmy seemed not to notice. He was all smiles and attentiveness, which is not an easy role for a man of his size and normally gruff demeanor. Had I not known better I would have guessed that he was quite taken with her. It was obvious that Lilly thought so, too. She kept lowering her eyes and smiling.

Jimmy took a chair opposite her across a battered wooden table. He clasped his hands like a supplicant and leaned forward, every inch of him solicitous. "Now I know this may be difficult to talk about. But I want you to do your best."

Lilly gave him a pained look, and then turned her gaze downward. "I vill try."

There was a glint in Jimmy's eyes, and I could tell he thought she was getting ready to lie through her teeth, and that he'd like nothing better than to ratchet up the tone a bit; give her a taste of the third degree. Of course you couldn't do that with a woman, at least none of the rough stuff. In fact most detectives I knew preferred to play it soft when they interrogated a woman. It was just a smarter way to go. Once a dame turned on the faucets there was no hope of getting anything else out of her.

Jimmy started slow. "So how did you come to know Louie Grosso?"

"He vas hired to be the security man for zee real estate company I vork at. He is supposed to check on zee buildings ve own, especially zee empty vons." Lilly patted her blond curls, assuring herself they were in place.

"And he had contact with you? In order to do his job, I mean."

"Yes. I have zee keys to zee buildings. Zo, ven he needed keys he vould come to zee office und I vould give zem to him."

"And one day he just attacked you? For no reason?"

Lilly gave him an expressive shrug. "He had a reason. He vanted vhat I didn't vant to give him. So he force me to." Lilly took a small handkerchief from her purse, getting ready for tears that were just around the corner. Jimmy noticed it, too, and he threw a half smile toward the mirrored glass of the observation room.

"And where did this happen? When he forced himself on you."

"At my office. ABC Realty on Second Avenue."

"And this was when?"

"Three veeks ago. July twenty-fifth."

"And do you remember what time of day?"

"It vas just after five o'clock. I remember because I vas just about to close zee office up for zee day."

"And after the attack did you call the police, or go to the precinct?"

Lilly shook her head.

"Why not?"

Lilly looked down at the table. "I vas afraid." Her voice was almost a whisper, barely audible.

"What frightened you? I mean after it was over. After Grosso had left."

"He had a gun. He showed it to me vhen he vas finished, und he said if I told anyvon he vould come back and he vould kill me."

"But you told Judge Reed?"

"Yes."

"And you weren't afraid to do that?"

"Yes, I vas afraid. But my boyfriend, he said I had to tell zumbody. Und he said I could talk to this judge who vas a relative of his."

"That would be Oliver Marks."

Lilly looked at him sharply, surprised he had known the name without her telling him. Her eyes became suspicious. "How do you know zat? How do you know Oliver's name?"

Jimmy gave her an innocent smile. He had led her into this. He wanted her afraid, or at least concerned that we knew more than we were supposed to. He also wanted her to feel uncertain about how he really felt about her, about whether all the flirting had merely been a game to set her up. Most of all he wanted to use it to throw her off stride, so she would start making the little mistakes he needed her to make. He continued to smile at her. "Your name was in the judge's address book," he finally said. "So we checked you out, found out you were dating his brother-in-law. There was nothing in the book about the judge trying to help you with Grosso."

Lilly's eyes darted about. She reminded me of a mouse who suddenly found itself locked in a room with a cat.

"I asked zee judge to keep everysing confidential. I vas afraid of zis Louie Grosso."

Jimmy nodded, raising her hopes that the answer had satisfied him. Then he dashed those hopes. "Strange he didn't write anything down. The date this attack happened, the time, the place. Even Grosso's name. None of it was written down. Just *your* name." He looked at her, his face curious. "You did tell him Grosso's name, didn't you? I mean he must have asked who it was who attacked you and you must have told him, right?"

Lilly twisted on the hard, wooden chair, and her accent got even thicker, more pronounced. "I don't know vhy zere vas nossing. Maybe zis Grosso takes zee notes vhen he kills zee judge."

Jimmy's eyes widened. "So you think he killed the judge?"

Lilly seemed completely befuddled now. She huffed and her

body seemed to swell up a bit. I couldn't tell if it was from out-rage, or simple frustration, but for a moment she looked as though she might explode. "Of course," she snapped. "Zat is vhy I am here, no? I tell zee judge vhat zis Louie Grosso did to me, und zee judge goes to him und zen Grosso knows zee judge is after him, zo he kills him."

"Did Grosso tell you that? Did he tell you he killed the judge?"

Lilly stared at him; blinked several times as if trying to de-cide how to answer. She seemed utterly confused now. But if Jimmy was right, that someone had given her this song to sing, and that someone was none other than Manny Troy, the confu-sion made perfect sense. Given Troy's power, Lilly would have expected us to buy anything she said, not sit her down in a hot airless room and try to break her story. Standing behind the mirrored glass, I could almost see her mind working out differ-ent answers, deciding whether or not to elaborate on the tale she'd been given. Finally, she made up her mind. She shook her head. "No, Louie Grosso didn't tell me anysing." She had decided to sit tight and stick to her story.

Jimmy eased back in his chair and looked at her. He seemed unfazed by her answer and I could tell he had expected it. I could also tell he was ready to turn the screws a bit more, put the finishing touches on his own game. The silence grew. Jimmy scratched his chin. "Okay, let's say you're right. Let's say Grosso killed the judge." He inclined his head slightly. "From what I know about him, he's sure capable of committing murder." He threw in a small grimace as if something he had said bothered him. "But there's one thing I don't understand." He added the next comment almost as an afterthought. "I don't understand why Grosso didn't kill *you.*"

Lilly's eyes widened. She shook her head again, this time in utter confusion. "Because I did vat he vanted." She spoke the words as though she were being forced to explain something that any fool would know.

Jimmy gave her a patient smile. "No, I mean later, when Grosso thought the judge was out to get him. Why didn't he kill you *then?*"

She stared at him, eyelids blinking.

"I mean why not kill you *instead* of the judge?" He leaned forward, all sincerity now. "It makes sense, right? What we had was a 'he said, she said' situation." He gave her another patient smile. "At least we had that unless he upped and confessed when the judge confronted him, and I can't quite imagine a guy like Louie Grosso doing that." He waved the idea away. "So what we most likely had was you saying that Louie sexually assaulted you, and him saying, no, that's not true, and unless we've got a third party, a witness to what really happened, or some physical evidence, then the cops and the DA and even the judge are stuck. Nobody can do nothin' about it. You see what I mean?"

Jimmy didn't wait for an answer, but I doubted any response was on the way. Lilly just sat there, her rapidly blinking eyes giving her the appearance of someone in a state of shock.

"So if he's gotta kill somebody, why the judge? I mean why not kill the victim, the person who's pointing the finger at him?" Jimmy gave her his sincerest look, followed by a small shake of his head. "The other way around just doesn't make sense. See what I mean?"

Lilly's lips began to move, but the words refused to form. Finally she forced them out. "You sink he vould kill me now?" I heard a tremor in her voice, and from my position off to one side I could see her hands twisting together beneath the table.

"Now?" Jimmy said it as if the thought had never occurred to him. He seemed to consider the idea. "Yeah, I suppose he might. He's a dangerous guy." He seemed to catch himself, to suddenly realize he had said something he shouldn't have. "But you don't have to worry. We're gonna be watchin' out for you real good."

I could tell from the look on Lilly's face that Jimmy's assurance didn't provide a great deal of comfort.

There was a big grin spread across my face when Jimmy returned to the squad room after escorting Lilly Straus out of the building.

"I think I'm gonna put you up for an Oscar."

He gave me a pronounced wink. "You think I made the lady a little nervous?"

"I think you scared the shit out of her."

"I hope so."

"Any specific reason?" I paused, grinning again. "Other than the fact that you're a sadist who likes to frighten middle-aged bimbos?"

"Ah, now, don't call the lady a bimbo. She was just tryin' to do her civic duty." He gave me another broad wink. "But I doubt she'll be runnin' to Manny Troy with any complaints. I don't think she'll want any more of his suggestions."

"So while the lady's hiding under her bed, what's our next play?"

"I think it's time for us to have a talk with Louie Grosso. I wanna find out why certain people are tryin' to paper his ass with a murder charge."

{ 17 }

It was eight in the evening when Walter Morgan made his way to Jake's table at the Ginger Man. It had been Jake's suggestion, a private dinner to "smooth over any bad feelings," and Morgan had quickly agreed, an acquiescence driven more by curiosity than any interest in peacemaking.

Morgan's gaze roamed the room as he took his seat, an act of *cop's eyes* that brought a smile to Jake's lips. Satisfied that no one untoward was seated close by, Morgan offered Jake his own brand of smile. It was sly and suspicious and made Jake think of two foxes meeting in a barnyard.

"Interesting place, this." Morgan made a show of surveying his surroundings again. "The wife loves it here—loves all the polished brass and potted plants and cute pictures on the walls. Me, I never understood why they named a French restaurant after a book, especially one written by some guy from Brooklyn who went and became an Irish citizen. Did I ever tell you that I met him once . . . J.P. Donleavy?"

"No, you never did."

Morgan waved the information away. "Not important." He smiled again. "Anyway, the food's good here and you're buying. What more could I want?" He chuckled at his small joke and inclined his head to one side. The gesture was as cold as the laugh, followed by: "So how've you been, Jake?"

"Good, Walt. But worried that you and I got off on the wrong foot in this Reed business."

Morgan gave him another cold smile. Jake was certain it was a smile he used with subordinates who had displeased him. But tonight Morgan was wearing civilian clothes and his displeasure didn't seem to carry the weight it might with gold stars gleaming on his shoulders.

Morgan drummed his fingers on the table. "I don't see why us being on the wrong foot should worry you. The commissioner seems willing to go along with you on reopening the case. That's all that matters."

Jake leaned forward like a conspirator. "That's what I see as the problem. The PC deciding between what you thought was right and what I wanted to do. I feel it's put a wall between us that I'd like to take down."

The waiter came and they ordered drinks, a Johnny Walker over ice for Morgan and Irish whiskey neat for Jake. Morgan's eyes never left Jake as they ordered. It was as though he hoped to ferret out some lie that was there to be found. "I don't see any need for worry." He offered Jake an innocent shrug. "You got what you wanted. Go with it."

"I'm worried because that whole Reed thing was bad from the start, and I want to put an end to it, not make it worse. I'm worried because you and me and Jimmy Finn were in it together right at the beginning, and we knew something was wrong, but there wasn't a damned thing any of us could do about it, because Manny Troy and Commissioner Parker and half the politicians in the city had already decided just how it should turn out."

Morgan raised a hand, stopping him. "Look, it's over and done with. That's my whole point. Troy and Parker and the rest of them, all they wanted was for Reed to be a martyr, the would-be Democrat governor of New York cut down in his prime." Morgan let out a snort. "I don't think they cared who killed the judge, just so long as the press clippings looked good. Something the next candidate could use to get a leg up on Tom Dewey."

Their drinks arrived and Jake let Morgan's comment pass. Instead he turned their conversation to political matters within the department, a topic that carried them through dinner and on into coffee and brandy, and one that seemed to put Morgan in a friendlier, less suspicious frame of mind. Now Jake was ready to turn the conversation again.

"You know, I'd like to go back to something you said earlier." Jake paused and sipped his Rémy Martin.

"And what's that?"

"You were talking about Judge Reed being used as a martyr by Troy and the other politicians. I know that's how it turned out. But I've always wondered if that was their primary concern. Or if maybe that just helped them hide something else, something they didn't want anyone to know about."

"Like what?" Morgan's eyes had grown suspicious again. "You back on this kick that an innocent man was sent to the electric chair?" There was a sneer in his words, although Morgan managed to keep his face neutral.

Jake looked down at his drink and smiled. He had no intention of giving Morgan ammunition that would produce another battle with the PC. He had asked Morgan here to put pressure on him, to get him off Molly's back and to pry whatever information he could from him, not to give him something more to fight with. "Not at all. We got off on the wrong foot with that innocent man routine the first time." He looked up, eyes steady. "Look, there's no question in my mind that Louie Grosso deserved what he got. I'm not about to turn him into a victim. I'm just not convinced that someone else didn't have a hand in Reed's murder."

"Who do you have in mind?" A cunning look spread across Morgan's face. "The wife?" He let out a small laugh. "You sure didn't think so back then."

Jake ignored the jab. "What about Mrs. Reed's brother, Oliver? Or maybe Owney Ryan?"

Owney Ryan's name seemed to light a spark behind Morgan's

eyes. "Why Ryan? What was his connection to the judge? I mean, I know he was connected to Grosso. You thinking he *sent* Grosso to whack Reed?"

Jake gave him a noncommittal shrug. "Everybody *was* connected to him—Grosso, Mrs. Reed's brother, maybe even the woman Grosso was supposed to have raped."

"How was she connected to him?" Morgan seemed genuinely confused by the suggestion.

Jake decided to be more circuitous in answering that one. "Back then did you ever hear about any business ties between the judge, Ryan and Manny Troy?"

Morgan's eyes widened slightly. "Never, not once." He shook his head. "I mean Troy was always rumored to be part of shady deals that were going down, but that goes with the territory of being party boss. There was never any proof of anything crooked, and the deals that were out in the open were always on the up and up. As far as Ryan was concerned, everything he did was crooked. But the judge . . ." He shook his head. "I never heard anything about the judge."

Jake nodded. He was willing to accept Morgan's claim of ignorance. "There was an interesting real estate deal going on at the time the judge was murdered. It involved the old slaughterhouse on First Avenue, which, by the way, had a labor contract with the union Owney Ryan ran."

"The one that was sold so they could build the UN."

"The same." Jake leaned forward and lowered his voice. "Just about four months before that deal went down, Owney was given a fifty percent share in the slaughterhouse." He watched Morgan blink, then twist slightly in his chair. He had the look of a man who knew something was coming, and who could already tell he wasn't going to like it. "The slaughterhouse wasn't sold directly to the UN. First it was bought by a Manhattan real estate company."

"Which one?" Morgan was almost cringing now.

"ABC Realty, the same company that employed Lilly Straus and Louie Grosso, and which, according to its incorporation papers, had two very interesting officers—Vincent Murtaugh, one of Manny Troy's henchmen, and Oliver Marks, Judge Reed's brother-in-law."

Morgan closed his eyes. "And both of them fronting for Troy and the judge, with Owney getting his dough up front so he'd never be tied into it as a partner."

Jake smiled. No one had ever said that Morgan wasn't a smart cop. "Yeah, that's the way I see it, Walt. That, plus Ryan having his boy Grosso on the real estate company's payroll just so he'd have some eyes inside. After all, Owney had to protect his investment. The bank records don't show any money actually changing hands between the slaughterhouse and ABC Realty until the deal with the UN was completed. It was never out in the open, of course, but I imagine Owney played a big part in getting the slaughterhouse owners to agree to those terms."

Morgan snorted. "I bet he did. I can almost hear the sleazy little mick. *Sell your slaughterhouse to my friends on their terms or my union will put your slaughterhouse out of business.*" He eyed Jake. "Do you have bank records that show the dough going into Troy's personal account?"

Jake nodded. "Also into Mrs. Reed's account. She got the judge's share. I managed to get *unofficial* copies on both accounts after the case ended. And the records are still sitting there on microfilm. We just need a court order to get an *official* copy."

"So you think the judge might have been killed in a falling-out over money. That Ryan sent Grosso in to kill him, and then set Grosso up for a fall with a phony story about him raping Lilly Straus and the judge going after him for it."

"That's one of the theories . . ." He paused. "At least part of it."

Morgan sat there, staring into his drink, considering what Jake had told him. Suddenly his eyes shot up. "But that would mean Troy was involved, too. At least at some level. He's the guy who tipped us off to Grosso." Morgan stopped cold, realizing what he had said.

Jake gave him a long look. "And that's part of my problem. It's one of the reasons I wanted us to talk."

"Because I gave you Willie Riley as the finger on Grosso leaving the judge's house."

Jake nodded. "And Willie went back on that story later when Jimmy and I interrogated him. He said he was told what to say."

Morgan's eyes became a mix of eagerness and anxiety. "But

that never came out at Grosso's trial. Your reports on that interrogation never became part of the case record."

"That's right. Because Riley never testified. But the report still exists. And that gives me a bit of a problem, since the report also identifies you as the person who got the original information from Riley."

Morgan stared at the table and rubbed his forehead with the fingers of one hand. After almost a minute he looked up. "Troy's the one who gave me Riley. He said he didn't want it to come from him because he was already too involved. He asked me to go see Riley and then pass it on to you and Jimmy. I was supposed to tell you Riley was one of my snitches." Morgan clenched his jaw and slowly shook his head. "I did it because I knew he'd owe me if I did." He looked down at the table. "And because I knew Manny Troy was someone you could count on to pay up on a debt."

Jake nodded. "I was hoping it was something like that. That you were conned into it."

Morgan fidgeted in his seat. "So what happens now?"

Jake shrugged. "So now the report stays buried in my files."

"No one will see it?"

"No one but me."

Morgan nodded. The message was clear enough. "I owe you." He spoke the words as though they might choke him.

"Don't worry about it." Jake smiled across the table. "All those years ago we all played into the same game. And besides, it's like you said. I know you're a man I can count on to pay up on a debt."

{ 18 }

Louie Grosso lived in a two-room walk-up that overlooked the Third Avenue El. It was a rat-trap, which contrary to Hollywood was exactly the kind of joint most thugs called home.

Jimmy and I unbuttoned our coats to free our pistols and took up positions on either side of Grosso's door. We had no reason to believe he'd be violent, but then we had no idea who else he might think was looking for him. You never knew with a hood. They were always expecting unpleasant company of one sort or another, and that didn't always mean cops.

Jimmy knocked and we heard heavy footsteps approach the door.

"Yeah?" The solitary word came as a deep, gravelly growl through the door.

"Police, Louie," Jimmy announced. "We need to talk."

"So talk. I don't gotta look at you to do that."

"Be polite, Louie, and open up."

"Fucking shit. Gimme a second."

We heard him move away and gave each other knowing looks. Louie was putting something away that he didn't want us to see—probably a weapon. About thirty seconds went by before the bolts of two locks turned and the door pulled back.

Louie Grosso stood before us in a sleeveless undershirt. I had never seen the man before and his size alone impressed me. He was a little bigger than Jimmy, maybe six-two, and he was burly with the kind of heft that doesn't come from a gym—big and bulky beneath a thin layer of fat, the kind of body that looks as though it could pick up a car and toss it. He was also a hairy sonofabitch with tufts bursting out of his undershirt like a reemerging forest and sweeping across his shoulders and biceps. His head was square with a black cap of medium-length hair, brown eyes that were set a bit too close together and a flat nose that someone had tap danced on more than once.

"So the door's open. So talk." Grosso growled out his words like some kind of jungle animal.

Jimmy gave him the cold eye. "This could take a little time. So be nice and invite us in. Otherwise we'll have to take a little ride to the precinct."

Grosso gave us a sneer that said getting him there might not be in the cards, but Jimmy ignored it and just stared him down. Finally, Grosso stepped back and let us inside.

The two rooms that Grosso called home could get you cited by the Humane Society if you kept your mutt there. The combination living room, dining room, kitchen was dominated by a sink piled high with food-encrusted pots and dishes, and a beaten-up stove and refrigerator that years ago might have been white. Across the room from the sink sat the only usable furniture, a sofa and a solitary armchair, both of which looked like a gorilla had tried to eat them. A rickety table stood in front of the sofa, its surface littered with an overflowing ashtray, a collection of empty beer bottles and a plate of uneaten pasta so old it had become hard and brown. Behind the sofa was a door that must have led to the bedroom. I was immediately thankful I didn't have to look in there.

Jimmy and I took the sofa, both of us sitting on the very

edge to reduce the amount of contact. It also gave us a scenic view of the kitchen sink. Grosso sat in the armchair, which put him a little closer to me than to Jimmy.

Jimmy started it off. "So where you workin' now?"

Grosso shrugged. "Here and there."

"No one special place?"

Another shrug.

"What about ABC Realty over on Second?"

Grosso's eyes narrowed slightly. "You been checkin' up on me?"

"Always." Jimmy grinned at him.

Grosso snorted. "I work for 'em from time to time. Mostly when they gotta evict somebody. I go tell the deadbeats that it's time to leave."

"And they leave." Jimmy said it as a fact.

Grosso smiled. "Yeah."

"Then you must know Lilly Straus." It was my turn now.

The question, and the fact it had come from me, seemed to throw him for a moment. He gave me a hard look. "Yeah, I know her. What of it?"

"You ever take the lady out?" This one came from Jimmy, and again the change in questioner seemed to throw Grosso off stride.

He turned slowly to Jimmy, as if the effort of going from one questioner to another was more than he cared to handle. "No, I never took her out."

"You ever go to bed with her?" This one from me.

Grosso's head turned slowly again. "The broad's a lush. I wouldn't fuck her with *your* dick."

Jimmy let out a derisive snort. "Shit, Louie, I didn't know you were so particular. I figured you for a guy who'd fuck a hole in the wall, there wasn't anything else."

Grosso glared at him. "Yeah, well you figured wrong, flat-foot."

A slow smile crept onto Jimmy's face. I'd seen it before. It was like a warning sign that someone was close to getting smacked. "You ever hear of Judge Wallace Reed?" The smile was still in place as he asked the question.

"Yeah, I heard of him. He got croaked about a week ago." He

returned Jimmy's smile. "Too bad. He was a good judge." He paused and added, "For guys like me."

We ignored the crack. "He ever talk to you?" I asked.

"Nah. I never had nothin' to talk to him about. Besides, way I hear it, he never talked to guys he was gonna help out." A sly look came over his face. "He only talked to intermediaries, if you know what I mean."

Grosso's use of the word surprised me, but what he was implying surprised me even more.

"You sayin' the judge could be reached?" Jimmy asked.

Grosso looked at him with a touch of surprise. "I thought that's what you was askin'. I figured you was lookin' into some of the things he done." He gave us a big, exaggerated shrug. "Hey, everybody knew if you had a case comin' up before him, you could go to certain politicians and they'd reach out to him." He let out a barking laugh and there was a sneer spread across his face. "I guess everybody knew it except you guys."

I could see that what he had said had grabbed Jimmy the wrong way. Not that the judge might have been dirty. We already knew about his little real estate scam. It was Grosso's sneering implication that the cops were too stupid to know that Reed could be reached. I decided to step in and take over the questioning and give Jimmy time to cool off.

"So the judge was dirty." I said it as a fact to see where Grosso would go with it. He seemed to enjoy playing the big man, letting us know he knew things we didn't, and I thought I'd let his ego run a bit and see what else came out.

But he wasn't quite that dumb. His eyes narrowed and the smile faded. "Look, I'm only sayin' what I heard. Just barroom talk, nothin' I could swear to, understand?"

Jimmy's eyes had narrowed as well, but in a different way, and I could tell there was going to be no cooling off, no keeping him out of it. "The judge ever talk to you about Lilly Straus?" he asked.

Grosso's head snapped around. "What the fuck you talkin' about?"

"I'm talkin' about you rapin' her, and her goin' to the judge about it. And I'm talkin' about the judge comin' to see you, and maybe you gettin' a little pissed off and decidin' to do somethin' about it."

Grosso was up out of his chair, eyes blazing. "What the fuck you tryin' to pull? You tryin' to say I raped that fuckin' douchebag, and then I killed a fuckin' judge to cover it up? What kind of dumb fuckin' frame you tryin' to pull here?"

Jimmy and I both stood with him. With a guy like Grosso you didn't give him any edge, like being able to kick one of us in the teeth to bring the odds to even money.

There was a faint hint of a smile on Jimmy's lips, a touch of pleasure that he had gotten to Grosso. "Sit down," he snapped.

"Fuck you," Grosso snapped back. "I know what you pricks are up to, and I ain't fallin' for it. If I had a problem with that broad, I woulda solved it with her, not with no fuckin' judge. Somebody told you bulls to lay a frame on me. But it ain't gonna work."

"What if I told you we got somebody who says they saw you comin' out of the judge's house the day he was killed?" Jimmy was pushing it now, harder than he should.

"I'd say fuck you, I ain't playin' patsy for you or nobody else. I'll kill you both first; then I'll go get the guy who fed you this crap and I'll rip his fuckin' lungs out."

It had gone over the edge now and Jimmy sensed it a second too late. Grosso's words brought Jimmy's hand to his holster, but before he could do anything the big man's right fist caught him just over the ear. It was only a glancing blow, but still packed enough power to send Jimmy two steps back toward the sofa.

I didn't wait for any more. I pulled my blackjack out, and as Grosso turned to me I laid it upside his head with every bit of power I could muster. He went down, but only to one knee. I couldn't believe it. Three ounces of lead hitting with all my 180 pounds behind it should have put him down for the count. He looked up at me, eyes not even glazed, and started to get up. I bent at the waist and laid one along the side of his knee. That dropped him to all fours, but almost immediately he started to push himself up and I let him have it again, this time on the back of the head, the blow so hard I almost came off my feet.

This time he went down, and Jimmy was on him, knee pushed into his spine as he pulled his hands behind his back and cuffed him. "Jaysus. It's like tryin' to knock out a mule."

It had gone too far, a lot farther than we had wanted or expected. I looked down at Jimmy, who was still straddling

Grosso. He shook his head, indicating he didn't know how he had let it go so wrong, so fast. When he spoke I could hear the regret in his voice.

"Let's get him to the precinct. We'll have to book him on assault. There ain't nothin' else we can do."

"The crazy sonofabitch went berserk." Jimmy shook his head and I could tell that he couldn't quite accept how everything had turned out. Grosso was in a holding cell charged with assault. It was exactly what we had wanted to avoid. Now we'd have to book him, and then the pressure would begin to charge him for Judge Reed's murder as well.

We were seated at our desks. The squad room was almost empty but we still kept our voices low as we tried to figure out our next step.

"I screwed up," Jimmy said. "I let him get to me, and then I had to rub his face in it to go one up. I never thought he'd go ape like that."

"So what do we do now?" I asked. "We can't let him go. He'll go out and get Lilly Straus for sure."

Jimmy ground his teeth. He had put us in this box and he knew it. He drew a long breath and shook his head again. "I know. I just don't wanna charge him with the judge's murder. Everything we've got against him is a load of crap. Shit, Grosso couldn't be more right about it being a setup. Thing is, I just don't know *why* he's being set up. What I do know is that once we charge him, once the ball starts rolling toward the courts, it'll be hell to stop."

"Let's see if he's got an alibi for the night the judge was murdered," I suggested. "If he's got one, and it's solid enough, the DA won't want to touch it. The newspapers are sure to play any trial hot and heavy, and the DA isn't gonna want a sure loser."

Jimmy nodded. "Yeah, you're right. It's our only hope. 'Cause about an hour from now Manny Troy's gonna be so far up my ass I'm gonna want him to put a ring on my finger."

"I was workin' that night." Grosso sat in our windowless interrogation room, his hands again cuffed behind his back. There was a bandage on the back of his head and a good-sized bruise on one temple. Other than the small cut and the bruise he didn't look any the worse for wear after going a couple of rounds with my blackjack.

"Anybody see you workin'?" Jimmy asked.

"Yeah. Lots of people."

Jimmy and I glanced at each other. It was the first bit of good news we'd had. "Give us the names," I said.

Grosso rattled off the name Joey Hannon, a low-level thug I knew only by reputation, and finished off with Owney Ryan, himself.

"You sure they'll back you up on this?" Jimmy asked.

"Hey, the three of us went to the Garden to see a fight." He inclined his head to one side. "Mr. Ryan, he likes to have a couple of his guys with him when he goes places."

"Who was fightin'?" Jimmy asked.

He gave us the names of two ham-and-eggers I had never heard of before. He said they were middleweights.

Jimmy and I put Grosso back in his holding cell and returned to our desks. Jimmy glanced at the clock on the wall. It was nearly four.

"You gotta pull duty at the Reed house tonight. You wanna grab some time with your old lady, this would be a good time. I'll drop you at your house; then I'm gonna scout up this Hannon thug, see what he has to say about Grosso's story. Then I'll see if I can track down Mr. Owney Ryan."

"You find Ryan, I'd like to be there when you brace him," I said.

Jimmy nodded. "I locate him, I'll give you a call at the Reed house."

I had gotten Jimmy to stop at a street stall so I could pick up some flowers for Mary. It was just a little summer bouquet, nothing that would look like the guilt offering it really was, and it made Mary's face light up like a Christmas tree when I waltzed in the door.

She took the flowers and stared at them for a long minute. A small tear formed in the corner of one eye and it brought the guilt rushing back. I stroked her arm softly. "I can't bring you flowers if it's gonna make you cry," I said softly.

"I can't help it." She sniffed deeply, forcing the tears away. "These days everything makes me weepy." She touched her stomach lightly with the fingers of one hand and raised her eyes to mine. "Anyway, we can't afford flowers. Even if I love them, and love you for bringing them. They cost too much, what with all the expenses that come with a new baby."

"These were just from a guy selling them on the corner. They weren't that pricey."

She gave me that raised-eyebrow look that wives are so good at. "And where do you think *he* got the flowers? I'll tell you where. He got them from some flower shop, and then he added his own bit of profit to the price."

I laughed and bent down and kissed her nose. "These guys who sell flowers are all down-and-out types. Most of them are fresh out of the service with no job in sight. They buy their goods at the wholesale flower market, same as the shops. I see them down there, all these street-corner guys, buying an armful every day to sell during rush hour." What I didn't tell her was they bought the *leftover* flowers, the ones past their peak, so they could peddle them for what seemed a bargain to the people who grabbed them up. Especially guys headed home who had maybe forgotten a wife's birthday, or an anniversary, or guys who had gotten home late the night before and had found a stone-faced woman sitting across from them at breakfast.

Mary gave me a coy look. "Well that's all right, then . . . if you're sure it didn't cost a lot." She paused. "Especially since you're a husband I never see anymore." She raised her hand to stop any objection, although my conscience wouldn't allow any to be made. "Oh, I'm not complaining, you know that. I love the extra money you'll be getting. But not for greed's sake. Only because we need it so." She touched her stomach again, drawing my eyes to the enormous bulge that had replaced the tiny waist of the woman I had married.

"It looks like it's getting so close," I said.

She nodded; then her eyes took on a look of concern. "You mean I've started to look like a big old cow."

"No, not at all." I put all the sincerity I could into each word. "It's just that your stomach looks . . . looks . . . like it's so *full*, like the baby's ready to come any day now."

"See, you do think I look like a cow." Her eyes began to tear up again. "And that's just how I feel, like a big, fat, enormous cow. And that's probably why you're never here, because it's like coming home to some awful woman who belongs in a barnyard."

The tears were rolling down her cheeks, and I stood there, realizing I had somehow brought it all on and feeling utterly inept; helpless to make it stop. Earlier in the day I had used a blackjack on an enraged thug who had wanted to break both Jimmy and me in half. Now, compared to my weeping wife, dealing with Louie Grosso seemed like child's play.

I went to her and took her in my arms, hoping that would work. I stroked her back, and wondered if it hurt. She had told me before that her back always hurt now, and I thought maybe I should offer to rub it. Before I could say anything she started to talk, but so softly I had to lean down, bring my ear closer to her mouth so I could hear what she was saying.

". . . I saw her picture in the paper."

"Whose picture did you see?"

"The one you're guarding. Mrs. Reed. She's very beautiful, isn't she?"

"You don't have to call her Mrs. Reed, you know. She's two years younger than you are."

"Is she?" She was quiet for several moments. "Do you think she's beautiful?"

"I never really thought about it," I said, quick with the lie. "She's just a job. I'm just making sure nobody hurts her. Besides, I don't really see her all that much, unless she goes out. Mostly, I just make sure nobody gets in the house."

"But you went to the Stork Club with her. You told me about that. You must've *looked* at her, for Gawd's sake."

I had never told Mary about our second visit to the Stork, or anything else about the time Cynthia Reed and I spent together. Not even the innocent stuff. I was glad now that I hadn't. "I've looked at her, sure. But mostly when I have to go out with her I'm watching out for other people, people who might want to hurt her. I'm not spending the night gazing into her eyes."

Mary leaned back and slapped my arm playfully. "You better not be goin' all moonstruck with another woman."

The lie still burned in my throat, but I managed another with little difficulty. "I save all my moonstruck looks for you."

Mary hugged me tight, as though I might try to get away. "You better. Your child will never forgive you if you don't, and neither will I." She pushed me away, suddenly all wifely business. "You should eat something before you have to go. I've got some cold chicken in the Frigidaire and I can fry up some potatoes to go with it."

My guilt was growing worse by the minute. "Just the chicken's fine. I don't want you standing by a stove. It's too hot for that."

Mary came against me again, returning her head to my chest. "I love that you're so good to me, Jake."

{ 19 }

I could hear Cyn's voice as I came in the front door. It was filled with a mix of fear and anger, so close to hysteria I thought at first that she was being attacked.

"You can't do this. I won't let you. Don't think for a minute I won't do whatever it takes to stop you."

Her voice was coming from the small parlor. I unbuttoned my coat and placed my hand on my weapon as I started moving slowly down the hall. I was almost to the door when another voice stopped me cold.

"Dammit, Cynthia, no one is trying to do anything to you; certainly not to cheat you out of anything." It was the low, angry growl of Manny Troy, yet this time there was also a touch of something else hidden in the words—uncertainty, nervousness, I couldn't be sure.

"And you better not ever, Manny. Not *ever*. Just don't forget that I *know* things. And I also know what to do with them if I have to."

I hesitated, trying to decide how to play it. If anyone came through the parlor door I'd be caught out like some amateur snoop, and I didn't want either Troy or Cyn to think I'd been eavesdropping, so I did a quick about-face, returned to the front door, pulled it open and closed it with a sharp crack. The sound produced immediate silence and as I started down the hall Troy emerged from the parlor and gave me an angry look.

"Downing, you'll have to wait outside. Mrs. Reed and I are discussing some private matters." He snapped the words out like commands, which of course they were. Manny Troy didn't make requests of city employees, not even ones who wore badges and carried guns.

Cyn suddenly appeared behind Troy. "I'll give the orders in my own home, if you don't mind." She stepped around him as she spoke, her eyes harder and colder than I'd ever seen them.

Troy stiffened, his face flushing a deep red. Then he spun on his heels and returned to the parlor.

Cyn ignored him. "There's some coffee in the kitchen, Jake. I'll let you know when Mr. Troy and I have finished our business." Then she, too, returned to the parlor, this time closing the pocket doors behind her.

It was quarter past eight when Cyn came into the kitchen. She was wearing a pale blue dress made of that light filmy fabric she seemed to favor. It always made me think of the song lyric that spoke about gossamer wings, and it always made me look at her long and hard, and when I did it always made me think of other things as well.

"Did you get some coffee?" she asked.

Before I could answer she moved against me, brought her hands up behind my neck and kissed me. When she pulled away she stared up into my face, just the trace of a smile on her lips. "I've been thinking about you all day. I've been thinking about how good it would feel to be in bed with you, to have you inside me."

I could feel myself growing, and she pressed against me, her little smile turning into a laugh. "I think you like that idea. At least your friend seems to like it."

"Yeah, I like it. I like it so damned much I can hardly think of anything else whenever we're in the same room." I put my hands at the small of her back and pulled her to me. Her hips came forward and her pelvis began to grind against me, then she rolled her head back, closed her eyes and let out a small, hungry groan.

"Take me upstairs, Jake," she whispered. "Take me there right now."

We lay in Cyn's bed, our bodies slick with sweat and the smell of sex. I tried not to think of Mary, or of the dead judge who had slept in this same bed—slept here every night until someone, maybe even the woman I was lying next to, had taken a bronze gavel and turned his forehead into jelly.

I rolled onto my side and placed a hand on Cyn's naked hip. Her eyes were closed, but she wasn't asleep, and she moved pleasurably to my touch. "You never told me what you and Troy were fighting about," I said.

Cyn opened her eyes, gave me a dreamy look, and then closed them again. "We weren't fighting." She seemed to consider what she had said, or what I might have heard. She opened her eyes again and turned her head toward me. "He was trying to cheat me out of something that's mine. I told him I wouldn't let that happen."

"What was it?"

"What you told me about. The real estate deal they had."

"You want the judge's share." There was no question about her intentions, and none reflected in my words.

"I want the profits to go to his estate. It's only fair. It would have been Wallace's money if he'd lived. Manny and this Ryan man can't just take it, just because they . . . just because Warren was killed. I won't let that happen."

I ran my fingers along the side of her body. "What if the deal's crooked?"

She let out a harsh laugh. "What isn't crooked in this town?" She turned away, shook her head. "How many private little deals do you think my husband had in the short time we were married?"

"You knew about deals he had, things he did for people?"

"Not specifics. Just the people. He'd meet here with Troy and with other city officials, and I'd hear them talking about certain people—people who had some influence and who needed a little help with something in Warren's court. Then there was the money that always seemed to appear for no reason. Even a hatcheck girl could figure out that something was going on." She turned back to me, her eyes hard now. "Warren was a wealthy man when I married him. He was a public official most of his life, but he always had plenty of money."

"You told me his family left him well off. Not filthy rich, but rich enough."

She turned her head away. "I told you that because that's what *he* told people, that he'd inherited his money. But it wasn't true. At least not any significant amount. His people weren't rich. They weren't poor like mine, but they weren't rich either. His father owned a small drugstore and he worked in it until the day he died."

"So your husband sold the drugstore and invested the money." I was just saying it to get her reaction. She smiled at me like I was a fool.

"Yes, of course. He was a shrewd investor." She ended the sentence with another harsh laugh. "Would you get my cigarettes? They're on the bedside table."

I reached back for her cigarettes and managed to dislodge two books, knocking them to the floor. After handing Cyn her cigarettes I retrieved the books. As I returned them to the table one caught my eye. It was a dream book. I had come across others like it, but usually in the homes of Negroes, or poor immigrants. It was a book you used to interpret your dreams—special dreams—dreams that could help you pick winning numbers in the policy racket.

I propped myself up on one elbow and held the book out. Cyn glanced at it and sent a long stream of cigarette smoke in its direction.

"You play the numbers?" I asked.

"I did. Every day until Warren died."

"And you used the dream book?"

"Yes."

I shook my head, not quite believing it.

"What did your husband think about that?"

She took a long drag on her cigarette and blew it out. "What he thought about everything I did. That it was stupid. That it was just something his floozy of a wife did." She glared at me as if I, too, were saying the same thing. "But maybe I was just trying to hit the number. Maybe I just wanted to win, just wanted to take the money and leave. Maybe I was just tired of getting knocked around and I wanted to get away."

Cyn took another drag on her cigarette and then she laughed, either at what she had just said, or herself in general, I couldn't be sure.

She turned and looked at me, her eyes softer now. "Everyone has to have dreams, Jake. If you don't have dreams there's no point in waking up in the morning."

"What if you're old, and your dreams have passed you by?"

"Then you dream for your children." She ran her hand across her stomach as she spoke the words, and it made me think of Mary and the child she was carrying.

"The people I feel really sorry for are the ones who live their whole lives without children, the people who are alone in the world." She stared at me, trying to see if I understood what she was saying. "You see, people like that, they're the truly sad ones. They grow old and their dreams come to an end." She looked at me, her eyes very soft and very sad. "Without dreams, you don't have anything at all."

The bedside telephone interrupted her. Cyn tried to ignore it, but it kept ringing and she finally answered it. She listened, then said, "I'll go and get him." She raised her chin toward me.

I waited an appropriate time, and then took the receiver from her hand. "Detective Downing."

Jimmy Finn's voice floated across the line. "I found our friend Owney Ryan. You want to join me, get a squad car to drop you at Danny's Hideaway."

"I'll be there in twenty minutes," I said.

"I'll wait for you out front," Jimmy said.

Danny's Hideaway was on East Forty-fifth, between Third and Lexington. It was a show biz hangout, peppered with East Side hoods who provided a vicarious thrill for the boys and babes of

Broadway who wanted to put "a little danger" in their lives. Owney Ryan, given his reputation for piling bodies in meat lockers, was one of the favorites, and according to the gossip columns he had even put his own dough into a couple of Broadway plays.

Jimmy was standing out front as promised. He was grinding a cigar between his teeth, and as I exited the squad car he took my arm and led me a few doors down the street. He seemed a little edgy, and he didn't start talking until we were safely away from Danny's front door.

"I talked to that punk, Joey Hannon, and the little shit backs up Grosso's story. The two of them were playing bodyguard for Ryan the night Reed got iced."

"So now we get Ryan to confirm it and Grosso's off the hook."

Jimmy nodded. "It's all we need. The DA won't touch it, he's got two people saying Grosso was someplace else, not even if both of them sayin' it are goddamn hoods themselves. It's just too risky some jury might buy it." He gave me a wink. "And that means that not even Manny Troy can order us to pin this rap on Louie."

That was Jimmy's big worry, the thing that had been eating at him since we first walked in Judge Reed's front door—that Troy, or the commissioner, would take the case out of our hands and decide how it turned out.

I gave his shoulder a love tap with the side of my fist. "So let's go wrap it up with Ryan, and we'll be home free."

We went back to the entrance and swaggered through the front door, sure we were going to get what we wanted.

Danny's was a long, narrow room with a bar taking up the entire right wall and tables filling in every inch of remaining space. The bar was said to be the longest in the city. There were no stools, it was standing room only, and the massive expanse of mahogany easily accommodated more than fifty drinkers at a time. Tonight it was packed, keeping three bartenders busy.

I followed Jimmy down the length of the bar, through a cacophony of bluster-filled voices and phony laughter, to where Owney Ryan occupied a table at the rear of the restaurant. True to gangster form, Ryan was seated with his back firmly planted against the rear wall. Next to him, giving us a self-satisfied smirk as we approached, was Oliver Marks.

We both pulled up chairs without being asked and sat across from them.

Ryan gave us a cold smile. "Hello, boys. Wanna drink?"

"We'd love one, but we're on duty," Jimmy said.

Oliver gave out a little snort, offering it as his opinion of what Jimmy had said. It was his tough-guy role, played for Ryan's benefit, and just like the other time I'd seen him, it made me want to reach out and grab his scrawny neck and squeeze for about a minute and a half. Instead, I leaned forward and offered him a grin that told him what I was thinking, and then watched him twist nervously in his seat. It was a marvel to me that he and his sister could have come out of the same dick. But I guess it proved the old adage that the fastest sperm wasn't necessarily the brightest in the load.

Owney gave Jimmy another big, phony smile. "So, what's your business, sport? From what I hear, you already locked up one of my boys. That oughtta be enough for one day, don't ya think?"

"That's why we're here, Owney." Finn offered up his own smile, so big and friendly it almost made me laugh out loud. "We've been lookin' at your boy Louie for the Judge Reed murder, but it could be we went and locked up the wrong man. Seems like Louie claims to have an alibi. Says he was at the Garden with you and Joey Hannon that night, watchin' a pair of pugs duke it out." Jimmy leaned forward and lowered his voice as if sharing a big secret. "Hannon tells me Louie's story is on the up and up."

Ryan's eyes narrowed noticeably at the mention of Hannon's name. Then he caught himself and matched Jimmy's big smile. "Ah, now, I hate to say it, but I think Joey's got his dates mixed up." He inclined his head toward Oliver. "It was Ollie here who was with Joey and me that night, not Louie Grosso. That's right, ain't it, Ollie?"

Oliver gave him a vigorous nod. "Yeah, that's right, it was me and Joey went with Mr. Ryan. I remember it good, 'cause the next morning I woke up and read in the papers that my brother-in-law was dead."

Jimmy's jaw had tightened, and I decided I'd take over for a bit. "You remember who was fighting that night?"

"Yeah, sure." Oliver rattled off the names of the fighters, almost as if he'd memorized them. They were the same names Louie had given us, names we had already checked out and found legit.

"That surprises me," I said.

"What does?" It was Ryan trying to direct my attention away from Oliver. He was still smiling, but it looked like the effort was growing old.

"It surprises me that one hood wouldn't back up another's alibi. Seems like maybe Louie Grosso is being tossed to the wolves, doesn't it?" I turned to Oliver. He was nervously licking his lips. He seemed to catch himself and blew out a long stream of smoke from the cigarette he was smoking. "Louie won't like that. He gets out on bail, he's gonna come around and ask why."

Ryan let out a low, rumbling laugh. It was more to ease Oliver's nerves than because he found anything funny in what I'd said. "Well, I'll tell you what surprises me. It surprises the hell out of me that two of the city's finest don't want honest citizens to tell the truth."

I laughed out loud at the term *honest citizens*, driving the smile from Ryan's face. His eyes narrowed into slits. "I'll tell you what else surprises me," he said. "That two smart detectives like yourselves can't read the goddamn writin' on the wall."

"And what writin' is that?" Jimmy leaned forward as he spoke. He looked like he might fly across the table.

Ryan shook his head and smiled again. "Ah, I'm sayin' too much. You boys are smart enough to figure it all out for yourselves. Every cop knows there are times when you should just back off."

"You saying this is one of those times?" I asked.

Ryan placed the fingers of both hands against his chest. "Me? What would I know about that? We're talkin' philosophy here, that's all. Besides, I'd never try and hand out advice to two smart boys like yourselves, now, would I?"

Jimmy pushed up from his chair and I followed the example. He stared down at Ryan with hard eyes. Then his features suddenly changed, as if he had just realized something. He gave Ryan another smile. "Ah, now don't worry yourself, Owney. We don't mind a bit of advice, now and then. In fact, sometimes it's a big help. We even like it when it don't have nothin' to do with the case we're workin' on. Say like a nice real estate tip, or somethin'." He stopped and scratched his chin, watching as Ryan's face hardened into a stone mask. "Of course, you never know. Real estate could have somethin' to do with almost anythin', couldn't it?" He gave Ryan a wink and a slight pull on the brim of his hat. "Be seein' you, Owney. Don't you go takin' any wooden nickels, now."

{ 20 }

It was seven-thirty when Molly walked into Jake's office at One Police Plaza. He was seated at his desk, the room lighted by a solitary desk lamp. He hadn't heard her, and she stood just inside the doorway watching him as he pored over a report, glasses perched on the end of his nose, pen in hand, looking more like a schoolteacher grading papers than the chief of detectives for one of the most sophisticated police departments in the world.

It was only the second time she had been to his office, the first being the day they had met. He was the newly named chief of detectives then, and he had called her in to discuss a high-profile murder case. But the meeting had produced much more. The chemistry had exploded between them, and a short time later they had begun to see each other. From that point on, because he was still married to Mary, discretion had made her stay away. It was not something he had asked her to do, but neither had he objected. It was an unspoken agreement that had become a parameter of their relationship, sometimes hurtful, but one she understood. So today, when he had asked her to meet him here for their dinner date, it was a clear signal that the days of hiding their affection were over. It had made her heart race like a schoolgirl's.

"The outer office was empty, and your door was open, so I just came in." She paused. "So . . . who's protecting the chief?"

Jake looked up at the sound of her voice. He removed his reading glasses so he could see her better. "I don't need protection, sweetheart. I've got my gat." He had spoken the words in the worst Humphrey Bogart imitation she had ever heard. Then he smiled. "I sent everybody home except Pete Tedesco. He's in the garage with the car."

"We're being chauffeured?"

Jake made a point of raising his eyebrows in disapproval. "In the cops we don't call it being chauffeured. We call it having a driver."

"Pardon me," she said, playing the game. "So . . . we have a *driver?*"

Jake pumped himself up to look as pompous as possible. "Of course. You've got a date with the chief of detectives—a very important man. He always has a driver."

Molly grinned at the self-deprecation. It was one of the first things that had attracted her to Jake, his refusal to take himself seriously. She hadn't known many cops, let alone chiefs, whom that could be said about.

She went around his desk, bent down and kissed his cheek. "What's keeping you late?"

He looked up and smiled. "The work of an exceptional ME."

Molly was momentarily puzzled. Then she realized what Jake meant and felt a rush of satisfaction. "You charged Radcliff."

He held up the papers he'd been reading. "I was just going over the paperwork to make sure we've dotted every 'i.' We're hitting him with second-degree murder. My boys couldn't find anything that pointed to premeditation. They think he just lost his temper and hit his daughter too hard. From what they were able to find out, it wasn't the first time he'd knocked her around. We've got neighbors telling us that little five-year-old was roughed up pretty regularly. This time they heard him screaming at the child and then heard her crying. So with what you came up with in the autopsy I think we've got him cold, but I've been double-checking everything just to make sure there's nothing we did, or failed to do, that his weasel of a lawyer can use to get him off."

Molly let out a satisfied breath. "God, you have no idea how good that makes me feel. The only thing worse than having a child on the table is discovering they've been abused. Every pathologist I've ever spoken with feels the same way. It just gives you an indescribably sick feeling. And it always makes you wonder how many others are out there who we'll never find out about because their deaths are ruled accidental."

"Unfortunate bicycle accidents." Jake reached up, took her hand and gave it a squeeze. "At least the bastard who hurt this child didn't get away with it, thanks to you. It's not much to celebrate, but it's something."

"Yes." She reached down and stroked his cheek. "But I don't want to celebrate that. Not tonight."

Jake nodded, believing he understood what she meant. "What shall we celebrate then?"

Molly glanced around his office and smiled to herself. "I'll tell you later."

They took a private elevator reserved for the commissioner and his chiefs and found Pete Tedesco waiting beside Jake's car.

"Hello, Doc." He was fighting off a grin. "Nice to see you."

Molly had always assumed that Pete knew about her relationship with Jake. He had been Jake's driver for the past three years, and was, after all, a competent detective. He was also completely loyal to his boss, and she was sure he had kept the secret as well as he could. Now he seemed genuinely pleased that it was out in the open.

They climbed into the back of Jake's official car. There was a copy of the *Daily News* on the seat. The headline read, *Ford to City: Drop Dead*. It alluded to President Ford's decision not to bail the city out of its fiscal crisis.

Jake saw Molly looking at the headline. He ran his finger beneath it. "Have you heard the joke that's going around?"

She shook her head.

"It's about those two attempts that were made on the president's life. They're saying it was only practice; that this time the mayor won't miss."

For dinner, Jake had chosen Sammy's Romanian, a Christie Street landmark that had long been a favorite haunt for the city's movers and shakers. Molly couldn't help smiling as she exited the car. They were certain to meet other high-ranking cops and city officials and she took it as another sign that the secrecy surrounding their relationship was at an end.

As they stepped inside they were greeted by a small, slender man in his early sixties, who seemed to bounce rather than walk, and who played host every night to the endless party atmosphere that always engulfed Sammy's. The restaurant had been described most accurately as an ongoing bar mitzvah, complete with a band made up of old men who could play everything Cole Porter had ever written, plus half the show tunes sent out across Broadway's footlights for the past fifty years. It was a boisterous, funny, madcap place that also offered the best Romanian garlic steaks in the city, topped off by egg creams made right at your table. It was pure New York, and its out-of-the-way location, and the reticence of its devotees, kept it a well-guarded secret from tourists.

There was no hope of a quiet table, of course, but the combined cacophony of music, laughter and boisterous waiters offered a reasonable guarantee that conversations would remain private. Jake increased that assurance by asking for a small corner table just to the right of the band.

They had just settled in and ordered drinks when a tall, well-dressed man in his mid-forties approached their table. Jake introduced him as Philip Caldwell, a name Molly recognized from newspaper articles. He was the Queens County Republican boss, a man who, even though his party was currently out of office, wielded considerable power in the city.

Caldwell was a handsome man, with distinguished streaks of gray running through his otherwise black hair, and the patrician good looks and bearing of someone who had gone to all the right schools. If Molly remembered correctly he was also a partner in a Wall Street law firm founded by his grandfather, which meant his money was old enough to garner respect among the city's blue bloods.

"What can I do for you, Phil?" Jake asked, as Caldwell took an offered seat.

"I just wondered if we could set up a meeting tomorrow. I'd like to discuss a case with you."

A smile flickered across Jake's lips. "The Radcliff case?"

Caldwell glanced at Molly. "That's right." He spoke the words with obvious reluctance.

"Tomorrow's a tough day for me, but we can talk right here." Jake raised his chin toward Molly. "This is *Doctor* Molly Reagan. She's the assistant ME who handled the post on Jim Radcliff's daughter. We won't be talking out of school in front of her."

Caldwell looked at Molly again and gave a weak nod. "I think your autopsy may be part of the problem. I spoke with Jim today, and he said your conclusions have pointed a finger at him. He insists those conclusions are wrong."

Jake reached out and placed a hand on Caldwell's arm. "Phil, do yourself a favor and step away from this one. We're charging Radcliff with murder two, and between you and me it's a lock."

"Jesus."

"Indeed. So unless your firm is representing him . . ."

"No, we're not." Caldwell snapped the words out reflexively before Jake could even finish. He shook his head, lowered his voice and leaned in closer. "Jake, murder two, isn't there some way to go for a lesser charge? I mean I know the DA would go along providing you boys didn't object. This—"

Now Jake interrupted. "This isn't a traffic ticket you're talking about, Phil. You're not talking about something that should, or could, be fixed. You're talking about a five-year-old child who was beaten by adult fists, beaten so hard her internal organs were damaged beyond repair, and who must have been in excruciating pain before she died. If you'd like, I'll have one of my people show you the autopsy photos."

Caldwell blanched. "No, that won't be necessary." He shook his head again. "I just find it very hard to believe that the Jim Radcliff I know could do something like that. Especially to his own child."

"Believe it, Phil. And if it ever goes to trial, you'll find out that it wasn't the first time that little girl was abused by her father."

"Jesus." Caldwell pushed himself up from the table.

"One other thing, Phil." Jake's voice had a sharp, cutting edge to it now.

"Yes, Jake."

"If it *had* been a traffic ticket, I would have said no to that, too."

Molly watched Caldwell's face redden. Then he nodded and turned away.

"Not very politic." She lowered her head, struggling to hide a smile.

Jake inclined his head. "I guess I'm not feeling very politic."

The waiter brought their drinks and took their dinner orders. When he left Molly leaned in close so she could be heard over the music without raising her voice.

"Jake, how much of what I just witnessed goes back to the Reed case?"

Jake cocked his head again. "Do you mean would I have gone for a deal if I wasn't in the process of reopening it?"

"No, that's not what I mean. I know you made a decision thirty years ago that was wrong. I know it's been eating away at you for a long time, and that it's something you never let happen again." She paused, trying to phrase her words properly. "But there's more to it. It's the anger I just saw. And that really interests me. I know what happened in the Reed case, how it all turned out, and the way you and Jimmy were outmaneuvered and pressured. You've told me all of that. What I don't know, what you haven't told me, are the particulars, the personal things that happened, the personal things you felt. You see, I think that's what's really eating at you; that's where the anger really comes from. It comes from the personal things that happened, and I'd like to know about them and understand them."

"Why? Why is that important to you?" There was no resistance in his questions, just honest curiosity.

Molly looked at him without speaking. "Because it's the key to what you're doing, the reason behind it all." She paused a moment. "Jake, I'd like to spend the rest of my life with you. I think you know that." She reached across the table and took his hand. "I love you, Jake. I have almost from the first day we met. And because I do, I need to know all of it."

Cyn was asleep when I got back to the Reed house. I didn't want to wake her, so I set myself up in the small parlor, dropped my hat over my eyes and went to sleep. Jimmy woke me at seven the next morning and I was glad I hadn't climbed into Cyn's bed. It would have been embarrassing to be caught out a second time.

"What are you doing here so early?" I asked, shaking away the cobwebs.

"I'm on the dodge," Jimmy said. "I figure the commissioner, or his lackey, Morgan, are gonna reach out and tell me to charge Grosso with the judge's murder. Every hour I stay out of their clutches buys me a little time to come up with somethin'."

I didn't see much hope in it, but I was willing to play along. "What do I do if they give *me* the message?"

A pained look crossed Jimmy's face. "There's nothin' you can do." He took me by the arm and walked me to a front window so we could see outside. "But listen up a minute. You gotta stay here until Mrs. Reed wakes up, those are our orders. But I want you to keep out of sight as best you can. I told the uniform outside to tip you if he sees Morgan, or anybody above the rank of lieutenant, headed for the house. He blows the whistle, you find yourself a place to hide. I don't care if you have to jump in a fookin' closet. Then, you beat it the hell out of here as soon as you square yourself with Mrs. Reed. You got it?"

"Yeah, I got it. What then?"

"Then I want you to pay Lilly Straus a little visit. I shook her up, but not enough to get her to spill. I want you to give it a try. We gotta get her to admit that she never went to the judge about Grosso. So, when you see her, let her know you're a cop, and that the little love affair she thought she was about to start up with you was nothin' but a con. Tell her how you were just checkin' her out on the sly, checkin' out her story about Grosso, and now that you have, how you don't buy any of it. In other words, shake her fookin' tree as hard as you can . . ."

"And see what falls out," I said, finishing the sentence for him.

* * *

Cyn wasn't at all disappointed when I told her I had to leave her in the care of the uniforms because I had a job to do. I didn't say what that job was, and she didn't ask, didn't really seem interested. She seemed cold and aloof and said she had some business to take care of herself, and that she'd be tied up most of the day. When I asked what it was she just brushed it off as something to do with the judge's estate. I could tell she didn't want me to push it, so I let it alone.

Lilly was in her office when I got there a little after ten. She looked up from her desk and didn't seem real thrilled to see me. Instead of the big smile I'd expected, she gave me a hard look, probably the same one she gave deadbeat tenants who came around to say they couldn't pay that month's rent. After the cold shoulder I had gotten from Cyn I figured it just wasn't my day for women.

I decided to hang tough and gave her my best boyish grin, hoping to soften her up. It still didn't make a dent. Her face was heavily made up, so much so she looked like she had layered it on with a trowel, and the bright overhead lights accented the hard edges around her eyes and mouth. But it didn't look like there were many soft lines under all that pancake anyway. Not for me, and not today. All in all she seemed to have recovered from her visit to the precinct. And no matter how much Jimmy had scared her then, it was pretty clear that somebody else had made it all go away.

"How have you been, Lilly." I sauntered up to her desk, hat in hand, the grin still fixed on my kisser.

"Vhat do you vant?" Her voice was crisp, sharp as a knife edge.

"Just stopped by for a little chat."

"About vhat?"

Her tone of voice had a bit of a snarl to it, and it made me glad she wasn't male and six-foot-three. I figured the jig was up so I flipped open my badge case and flashed the tin.

"This and that. You don't mind talking to cops, do you?" I had perched on the edge of her desk, crowding her, taking up as much of her space as I could.

"I knew you vere a cop." She snapped the words out with a touch of defiance.

"Oh, yeah? When did you find out?"

She sneered at me. "After I talked vit your partner zee osser day."

"Hey, that's too bad. It ruined my surprise. Who was it who told you?"

Lilly gave out with a little snort that wasn't very becoming but made her point. "It's not your business."

I leaned in even closer and lost the smile. "Hey, lady, everything's my business if I say it is. Especially Louie Grosso."

Lilly pushed her chair back. Her eyes darted toward the office door and I could tell she was hoping someone, even one of her deadbeat tenants, would show up. Then she gave up and turned back to me and her eyes were as hard as ever. I didn't have any idea who had put her at ease, but whoever it was had done one helluva job. Oh, she still wanted me out of there, all right. But it wasn't because she was scared.

"You lied about Grosso, didn't you?" I was still playing it hard, even though I knew it wasn't going to work.

"I don't know vhat you're talking about."

"You never even went to the judge about him, did you? That wasn't how you knew the judge. You knew him because of something else, isn't that right?"

Lilly's mouth twisted into an ugly sneer that exposed the harsh lines beneath the too-heavy layer of pancake. Now all pretense of being a pretty young woman fell away as anger revealed the well-worn dame she worked so hard to conceal. "You so smart, you tell me vhy I knew zee judge, vhy don't you?"

She threw it out like a challenge and I couldn't let it lie there, even though all good sense told me I should. I spread my hands and laughed. "Hey, Lilly, you're too smart for me. How could I know anything, right?" I leaned in, crowding her again, and widened the smile. "But maybe if I took a walk down First Avenue; maybe if I walked past a certain slaughterhouse . . ." I eased back and shrugged. "Hey, who knows what a dumb cop could come up with if he did those things?"

Lilly's eyes widened noticeably and she inhaled deeply through her nose in short, ragged little breaths. Her mouth was tight and hard, a thin line of pressed lips. Without a word she reached out, picked up the telephone and dialed a number. All I caught of it was the exchange—Butterfield Six.

"Ziz iz Lilly Straus," she said when the phone was answered. "I need to speak wis him." She paused and irritation crossed her face. "Yes, it iz wery important." She waited again, then a smile crossed her lips as someone else came on the line. "Zere iz a detective here. Zee young one. He iz talking about slaughterhouses." She paused, listening. "I tell him nossin. I just vant him out of here." Lilly listened again and the smile returned. "I vill tell him."

Lilly leaned back in her chair and stared up at me. The look on her face cut into my gut, the self-satisfaction so overwhelming it made her cheeks glow with pleasure. It also made me want to reach out and shake her until that look disappeared.

"Vhen you get back to your office zere vill be a message for you from zee commissioner. He vill vant to see you about zis little visit you pay me." Her eyes turned to ice and the smile vanished. "Now get out of zis office or I vill make anosser call."

I was afraid to go back to the precinct. If Lilly was right, there would be a message waiting for me, and it would be one I couldn't ignore. I needed to give Jimmy the time he had asked for, and I couldn't do that unless I kept out of sight. And that wouldn't be easy. By now the bosses would figure that Jimmy and I were on the dodge and that gave me only an hour or so on the street before the word went out to every beat cop that the PC wanted us found. That meant I needed a spot to hole up, and the best hideout I could think of was the last place they'd expect me to go.

I killed an hour on the street, then figured I was running out of time and headed back to Cyn's house. I stayed on the corner watching the uniform on the front door. After twenty minutes he went inside for a bathroom break, and I beat it across the street and made it through the front door before he finished. After he was back on the stoop I checked out the house and found it empty. The log we kept in the front hall told me that Cyn had gone out two hours ago, driven by the squad car that was regularly stationed outside. I went up to her room and stretched out on the bed, figuring that no one would look there if they came by checking for me. Another hour went by before I heard Cyn's voice in the downstairs hall.

I started down the stairs but pulled up short when I heard Manny Troy answer her. He was the last person I wanted to see, so I retreated to the second-floor landing and listened. They were in the large sitting room just off the front entry, and the angry voices of the other day were gone now, replaced by the clinking of ice against glass as drinks were poured.

"You're sure you understand what you have to do?" Troy asked.

"Please. I'm a lot brighter than you think," Cyn responded.

"Oh, I don't doubt how bright you are," Troy said. "That's never been a question for me. I watched you lead Wallace around like a pup until you caught him. He never had a chance." There was a lengthy pause before Troy continued. "Did you know I told him to stay away from you?"

"I suspected it." Cyn let out a cold laugh. "If he had listened it would have saved me a lot of bruises."

"You'll be well compensated for those," Troy said.

"Does that make it all right?" A hint of anger had crept into Cyn's voice now.

"I think we should let that one sit," Troy said.

There was a pause, then more clinking of ice on glass. "It's fine with me," Cyn said at length. "I just want everything cleared up and then I want to get the hell out of here."

"Just relax," Troy said. "Take everything nice and easy."

Cyn let out a harsh laugh. "I went to see my doctor this morning, and that's what he said. He told me to put my feet up and take things easy."

"Is something wrong? You're not ill, are you?"

"Don't sound so concerned, Manny. It's nothing that will keep me from doing what we agreed on."

Cyn's hand flew to her throat and she gave out a startled cry when she entered her room and found me stretched out on the bed.

"Oh, God, you scared me." She leaned back against the door, her hand still at her throat. "What are you doing here?"

"Hiding out," I said.

"Who from?"

"The commissioner, for starters. You can work your way down from there. Right now I'm just trying to avoid anybody above the rank of sergeant."

"Why?"

I waved away the question. I wasn't sure why, but I didn't want to tell Cyn about our Louie Grosso problem. "No special reason. It's just that the brass likes to stick their noses in every big investigation. Smart cops try to avoid that whenever they can."

Cyn walked to the bed and sat down next to me. "I just want this investigation over with. I don't care whether you do it, or your bosses do it. As far as I'm concerned, the sooner it happens, the better."

"Yeah, I couldn't help hearing you tell Manny Troy the same thing."

Cyn seemed surprised that I'd overheard her conversation with Troy, but any concern passed quickly. "I'm glad you heard. I want to leave, I want out of here as fast as I can make it happen." There was a long pause, as if she was considering whether or not to continue. "I'd like it if you came with me," she finally added. "I'd like it a lot, Jake."

That one stopped me cold. Dozens of thoughts rushed through my mind simultaneously. The first was Mary, and the child that was coming any day now. Then Cyn seemed to rush to the front of my brain and push her out. Cyn, beautiful, desirable, the most exciting woman I'd ever been with, and, though it twisted my gut to even think it, soon to be a very wealthy woman. God, it would be a different life, a life I'd only gotten a small taste of, a life where we could do just about anything we wanted without any worry about the next day, or week, or month, or even year. It shook me just thinking about it. Oh, I'd thought about it before—fantasized about it ever since I'd met her, even more since I'd become involved with her, there was no denying it. Why else had I kept things from Jimmy, things that would have made her look bad, things that would have made him even more suspicious of her. There was no question I'd become *full of her,* as my mother and her cronies used to say . . . *taken* with her; that was another one. Or was I just being taken? For a ride, maybe.

I sat up, took her shoulders in my hands, and turned her toward me. "Why me? Why do you want me with you?"

She looked down; then slowly raised her eyes again. "Do I have to tell you?"

"Yeah, you do. You know I've got a wife, and you know I've got a baby coming. You also know I'm crazy about you. So, yeah, I need to know."

Cyn lowered her eyes again, shook her head just a bit, then let out a breath as if she were giving something up she had held in for a long time. "We're good together, Jake. Real good. It's the way I always hoped it would be when I fell for somebody." All the sophistication seemed to be gone now. All of it stripped away from her. It surprised me, reminded me that she was just a twenty-three-year-old woman—still a girl in some ways—and all the sophistication I'd witnessed was mostly façade, painted on like Lilly Straus's makeup. She looked up at me now, her eyes fluttering just a bit. "It's the way I hoped it would be with Wallace. But that was just a dream, something that never turned out the way I wanted it to."

That last one didn't quite ring true, given what I'd heard Manny Troy say earlier. But the rest of it was something I wanted to believe, wanted very much, and that part made me nervous. "Maybe it's just a dream with me, too."

She shook her head, her eyes still lowered, avoiding mine. "Nobody's ever made me feel like you do, Jake."

It was what I wanted to hear. Christ, it was what every man wanted to hear. And every woman with half a brain in her head knew it. Mary rushed back, filling my mind. After all the years we had together, how could I agree to what Cyn was asking? How could I do this to her and to the baby she was carrying, a baby I didn't even know, who—if I left—I never would know? "You're asking a lot." My mind rushed at me again to add, *and you're offering a lot.*

Cyn looked up at me, her eyes slightly moist. She ran both hands along my chest. "I know. It's just . . . It's just . . ."

Jimmy's voice bellowed from downstairs, calling out my name.

"Shit," I muttered, as I pushed myself up and hurried to the top of the stairs.

"Yeah," I called.

Jimmy came into view below me. He stared up, eyes narrowed. "What the hell are you doin' up there?" he snapped.

"I'm hidin' out like you said," I snapped back.

"You alone?"

"No, are you?"

He looked down at the floor and shook his head. When he raised his eyes again there was a smirk on his face. "Get down here. I need to tell you somethin'."

Jimmy took my arm and led me into the front sitting-room parlor. He noticed the empty drinks glasses. "You and the lady havin' a cocktail?"

"Save the sarcasm. The lady was having one . . . with Manny Troy. That's why I was upstairs. She came up when he left and found me there about ten minutes ago." I gave him a hard stare. "That's all there was to it." It was a lie, of course, and Jimmy probably knew it as well as I did.

"All right. All right." Jimmy waved away my phony complaint and went to the drinks cabinet. "You think the lady'd mind buying us one? I know I need it, and you will once you hear what's up."

He poured us each a healthy shot of bourbon, handed me mine, then gulped his down in a single swallow. I put mine on a small side table without tasting it. Drinking on the job was the bane of most cops and something I didn't want to get started on. The thought rushed at me, made me want to laugh at myself. Climbing in bed with someone I was playing bodyguard to was something else, I supposed—or with somebody who my partner considered a potential murder suspect. I let out a long breath, picked up the drink and poured it down in two swallows.

"So what happened?" I asked.

"One of the commissioner's lackeys nailed my ass. A plainclothes captain. I never even saw the bastard coming. Hauled me straight up to the PC's office, where I got reamed so hard my rosy red Irish asshole almost lost its virginity." Jimmy shook his head and poured himself another. "The short of it is we charge Grosso today, or else."

"Or else what?"

Jimmy smirked at me. "There's some potato farms out in the far reaches of Queens need to be patrolled. You get the message?"

"So we charge Grosso and keep our detective shields?"

"He's gonna get charged anyway, boyo. You can write that one down in your book. The only question is where *we* work after he's booked, arraigned, convicted and sent up to Sing Sing. As far as all that goes, I could give a shit. Louie Grosso ain't exactly the kind of guy I'm gonna sit down and spill some tears over."

"Jesus."

Jimmy looked away, not quite able to meet my eyes. "Yeah," he said, his voice filled with disgust.

"There's no way out of it?"

"Not unless you came up with somethin' with Lilly Straus. But I don't suppose you did, because the commissioner made it *very* clear that I was to tell you to stop harassin' witnesses. He said he'd received a personal complaint."

"Not from her, he didn't. But she did make a call, and when she finished she told me the commissioner would be looking for me when I got back to the precinct. That's why I snuck in here and hid out."

Jimmy raised his hands as if to say, *so there it is*.

"No." I shook my head as vigorously as I could. "It wasn't the commissioner she called. It was a Butterfield Six exchange. I didn't see the rest of the number, but I saw that much. And that's not the exchange for headquarters."

Jimmy digested that. "No, it's not." He went to a table in the hall and came back with a telephone book. He started flipping through it. "It's not the meat cutters union, or the slaughterhouse, so it wasn't Owney Ryan," he said.

"What about where he lives?"

Jimmy shook his head. "He lives way uptown in Morningside Heights. That's a different exchange." He flipped some more, then stopped, jabbing his finger at the page.

I looked down and read where he was pointing. Democratic party headquarters, BUtterfield-6-7070. "Manny Troy," I said.

"There aren't many people the commissioner would snap to for, but he's sure as hell one of them."

"So what do we do now?"

Jimmy laughed, but it had a sour, angry tone to it. "We go do what we're told, like the good little detectives we are."

* * *

The assistant DA assigned to the Reed murder met us at the precinct for a final interview with Louie Grosso. One of the senior men on the DA's staff, Daniel Cox, had a reputation as a straight shooter. He was a tall, slightly overweight man, with thinning gray hair, and he looked every inch the successful attorney right down to a three-piece suit with a gold watch chain looped across the vest. He also looked like a man who'd seen enough political bullshit to recognize a setup when it stared him in the face. So Jimmy and I were just a little surprised by his enthusiasm. Cox, for reasons lost on both of us, actually seemed excited about charging Louie Grosso with Judge Reed's murder, so much so I thought he might jump up and dance around the room.

"I love it when you guys hand me a ground ball like this one." He spoke to us through a wide grin. "We've got this sonofabitch so cold they'll be dusting off the electric chair before the case even goes to the jury."

We had settled into chairs in the foul-smelling interrogation room as we waited for Louie to be brought in from a holding cell, and I just sat there staring at Cox, not sure I'd heard him right.

"You think it'll be *that* easy?" I finally asked.

"You'll never find an easier murder case," Cox replied.

"How so?" I could hear the skepticism in my words.

Cox looked at me, blinking several times as if he didn't understand what I meant. Then he leaned back in his chair, looped his thumbs into his vest and gave out with a laugh. "Son, I know you're new to homicide, but when you have a witness who sees the suspect leaving the murder scene just a scant few minutes before the body is found, and that suspect is a hood like Louie Grosso, who the victim has threatened with arrest, well then my boy, you've got yourself one *helluva* case."

"A witness . . ." An image of Willie Riley rushed to mind. He was just as he'd been when Jimmy and I had last seen him, seated in a booth at the Aces and Eights, a toothpick stuck in the corner of his narrow, pinched, double-dealing mouth. But before I could tell Cox what a two-bit four-flusher he had for a witness, two uniforms ushered a handcuffed Louie Grosso into the room.

Cox eased back in his chair and almost bristled with pleasure as he prepared to brace him. For Louie's part he just glared
at us; then dropped into a chair sullen and resigned. I could almost feel what was going through his mind. The man knew he
was being framed, and he believed that we were all a part of the
fix. To Louie that meant there was a score to settle, and to do it
right he needed to tear us apart, one after the other. He also realized he couldn't do us sufficient damage with his hands cuffed
behind his back, so he had decided to sit there, take whatever
we dished out and bide his time.

"I'm here to talk to you about Judge Reed," Cox began.

Louie glared at him. "There ain't nothin' to talk about. I never
even met the lousy thief."

"Watch your mouth," Cox snapped. "You're talking about a
man who was a respected jurist."

Louie threw back his head and laughed. It was a cold
sound, lacking any pleasure, and when it stopped he stared at
Cox with equally cold eyes. "Maybe you respected him . . ." He
let out a derisive grunt. "And maybe you're just as much of a
crook as he was."

Cox leveled a finger toward Grosso's nose. "You lowlife—"
He stopped in midsentence and jerked his finger back as Grosso
lunged toward it with snapping jaws. Now Grosso leaned back
and laughed—with real pleasure this time.

Cox seemed a bit ruffled by the bluff. His neck turned pink
above the white collar of his shirt, and the color spread gradually upward into his cheeks. It was like watching his anger
grow. Then he seemed to get hold of himself and a small smile
came to his lips. He leaned forward, defying Grosso to try
again, and spoke in a near whisper. "When I'm standing there in
court, questioning the witness who saw you leave the judge's
study just minutes before his body was found, I'm going to turn
around and look at you, Grosso. And when I do, in my mind, I'll
be seeing you just the way you'll be when they strap you in the
electric chair up at Sing Sing."

Grosso gave him another derisive grunt. "Who you got as a
witness, Counselor? Another piece of shit that Owney Ryan
handed you?"

Cox leaned back and again looped his thumbs into his vest. It seemed a favorite pose whenever he wanted to assert his authority or expertise. He steadied his gaze on Grosso. "I think we can do a bit better than that, Louie. I think the jury will like our witness quite a lot. Of course they always do seem to favor widows. And when they're pretty *young* widows they seem to like them even more. And Mrs. Reed, I think you'll agree, is quite a fine specimen of womanhood." Cox released his vest and began rubbing his hands together like a hungry man seated before an unexpected feast. "And then, of course, she'll be just a little bit frightened as she sits up there in the witness box. But the jury will understand that, too, and they'll sympathize even more, because they'll see that the very man she saw leaving her husband's study just minutes before she found his blood-soaked body is sitting only a few feet away from her." Cox's voice had slowly risen as he spoke, ending in a crescendo that seemed to shake the walls.

Jimmy and I sat stunned. Then we turned almost simultaneously and stared at each other. When I looked back across the table I saw that Grosso was shaking with rage. Still shocked by what I had heard, I sat watching his fury grow. It was like witnessing a volcano as it prepared to erupt; there was even a low rumbling sound in warning. Then Grosso roared out at us, "That's a fucking lie!" as he exploded from his chair and with one foot kicked out at the table that separated us.

The table and chairs were bolted to the floor to keep them from being used as weapons, but Grosso's kick came with such force that the two legs on his side snapped free and sent the table tilting toward the three of us.

Cox immediately jumped back, as Jimmy and I moved forward around the table. When I made my final move toward him, Grosso lowered his head and rammed it toward my chin. Seeing the butt coming I moved aside just enough so the blow caught me on the shoulder, but it was delivered with such force it still sent me spinning off to one side.

By that time Jimmy had his blackjack out and laid it upside Grosso's head in almost the exact spot where mine had connected a few days earlier. Jimmy must have hit him harder than I had—either that or Grosso's head was softened up from the previous blow, because he dropped like a stone and didn't so much as twitch.

Cox, his safety now guaranteed, stepped forward and glared down at Grosso's massive body. "Is he all right?" he asked.

"He'll live," Jimmy said.

"Then book the sonofabitch. First-degree murder. There'll be no deals, no pleas on this one." Without another word he strode across the room and out the door.

Jimmy looked down at Grosso again; then he slowly raised his eyes to meet mine. "Did we miss somethin' with Mrs. Reed? Because for the life of me I can't remember her ever telling us she saw Louie Grosso in her house." He paused, shaking his head. "Not that night, or any other."

"Must have slipped her mind," I said.

"Yeah, well, while I'm booking Grosso here, why don't you go and ask her about that."

Cyn was in the front sitting room when I arrived at the house. It had begun to rain and dark clouds had turned the afternoon to twilight. She was standing at the window when I entered, her back to me, her eyes fixed on the rain as it began to fall more heavily now.

"Hello, Jake. I thought you'd be back."

"Yeah, I bet you did." I walked toward her, but she didn't turn around. I stopped a foot away and continued talking to her back. "Jimmy and I just got a bit of a surprise. We just sat in an interrogation room and listened to a DA tell Louie Grosso that you saw him leave your husband's study on the night of the murder. We got to wondering why you never told us."

A long minute of silence dragged by before Cyn finally spoke. "I was afraid."

"Afraid to tell us?"

"Yes."

"Why?"

"I was afraid Louie Grosso would find out that I saw him and that you wouldn't be able to protect me from him."

I lowered my head and started to laugh. "Who thought that one up? Manny Troy?" The question was met with silence. I tried again. "I suppose you know that one bit of testimony will guarantee he gets the chair."

"Yes, I know."

"And that doesn't bother you? That your testimony will get him fried?" I waited and got nothing in reply. "I've never actually seen it, myself, but they tell me when they throw the switch the first time, the juice keeps running for about two minutes, and after the first minute the eyes just start to cook from the heat. They just bubble up and turn to jelly, they say, and then they run right down the cheeks. Of course they have a hood over the person's head so nobody has to see it."

Cyn's shoulders heaved ever so slightly and I realized that she was crying. But I didn't care. The whole thing made me sick to my stomach and I wanted her to have to face it. She said something, but I wasn't able to hear her.

"I missed that. You'll have to speak up."

"I said he isn't a nice man. He's killed other people."

"Yeah, that's true." I took her arm and turned her toward me. "But he didn't kill your husband, did he?"

She just stared at me, not answering, not doing much of anything. Her eyes had filled with tears but I didn't think they were for Louie Grosso, or even for what she was doing, and right at that moment I didn't like Cynthia Reed very much.

"I told you earlier today that I was leaving New York, and I asked if you'd come with me. You never had a chance to answer."

I stared at her, my anger building. "We'd be a pair, wouldn't we? Where would we go? San Francisco, maybe. It's lovely out there. I ended up in a military hospital there after Pearl. Always thought I might like to go back. Yeah, it would be nice. A nice easy life for two people who put Louie Grosso in the electric chair."

Tears began to roll down Cyn's cheeks, but there was no sorrow there. Her face filled with anger. She wasn't the sophisticated young widow anymore—maybe she never had been except in my mind. The person who stood before me now was the girl from upstate New York, the kid from the sticks all dressed up like somebody else. The glamorous woman, the role she had carved out for herself, and now with the judge's money in her pockets, the role she would continue to play out for the rest of her days, just didn't exist anymore. And I didn't think it ever would again. Not for me. For me all that had disappeared. For me she was just Oliver Marks's sister.

Cyn's face twisted into something I didn't recognize and she pulled her arm from my grasp. "Why don't you change it?" she snapped. "Why don't you just stand up in court and tell them that Louie Grosso is an innocent man? You could do that, you know. Of course you won't be a detective any more after you do it. You might not even be a cop. But you could do it, couldn't you? You could do it and then you'd be so much better than I am." She paused, staring at me with angry eyes—eyes that were filled with a contempt that I knew I deserved. Then she threw out her final line like a slap in the face. "But you won't do that, Jake, will you—you won't do it because it might mess up your *nice . . . little . . . life.*"

I turned and left without another word, the last thing to fill my mind the hard angry smile on Cyn's face.

Three days later, the day of Louie Grosso's arraignment, I awoke in my own bed. It was the third consecutive day I had done so, all need of guarding Cynthia Reed having evaporated with Grosso's arrest. I had not seen or spoken to Cyn since our final bitter encounter, although the angry smile I had last seen on her face still lived just behind my eyes.

Mary was delighted, and she made a point of making me lavish breakfasts each morning, even though I was far from pleasant company. I hadn't told her about Grosso, and when she read about him in the papers and asked, I dismissed the subject quickly and irritably. But if Mary noticed my anger, she kept it to herself. She was a bundle of energy throughout that time, constantly cleaning every crevice and corner of our home, sorting through old clothes, even taking down dishes we only used on holidays and special occasions and washing every one. Each time she embarked on a new project I offered to help, but she dismissed the need, claiming she was just keeping busy. If I worked half as hard I'd be a captain within the month.

I arrived at New York County Criminal Court at nine that steamy August morning and found that I'd walked into a circus with an overflow crowd that spilled out into Foley Square. The proceedings had been moved to the largest courtroom, but it still couldn't accommodate all the media who wanted a piece of the action, or all the judge's political cronies who wanted to see how the last act of his life played out.

Jimmy and I were seated at the prosecution table with Daniel Cox, who seemed more than a bit pleased with himself. Neither Jimmy nor I were doing much smiling, nor had we for the past few days. Mostly we had just avoided the subject of Louie Grosso. We had done the paperwork required, but other than that we had just kept our mouths shut and found other work to do. There was never a lack of bodies for a New York homicide detective.

Cynthia Reed was seated in the first row, directly behind us. She was dressed in black, her face partially hidden by a black lace veil. She looked as she always did, stunningly beautiful. Manny Troy sat at her side. He looked as he always did, too— hard and arrogant, a man used to getting his way . . . always. Today they weren't smiling either, and Cyn actually looked as though she very much wanted to be somewhere else. But she was there—at Troy's insistence, I suspected—the epitome of the sorrowful young widow, alone and frightened, yet prepared to confront her husband's killer. At least that was how I imagined Troy feeding it to the press.

Louie Grosso was the only player missing from our little drama. He was still in the Tombs—the city prison that was attached to the courthouse—where he was undoubtedly being given a final shakedown to make sure his appearance before the judge was nice and safe and free of weapons. Lawyers and judges liked the assurance of safety, I had learned. But I couldn't blame them. Briefcases and gavels didn't do too well against knives and guns, even though those same briefcases and gavels could do a world of killing all by themselves.

I was still daydreaming my private little thoughts when the bailiff began his "oyez," and I looked up to see Judge Mario Cicone make his way to the bench. He was a short, portly man with longish black hair that lacked even a touch of gray, though the judge was well into his fifties, and a large nose riddled with the burst capillaries of a drinker.

You could hide the gray hair, but not the red veins, I thought uncharitably. But then this was not going to be a very charitable day. At least it wouldn't be for Louie Grosso.

Cox had told us earlier that the *Reed matter* would be the first business taken up by the court. *It's been a zoo,* he had explained. *The afternoon papers wanted it done early so it made their first editions and the morning rags wanted us to hold off till the end of the day so the afternoon papers were fucked. We gave the p-yems what they wanted, and later, when the arraignment's over, we'll offer a special interview to the a-yems so they go away happy.*

I hadn't paid much attention to his chatter then, but now it had started me thinking. I leaned in and asked quietly, "Who are the morning papers going to interview?"

Cox inclined his head, indicating the row of seats behind us, and shielded his mouth with his hand. "They get the beautiful young widow. It was Troy's idea. When it comes to manipulating the press the man is pure genius."

A low rumble of hushed voices drew my attention to the spectators seated behind me, and I followed their collective gaze to a side door of the courtroom. There, Louie Grosso stood in the doorway like an immovable block of granite, as a trailing guard tried to shoulder him into the room. Slowly, impervious to the guard's efforts, Grosso's eyes roamed the crowded courtroom until they finally settled on the person he was searching out. Then his entire face filled with a depth of hatred I had only rarely seen. I followed his eyes to the source of that intense enmity and found myself looking at the lovely, veiled countenance of Cynthia Reed, distraught widow and primary accuser, and I wondered just how much I, too, might hate her if I found myself in Louie Grosso's place.

Grosso's glare lasted less than a minute before the first guard was joined by a second and together they shoved him through the door and into the courtroom. He barely seemed to notice and continued to move at his own pace, slowly, almost defiantly. He was dressed in a gray prison uniform that barely contained his massive shoulders, chest and arms, making him appear even more brutish than I knew him to be. His greasy black hair was uncombed and he hadn't bothered to shave, leaving a dark shadow along cheeks and jaw and neck. I supposed he saw no point in striving for a good impression, which was far from surprising. Had he merely read the newspapers over the past three days he would have found himself and his history described in the most contemptuous of terms. When added to the frame that had been so carefully built around him, even he would see that any such effort would be nothing short of foolish.

When he reached the defense table his court-appointed lawyer stood and placed a comforting hand on his arm, which Grosso belligerently shrugged away. Then his eyes fell on the prosecution table, and he took time to look at Cox and Jimmy and me, letting each of us know exactly what he would do given half a chance. And who could blame him? I thought. His massive hands were closed into fists, and I was grateful to see them held together with sturdy steel cuffs.

It hit me at once and I leaned in to Cox with a whispered warning. "They should cuff his hands in back," I hissed.

Just as I spoke one of the guards took Grosso's arm to guide him into his seat, and I watched helplessly as Louie leaned slightly forward, then mustering all the force he could, drove an elbow into the man's sternum, doubling him in half.

Before my hand reached the pistol at my waist Louie had the guard's weapon in his own hand, and with speed that belied his size he leaped forward, grabbed Cyn and pulled her across the spectator railing, spun her roughly and looped his arms around her body to bring her up against him like a shield.

Now, with the guard's pistol pressed against her temple, he stared down at Jimmy and me, sneering at the suddenly ineffectual weapons in our own hands.

"You wanna see the lady's brains on the other side of the room?"

There was a sense of glee in Grosso's voice that made his threat even more chilling. Slowly, Jimmy and I laid our pistols on the table, and Grosso turned and forced the other guard to do the same. Then he motioned to the cuffs, keeping the pistol hard against Cyn's head as they were unfastened.

Cox, who was between Grosso and us, had remained in his chair, apparently unable to move, and I could see the tremors in his arms and could actually hear his wrists rapping against the tabletop. Grosso obviously heard it, too. Free of the handcuffs, he looked down at Cox and grinned, and before either Jimmy or I could react, he redirected his weapon to Cox's head and pulled back the hammer.

The three distinct clicks the hammer made as it was drawn back sounded like three separate pistol shots in themselves, and they were followed almost immediately by a strong smell of urine coming from beneath the prosecution table. Grosso looked down at the spreading pool surrounding Cox's shoes and let out a loud, coarse laugh. Then he snapped the pistol back to Cyn's cheek and leaned his mouth against her ear.

"You gonna piss your pants, too, honey?" he hissed.

Cyn's eyes met mine, begging me to do something, anything.

I took a tentative step around the table. "Louie. Let's talk about this before it goes too far."

Grosso looked at me, eyes incredulous, and again he laughed. "You gotta be jokin'. Either that, or you're a bigger asshole than I think you are. You take one more fuckin' step and I'll put your brains on the floor, then hers right next to them. Got it?"

I raised both hands in surrender. I felt remarkably calm; all my fears directed to Cyn, not myself. "Louie, I'll do whatever you say. But use me as a hostage instead of her." He started to laugh, but I hurried on. "It makes sense, Louie. Think about what I'm saying. It would make things safer for you, because no cop is gonna fire his weapon if there's even the slightest chance he'll hit another cop. They just won't do it. It's a code we have. No matter what happens, never let a brother cop down, never put him in danger if there's a way to avoid it. So if you've got a cop under the gun, Louie, you've got a better chance of staying alive yourself. Think about it."

A contemptuous smile crossed Grosso's lips. "That's nice of you, you fuckin' punk." He let out a grunt. "You wanna keep me alive and safe, do you? What for? So you can watch them strap me in to the fuckin' chair and fry me, fry my fuckin' brains till they drip outta my ears?" Another grunt. "Fuck you. All of you." He pulled Cyn tighter against his chest. "And you too, bitch." He leaned in close to her ear again. "Why don't you tell everybody how you saw me kill your thief of a husband? Why don't you tell everybody how you saw me come outta the room where they found his body? Tell everybody your fuckin' story, you lyin' little cunt."

I could see Grosso's rage building. There was a slight tremor in his hand, making the gun barrel quiver against Cyn's cheek.

Her eyes were terrified now, and she stared only at me. It was as though I were the only other person in the room, the only one who could save her from the brute who was ready to snuff out her life. Her lips moved silently, mouthing my name . . . *Jake*.

Grosso began backing toward the door that led to Judge Cicone's chambers. I started slowly toward him, my hands still raised.

"Don't, Jake," Jimmy hissed.

"You should listen to your partner, punk." Grosso leveled the pistol at my head.

"Oh, Jake, please." It was Cyn, finding her voice. But I couldn't tell if hers was a plea to move forward and save her, or like Jimmy's, to stay out of harm's way.

Grosso turned his head so he could look at one side of Cyn's face. Then he looked up at me. "We got somethin' goin' on here, do we?" There was a leer in his voice. "I think maybe you should come with me, cop. I think that might be real nice."

"That's fine, Louie. We'll all go into the judge's chambers. Then you let her go, and I'll stay with you. All right?"

Louie jerked his chin upward, indicating I should follow. "You come along, cop. You put your hands behind your head and you follow old Louie and the little lady here."

"Jake. Don't follow him, Jake. He won't let her go no matter what you do."

Jimmy's voice rang in my ears, and somewhere deep in my brain I knew he was right. But the words were far away and fading fast. All I could see were Cyn's frightened eyes and the barrel of the pistol pressed back into her cheek. She wasn't speaking now, but I could still hear her saying my name . . . *Jake* . . . and I knew if I allowed Grosso to harm her I would hear her calling my name every morning when I awoke, and every night as I waited for sleep to come.

"I'm coming, Louie." I placed my hands behind my head and started toward them.

Grosso made me enter Judge Cicone's chambers first just to make certain no cops had slipped inside and set an ambush. He locked the door to the courtroom and a second one to an adjoining hall and then followed me while I checked the judge's private bathroom. When he was sure the chambers were secure he made me spread them against a wall and gave me a quick frisk to be sure I wasn't carrying another weapon.

"You're a thorough guy, Louie; you're playing it real smart." I struggled to keep my voice calm. "Let's play it even smarter now and let the lady go."

At the mention of Cyn, Grosso looked around and discovered that she had moved to the farthest part of the room, as far away from both of us as she could get. "Get your ass over here," he snarled.

"Listen, Louie, let's play it smart, let's—" I never had a chance to finish the sentence. Louie swung the guard's pistol and brought it down on my head, and all I saw was a flash of light before everything faded to midnight.

I have no idea how long I was out. I remember coming to and hearing a voice pleading for someone or something to stop. Everything else was a big blur. I tried to push myself up, but the room began to spin and seemed to slip out from under me, sending me back to the thick carpet that covered the floor. A second attempt worked better, and I made it to my knees. But that was as far as I got. Suddenly my stomach threatened to toss everything I had eaten for the past year, so I stayed on all fours taking deep breaths that I hoped would settle me down and keep everything inside.

The voice I'd been hearing was clearer now. "Please, don't. Don't do this to me. Please, please." Now I recognized it—Cyn's voice, pleading, almost begging.

My eyes began to clear and I saw her forced down on top of the judge's desk, Grosso beside her, partially on top as he ran his hand up under her black dress. Her body was twisting, legs flailing, as she tried to avoid his hand.

"Grosso." I growled out his name, or attempted to. It came out more as a croak in my ears. I staggered to my feet.

He pushed himself off her and spun to face me, his pistol leveled at my face. Cyn jumped up almost immediately and started to move away, but Grosso's free hand snaked out and snared her wrist and he yanked her back against him. "You didn't sleep long enough for me and the lady to have any fun. Maybe I should put you to sleep for good."

"No, please don't. Please don't kill him. I'll do whatever you want. Anything."

The words shocked us both, and both our eyes went to Cyn. Tears streamed down her cheeks and she was trembling so badly it seemed to start at her shoulders and move down the entire length of her body. She looked at Grosso and her eyes were more beseeching than any I'd ever seen. "Don't kill him." She repeated the plea through a quivering jaw. "Please don't kill him."

A lewd grin filled Grosso's face. "So I was right. You two do have a thing going." He began to laugh. Then he jabbed the pistol in my direction. "You've been fuckin' her all this time, haven't you? Investigatin' the judge's murder and fuckin' his old lady on the side." He jerked his head toward the courtroom door. "All those newspaper clowns in there, I bet they'd treat old Louie a lot better if he tipped them off to that little number." He laughed again, truly enjoying himself.

He still held Cyn by the wrist and he pushed her out to arm's length now and looked her over like some nag up for sale in some breeder's ring. He turned slowly back to me and smiled. "She good under the sheets?" He looked back at her, leering. "Oh, I bet she is." He extended the pistol toward her, and lightly ran the tip of the barrel against her lips. "I bet you use that mouth real good, too, don't you?"

"Louie!" I shouted his name as loud as I could, trying to distract him.

His head snapped around. "Get on your knees," he snapped.

"Goddamn you, Louie . . ."

"Get on your knees or I'll blow her fuckin' head off right now." His voice was so loud, so forceful, it seemed to shake the walls of the room.

There was no question in my mind he would do what he threatened. The man was suddenly crazed with rage, and I knew I was walking a line with him, one I could fall off any second. I dropped to my knees.

"Now crawl over here until you're right in front of me."

I did as he said, stopping just a foot away from his feet.

"Now open your mouth," he ordered.

Again, I did as I was told.

Grosso removed the gun from Cyn's lips and placed the barrel in my mouth.

"Now close your mouth." My obedience pleased him and he was almost giggling as he spoke the words.

The gun barrel was cold and it gave off a bitter taste of cleaning solvent and gun oil. To me it tasted like death, and as I looked along the barrel and past the cylinder I could see Grosso's hairy index finger twitching lightly against the trigger. Sweat formed along my forehead and began to drip down past my eyes. Louie saw it and laughed again.

He turned to Cyn and I could no longer see his face, but his voice was low and breathy and held an undertone of expectation.

"You gonna do what I tell you, now? Or am I gonna blow your boyfriend's head off?"

"I'll do what you want."

Grosso looked back at me. "You move one inch, punk, and this is what's gonna happen. I'm gonna pull the trigger of this gun and send your brains flyin' across the room. Then I'm gonna stick this gun in the bitch's mouth and I'm gonna blow *her* fuckin' head off. You understand me?"

I nodded as best I could.

"One inch," Grosso warned again. "That's all it's gonna take and you're both headed for the boneyard."

That said, Grosso turned again to Cyn. "Now *you* get on your knees."

My body began to shake with rage as I watched Grosso unbutton his trousers and remove his penis. It was enormous, already half engorged, and he reached out and grabbed Cyn by her hair and forced her to him.

We were kneeling side by side, Cyn slightly in front of me, and her head, blessedly, blocked me from having a clear view. But there were still the sounds and the movement of her head. After a short time Grosso's breathing began to come in short, urgent gasps. Then small groans came from him. I closed my eyes, wishing I could close my ears as well. I felt helpless, emasculated, and I wanted nothing more than to jump up and grab Louie Grosso by the throat and choke the life out of him. But it would be a death sentence, first for me and then for Cyn. There was no question Louie Grosso, mad as he was, would do exactly what he had threatened to do.

I don't know when I first noticed it; I was trying so hard to notice nothing at all. It just seemed to happen. Louie's groans increased, both in rapidity and intensity, and as they did the barrel of the revolver began to move about in my mouth. But not just move. It seemed to move loosely, as though it was no longer held by a firm hand. Slowly I began to ease my head back, testing at first to see if he'd notice, then more, inching the barrel past my lips, moving it out and away, my body tensing, preparing to strike at the last possible moment before Louie realized what was happening.

Louie let out a long groan as the barrel flopped free, now so loose in his hand it almost fell to the floor. I could feel his whole body stiffened as he realized somewhere in his besotted mind what was happening, and my hand shot out, grabbing his wrist and driving it up and away. The pistol exploded as I pushed myself up, and I felt Grosso's body stiffen as he let out a terrifying scream. I slammed the top of my head into his jaw once, twice. I reared back to do it again and saw that Grosso was ignoring my attack. Instead his free hand was twisted in Cyn's hair as he tried to pull her from him, tried to free his penis from the teeth that had sunk into it and continued to bite down, producing his terrified screams.

I reared back and drove my right fist into his face, my left still clamped on his wrist, stopping him from bringing the pistol to bear on either of us. Then out of the corner of my eye I saw the bathroom door open and Jimmy swing into the room, his own pistol out in front in a two-handed shooter's grasp.

I heard his voice shout, "Hit the floor," and without thinking I released Grosso's wrist and threw myself to the side, grabbing Cyn as I fell, shouting at her to get down, pulling her with me.

Jimmy's .38 barked once, then a second and third time, and out of the corner of my eye I saw Grosso's body fly past and heard it hit the floor like an oversized side of beef.

Jimmy was standing over Grosso before I even got to my knees, and he kicked his pistol across the room, then bent and felt the pulse in his neck. "He's still alive. But he won't be fightin' anymore today." I watched him shake his head. "Hell, he might even survive this, fookin' ox that he is." He stepped back and his eyes roamed Grosso's body, looking for any sign of another weapon. They stopped when they reached his middle. "Jaysus Christ," he hissed. "She almost bit the fookin' thing off."

I put my arm around Cyn's shoulder and drew her to me. She was shaking so hard her head banged lightly against my jaw.

"I wish I had," she whispered, the words spoken so softly I could barely hear her. Then she seemed to sense what had happened and she bent over and began to spit on the carpet as if cleaning her mouth of all the filth, the humiliation. Suddenly her stomach began to heave and I eased her to her feet and led her to the bathroom.

When we came out I stared across the room at Jimmy. "You came along the ledge and through the window?" There was a bit of incredulity in my words.

"And I almost pulled a Cox and wet my drawers doin' it."

I nodded, almost laughed, but found I couldn't. "Thanks," I said.

"Not a problem."

"I'm going to take Mrs. Reed home," I said.

He gave me a long look. "There's reports need to be filed, you know. Statements that will have to be taken."

"Tomorrow," I said. "If the brass bitches, tell Manny Troy to throw his weight around. He's good at it, and it's the least he can do."

Jimmy grinned at me. "I'll tell him you said so."

"Do that," I said.

We were driven to Cyn's house in a patrol car, with the two uniforms instructed to remain outside and keep the press and anyone else away. Though he lacked the formal authority, Manny Troy had issued orders that no one, not even the commissioner himself, was to be allowed inside. There was little question the order would be obeyed.

When the door closed behind us Cyn took the phone off the hook and turned to face me. She was pale, nearly ashen, and her hands and arms were still trembling badly. "I want you to stay with me tonight." Again, her voice was so soft I could barely make out the words.

"I want to stay," I said. "I want to stay tonight and tomorrow and the next day. You're going to have to tell me to go away."

She looked at me and tears filled her eyes. I moved forward and took her in my arms and held her for a long time. It was all I wanted, all either of us could handle, just to hold each other. Then, without a word spoken between us, I picked her up and carried her up the stairs.

It was nine o'clock the next morning before Jimmy Finn was able to get into the house. He grabbed me as I came down the stairs and pulled me into the small sitting room.

"I tried to get to you last night, but the phones were down and the uniforms on the door wouldn't let Christ himself inside."

"What's wrong?" I asked.

"I tried, dammit. I really tried."

"What, for chrissake?"

"Mary had the baby about eight o'clock last night."

The hospital was only a few blocks from our home in Park Slope, and the patrol car that drove me there used its lights and siren to cut through the morning traffic, and I made it there in less than half an hour.

It was a beautiful, glorious morning, a cloudless sky with a bright sun, yet unseasonably cool, very much like days Mary and I had shared in San Francisco while I recuperated from my war wounds. Thoughts of those times had come rushing back to me as the patrol car fought its way through the city's streets, and it made me feel schizophrenic, leaving Cyn after promising to stay, rushing to Mary, my mind filled with all the love she had given me, all the hopes and concerns we had shared for all these years—and now a child that was *ours* together. There was guilt, too, of course, but it was overwhelmed by my confused state of mind. Yet I never thought to prepare excuses for my failure to be with her at that most important time; reasons why I had missed the birth of my first child—a girl, Jimmy had said, healthy and happy and eight pounds even.

I bought flowers in the hospital gift shop and a small, white teddy bear with a pink bow, and both occupied my hands when I entered Mary's room. Her eyes were closed and I moved to the side of her bed, bent and kissed her lightly on the lips. Her eyes opened and she stared at me with unconcealed anger, and something else, something I had never seen there before—the look of someone betrayed.

"You came." She glanced contemptuously at the flowers and the stuffed bear. "I wondered if you would."

"Why would you wonder that?" The words almost choked me as I spoke them.

"I can read is why. Do you think I'm so much a fool I can't even do that?"

"What do you mean?"

She picked up the newspaper that was beside her on the bed and swung it at me, and I dropped the bear catching it. It had been lying face down so I had not noticed what now stared back at me, a photo filling the front page of the *Daily News*, a photo of Cyn being led from the courthouse by a young New York City detective, his arm around her protectively, her eyes still filled with fear, her head pressed against his shoulder. She looked astonishingly beautiful and vulnerable, and in desperate need of comfort. Jimmy was behind us in the photo, and we were all moving through the crush of press people, trying to reach a patrol car parked in front of the court. The kicker on the photo read: *Hero Detective and the Woman He Saved*. There was a small photo, a police mug shot of Louie Grosso, set inside the other, and it made him appear every bit as brutish as he was in life. I was afraid to read the story, afraid of what it would say, and I lowered the paper and stared down at Mary's angry eyes.

"I'm sorry." It was all I could think to say.

"And what are you sorry about, Jake? Are you sorry you couldn't be bothered to be here when your beautiful daughter was born? Are you sorry you weren't with your wife for the seven hours of labor? Or maybe you're sorry you were *too busy* with another woman while all that was going on? Or that you couldn't tear yourself away when even your partner was sent out to find you?"

I started to speak but Mary shook her head violently, stopping me. "Oh, they told me at the precinct how they were trying to get to you, but that you were at the *Reed house*, protecting that *poor, poor* woman, and how *nobody* was allowed inside at *her* request." She glared at me. "And what about *my* request,

Jake? What about *my* need to have my husband here while I was delivering *our* child?"

"I'm sorry, Mary?"

"But *what* is it you're sorry about, goddammit?" Her words were shouted, demanding a final answer.

"I'm sorry about all of it, Mary."

"So you deny *none* of it? You have excuses for *none* of it?"

I lowered my eyes, and there at my feet found the small, white bear looking back at me. "I can't. I wish I could."

Mary stared at me for more than a minute without speaking. Then she closed her eyes and drew a deep breath. "Get out of my sight. Go see your child. See your daughter, Jake. Hold her and let her know there's a father in her life. Don't let her spend her first day of being without even that." She drew a long breath. "Let her be older before she finds out what a sonofabitch you truly are."

Mary's eyes had remained closed when she spoke and they were still closed as I picked up the bear and started for the door, and I knew then that she would never look at me again without a feeling of contempt in her heart. Her final words stopped me before I reached the door.

"Her name's Kate, in case you care."

I turned to look at her, perhaps even to object, but her eyes were still closed, shutting me out.

I held my child as long as the nurse allowed; then waited for the next time so I could do so again. It was a strange feeling, as much frightening as it was joyously uplifting. So small she was, so soft, so very much her mother's daughter in the shape of her eyes and nose and mouth. Her hair coloring was mine, and her ears, I thought, and I felt an undeserved swelling of pride in the fact that she looked like me at all.

I went back to see Mary while I awaited turns with Kate. The first time she was asleep, or pretending to be, and I sat next to her for a while before I left to hold my child again. The next time I returned to her room her sister, Rita, was there, and together they glared at me as though I were some unclean thing that had somehow slipped by the nurses.

It felt strange, because Rita had always been fond of me. She was older than Mary by ten years, and had always been protective of her little sister, a strong, solid, maternal woman with three kids of her own, who had treated the two of us like a fourth and fifth child. Now her contempt compounded her sister's and left me feeling beaten and alone.

Jimmy came early in the afternoon. He brought a stuffed bunny for the baby and some more flowers for Mary. The precinct would send flowers, too, and there would also be some from individual cops in our squad. It was customary, required treatment for a new mother, and before she left the hospital Mary's room would look like a small flower shop. It was what we did, we cops. We surrounded our women with flowers at births and funerals, and then we forgot them, along with our children, and we allowed the things outside our homes to dominate our lives.

Jimmy raised his eyebrows as he left Mary's room. He took me by the arm and led me slowly down the hall. "She's a bit pissed, your wife is. She didn't say anything, and she tried very hard to be pleasant, but you can tell it's there." He hesitated. "You told her, fessed up to it?"

I nodded.

"They say you never should. They say you should lie through your fookin' teeth, because it's what they really want to hear. But I'm a bachelor, so what the hell do I know?"

"She saw the *Daily News*."

"Ah, I was afraid she would, or that some sonofabitch would show it to her."

"It was there on the bed when I got here."

"Damn. Not much chance for a bit of fibbin'. That picture, well, it kind of said it all, didn't it?"

"I don't think I would have lied to her anyway." I looked at Jimmy a bit sheepishly. "I never had . . . not until all this started."

Jimmy looked down at his shoes, shook his head. "Cynthia Reed's gone," he said.

It came out of the blue, and at first I didn't think I'd heard him right. Then my cheeks stung as though I'd been slapped. "What do you mean, gone?"

"Gone. Out-of-town gone is what I mean." I started to object but he took my arm again and began walking me farther down the hall. "I waited for her, like you asked. To tell her you had to leave. She came downstairs about an hour later and I told her about the baby coming, and how you'd gone to the hospital."

"What did she say?"

Jimmy shook his head. "Nothin' really. She just kind of stared past me and nodded that she understood. I started to tell her that you'd be back, but before I could Manny Troy showed up and he spent an hour talking to her. When they finished she went upstairs, and Troy told me she'd be leavin' town for a while, and that I should take off and let her get herself packed."

"Did you see her go?"

"Yeah, I waited outside. Fuck Troy, I figured. I wanted to see what was goin' on. She left about an hour later in his car. She had two suitcases with her. I tailed them. He took her to Grand Central, but I didn't go inside. I didn't want to take a chance he'd spot me. I figured you and me, we're close enough to a pile of shit as it is."

I stood there shaking my head. "I don't understand." I stopped walking and turned to him. "She didn't leave a note, nothing at all."

Jimmy shook his head. "Troy said she'd be back for the trial. That's all."

I shook my head again. "No, that can't be." I turned and looked back down the hall toward Mary's room, then toward the nursery where my daughter slept the sleep of innocence. "That's it. It was all for nothing." I spoke the words to no one in particular; perhaps only to myself.

Jimmy gave my shoulder a squeeze. "You got hooked on a broad, and it wasn't to be. It happens sometimes."

I shook my head. "No, she'll call. I know she will."

(21)

"Did she ever call?" Molly asked.

Jake smiled across the table. "No, she never called. The next time I saw her was at Louie Grosso's trial."

They had finished their garlic steaks and had survived an hour and a half of Sammy's bar mitzvah band and were now down to after-dinner drinks. Jake took a sip of his. "We were all surprised that Grosso survived. I think Jimmy was hoping he'd croak so there wouldn't be a trial; there wouldn't be that trip to Sing Sing and the electric chair."

"That's understandable," Molly said. "He deserved what he got in the judge's chambers. If he'd had the decency to die it would have made it all nice and clean . . . instead of the way it was."

Jake nodded. "Yeah, it would have, but I guess Louie didn't see it that way. Anyway, Cynthia Reed came back for the trial. It was a bit odd, because it was almost a year later, and the trial had been scheduled to start six months after the arraignment. But the DA kept postponing it, saying he had a witness who couldn't appear. It turned out that witness was Cynthia. I think she was also hoping the trial wouldn't take place. Either that Grosso would die or that they'd find some way to convict him without her testimony."

"You can't blame her, considering what she went through at the arraignment." Molly's words were honestly sympathetic.

"That's the other thing that was kind of odd. There was no reluctance when she got there. She was cool and calm when she testified—like water rolling off a duck. She sat up there on the witness stand and stared down at Grosso like she wished they'd take her up to Sing Sing and let her throw the switch herself."

He leaned back in his chair, remembering it all. "It was odd with Grosso, too. When he came into the courtroom he looked at Jimmy with pure hate. The look he gave me was equally murderous. But when Cyn took the witness stand he stared at her and she stared back, and I swear to God it was as though he was reliving what she did to him, because there was real fear in Louie Grosso's eyes."

Molly took a sip of her drink, and then toyed with her glass. She seemed hesitant, thoughtful. When she finally spoke the reason for her hesitancy came out. "Did you ever get a chance to speak to her?" There was a catch in Molly's voice, a fearfulness about what her question might produce. But it was something she very much needed to hear.

Jake looked down and toyed with his own drink, not really wanting to hold Molly's eyes. "Yes, I did." A small, bitter smile played at the corners of his mouth. "I had to. So much of my life had changed because of her." He picked up his glass and took a long sip. "I was still living with Mary, of course, but it was day and night from what it had been. We were together for Kate's sake; that and because Mary, devout Catholic that she was, believed divorce was wrong. But aside from our daughter we pretty much lived separate lives, slept in separate bedrooms, the whole thing." Jake seemed to sense a note of self-pity in his voice and he looked up at Molly and let out a long breath. "Yeah, I know, I'd bought and paid for it myself. There's no way

I can lay the blame off on Cynthia Reed, or Mary, or anyone else, much as I'd like to. I own it. It's all mine."

Now Molly looked down, avoiding Jake's eyes. "You were very young," she said. She was making excuses for him, and they both knew it.

"I was twenty-five. But you're right, that is young, even though you sure as hell don't think so at the time. But I knew what I was doing. I'd gotten myself all caught up in the glamour of the woman. She was like no one I'd ever known before." He gave his head a small, almost imperceptible shake. "Except she wasn't really anything like that at all, if you know what I mean."

Now Molly looked up and smiled. "She was very young, too. A young girl from a small town. It was everything that surrounded her that seemed glamorous. It wasn't Cynthia Reed."

"All that phony café society." Jake laughed. "God, it was so ridiculous and superficial. But it didn't seem at all like that back then. Sitting in dining rooms with movie stars and big-name politicians, even European royalty for chrissake; being *ever* so sophisticated, each and every one of us, and all right there in the lofty presence of gossip columnists, no less; all the celebrity wannabes who'd lick their boots for just one line of ink. Being 'one' of them." He made little quotation marks around the word "one." Then he laughed again. "And I was so taken with it. Christ, when Sherman Billingsley found out I'd been at Pearl Harbor and told me I'd be welcome at the Stork any time I cared to drop by, I nearly floated off the floor. Never mind that it would have taken a week's pay for me to drop by for one night."

"It was a big thing back then," Molly said.

"Only if you took yourself seriously. And in those days I was a young man who was very full of himself."

"They say all young men are. At least until they get their tails kicked a few times." Molly leaned forward. "So what happened when you spoke to Cynthia Reed?"

"Nothing." He looked down and smiled again. "I went up to her after she testified, all hat in hand, but really seething inside, just not wanting her to know it, not wanting to give her the satisfaction of seeing how much she'd hurt me."

"So you'd accepted the fact that you'd been in love with her."

"Oh, yeah. There was no getting away from that. But I knew I'd been in love with Mary, too. Looking back it was completely schizophrenic."

Molly shook her head. "I don't think so. I think maybe you were just in love with what you thought Cynthia Reed was."

"Oh, there was that. But, no, it was more."

I found Cyn standing in the hallway outside the courtroom. She was dressed in a peach-colored dress that went to midcalf, and it made her look long and sleek and willowy . . . and very, very appealing. She had put on some weight since I'd last seen her, but it had gone to all the right places; taken away the last trace of girlishness and made her seem a bit more womanly.

"Hello, Jake. How have you been?"

I couldn't reply at first. All I could do was look at her. Her blond hair was a bit longer than I remembered; her blue eyes like a summer lake, so deep and warm that you could fall in and be lost forever. I just kept looking at her, unable to help myself. Then slowly everything that had happened came floating back, and the anger that had been inside me for the past year began to surge up and I had to push it back down to keep from shouting.

"I've been fine. How have you been?"

She tilted her head slightly to one side. "It's been an interesting year. How is your daughter?"

The question took me by surprise, the fact that she knew the baby had been a girl. Then I realized that Jimmy must have told her. "She's well. Growing bigger every day."

"Does she look like you?"

"A bit, but mostly she looks like her mother."

Cyn smiled and nodded, but whatever caused her to do so she kept to herself. All the talk about my daughter was getting on my nerves, so I decided to put an end to it and just ask her what I needed to know.

"Why'd you leave without a word . . . or a note . . . or even a telephone call?"

She looked at me for almost a minute without speaking, her eyes as sad as I'd ever seen them. "I thought it would be best." She spoke in a very soft voice, and then hurried on before I could interrupt her with another question. "I thought I'd caused enough problems in your life; I didn't want to cause any more. Leaving New York seemed like the best thing for everyone. You. Me. *Everyone."*

The implication that it was also good for my daughter— maybe even Mary—brought my temper up again. I sneered at her. "I suppose it was. Good for everyone, I mean. I read all about your late husband's real estate deal going through. It'll be a big thing, having the United Nations here in New York. Profitable, too, for the people who sold the land. I imagine it took you a bit of time to count up all that money."

Cyn's head moved back slightly as though I'd slapped her. She drew a breath and her eyes hardened momentarily. "I guess we've all done well. I read about your promotion. You and Jimmy, both—the two of you becoming sergeants." Her eyes softened again, almost as though she'd willed it, perhaps even regretted what she'd said. "I was happy for you, Jake. Truly happy."

I glared at her. "Yeah, Manny Troy took care of us all. You got your real estate money. Jimmy and I got our stripes." I stared at her, my eyes as hard as I could make them. "Now it's Louie Grosso's turn."

Cyn stared at me for another long minute. "So we all got what we wanted. Is that what you think, Jake?"

I kept staring at her with hard eyes. "I guess I don't really know, Cyn. Did you get everything you wanted?"

She gave me a very small, very sad smile. "No, Jake. It didn't even come close. But life always seems to work out that way, doesn't it?" She smiled again at the notion. "When you're a kid growing up you don't think it will be that way. You're sure that somehow you'll get everything you want. But it just never happens." That said, she raised her chin, gave me another small, sad smile, turned slowly and walked away.

"And you never saw her again?" Molly asked.

"No, I never saw her or spoke to her, not in thirty years, not once in all that time." Jake paused. Then he drew a long breath. "But I will soon."

Molly raised her eyebrows. "You will?"

Jake nodded. "She's back in New York."

He laid the statement out there and left it. Molly just stared at him. Finally she shook her head. "You are truly a wonder, Jake Downing. And when did you find that out?"

"Just a few days ago. I asked one of my people to run a trace on her. I figured when we finished this investigation I'd have to talk to her one way or another, and I wanted to be sure I still knew where she was."

Molly's eyebrows rose. "Still?" she asked.

Jake gave her a weak smile. "After Grosso's trial, after she left again, I couldn't stand not knowing where she was. So I did some checking and found out she was living in Los Angeles. My man started from there and found out she'd moved to New York about three months ago." Jake played with his drink, buying time. "Years back she married a successful LA lawyer. He died not too long ago. They had a son who just graduated from law school. According to my man, the kid's been hired by a law firm here, and Cyn's bought herself an apartment so she can be close to him."

"But you never contacted her? Not in Los Angeles, or since you found out she was back in New York?"

"No. At first, thirty years ago, when I found out she was in LA, I really thought I would. I even went over in my mind just what I'd say to her when I did. But I just couldn't bring myself to do it, so I kept putting it off, and before I knew it two more years had gone. When I finally decided I'd do it I ran another check on her, and I found out that she'd remarried and that she and her new husband had a kid." He gave her a weak smile. "So I never did."

"Where is she living now?"

"She bought a co-op on Fifth Avenue, up near the Metropolitan Museum."

"Pricey."

Jake inclined his head and smiled. "I guess she put that UN money to work for her. Or maybe her second husband had a bundle of his own."

"You said he died."

"Almost a year ago. According to my man he was quite a bit older than Cyn. She seemed to have a penchant for older men, didn't she?" He gave Molly a wry smile that she found just a touch cynical. "The husband's name was William Morrisey. Quite a bigshot in LA legal circles. The son is named after him."

Molly finished off her brandy. She stared across the table, unable to hide the worry in her eyes. "I guess we better get moving on this investigation. I'll give Barry Hamilton a call in the morning and see how close he is to finishing the forensic work."

"I called him this afternoon," Jake said. "He thinks he'll have it wrapped up in another two or three days."

{ 22 }

It took Barry Hamilton six days to finish the forensic work, but Jake had expected it. He'd never known an FBI scientist who could finish anything in the time specified. Tardiness was something that seemed to be infused in each and every one of them as soon as they got within spitting distance of the Potomac River.

"I like to think of it as *scientific caution*," Hamilton said when Jimmy Finn made the same point at the start of their meeting. They were gathered around the large conference table in Jake's office at One Police Plaza—Jake, Jimmy, Molly and Hamilton, along with a court stenographer, there to record the results of their separate investigations into the thirty-year-old evidence.

Jimmy gave Hamilton a wink and a smile. "Ah, scientific caution. That's what it is." He glanced at Molly as if noting her presence and reminding himself he'd have to watch his language. "Well, I guess if I was workin' on a per diem I'd be a touch cautious, too." He gave out with a little chuckle. "Hell, I'd be so . . . *scientifically cautious* . . . I probably wouldn't get out of bed for the first three days."

Hamilton lowered his glasses to the edge of his large nose and stared over the tops at Finn. "Are you implying something?" He was clearly not amused by the comment.

Jimmy grinned at him. "*Caution.* I'm implying caution."

Molly rapped on the table, drawing everyone's attention before Jimmy's teasing turned into an FBI-versus-cop donny-brook. "Let's get started. If no one objects I'd like to open it up with my report." She glanced around the table and, finding no objections, nodded to the court stenographer, indicating that she could start recording the proceedings.

The stenographer gave the date, time and persons present, and then signaled Molly to begin.

"I'm Dr. Molly Reagan, assistant medical examiner for New York. Over the past several weeks, at the request of the New York City Police Department, I reviewed the results of Judge Reed's autopsy and, like Barry Hamilton, all the physical evidence and crime scene photos. Mr. Hamilton and I have talked about the areas of evidence we jointly reviewed and are in agreement about the findings, so I'll stick to the area Barry did not consider, the autopsy results and their relationship to the crime scene photos and the excellent and very detailed written description of the judge's study, which was where his body was found." She nodded to Jimmy, who had written that description thirty years earlier.

"First, there is no question about the cause of death. It was due to massive blunt trauma to the upper, frontal portion of the skull—the forehead, to keep it in layman's terms. The wounds correspond in size and shape to a bronze gavel found at the scene, which, based on a partially detached inscription plate and a subsequent statement given by Judge Reed's wife, was an award the judge received prior to his death and normally kept on his desk. Blood and tissue found on the gavel were identified as belonging to Judge Reed, further establishing it as the murder weapon."

Molly glanced at her notes and then continued. "The damage to the skull was massive, with approximately five centimeters of the forehead forced inward, sending shards of bone into vital areas of the brain and causing extensive destruction of tissue and almost instantaneous death." Molly paused to look around the table. "What's interesting here, and what was *not* reported in the original autopsy findings, was that there appear to have been two clear and separate attacks—the first relatively minor, the second unquestionably fatal."

From the corner of her eye, Molly saw Jake lean forward. She had not told him her conclusion. She had withheld it, wanting an opportunity to review Hamilton's findings on the evidence they had studied jointly. That way she could be certain there would be no prickly contradictions. Now, with that certitude in hand, she picked up sets of crime scene and autopsy photographs and passed them to the other members.

"As you can see, there was a great deal of blood surrounding the victim's head when the body was found. This is not uncommon, since head wounds bleed quite heavily. But it *is* unusual in cases of near-instantaneous death, because as you all know, once the heart stops, so does the flow of blood. Outside of seepage caused by gravity, dead bodies simply do not bleed." She picked up a photo taken at the autopsy after the wounds had been cleaned. "In this photo you'll see a deep laceration just to the left of the more serious and fatal wounds. The original autopsy report indicates that this was a superficial blow struck just before the more fatal blows. I don't know if the ME who performed this post was just careless, or if he did not have access to the crime scene photos. Regardless, he was clearly wrong. Using the photos, it's obvious that a first blow was struck, and that Judge Reed fell to the floor, either unconscious or badly stunned. He clearly lay there for a period of time—long enough to deposit a substantial amount of blood on the floor in the area around his head. He did not get up and move about leaving a *trail* of blood. *All* the blood, except for splatter patterns, is in the area where his body was found." Molly picked up another photo showing a close-up of the fatal wound. "This wound, which was the culmination of numerous blows, produced massive, catastrophic injury, which resulted in death within seconds. Furthermore, based on the splatter patterns on a nearby wall and on the side of his desk, I believe Judge Reed was still on the floor when these mortal blows were struck.

This position of the body added to the severity of the injury, since the head could not recoil from the force of the blows, or in any way move so as to lessen their impact. I would also have to conclude that the blows, which were clearly repetitive and well beyond what was needed to produce death, were administered in a state of frenzy, caused either by rage or hysteria."

Jimmy Finn raised a finger. "Jimmy Finn with a question," he said for the stenographer. "Did these blows—the fatal ones—require a great deal of physical strength?"

Molly shook her head. "Not at all, Jimmy. The gavel, as you know, was bronze and quite heavy. Add to that the fact that the judge's head was in a fixed position—kept from moving away by the floor—and that would negate the need of great physical strength to bring about death."

"Jimmy Finn again. So the blows could have been administered by a woman?"

"Yes. They could even have been administered by a nine- or ten-year-old child."

Jake leaned even farther forward. "Jake Downing with a question. Is there any indication that Judge Reed was attacked by more than one person?"

"Not from the autopsy alone," Molly said. "Not even from all the combined evidence. But using the autopsy evidence in combination with some things Barry Hamilton uncovered, it is clear to me that there is a distinct possibility that more than one person attacked the victim."

All eyes turned to Hamilton, who seemed to preen just a bit under the sudden attention. He turned slightly in his chair, as if offering a better profile, puffed himself up and adjusted his notes on the table in front of him.

"Barry Hamilton, forensic scientist, Federal Bureau of Investigation, retired." He nodded to the stenographer and then looked at each of the others at the conference table. "First, let me start with the man convicted of murdering Judge Reed. Based on all the evidence—which I must say was considerable and extremely well preserved—there is absolutely nothing that would place Louis Grosso in the room at the time of Judge Reed's death. In fact, there is nothing that would place him in that room at any time whatsoever."

Hamilton smiled, looking like some forensic deity pleased with his godlike pronouncement. "That said, let's see if we can reach a logical assumption about who *did* kill the judge."

Hamilton spread his arms wide. "As you all know, the most difficult murder to solve is one that occurs in the home of the victim, especially if the murderer is someone who was rightly and regularly in that home, and who therefore can easily explain away the presence of trace evidence placing him or her at the scene of the crime. In short, fingerprints, clothing fibers or bodily fluids of a spouse, or lover, or even a close friend that are found in the vicinity of the crime cannot be considered proof that they were present when the crime was committed, since that evidence might have been left there on any number of previous occasions." Hamilton raised a lecturing finger. "But certain *kinds* of evidence are a different matter. And in this case we have exactly those *kinds*. We have fingerprints that could only have been left during, or immediately after, the murder.

"If you recall, I told you at our initial meeting that several patent prints appeared to be on the gavel beneath a covering of blood. This, given the technology available in 1945, was beyond the recovery abilities of the forensic experts working the case. Today's technology, however, made it possible to retrieve those prints." He paused for effect. "In fact, while retrieving them, we also uncovered several latent prints beneath both layers of blood, as well as another patent print and a partial plastic print, both of which were considered too damaged for identification back in '45. Using today's recovery techniques, however, I was not only able to identify each of those prints, but also to provide evidentiary support for Dr. Reagan's theory that two separate attacks may have occurred."

Hamilton stopped and pointedly looked at Jimmy Finn. "Let me say right at the outset that Detective Finn made this all possible by getting everyone concerned printed, and given the political stature of many of those involved, I'm sure this was no easy task."

Jimmy seemed pleased by the unexpected compliment. "I just told them we needed their prints to eliminate them from the killer's. Of course I was really hoping one of them would turn out to *be* the killer and make the whole job easier."

Hamilton nodded sagely. "Well, without those prints we could not have gotten as far as we have today. And I think you were right. I think those prints did point a finger at the real killer."

Jimmy started to speak, but Hamilton raised a hand, stopping him. "In good time. First the prints." He drew himself up, ready to make his pronouncements. "The patent print under the blood belonged to Manny Troy. This means that he held that gavel with bloody hands before it was subsequently dropped and again covered with a layer of the judge's blood. Beneath everything I also found the latent prints of Judge Reed, as one would expect, and of Mrs. Reed, as one would also expect, since they occupied the house and had occasion to touch the gavel before it was used as a murder weapon. Mr. Troy's latent fingerprints also appear on the gavel beneath the blood, indicating that he handled it prior to it being used as a murder weapon. There are no other latent prints, and according to police reports a housekeeper cleaned the room two days before the crime was committed." Hamilton raised another lecturing finger. "This would lead me to conclude that both Manny Troy and Mrs. Reed had the weapon in their hands after it was supposedly cleaned by the housekeeper and before the first attack.

"Second, the patent print, the one created by the transfer of the judge's blood to the gavel by a finger also identified as Manny Troy's, would tell me that Troy also held the murder weapon after the first attack, and then dropped it into the blood on the floor.

"And finally, we have two plastic prints, each one left when fingers were pressed against the bloody surface of the gavel. One on the *head* of the gavel, one on the handle. These prints belong to Mrs. Reed, and they tell us that she picked up the gavel by the head and then transferred it to her hand *after* Troy dropped it."

Now Hamilton really puffed himself up. "And here is the most interesting finding of all. Mrs. Reed's plastic print on the head of the murder weapon is partially covered by splattered blood." Hamilton's finger shot up. "This is *not* a case of it again being dropped into the pool of blood on the floor. There is a definite, recognizable pattern here, one we have all seen many times in many murder cases. This is clearly a case of blood splattering onto the head of the gavel as it struck something with considerable force."

"Like the judge's noggin," Jimmy offered.

"That's what we think," Molly said.

Jake leaned forward. "So your theory, based on all the evidence, is . . . ?"

Molly looked at Jake with a hint of sadness. "Our theory is that Manny Troy got into an argument with the judge; that in the course of that argument he hit Judge Reed with the gavel; that somehow during that fight he got the judge's blood on his fingers and transferred it to the handle of the gavel. Then, when the judge was lying on the floor, Troy dropped the gavel into the pool of blood that had formed around his head, causing his patent print to be covered by the judge's blood. Subsequently— and we can only guess whether she was present during the initial attack—Mrs. Reed picked up the gavel and repeatedly struck the judge as he lay on the floor, thereby administering the mortal blows."

Jake remained quiet for nearly a minute. Molly watched throughout that time as various emotions played across his face. First came uncertainty, while he seemed to sift the facts as they'd been laid out, then a gradual assurance that those facts were believable and true, and finally a look that to Molly's mind came frighteningly close to triumph.

Jake looked around the table, taking in everyone in turn. "Thank you." His voice was slightly strained. Then he drew a deep breath and his words became stronger. "I should have had these answers thirty years ago, but those were different times. I won't make excuses. I probably would have had them if I'd had the courage to go after them." He looked down at the table; then back at each of them. "Now, thanks to all of you, those answers are here in this room." He turned to his old partner. "Well, Jimmy, what do you think?"

Finn nodded soberly. Molly noticed that he did not smile, did not show any joy over the results. "I think we need to have a long-overdue talk with Cynthia Reed."

"I think that's a lovely idea," Jake said.

Jimmy gave him an uncertain look. "Yes, lovely," he said.

Molly noted that there was no conviction in his voice.

{ 23 }

Her name was no longer Cynthia Reed, and she was no longer the twenty-three-year-old woman whom Jake had known and loved and lost some thirty years ago. She was now a middle-aged lady of fifty-three, a woman with a son not much older than she had been at that time. Still, the prospect of seeing her again had set Jake's nerves on edge. Jimmy now added to that tension by dropping a battered manila envelope in his lap.

They were in the back of Jake's car, and he stared at the envelope as though it were something that might bite him. They were headed north to Cyn's Fifth Avenue apartment. A telephone call from Jake's aide and driver, Pete Tedesco, had secured the appointment, although it had been far from a request. At Jake's instruction Pete had merely advised her that the chief of detectives would arrive at her apartment within the hour. She was to remain there until he did. If she did not, uniformed officers would be sent to find her and she would be brought to the nearest precinct. Cynthia Morrisey, as she was now known, had assured Pete that she would be there when the chief arrived.

"Are these what I think they are?" Jake ran a hand over the well-worn envelope, feeling the outline of what lay beneath. He looked at Jimmy. "The case notebooks you never turned in?"

Jimmy stared straight ahead and nodded. "I never understood why I hung on to them all these years. Now I do." He turned to Jake. "I want you to read 'em, Jake. *Before* we get there."

"Why?"

"Because they're *my* perspective of what happened to us all those years ago. Especially what happened between you and her."

"And you think it'll make a difference? Today?"

"I dunno if it'll make a difference or not. I just think it's important that you read how it was back then. At least from someone else's viewpoint."

Jake didn't respond. He simply opened the envelope and withdrew the three notebooks inside, opened the first and began reading.

His old partner's cramped scrawl came back to him quickly and he read through Jimmy's long-ago observations with surprising ease.

Jimmy's suspicions about Cynthia Reed were right there at the outset. To him she was a prime suspect with a clear motive of financial gain. The only question in Jimmy's mind was the possible involvement of a third party. Her brother, Oliver, was the first who came under suspicion. Then the possibility that he had brought in one of the thugs he'd come to know through Owney Ryan. That theory disappeared after Jimmy met Oliver. *Doesn't have the guts, or the brains,* was the solitary comment he'd made. Later, Bobby Ramirez, the saloon singer Cyn had once dated, figured in, but Jimmy soon dismissed him as well. Ramirez was a small-time operator with a big-time addiction to the ponies. A fifty-dollar bill would have bought and paid for him and sent him scurrying to his bookie—not exactly someone you'd trust to bump off a prominent judge. Not unless you were stupid, and Cynthia Reed was far from that. That left Cyn, herself, as the only person with the motive and opportunity *and the toughness*, Jimmy noted.

Jimmy also recorded again and again the way Cynthia Reed manipulated those around her. At the top of that list was Jake himself. As he read Jimmy's observations Jake knew that every one was true. From the very first moment they had met, to the last morning he had spent alone with her, Cynthia Reed had used him.

As he turned to the last page of the last notebook he sat staring at Jimmy's final observation. It was made on the day his daughter was born, the day Cynthia Reed left New York and his life.

Jake stared at the notation for several minutes and then turned the notebook so Jimmy could see it. "You believed this?" He ran his finger beneath the final words, making certain Jimmy knew exactly what he meant.

"I did, yes," Jimmy said. "And I still do."

Jake stared out the window. It was a beautiful October day, Indian summer with the temperature reaching into the high seventies. They had just turned onto Fifth Avenue and to his right Central Park raced by like a wondrous forest set down in the middle of the city. "I don't see how you could. Not then or now."

Jimmy gave out a little snort. "You never did see things very straight when it came to that lady."

Jake's car pulled to the curb in front of Cynthia's building.

"I guess that would be a tough one for me to argue."

"It would, indeed. Especially with anyone who was there."

The door to the apartment was opened by a tall, slender man who Jake guessed to be in his late twenties. He had wavy black hair and green eyes, and a cocky air that rolled off him like sweat.

Jake flashed his tin. It was something he had little occasion to do, but thoroughly enjoyed when he did, the chief of detectives' badge being a real eye-popper. It didn't seem to impress the young man at all, so he introduced himself along with Jimmy and told him they were there to see Mrs. Morrisey.

The young man gave Jake a hard look. "I know who you are,

Chief. My mother told me you were coming. She also said you were old friends, so I was a bit surprised by the way your aide announced your visit on the telephone. I'm Bill Morrisey, Mrs. Morrisey's son."

He handed Jake a business card that identified him as an attorney with a Wall Street law firm. Jake had heard of the firm but had never dealt with it. But then, prestigious law firms didn't usually have the city's criminal element on their client list, at least not the criminals who robbed and murdered with knives and guns. Jake eyed Cynthia's son and passed the card on to Jimmy without comment.

"I'm not giving you that card for any other reason than to let you know I'm an attorney, and that I expect to be present if your visit with my mother involves anything more than reminiscing about old times."

Jake held back a laugh, glanced at Jimmy and saw he was doing the same. The kid was so full of himself he deserved it. But you didn't laugh at someone who was standing up for his mother, at least not in any circle Jake cared to be a part of—not even if that mother had bumped off her first husband thirty years ago. And no matter what she had done, it didn't involve the kid. He was just doing what he had to do to be a good son. Jake would have done no less himself. Sure, the kid was cocky, your typical pain in the ass lawyer, but Jake had to admit he liked his style. It was going to be a shame to slap him down, but it was no time to play it soft.

He gave the kid his own hard look and finished it off with an unfriendly smile. "Well, if that's your position, Counselor, I think you better hang around. Now if it's not too much trouble, I came here to see your mother, not stand in the hall and chat."

William Morrisey's jaw tightened under the rebuke. Then he turned on his heel and grudgingly led them across a sizable foyer, through a set of double doors that opened onto a spacious and well-appointed sitting room, then out to a wide terrace that overlooked Central Park.

As he stepped onto the terrace Jake found himself looking down at a woman kneeling before a long terra-cotta planter. Her head was covered by a wide-brimmed sunhat and was bent to her task so that her face was fully obscured. She held a gardening trowel in one gloved hand and was busy manipulating rich, loamy soil. Slowly, as if she had heard them, she placed the trowel to one side and looked up.

"Hello, Jake," Cynthia Morrisey said. "I was just putting my plants to bed for the winter. Seems I'm becoming an old lady and flowers have become my greatest passion." She smiled at him. "You look quite wonderful." She hesitated a moment, and Jake sensed a touch of nervousness. "I read about your wife. I'm very sorry for your loss."

"Thank you. It's kind of you to say so."

Cyn's eyes moved to Jimmy and she suddenly smiled. "And this is Jimmy Finn, isn't it?" Her eyes seemed to twinkle with a touch of mischief. "My, if it wasn't for the loss of that wonderful red hair, I'd say you hadn't changed a bit. But the white is quite distinguished." She raised a hand and touched her own still-blond hair and smiled again. "Mine isn't at all distinguished, so I keep the color as it used to be."

"You look beautiful, Cyn," Jake said. "And well."

"And you haven't lost any of your charms," Jimmy added.

Cyn stood, removed her gardening gloves, and looked at each of them. She seemed quite amused. "Thank you. It's been a long time since either of you paid me a compliment." Her eyes settled on Jimmy. "In fact, I don't think you ever did." She paused. "Except, perhaps, that one time, that day I left. You said I was doing a good thing."

"I remember," Jimmy said. He felt Jake staring at him, but refused to look.

Finally Jake turned his attention back to Cyn. "We need to talk to you. We've reopened the case . . . the judge's murder."

William Morrisey immediately stepped forward. "I think I should be here for this, Mother. Having a lawyer present is the smart way to go."

Cyn looked at her son and smiled. "I know it is, dear. But in this instance it's not at all necessary. Jake and Jimmy and I have a history here. We can deal with it without any help."

"Mother, I have to insist. This is just—"

"You can insist all you want, my darling. I know you're trying to look after my interests, but it's not the way I want to handle this. You'll just have to accept that." She turned to Jake and smiled. "It took my husband several years, but he finally convinced our son to go to law school. I enthusiastically supported that idea without ever realizing that it would turn my wonderful, loving child into a lawyer." She laughed and looked back at her son. "Please go inside, dear. If things become unpleasant, I promise I'll call for you immediately."

William Morrisey drew a long breath and studied the floor. Then he raised his eyes and gave Jake as hard a look as he could manage, even though his mother's words had decimated any threat he might hope to make. A small smile of resignation touched the corners of his mouth and he turned slowly and reentered the sitting room, closing the terrace doors behind him.

Jake watched him leave and turned back to Cyn. "Interesting young man."

"Yes, and a good son. All I could ask for."

Cyn removed her sunhat and shook out her blond hair, and Jake realized how kind the thirty intervening years had been to her. There were lines that hadn't been there, of course, around the eyes and the corners of her mouth, but they seemed to add to, not detract from, the finely etched bone structure, and her full lips and deep blue eyes still had the ability to draw you in and make you think of things you shouldn't. At least they did for Jake.

Cyn seemed to sense it, and she gave Jake a small, satisfied smile. Then she led them to a circular wrought-iron table and suggested they sit. The table was next to the terrace railing and offered a full view of Central Park. It was spread out twelve floors below, a lush carpet of trees and grass complete with miniature people moving along the crisscrossing paths, a view seen by only a select few of New York's millions and one that required a great deal of money to call your own.

Cyn asked if they'd care for anything to drink, smiled when they each declined.

"You've done well." Jake struggled to keep any bitterness from his voice. "I remember you telling me what you wanted from life. You seem to have gotten it."

Cyn cocked her head slightly as if thinking over what he had said. "In some ways I think so," she said at length. "In other ways, no." A mellow smile came to her lips. "But I learned something over the years. I learned that it's all right to want the best for yourself and for those you love, and that you should work very hard to try to get it. I also learned that no matter how much you want it, no matter how hard you work to achieve it, sometimes it just isn't possible and you have to settle for what you *can* have. And I learned that it's all right to be grateful for those things, too." She laughed at herself. "That last part's the hardest to learn. But it's also the part that makes life livable."

Jake surveyed the terrace and the view. "You don't seem to have been forced into many second choices."

Again, Cyn smiled. "You might be surprised." She folded her hands on the edge of the table. "So you're here to talk about Wallace's death, and how Louie Grosso didn't kill him." She looked at each of them. "But, of course, we all knew that thirty years ago, didn't we?"

Jake sat back and studied her. "You're a tough lady, Cyn. But, then, you always were. It was something I couldn't see all those years ago, even though it was right there in front of me."

"Yes, it was. I had to be if I hoped to survive."

"And Louie Grosso goin' to the chair doesn't bother you?" It was Jimmy this time, an unreadable look on his face.

She gave him a level stare. "Does it bother you, Jimmy Finn?"

Jimmy scratched his chin. "Sometimes. Not a helluva lot. But sometimes there's a twinge of . . . somethin'. Call it conscience, for lack of a better word."

Cyn turned to Jake. "And does it bother you, Jake?"

Jake gave a long and slow nod. "Yes. But mostly because his corpse became my stepping-stone. As for the man himself? No. The world was a much better place without Louie Grosso in it, and there were probably a number of people who lived longer or healthier lives because he left it."

Cyn's eyes hardened. "I don't regret Grosso's death one bit. Nor do I regret my husband's death." She paused momentarily, allowing her words to settle in. She looked at each of them in turn, and then continued. "You see, Louie Grosso and Wallace Reed were very much alike. They were cruel men who enjoyed hurting people they considered weak and vulnerable. Oh, they weren't alike on the surface. Wallace allowed very few people to see what he was capable of . . . just those who suffered from his cruelty." She let out a small, bitter laugh. "Who knows, perhaps Louie Grosso had a gentle side that few people saw."

"That's unlikely," Jimmy said.

"Yes, well . . ." Cyn lowered her eyes. "Barring intellect and position there was little difference between them." Slowly, she raised her eyes and looked at each of them again. "And I felt nothing but relief when each of them left this earth." She fixed her eyes on Jake. "Do you understand why, Jake?"

"I understand why you felt that way about Louie Grosso. I was there. I saw what he did to you; what he did to both of us. I didn't know the judge."

"Do you remember the scars on my back, Jake?"

Jake nodded, recalling the small, jagged scars that were always hidden by her clothing. "Yes, I remember them."

"Then you knew Wallace Reed."

Jake let the moment draw out. "Did you kill him?" he finally asked.

Cyn looked out toward the park, as if annoyed he would think her foolish enough to answer that question. "Do I need my son now?"

"That's entirely up to you," Jake said.

She turned back to him. "No, I don't think I want to do that—not yet."

She unfolded her hands and ran her fingers through her hair. Then she clasped her hands together, held them before her momentarily, and then slowly returned them to the edge of the table. It had all the earmarks of a nervous gesture, a tell, the very thing every good interrogator watched for when bracing a suspect. But there was something about it that felt wrong, something that Jake couldn't quite put his finger on.

Cyn looked off toward the park. "Some people say that when I got on the witness stand I killed Louie Grosso. Did you know that?" She turned back and looked at Jake, then Jimmy. "Some people say all three of us did."

"We're here to talk about the judge," Jake said.

"Yes, we are, aren't we?" Cyn unfolded her hands again, and brought the fingers of one to her throat. Then she began to softly stroke herself. "I guess I always knew you and I would have to do that one day. I just didn't think it would take so long for it to happen." She spoke directly to Jake; spoke the way she used to speak to him all those years ago; spoke as if they were alone, as if Jimmy wasn't there, as if her son wasn't sitting in the next room . . . as if none of that even existed.

Jake leaned forward. He wanted that one-to-one intimacy, wanted to maintain the feeling that they were just talking to each other. "We've been reviewing the evidence that we gathered after the murder. We've even applied some new technology we didn't have back then. The results have been interesting. We've come up with some things we didn't know before, things you can help clarify for us."

She looked at him as though the request was a bit odd. "Why does it matter to you? It's over with, finished." She paused and seemed to rethink the question. "Is it because I left?"

The question jarred him and he didn't know how to respond. Perhaps it even frightened him. He wasn't sure. He only knew he didn't want to deal with it. Not now. So he retreated to the safety of being a cop.

"Tell me about that day, Cyn. The day the judge was murdered. Tell me everything you remember about it. Everything you didn't tell me thirty years ago."

"It's been such a long time, Jake. And so much has happened. I'm not sure how much I still remember, or how well." She looked at him as innocently as she could, and she knew he could see it . . . the lie, big as life, sitting right there in her eyes.

She turned away and stared out toward the park again, and again Jake had the feeling that there was no one else there for her—just the Jake Downing of thirty years ago, just that young inexperienced detective and a beautiful young widow . . . Cynthia . . . Reed.

"You think I'm going to agree to a third? A goddamn third? Not likely, my friend. Not when it's my name that sits on that decision. Not when it's my ass that's hanging out in the breeze if anyone raises questions of judicial impropriety." The words roared through the door, so loud they seemed to shake the walls of the house.

I could hear someone reply. The words were clearly angry, but they weren't shouted. It was a man's voice, to be sure, low and a bit gravelly, but that was all I could tell.

The shouting had begun five minutes earlier, Wallace's voice roaring so loudly that I could hear him all the way up in our bedroom on the next floor. He'd been working in his study all afternoon, and that meant he'd been drinking. It was always like that when he worked at home. He drank as he worked; just a little at a time, spread over many hours until it built up and built up and finally changed him; until it brought out all the anger and the violence that he kept hidden inside and never wanted others to see.

My fear began to build as I listened to him shout. This was how it always started . . . every time he hurt me. Something would enrage him, I never knew exactly what. Something that had not gone as he thought it should: a higher court overturning one of his decisions, some political slight, an expected invitation that had not been forthcoming, an honor not bestowed, a disrespectful prosecutor, a disrespectful defense attorney, rain on a day he had planned to play golf, something, anything, and then someone would have to become his victim, someone would have to be punished for whatever or whoever had offended him, someone close and handy and vulnerable. Often that was me.

I came down the stairs and went to the far end of the hall, trying to keep out of sight. And I listened to Wallace shout. I had to. I had to know what had made him so angry. I had to know when the person he was shouting at left his study. I had to know both of those things, because I knew if this argument didn't go the way he wanted, if he didn't get whatever he was shouting about, he'd come looking for me because he'd need to show how powerful he was, need to soothe his frustration, and I wanted to know when that would be so I could keep out of his way; so I could hide.

I stood beside a large grandfather clock, using it to secrete myself in that dark corner of the hall, and I listened as the shouts grew louder and angrier. It was then that I heard the first crash. It sounded as if a chair had been overturned, and it was followed by grunting and low curses, the sounds of men struggling; then something heavy falling to the floor, and a long period of silence.

I waited, wondering if I should go to the door, wondering if I should see if someone was hurt, but I was too frightened. Then the door to the study opened and I flattened myself against the wall, using the clock to keep myself hidden. There was a pause outside the study door and for a moment I thought my pounding heart had given me away. Then I heard heavy breathing and footsteps moving away toward the stairs, and I peeked out from behind the clock and saw Manny Troy as he started down the staircase.

I didn't know what to do and I stood there for a long time, afraid that if I went to the study door I would find Wallace sitting at his desk glowering over what had just transpired. And he would see me, of course, and all his anger would be redirected, just as it had been in the past, just as it always was whenever I proved convenient and close at hand.

Finally, I couldn't stand the silence any longer and I moved cautiously to the door, not certain what I would do if I found Wallace waiting for me. I had tried running once, but that had only made things worse. Sympathizing sometimes worked, or joining him in his anger, so I began thinking of things I could say about Manny Troy, things that would let Wallace know that it wasn't I who had hurt him; that I was on his side; that I, too, was offended by whatever Manny Troy had done; that in harming him, Troy had harmed me as well. Then I entered the study and saw him. He was on his back behind his desk and there was blood all over his face and on the rug near his head. The desk chair was overturned and the gavel that was always on his desk was lying on the floor next to him. I called his name and moved closer . . . but . . . but . . .

"What happened, Cyn? Tell me what happened."

The sound of Jake's voice brought Cyn back. She'd been staring out at the park and she couldn't tell if she'd actually been speaking to him, if she'd told him anything at all, told him about the fear she'd felt; about Wallace and Troy and what had happened in the study; or if she'd only replayed it all in her mind and never spoken a word.

She brought her eyes away from the park and looked at him. "What do you want to know?" Her voice was distant, uncertain.

Jake leaned forward in his chair. "You heard them arguing, and then the sounds of a struggle. Then you saw Troy leave and you went into the study and found Wallace on the floor. What happened then?"

"What happened? I don't understand."

Jake took a breath, forcing himself to be calmer, more in control. "Did you touch him?"

Nothing.

"Did you feel for a pulse?"

Cyn shook her head, a gesture so small he couldn't be sure if it meant anything or not. He repeated the question.

"I don't think so. I don't think I did."

"Did you pick up the gavel that was lying beside him?"

Cyn's eyes suddenly snapped to his. At first they were questioning, and then a hint of concern seemed to pass through them, until they finally seemed to fill with a deep sense of sorrow and regret. Then she looked back toward the park.

Wallace stirs and groans. His fingers go to the wound on his forehead and he touches it gingerly. He struggles to rise, to pull himself up from the floor, but the pain must be too much because he falls back.

Then he sees me kneeling beside him. He stares at me, clearly confused, uncertain about what has happened.

Did Manny Troy hurt you?

I am reaching out to him when anger suddenly rushes into his face, fills it so quickly it startles me, makes me begin to pull away. But his hand lashes out and he grabs my wrist and the strength of his grip surprises me. Just moments before he was unable to raise himself from the floor. Now he seems so strong. Now his hand is crushing my arm, his grip so fierce that I'm afraid the bone will shatter in his hand.

Wallace, you're hurting me.

He glares at me with unbelievable hatred. *You bitch. You filthy bitch. You love to see me like this, don't you?* Wallace gasps for breath, struggling to find the words, and I can't understand how he can sound so weak and still be crushing my arm.

You love to see me down and beaten. But I'm not beaten and I never will be. I'm fine, whether you think so or not. I'll have to teach you the difference, won't I?

Don't hurt me, Wallace. Please don't.

I hear begging in my voice and the sound suddenly disgusts me. I try to pull away, but he yanks on my arm and I fall forward, and suddenly my hand is on the head of the gavel and I pick it up.

Bitch! he roars.

I pull away from him and stand, ready to run, but not knowing where to go. If I run, he'll find me. Sooner or later he will, and there is nothing I can do about it.

He starts to get up and his face has turned into a mask of rage. *I'll fix you, you bitch, you two-timing little slut. I'll beat you like you've never been beaten in your life. I'll make you scream. I'll make you beg for it to stop. But it won't. Not until I say so. Do you understand me? Do you?*

Cold enters my body. It comes suddenly and it's like nothing I've ever felt before. It is calm and soothing, and yet it simmers inside me like a boiling pot. But cold doesn't boil, does it? So strange. So very strange. I can feel the gavel. It's heavy, solid, and I turn it so the handle slips into my hand, and I feel my fingers wrap around it as I stare down at Wallace still struggling to gain his feet.

No you won't, Wallace. You won't ever again . . . and I strike out with all my strength and watch him fall back to the floor, his head hitting so hard that it bounces off the carpet, and I drop to my knees and raise the gavel above my head and I bring it down again and again and again . . .

Again Cyn's eyes returned from the park, and she looked Jake squarely in the eyes. "I don't know, Jake. I don't know if I picked up the gavel or not."

Jake inhaled deeply. "We found fingerprints on the gavel, including some that could only have gotten there at the time of the murder. Several of those prints were yours." He lowered his eyes, and then raised them again, and they were suddenly hard and unforgiving. "We weren't able to lift those prints thirty years ago. Now we can."

Cyn looked at him, but remained silent. She didn't seem up-set by what he had said, or frightened, or even concerned. Jake decided to change tack and see if he could find another button to push.

"Before we get to the prints, tell me about Manny Troy." She continued to look at him, unfazed. "Why didn't you tell us that you saw him leaving your husband's study just moments before you found his body?"

Cyn looked away for nearly a minute before she spoke. "I didn't see any point in it," she finally said.

Jake studied his shoes. "I see. But you did see a point in ob-structing our investigation."

"I don't think I did that." She looked away again. "I've been married twice, Jake, both times to lawyers, each of whom kept libraries in our homes, and I have some small understanding of the law. One of the things I understand is that no citizen has a legal obligation to tell the police anything."

Jake looked up, his eyes hard and unrelenting. "That's right, Cyn. A citizen doesn't have to volunteer information or even an-swer a question. But if that citizen chooses to do so, he can't lie or mislead an investigation." He leaned forward, eyes even harder. "A funny thing, Cyn, but since we reopened this case I've been reading all the old reports over and over again. One of those reports dealt with the first time I spoke to you. It was in the garden of your house. Do you remember?"

"I remember, Jake."

"Good. Because that's when you told me how you found the body. It was a voluntary statement, according to my report, and it explained how you'd been upstairs getting dressed because you were going out to dinner, and how you came down to tell your husband you were ready."

"Yes, I remember."

"I also asked you a question then. I asked if you'd heard the sound of anyone breaking in, or the sound of a struggle, and you told me you hadn't, that you'd been taking a bath and the water had been running." He looked at her steadily. "But I'd re-member that part even without the report, because when you said it all I could think about was you sitting in that tub."

Cyn looked away again, but this time she was smiling. "I

know." Her voice was very soft. "I remember it as clearly as you do. I could tell exactly what you were thinking."

Jake felt his anger rise. "And you knew exactly what you were saying."

"Yes." She was still looking away and her voice was still very soft.

"Well, what you did when you told me that was clear and simple obstruction, lady." Jake could feel Jimmy twist in his chair. He knew he was on shaky ground, that he was pushing it far beyond where he should.

Cyn turned back to face him, her eyes as hard as his now. "Don't try to bully me, Jake. Men have tried that all my life. I'm not a fool. I know there's no statute of limitations on murder. But there is on obstruction. So, please, respect my intelligence that much." She drew a deep breath. "Now, if you think you can prove that I killed my husband when I was alone with him in that room thirty years ago, then do so. But don't try to play the big, powerful chief of detectives and bully me into a confession."

Jake sat back and gave her a grudging smile. She had taken his bluff and thrown it back and had hit him squarely between the eyes. Sure, he had fingerprints. He even had her two statements—then and now—that showed she had lied. He could prove she had motive; that she had opportunity. He could even bring out the sleazy real estate deal her husband was involved in, and how she had learned about it and pressured Manny Troy to give her Reed's cut. But it was all after the fact. When it came down to Wallace Reed's murder, she was right. He could prove she had gone into that room. He could even prove she had picked up the murder weapon. But he couldn't prove she had used it to kill her husband, and no DA in his right mind was going to take this thirty-year-old evidence into court, no matter how compelling it was, and charge the widow of a famous judge with his murder. End of story.

He drew a long breath. But that was only the half of it. He could still charge her and let the DA refuse to prosecute. He could still tell the world that Cynthia Reed and Manny Troy had been the last people, the only people, with Wallace Reed before he died. He could clear Louie Grosso's name; prove that he hadn't killed Wallace Reed. And he could prove that they had all known that dirty little secret thirty years ago—cops and killers alike—and despite knowing it they had all stood by while the State of New York sent Louie Grosso off to Sing Sing and the electric chair. He could do that much for himself. And that's what it was about, what it had always been about.

Jake looked across the table that separated them. Cyn was staring back at him, but her eyes were no longer hard and angry. It was almost as if she sensed his need to finally bring it all to an end, and his frustration in knowing he could not.

He gave her a cold smile. "You always knew how to take care of yourself, Cyn."

"I had to, Jake. I learned early on that no one else would."

He looked down and smiled. "Well, you did a fine job of it." He paused and shook his head. "You even took Manny Troy for a ride—all that power and he probably never knew what hit him." He looked up, wanting to see her eyes now. "I'd like to have been there when you told him you saw him coming out of your husband's study. He must have been ready to wet his pants. He probably wanted you dead, too, probably would have paid someone to do it. But, of course, that's why you made him provide you with around-the-clock police protection. You *did* do that, didn't you? It *was* your idea, not his?"

"Yes, it was my idea."

"And then when you found out about the real estate deal—found out from *me*—you hammered him with that. He must have been glad as hell to see you leave town."

"I believe he was."

Jake shook his head. "I guess I was the only one who wasn't." His look hardened. "But I didn't understand very much of it then, didn't understand how you'd used *all* of us."

"I left because of you, Jake. You were the reason, the only reason. I left because I loved you. I didn't plan on that part. I didn't even want it to happen. It just did."

Jake threw back his head and laughed. It was a bitter sound, long and harsh and unforgiving. When he had finished he stared across the table, holding her eyes. "Jimmy wrote the same thing in his notebook. It was one he never turned in, one he only showed me today. He said you left because you loved me. He even told me today that he still believes it."

Cyn looked at Jimmy, watched him nod and turn his eyes away.

Jake slapped his hand on the table, drawing her eyes back. "Well, I don't believe it, lady. Not for a New York minute. So you better go get your son. You better get him and tell him it's time for him to join us, because dear old Mom is definitely going to need a lawyer."

Cyn pressed her eyes shut, as if driving away something she wasn't ready to face. "I don't want to do that," she said when she opened them again.

"Then get whoever you want, if you don't want him."

"It's not that."

"Then what is it?"

She held Jake's eyes for a long, lingering moment. "It's not how I want my son to meet his real father."

Jake stared at her, unable to speak. His body seemed to sway. Then it fell back in his chair as though he'd been struck. Several moments passed. Finally his lips moved as he tried to speak. No words would come.

"I was pregnant when I left, Jake. It was why the trial was delayed. The district attorney knew. I had to tell him. But he was an old friend of Wallace's and he promised to keep it secret." She smiled wryly. "But, of course, silence suited his purpose. I don't think he wanted prospective jurors to read about it in the newspapers, and he certainly didn't want a pregnant, unmarried widow sitting on the witness stand. It *was* 1945, and unmarried, expectant mothers weren't held in very high esteem."

Jake sat forward, finally finding his voice. "Why didn't you tell me?" His eyes were hard again, angry again.

"How could I? Your wife had just given birth to a daughter. How could I make you choose? And what if you chose me? Could I force your daughter to grow up that way?" She shook her head. "I grew up with nothing, Jake. I couldn't do that to another child." She paused again. "No matter how much I wanted to be with you, I just couldn't do that. As for our child, I knew I could give him what he needed . . . with you, or without you."

"I had a right to know." The words came out in an angry growl. Jake stared at her, his eyes as unforgiving as any she had ever seen.

Cyn's own eyes hardened. "Did you?" She paused and drew a long breath, clearly using it to calm her rising anger. When she spoke again the soft tone of her voice belied her words. "How dare you sit there and play the injured male? You knew what you were doing thirty years ago. You knew when you climbed into my bed that you had a wife at home, a wife who was carrying your first child."

"And you didn't?" Jake snapped out the question in an angry hiss. "I don't recall making a big secret of it."

Cyn gave him a long, level stare. Her voice remained calm. "Yes, I knew, Jake. And I accepted what I did. And I still do. I used you, Jake. I was frightened and I used you. I was alone. There was no one I could turn to. And then *you* came along, and I could tell you were attracted to me. And I used that. I was reaching out for anything I could find, anyone who would care about me, who would care enough to help me. It was something I'd been doing all my life. It was the reason I married Wallace. Only that didn't quite work out the way I planned. I was hoping it would be different with you; that I could make you want me; make you love me."

Suspicion momentarily filled Jake's eyes. "You're doing it again, aren't you? You used me thirty years ago; now you're using me again."

"No, I'm not, Jake."

He held her eyes. "I think you are. Your son's name, it's William Morrisey, the same as your second husband."

"He was born years before I met Bill Morrisey. But Bill loved him from the day they met and he adopted him and gave him his name." She paused, then reached out and took Jake's hand. "Have you found someone to love, Jake? Someone who loves you, too?"

Jake stared out at the park and nodded. "Yes, I have."

"I'm glad, Jake. I did, too. I found that with Bill Morrisey. He was a wonderful man, a wonderful father." She smiled, more at herself than at him. "You see, I finally found what I'd been looking for all those years ago. I found someone who wanted to take care of me, who wanted to love me. And even better, wanted to take care of my son, and to love him, too." She smiled again, as she sat back in her chair. "But I don't expect you to believe me.

There have been too many lies between us. So you can find out for yourself. The original birth certificate is still on file in Los Angeles. You can call and check any time you wish. Or you can arrange to have the police out there do it for you. Our son was born on May 18, 1946. The birth certificate gives his name as it was when he was born. The last name is Marks, my maiden name. The given name is Jake."

Jake fell back in his chair again, unaware that Jimmy had gotten up and was standing beside him. He reached down and handed Jake the business card the young man had given them at the door: *J. William Morrisey, Attorney at Law*.

"It's over, Jake," Jimmy said. "Over and done with."

Jake looked up at him. His eyes widened, not wanting to believe what Jimmy had said. He shook his head. "No. No, it's not. I've waited too long." He continued to hold Jimmy's eyes. "What about Louie Grosso, Jimmy? What about sending an innocent man to the chair?"

Jimmy reached down and squeezed his old friend's shoulder. "This was never about Louie Grosso. It was never even about Wallace Reed. Face it, man, they were both bastards who got what they deserved. Just like we all got what *we* deserved—having to live with all the ugliness of it for all these years."

Jake stared at him. "If it wasn't about Grosso and Reed, then what was it about?"

Jimmy looked at Cyn, then back at Jake. "This part—what we're doin' here now? What you've been hauntin' yourself with for the past thirty years? This part is what it's always been. It's about you and this lady sitting across from you. It's about getting back at her for what you think she did to you. Nothing more, nothing less. But that's over now. Unless you want to lose even more. Unless you want to lose this son you didn't even know you had." He squeezed Jake's shoulder again. "That's the size of it, Jake. And I'll have no part in it. Not anymore. It's time for me to take myself home. And it's time for you to put this madness away and go and meet your son."

Jake felt his arms and legs begin to tremble. It felt as though something had been wrenched from his body, leaving him weak and hollow. Sweat ran along his body, and his fists tightened involuntarily. He looked across the small circular table at Cyn, and his body shuddered. When he spoke, his voice was no more than a croak. "Can I?" he asked. "Can I meet him that way?"

Cyn nodded almost imperceptibly. "Yes, you can, Jake. And I think it's time you did."

Also Available From Akashic Books

BEULAH HILL by William Heffernan
281 pages, a trade paperback original, $13.95, ISBN: 1-888451-40-8

A novel of rare literary distinction—an erotic thriller combined with a true mystery, and a look back at a little-known part of the American societal patchwork.

"The whispered revelations that come spilling out of *Beulah Hill* are like ghostly voices you sometimes hear in the attic—soft, sad and disturbingly urgent."

—*New York Times Book Review*

CITYSIDE by William Heffernan
304 pages, a trade paperback original, $14.95, ISBN: 1-888451-47-5

"Heffernan whips up a superior potboiler in this tale of corrupt newspapering, brutal cops, and greedy doctors . . . Heffernan takes the reader behind the scenes of tabloid journalism, describing in fascinating detail the attendant perks, backscratching, and hypocrisy. Writing with verve, enthusiasm, and a flair for unconventional detail . . ."

—*Publishers Weekly*

BROOKLYN NOIR edited by Tim McLoughlin
350 pages, a trade paperback original, $15.95, ISBN: 1-888451-58-0

Contributors include: Pete Hamill, Nelson George, Sidney Offit, Arthur Nersesian, Pearl Abraham, Neal Pollack, Ken Bruen, Ellen Miller, Maggie Estep, Kenji Jasper, Adam Mansbach, C.J. Sullivan, Chris Niles, Norman Kelley, Tim McLoughlin, Nicole Blackman, Thomas Morrissey, Lou Manfredo, Luciano Guerriero, and Robert Knightly.

"*Brooklyn Noir* is such a stunningly perfect combination that you can't believe you haven't read an anthology like this before. But trust me—you haven't. Story after story is a revelation, filled with the requisite sense of place, but also the perfect twists that crime stories demand. The writing is flat-out superb, filled with lines that will sing in your head for a long time to come."

—Laura Lippman, winner of the Edgar, Shamus, and Agatha awards